AN ENTANGLE

BOOK 3

Love Affair

Tommy's Memoirs

GINA MARIE MARTINI

PAGE PUBLISHING, INC.
Conneaut Lake, PA

First originally published by Page Publishing 2021

ISBN 978-1-6624-3569-0 (pbk)
ISBN 978-1-6624-3570-6 (digital)

Printed in the United States of America

The Entanglements Novels by Gina Marie Martini

Love Affair: Tommy's Memoirs
Moonlight Confessions
The Mistress Chronicles

For the lights of my life, my sons, Joe and Anthony

*Kindness is the language which the deaf
can hear and the blind can see.*

—Mark Twain

ACKNOWLEDGMENTS

The artworks mentioned in my story deserve thoughtful recognition.

- *Love Scene* by Giulio Romano, located at the Hermitage Museum, St. Petersburg, Russia. This romantic-looking painting mesmerized me! I had to mention it in my story.
- *The Boulevard Montmartre at Twilight, 1897* by Camille Pissarro, location unknown. This painting was allegedly stolen by German soldiers during World War II, then later recovered and sold with no record of who purchased it in 1941. The mysterious history behind this piece made for a delicious, fictitious plot for my story. Pissarro crafted many pieces of the Boulevard Montmartre at various times of day, night, and season.
- *Water Lilies* by Claude Monet. Monet created numerous paintings of the water lilies and gardens outside his tranquil home in Giverny, a lovely, harmonious village nestled in the Normandy province of France.
- *Venus and Adonis* by Peter Paul Rubens, located at the Metropolitan Museum of Art, New York.
- *Dogs Playing Poker* by Cassius Marcellus Coolidge, commissioned by Brown & Bigelow. Several versions of *Dogs Playing Poker* were created by Coolidge.

I would like to recognize these true-crime books and the authors who depicted details about organized crime in Las Vegas during the era in which my fictional story transpires:

- *The Battle For Las Vegas: The Law vs. The Mob*, by Dennis N. Griffin,
- *Leaving Vegas: The True Story of How the FBI Wiretaps Ended Mob Domination of Las Vegas Casinos*, by Gary Jenkins, and
- *Casino*, by Nicholas Pileggi.

An endearing shout-out to my friend, Pegge Dixon, for your valuable contribution and prime editing skills.

My deepest gratitude to special friends and family who took time out of their hectic lives to review my story in advance and offer feedback. I value all of you for your friendship and support: Darlene Ashford, Donna Barent, Joanne Colavolpe, Sally Diglio, and Carolyn Lubitski.

PROLOGUE

The first death threat was received on April 1, 2010. An April Fool's Day joke was my initial thought. The US Postal Service delivered the typed letter to the Montgomery, the hotel and casino I owned along the exhilarating Las Vegas Strip. How could anyone take a death threat seriously when sent via snail mail?

Phyllis, my executive assistant, found the note mixed in with the stack of daily mail dropped off at her desk promptly at eight o'clock.

Gavin, an eighteen-year-old mail clerk, placed the pile carefully in the empty tray on Phyllis's desk, secured with a broad elastic band.

She smiled at Gavin, happy he respected her compulsion for organization.

Phyllis worked her way through the stack of envelopes, using a sharp letter opener. Junk mail would be discarded in the recycle bin. Correspondence she needed to tend to was placed inside a manila folder labeled "Daily Tasks" that she'd complete later. Phyllis imprinted the date with her stamper neatly in the upper right corner of the documents that required my attention.

Usually, Phyllis would tap on my door before entering, quietly step toward my desk, and leave the neat stack of date-stamped documents on the top of the desk tray fastened with a binder clip. But on the morning of April 1, Phyllis raced inside my office, waving a piece of paper in front of me, disrupting my review of a supplier's contract renewal. "You need to see this right away!" she shouted, rushing toward me, handing me the paper.

My eyes caught Phyllis's serious expression beneath her bright red glasses. "What's this?"

"Read it," she demanded as her fingers combed through her thick blond hair.

The note read, *I'll bring you and your business down. Your days are numbered, Tommy.* My cocky reaction to laugh it off, crumple the paper, and toss it into the garbage pail was suspended when Phyllis tugged at my elbow.

Phyllis insisted we involve the police. Maybe it was a threat from a competitor or a disgruntled employee, she thought.

I calmed her shaken nerves and tossed the crinkled letter toward the wastebasket like a Kobe Bryant jump shot.

Phyllis blocked my play, catching the document. "At least let me file this."

I shrugged in agreement.

Phyllis maintained an extraordinary filing system. She probably created a folder labeled "Threats 2010." It was possible one had already been established.

Recently, necessary budget cuts occurred, and my management team laid off some low-hanging fruit. A few people were pretty angry about getting axed. I might have given the order for the cuts, but I didn't conduct exit interviews. Human resource representatives and department heads dealt with the chopping blocks.

No one else received hate mail—only me.

A week after the threatening letter was received, Phyllis and I were reviewing the March financial report, sorted by each hotel I owned. Over the years, I extended the Montgomery chain to multiple locations in the US, the Caribbean, and Europe.

At approximately seven fifteen in the morning, a shockwave of thunderous booms detonated from outside the hotel. The blast sounded close enough to feel a rattling vibration in my office on the second floor.

Phyllis and I jumped from our chairs and rushed to the window to see what triggered such an angry, loud roar at this early hour. A dark gray cloud of smoke wafted through the air with orange sparks of fire blended through a smothering puff of fog. But we couldn't confirm the cause from where we stood.

My cell rang from an unknown caller before I had a moment to process a potential evacuation and contact security. I answered the call in a frenzied state, in case someone had an explanation for the fire raging outside or if we needed to vacate the building. I clicked my cell to speaker so Phyllis could listen in.

A nondescript, robotic-sounding voice said, "The heat is on now, Cavallo. Next time, pieces of your body will be charbroiled like your car." An abrasive click ended the call.

My office phone started to buzz, distracting me from the fire outside and the intense threat, *charbroiled like your car*. Was my beautiful Aston Martin DBS a casualty of the explosion? I picked up a line while Phyllis darted to her desk to answer another call.

Logan, a security officer, raced through the door, providing the serious details of that crashing blast. He confirmed my luxury car exploded in the parking lot. The security team had already alerted the Las Vegas Metropolitan Police Department and confirmed the damage had been contained to the lot.

Sirens blared, telling me help was on the way.

Phyllis kept me calm, insisting I stay in the office while Metro and firefighters controlled the scene outside. A few cops were on their way up with their little notepads and list of questions to investigate the crime.

I had never been a big fan of law enforcement. I didn't expect to say much. Talking to the police could amplify the danger.

Two Metro officers strode in, wearing the official tan uniform, toting badges and weapons, merely to take my statement. I wanted to keep this low-key, but in walked the Clark County sheriff himself, overseeing the investigation. What did I do to deserve his attention?

"Well, Mr. Cavallo, this is quite a conundrum. I hope you can clear up this disaster and tell us who your latest *fan* is," he said.

Phyllis acted as a witness to the ominous message received on my cell moments after the detonation. She sang like a canary. She handed the sheriff the crumpled letter received on April 1, while my head bobbed in agreement with her description of the events.

"Anything else you'd like to add, Mr. Cavallo, like a suspect's name?" he strongly suggested with a raised brow.

My head shook. "She covered everything."

"I find it hard to believe that a man in your line of work, with somewhat of an *interesting* past, is unaware of his enemies. You must have some idea who'd threaten you to this degree."

"I've no idea who made that call or who'd be insane enough to destroy such a beautiful car. People love me, Sheriff!" I smirked.

"Uh-huh."

I released a snicker, acknowledging the fact that he knew about my checkered history as the owner of the Montgomery with alleged illicit associations. Clearly, the sheriff wasn't convinced, but I couldn't quite sort out and explain the chaos strangling my brain cells. Professionally speaking, I wouldn't want my hotel guests to take their business elsewhere or fear for their lives if the media launched a shit-show, focusing on a potential hit on my life.

I gave the cops nothing except a list of the employees who were recently terminated. Maybe that was a big mistake. I knew none of the people on that list would go to these lengths to threaten me for losing their jobs. Roles they were paid copiously for, receiving generous severance packages, despite their inadequacies.

Fortunately, I wasn't driving my Aston Martin when one of my enemies chose to launch the explosive device that burned the luxurious vehicle from the inside out. Damn, that was a hot car, complete with all the bells and whistles I had picked up for about 270 Gs.

After the fire was extinguished, I learned the sporty red convertible took out numerous cars parked near it in the hotel lot. A pipe bomb activated that first crashing sound, followed by the hazardous combination of gas and oil, sparking more booms and flames in a domino effect.

Some passersby were mildly wounded. At least there were no severe injuries or fatalities, seeing that it happened at seven fifteen in the morning. And on the bright side, I didn't drive my Lamborghini that day.

That bomb was personal. I had been targeted.

The truth was, I pissed off a lot of people in my life. Ruthless men, who would have me shot and buried while still breathing, offering no remorse. Any one of the maniacal men who crossed my mind would love to bump me off and take credit for it.

When the next menacing warning occurred a few days later, I had to do something. A video of my son, Danny, and his family at their home was emailed to me with the message, *We're watching.* I could handle someone intimidating me, but this threat targeted my son. Without startling him, I took security precautions. My men monitored Danny's every move to assure his safety without him knowing.

My stress level rose. I started popping anxiety pills like M&Ms.

The creation of my memoirs circled within my mind for years, but it wasn't until the late eighties when I began writing. Information expected to join me in the grave someday would spook my enemies if they knew I put certain unsavory details in writing. Sending me six feet under before my book became published might have been someone's plan.

I put my affairs in order. My will was updated to ensure my loved ones would be taken care of. An additional insurance policy, my life story, would be ready to launch if I died before its completion. I left copies with key people in my life. Caring friends, whom I loved and trusted with this information, would do right by me to ensure my book went to print to find a potential killer.

Should I die under suspicious circumstances, the suspects would be acknowledged in my book. Some pretty vicious people wanted me dead—with good reason.

Writing a tell-all book was not an endeavor I planned to accomplish. Revealing sordid details about my life and loved ones for public consumption—not my typical style. But there was someone special out there who should know the whole truth. Facts about some pieces of my past that I couldn't divulge to her years ago would be exposed. A form of absolution of my sins while tipping the scales with the emotional baggage I carried for years.

This project, much like me, had been a work in progress from the beginning. So the beginning would be the best place to start.

"Somebody to Love"

CHAPTER 1

ROCKY CAVALLO

A Chinese proverb I read once said, *To forget one's ancestors is to be a brook without a source, a tree without a root.* Twenty-five years, the average length of a generation, validated the rationale that millions of people shared in the responsibility of every individual's existence. Our origins motivate us to start our journey and move along the path called destiny.

I didn't materialize into a prosperous tycoon without struggles, compromises, and dipping my toe in a sea of corruption. Surviving hurdles to achieve and maintain success were qualities sewn into the fabric of my soul, thanks to the characteristics inherited from my ancestors, particularly on the Cavallo side. I descended from mighty strong, stubborn roots.

The year was 1919 when Ronald "Rocky" Cavallo, my pop, was born in Reno, Nevada, the son of Egisto Cavallo and Elvira Montgomery-Cavallo.

Grandpa Cavallo was born in the lovely seaside village of Naples in southern Italy. At the tender age of two, his family emigrated to this country, making Brooklyn, New York, their new home. A sizable Italian community had already been established, allowing them to blend in and feel comfortable in the vibrant city. Grandpa Egisto was the youngest of five children. Three of his older siblings died from, of all things, the flu. The harsh New York winters were to blame, so the Cavallos drifted west and eventually settled in Nevada.

Grandma Cavallo's family originated from the antiquated countryside of Canterbury, England, before relocating to the US in Nevada. The Montgomerys weren't too pleased she married an Italian. Let's face it, people in most ethnic groups labeled poor Italian immigrants as undesirable options to marry in the early 1900s. But fate stepped in, and love ignited.

My grandparents were big dreamers with hearts of gold. Their love story began like the Capulets and the Montagues but with a much happier outcome. Grandma didn't allow her family to control her heart. If she had, I wouldn't have existed.

Grandpa relied on his background in construction to earn steady pay, while Grandma worked at a flower stand for extra money. When she became pregnant with my father, she continued working long hours to ensure they had food and shelter for their baby. Despite their financial issues, they were happy, fun-loving people whose idealistic visions carried them throughout life. No matter how little they had, they never lost their faith or their sense of humor. Family meant everything to them.

Pop shared fond memories he carried, learning the construction trade from his father since he was a toddler. He'd accompany Grandpa at some jobsites. At the age of five, he stumbled over a bag of dried cement and fell into a pile of rocks, headfirst. He didn't cry, although he developed quite a lump on his head. The crew considered him a tough kid, earning him the nickname Rocky, in jest, but that nickname stuck throughout his life.

My father worked hard alongside his pop in construction, but that industry didn't interest him as a long-term career. When he was of age, he courageously enlisted in the Army like many young men when the calling for higher education didn't ring. College wasn't part of his future. He craved adventure more than a desk job or a blue-collar career.

Pop met my mother, Mary McGee, after he sustained an injury. Not a war injury, mind you. He fell off a ladder and twisted his ankle.

From a young boy's perspective, Pop made his tale sound so much more dramatic and dangerous than it was.

Mom had been working as a nurse-in-training assigned to tend to Pop's wounded ankle. That cute Irish nursing student wouldn't leave his thoughts.

Pop was a handsome man with ash-brown hair, standing at a medium height with an average yet muscular build. He flaunted confidence like thousand-dollar bills. The next opportunity he had, my father stormed into that Nevada Hospital with a rose bouquet and a request to court the woman he desired.

If he didn't suffer that sprained ankle, he wouldn't have met Mom.

They purchased a small ranch-style house in Carson City after they married in 1940.

My brother, John, was born on April 27, 1941, a spring day in which the rain poured in droves, causing major floods through the streets and within basements. Pop joked about needing a boat to get Mom to the hospital on time.

At some point after John's birth, my parents realized something wasn't right with their baby. They'd smile at him, which would make him smile. Mom sang to him, but John wouldn't respond to her voice. Any reaction he offered was due to their adoring expressions.

He couldn't hear.

Remember, this was the early 1940s. Newborns at that time were not checked for hearing challenges before they left the hospital. Auditory tests were not as robust as the tools and resources existing today to identify hearing losses.

John would make cooing sounds as most babies did, but when Mom or Pop called out to him, he'd never turn his head at the sound of their voices.

Naturally, their hearts broke when John's doctor explained his impairment. Guilty feelings crept up because it took them time to realize something was wrong with their baby—a devastating blow to conquer.

Friends had commented on this perfect-looking infant. How could a baby this handsome be born with such a deficiency?

The doctor advised that the closest school offering a remarkable program for hearing-impaired children was located in Utah.

Fortunately, Mom and Pop were able to take control of the situation and make decisions in their son's best interest. They moved to Ogden, Utah, once Pop's transfer to the Army base in Ogden was approved. The base dwelled in proximity to the School for the Deaf and Blind.

My parents wanted to learn all they could about raising a deaf child. They didn't want their son to stand out like a sore thumb or be excluded from activities with other kids.

They wanted to learn sign language immediately to communicate with John as a baby. Nothing could stop my ambitious parents when determined to beat the odds and defy every obstacle against them, embracing a different type of normalcy in life.

Mom brought John to the School for the Deaf and Blind to learn how to sign and practice those skills, while Pop worked hard to pay for the added expenses outside their budget.

After Pearl Harbor was viciously attacked on December 7, 1941, Franklin Roosevelt declared war on Japan. With the fascist camaraderie of Germany, Italy, and Japan heightening, Germany and Italy wasted no time declaring war on the US.

Pop soon deployed into World War II with little warning, despite my mother's concerns. The fact that he had been raising a disabled baby wouldn't prevent him from his duty. He signed up with the military to protect the citizens of our great country.

When Pop deployed, destination unknown at that time, Mom was left to tend to John, an eight-month-old deaf baby, on her own. Years later, Mom explained the pain she felt, hiding the fear that coursed through her veins. The thought of her husband leaving her to raise a baby with special needs alone frightened her.

Adding to her stress level, Mom couldn't contact Pop while stationed in Europe. His actual location had been a mystery. Local politicians wouldn't help her trace his whereabouts. Her intuitive nature told her that he was still alive.

One of Mom's letters had delivered successfully to Pop's base in Exeter, a city along the southwest corner of England—his secret setting. He read about the challenges Mom endured raising a deaf baby, although she sugarcoated the situation, reassuring him that she had everything under control, and John was adapting to life without the use of his ears.

A wrinkled photo of his beautiful wife holding John as an infant kept his memory pumping overseas, knowing he had the love of a good woman and a son waiting for him at home. Her letter substantiated the love between them, keeping him focused on his mission so he'd return home safely.

Shortly after midnight on May 4, 1942, Exeter was bombed, destroying 75 percent of the city center, injuring 583 people, and taking the lives of 156.

Pop had been buried beneath a pile of rubble of what was once someone's home.

Rescue workers found him alive with a few broken bones, burns, and a head wound. He remembered very little after feeling the fierce blow to his head. He awoke in a British hospital. Memories of how he got there were lost entirely.

When Mom heard of his injury, she pushed relentlessly with the powers that be to send him home instead of keeping him in England. With her nursing skills, she insisted she could care for her husband better than the British hospital staff.

For the rest of her life, Mom believed she won the battle, ensuring Pop returned home to her because of her strong will. She never gave up fighting for her family.

Truth be told, my father suffered psychological issues. He didn't speak from the moment his eyes opened in that British hospital. Shock, maybe. Post-traumatic stress disorder wasn't a common label then.

If he were mentally stable, he would have been ordered back into the vicious battle to defeat our enemies once his flesh wounds healed. His inability to communicate effectively fostered his safe return home to his family due to "combat exhaustion." Pop's homecoming had nothing to do with Mom's obstinate confrontations with the military brass.

After months of separation, tears drizzled from Pop's eyes at the beautiful sight of her shape and warm, welcoming gray eyes. Unfortunately, he couldn't carry a conversation with her. Not even when he saw John, a precious toddler, taking steps on his own by then.

No one forewarned my mother about Pop's fragile state. She realized Pop was incapable of speaking when he'd open his mouth and no words released. She knew he heard her. Revisiting sign language, she hoped he'd recall the language he started to learn before his deployment. At least they were able to communicate using sign language.

One morning, after Pop had been home for a couple of weeks, John cried restlessly, red-faced, waiting for a diaper change.

Mom was taking a shower.

Pop gingerly stepped closer to his crying son and cautiously lifted him from his crib to soothe him. He changed the dirty diaper, a task he hadn't performed since he returned. Then he kissed John's wet cheek, wiped his tears, and muttered words with a raspy voice for the first time, "That better, Johnny boy?"

Mom screamed, bursting with excitement after hearing those delightful words leave her husband's lips in a crackly manner. She slipped, stepping out of the shower, and darted toward the voice she recognized with a towel loosely draped around her body. She ached to hear the rugged sound of his voice again. Mom threw her arms around him and John, offering the warmest hug filled with gratitude. "Your pop is back, Johnny!" she said with tears of joy flowing. "My husband is back."

From that point on, Pop began to speak normally again. The tranquility of home resurrected his mind, reassuring he resided in his safety zone with his family, without the threat of bombs exploding or bullets spraying. Exeter became a prime target for Hitler to terrorize. Multiple air raids occurred in that area prior to the most disastrous attack on Exeter that nearly killed my father.

Once Pop started speaking again, life returned to normal for my parents. At least what they considered normal.

I entered the world on March 11, 1943, at the Thomas Dee Memorial Hospital in Ogden.

Maybe the infamous Exeter Blitz that injured Pop actually saved his life. We'd never know what might have happened to him if he didn't return home after his brief mental incapacitation. When he fully recovered, he remained stationed on US soil at the Ogden base.

I certainly wouldn't have been born if Pop hadn't sustained those injuries in World War II. Wounds that brought him home to be with Mom triggered my existence, starting me on my destined journey.

CHAPTER 2

MARY MCGEE-CAVALLO

The Irish heart is warm and wide, a place where love and peace abide—a saying written on a plaque that always hung on our kitchen wall. Ireland, a beautiful land where I felt a treasured connection, thanks to my mother's roots. The Irish were considered a superstitious bunch. Mom used to tout tales about mystical leprechauns, magical cures, the evil banshee screech, and dreaded curses.

Mary McGee, my mother, was born in Carson City, Nevada, in 1921. Her parents emigrated from the beautiful fishing town of Kinsale in County Cork, Ireland. Tim McGee's fishing pole was practically attached to his arm, and his sassy wife, Maureen, cooked extraordinary delicacies. Grandpa caught a variety of trout and bass from Lake Tahoe. Grandma sold his daily catches at a small fish market they ran near the lake until Grandma's unfortunate death from breast cancer at the age of fifty.

Grandpa Tim lived with diabetes. He was a true Irishman who loved his whiskey as much as he loved fishing. He passed on two years after Grandma. My mother kept her parents' memories alive, always telling exciting stories about their life in Ireland and their adventure of relocating to America.

Mom was raised to believe in the power of love that united families. She fell in love with a confident, strong-minded soldier, and she couldn't wait to start a family.

After giving birth to a deaf son, Mom feared having another child. When she discovered she was pregnant with me, her concern about my health festered. She insisted on having tests performed immediately following my birth. When the doctor in Utah told her I was a normal, healthy baby, she didn't believe him. She performed her own test, calling out to me when my back faced her. She felt relieved I always looked for her when I heard her voice.

Raising a disabled child kept Mom home, although she volunteered at the School for the Deaf and Blind, meeting parents going through the traumatic emotions of raising a child with a hearing deficiency. Mom understood their fears and anxiety. She attempted to reassure them with hope and coping mechanisms. This school offered a kaleidoscope of opportunities to help deaf children navigate the world.

Mom favored her dad in the looks department. She used to say I reminded her of Grandpa Tim's handsome features that she also acquired: medium-brown hair, a sculpted face with a pronounced chin, and catlike eyes an unusual color of gray with a touch of green flecks.

My mother was a sweetheart of a woman and the glue that bonded our family. She kept us in line, dishing out responsibilities, building our skills. Whenever I inhaled the fragrance of lilacs, I'd think of the sweet perfume Mom loved. The rich, intoxicating scent reminded me of her bright smile and the slight musical brogue of her voice. She was fun-loving but a tough disciplinarian when warranted. Her adoring facial expressions projected warmth and kindness, but watch out if she was angry! That Irish temper could ignite a fire.

Numerous memories were engraved of Mom humming melodies and reading us bedtime stories before we could read ourselves. She'd read aloud while using sign language to entertain us both. I wasn't much of a reader as a boy, but John loved to read. Because he couldn't hear, he valued and relied upon his other senses.

My brother missed out on so much without the ability to hear our voices, radio broadcasts, cheers at a ball game, and music. I wouldn't know what to do if I couldn't listen to music. Simple things that most people took for granted every day, John would never experience. I couldn't be jealous if Mom gave John extra hugs or applauds for any achievement he made. Life was far more difficult for my brother.

CHAPTER 3

The Korean War began in 1950, and Pop got deployed against Mom's wishes. I was seven at the time. John was nine.

Grandpa Cavallo had passed away after a fierce fight with lung cancer that year. He never smoked a day in his life. In those days, the construction industry used asbestos, attributing numerous bouts of cancer to people who regularly breathed in the dangerous fibers. The hazardous impacts of asbestos were unknown at that time.

Grandma Cavallo had moved in with us, seemingly disoriented after losing her husband so tragically, watching him die a slow, painful death. She became equally concerned about her son's well-being when Pop started to walk out the front door, headed for battle. "Don't you die on me too!" she shouted a dramatic, heart-wrenching farewell to her only child, hugging him tightly like she'd never let go.

I felt the stress my mother and grandmother endured, missing Pop. His safety overseas was a great concern. They tried not to let their fears show, always wearing a brave face for my benefit.

In 1952, before the war ended, Pop had been scheduled to return home. He was injured again but lucky to pull through with only a broken leg and some burns against his flesh that never fully healed. Over the years, whenever he spent time in the sun, the damaged skin wouldn't tan the same shade as the rest of his body. Fortunately, he wasn't a sun worshiper.

Another soldier he met in Korea, battling the same brutal fight, saved his life. Pop and our family owed a man named Fred Meade. A grenade landed behind a circle of soldiers, catching Fred's eye. Their enemies had discovered where they were stationed. Fred shouted with fierce intensity, "Move!"

If they hadn't run instantaneously, several men might have died from the explosion.

Fred's injuries were far more severe than Pop's or the other soldiers he saved. Fred ensured his brothers ran from that threat before he did. When that grenade blew, a good chunk of Fred's foot burned off, sending his body flying several feet off the ground, leaving shrapnel throughout parts of his left side, and similar burns my father had endured. He survived the trauma after struggling through several surgeries. The man lived with limited function in his left arm and leg for the rest of his life. Fred saved several men that day, including Pop.

Pop never returned to the Army after his tour in Korea. He retired from the military as a sergeant first class.

As I entered my teen years, I attempted to ask him questions about the war.

My father rarely talked about the horrible incidents experienced through every sense of his being. Sights, sounds, smells, wild emotions, and the bitter taste of stench in the air overpowered his chaotic mind. "I could never erase the fury of violence witnessed, but my love for your mother and you boys rescued me," he said without revealing the specifics about the tragedies he endured.

CHAPTER 4

John Cavallo

I never thought my brother differed from anyone else. His disability became a typical, familiar circumstance in our home. Life with a deaf brother, using sign language, had been my "normal" since birth, so we could communicate as a family with John. It was essential to my parents that John never felt out of place in the world.

John made friends at his school, but he attempted to keep up with my friends and me.

If any kid in the neighborhood made fun of my brother, I'd knock his teeth out. Trust me, it happened. I punched out Davey Mitchell's front teeth when I was ten years old because he didn't want the deaf kid to play with us.

Pop beamed with pride because I stood up for John, even though I was the little brother. He expected me to always ensure John's safety, especially after the injury—the horrible accident that cost him the use of his legs, leaving him wheelchair-bound.

Mom had been the disciplinarian in our home. What she said was law, and she didn't like fighting. I got grounded for two weeks for punching Davey. It was well worth it, though.

No one in that neighborhood said a bad word about John again, at least not in my presence. Word got out they'd catch a lickin' if they did.

John's school offered specific programs for children and adults to teach them communication skills, enhance their abilities to find employment, and live independently despite their limitations.

Pop believed John resembled his Italian father with his jet-black hair and olive complexion. But his crisp green eyes were inherited from Grandma Cavallo's British roots.

After John turned sixteen, he met Judy, his first love from the School for the Deaf and Blind. Judy always pulled her bright yellow curls into a ponytail with a daisy tucked between the strands behind her ear. Poodle skirts were a popular trend for teenage girls at that time. Judy owned a variety of poodle skirts in different shades, fabrics, and various-colored poodles.

Watching John and Judy communicate fascinated me. Their fingers and movements were fast, fluid, and furious. They would often use their own voices when they were passionate about a topic or if they fought, forgetting their disability at the moment. Then they'd spend time making up.

I knew John and Judy were screwing around in his bedroom. Hard not to know since there was no volume control on those two. They were deaf, but they weren't mute. I'd wander outside to shoot baskets when the moaning started.

One day, Mom returned home earlier than expected from the market and heard them going at it.

John and Judy had no clue Mom came home. They couldn't hear the door open, but they sensed the vibrations of her screaming at the top of her lungs when she realized her sweet, precious teenage boy discovered girls and the elation of sex.

That might have been Mom's first realization that John was a regular teenager in spite of his disabilities.

CHAPTER 5

Pop had married the love of his life like his father did, but he also loved money, which was something his parents didn't have or care about. Pop made some wise investments that really paid off. Not only did he have a good head for numbers, he was a true idealist who always envisioned the bigger picture.

He invested his entire life savings and acquired a loan to purchase a hotel in the early sixties when the glamour of the Vegas Strip had beefed up. He named the hotel after his mother, using her maiden name. The Montgomery Hotel and Casino, a classy establishment that, at that time, rivaled the Sahara, the Tropicana, and the Stardust.

Grandma beamed with ecstasy when she learned that he named the hotel after her surname. Her son survived another war, later to transform into a sensational entrepreneur. Unfortunately, she passed away before she saw the hotel, her namesake.

My parents purposely stayed busy after her funeral, diverting the anguish felt for losing such a loving and caring woman. They packed up our things, and we left the state of Utah to move to Las Vegas permanently. We lived at the hotel until profits poured in to buy a new family home. It didn't take too long before the Montgomery proved its success financially. People flocked to the hot new hotel and casino on the Strip.

Soon, Pop wanted us to live normally, off the hotel property. We moved into a Tuscan-style stucco mansion with seven thousand square feet of space in Henderson.

The place had an in-ground pool and a basketball court prominently situated on ten-acres of land. The lawn was perfectly clipped. Ripened peaches and apricots hung from trees, begging to be picked. The sweet aroma awakened my senses through open windows on breezy days. An elaborate display of vines with the richest-looking strawberries draped loosely over a wall of white columns. Behind the columns, a horseshoe and bocce court were set up for my parents to enjoy when entertaining guests. It was quite an upgrade from our Utah house.

With John's impairments, Pop always said the Montgomery would be mine to run someday. He dreamed of the two of us building an empire together, father and son. And from that day on, I was groomed to be a businessman.

Pop insisted I acquire a college education. The partying and the girls were the best part of my college experience. I skated by with a C average and soon earned a bachelor's degree in business from the University of California in Santa Barbara, one of the biggest party schools in the country. My education and love for business were Pop's dreams, not mine, but I had a blast.

Suddenly, the weight of responsibility fell on my shoulders like a ton of bricks. Pop said, "Tommy, your grandpa died much too young. Who knows what damage the war did to my mind and my insides? If anything happens to me, you need to take care of your mama, John, and the Montgomery. I know I'm leaving them in your capable hands, son." Mere words he drilled into me for years declared the Montgomery as my destiny.

In 1963, tragedy struck our family. Mom was diagnosed with the disease that took her mother's life—breast cancer. She was an angel on earth who earned her wings in heaven too early. Unfortunately, we lost her to that horrible condition a few days after my twentieth birthday. I never enjoyed my birthday again, thinking about my mother's illness and her harsh struggle to survive fighting that severe uphill battle—only to lose the war.

The bright light in Pop's eyes that once gleamed vibrantly had vanished. He spent more nights at the casino, nose to the grindstone, keeping himself busy.

Mom's death was a devastating loss for John, maybe more than the rest of us. She was home every day to keep him company. She pushed him to join social groups to meet people, whether they were handicapped or not. Mom's encouragement helped John conquer his fear of living life without limits.

She urged him to look for jobs after we settled in our Vegas home. Something on his own without Pop's influence to build his esteem. No one felt as proud as she did when he achieved that critical goal, knowing he could contribute to society without Pop padding his way.

Independence had been instilled within John, but our father always ensured his needs were fulfilled to simplify his life. Ramps were built for John's wheelchair to access the house. He had purchased a van to easily store John's wheelchair when we drove into town.

Pop hired a driver named Buck who knew sign language. Buck and John became good friends. Buck used the van to drive John to work or anywhere he needed to go. John snagged a job sorting mail at the post office.

Pop allowed John to choose the type of work he desired, abiding by Mom's wishes. My father had been too busy controlling *my* future, molding me into a junior entrepreneur, to care about John's employment choices. He never thought his deaf son could run a booming business like the Montgomery. At that time, there were limited resources to allow people with disabilities the privilege. He would have found tasks for John at the Montgomery to handle, but he felt proud that John secured a position he enjoyed and succeeded at.

In Mom's honor, Pop hung a lovely twenty-six-by-thirty-eight portrait of her, centered on the living room wall. Whenever I needed to feel close to her, that was where I could be found. None of us were quite the same without her.

CHAPTER 6

SADIE MEADE

Fast-forward to 1968. Saturday, February 3, to be exact. The day I took the plunge. I wished it were into a pool.

My Saturdays were often spent lounging in the pool, catching some rays, and waiting for night to roll around. Gambling with the boys along the Strip, a few drinks, picking up girls, not necessarily in that order. Life was simpler before I met Sadie Meade, my bride.

Sadie's father was Fred Meade, the soldier who saved Pop's life in the Korean War.

"If it hadn't been for Fred, I wouldn't be here. Pieces of my body would've been shipped home in a bag," Pop said. He owed Fred his life. If Pop died, the Montgomery would cease to exist.

Pop learned from mutual friends that Fred had been struggling financially. His family lived on the East Coast in a small fishing town outside of Boston. He wanted to help his war buddy and hero, so he offered Fred a job and relocated his family to North Las Vegas.

Don't get me wrong, Sadie and I easily became friends. She was a beautiful girl with the face of an innocent angel. Bright blue eyes and silky blond hair. Petite with a set of killer legs. Her legs and what connected them made up for her flat chest.

Of course, I sampled her body before the wedding. That was how I got into this mess. I wouldn't call this a shotgun wedding, but she was definitely knocked up, and her finger pointed straight at me.

Pop felt ecstatic! He'd been hounding me to settle down and find a nice girl to marry. I was only twenty-four.

I remembered my discussion with Pop when I first told him she was pregnant. I explained I wasn't ready for marriage, especially to a woman I didn't love.

"You're going to be a father, Tommy. Do the right thing. If you didn't want to get married, you should've worn a frickin' rubber."

The responsibilities that accompanied a child entering my life forced me to settle down. My father's philosophy corroborated my need to successfully handle the stresses of running the Montgomery since I'd have a family to support. Marrying Sadie proved myself worthy in Pop's eyes to take over the family business before passing it down to my children someday. And my first child was unexpectedly on the way with Sadie.

Just because Pop found Mom and fell in love instantly didn't mean Cupid would point his arrow in my direction.

If only I understood what the hell I was getting myself into that one drunken day after a few too many Jameson shots in a hotel room with Sadie. One erotic romp led to a life sentence.

I found myself staring at my dazed reflection in the back room at St. Francis Church, waiting for my bride to arrive. If I had a gun, I might have shot myself. I never planned to marry anyone before my twenty-fifth birthday.

Pop wanted me to have a wife and kids, but that wasn't my priority. Maybe if I met the right woman, marriage would have felt natural. I sure enjoyed myself looking for her. That perfect woman— if she existed. Sadie wasn't *the one*.

Working along the Strip in Vegas was any young man's fantasy. I learned about all functions of the Montgomery's operations—from the front desk processes, to the casino pits, to the entertainment. The entertainment was my favorite part. I had a charming way of getting many a dancer out of her clothes. But that all changed after Sadie's baby announcement and the clanking sound of wedding bells.

CHAPTER 7

THE TOSCANO FAMILY

The deafening sound of silence seized the back room of the church where John and I waited on my wedding day. Stressed—an understatement to describe how I felt moments before marrying a girl I knew in a physical sense through a moderate friendship.

For a man with the inability to hear or speak with a clear voice, I had never known John to be so quiet. He sat upright in his chair, staring through a stained-glass window that overlooked the muted street, fiddling with his bowtie.

Instinctively, my head lowered before a statue of Saint Francis of Assisi embracing a lamb. My fingers played with the ends of my brown strands. I chanted the Our Father to myself when heavy footsteps and rambunctious laughter disturbed the peaceful moment. The side door creaked, and in strolled Pop with Carmine Toscano, our new business partner.

Carmine wore a formal dark-gray suit. His large-brimmed hat hid his widening bald spot. An oversize mole positioned near his chin on the left side of his face always caught my eye. He could have at least plucked the hair sticking out of it, but I wouldn't dare tell him. No one would. I tried not to stare at that mole when he shook my hand, saying, "Tommy, hey, good luck with your marital future, son. She's a lovely woman you got there."

Out of respect, I held his hand firmly and said, "Thank you, Carmine. It was nice of you to fly out from Philly for the wedding."

"We're practically family, my boy. The Montgomery blood runs through all our veins now."

I offered no reaction to his unholy statement.

My father pictured a more luxurious hotel and casino to enrich our ranking among the competition on the Strip. To honor Grandma Cavallo's British heritage and my mother's Irish roots, Pop envisioned a European look, adding a flavor of those countries to our hotel. No other hotel on the Strip offered such a remarkable theme at that time. The three wings of the hotel were to be recreated with the effervescent flavors of England, Ireland, and Scotland.

At first, I thought Pop's visions were too fantastic for any contractor to oblige, but Pop knew about construction from his days spent working with his father. Miniature models of our hotel were created to lay out the incredible architecture. Murals with scenic pictures of the countries' landscapes were painted, sculptures were replicated, and flags were assembled. I knew Pop's futuristic concept could be a gold mine, but he needed money, investors to help fund the pricey renovations.

Enter Carmine from Philadelphia. Why would someone from Pennsylvania want a piece of our business? The Montgomery was our hotel, yet Carmine's recommendations carried a lot of weight with Pop, along with the weight of his wallet.

Pop told me not to worry about Carmine. He'd deal with the man directly. However, if our hotel and casino didn't make this man money, Pop would have to answer for it. I never liked the way that sounded. Pop didn't allow Carmine total control. The hotel was our family business, our livelihood. Pop ensured 51 percent of the Montgomery was in his name.

The Mafia influenced the Vegas Strip since Ben "Bugsy" Siegel opened the Flamingo back in '46. The Strip lured millions of tourists annually, leading to a substantial income, an investment in which the mob wanted a cut. If the mob didn't have their hands in a Vegas hotel by the late sixties, most likely Howard Hughes did.

Carmine's primary business was in tea. He imported various teas from around the globe. Who knew there were so many types of tea? He sold his products under the company name, the Heavenly Tea Emporium. The tea business, not Carmine personally, became our partner on the books. There was a valid reason for that. Carmine was a Mafia underboss. Untouchable by anyone inside or outside the organization, except cops. He made some kind of business offer to Pop that was too good to pass up.

Carmine's older cousin, Aniello Toscano, was the head of the Toscano family—*il capo di tutti i boss*. The boss sat back and reaped the financial rewards of his organization, delegating tasks to Carmine and his soldiers.

Besides the tea company, the Toscanos searched for another legitimate entity to seek their corrupt teeth into. The Mafia always looked for productive ways to generate income for the boss. Unfortunately, they saw potential in our pride and joy, and we served a variety of the Toscanos' fancy tea flavors to our guests.

Their crew of thugs hung around the casino every night. We never made money on those wise guys. That was how the business rolled. They'd request credit at the tables, try to beat the system to win, and cause a commotion with the innocent dealer when they lost. What was the benefit of having these guys in our lives and business? To answer my own question, if the mob didn't get what they wanted, they'd destroy the Montgomery, and we'd be lucky to remain breathing.

Carmine didn't always fly out to Vegas to see Pop. He was busy performing the duties of an underboss. His trusted business associate worked directly with us, a capo, or captain in the organization, nicknamed Fat Nicky. And man was Fat Nicky fat. If I had to guess how much this guy weighed, I'd say over four hundred pounds, easy. How much did a guy have to eat to get that fucking fat? Only Carmine called him Fat Nicky to his face, to my knowledge. Nobody else dared to call him that directly.

Fat Nicky's presence simply entering the room was enough to scare the shit out of somebody. That big, tall walking heart attack waiting to happen strutted around with no expression and no personality. He was Pop's main contact, and he inserted himself into our business.

While Fat Nicky oversaw the casino operations, Marty Carbone was a newly appointed soldier who handled Carmine's drug trade in Vegas. Millions of dollars were collected from that branch of the Toscano business annually.

Marty's predecessor got popped along with several street dealers. A war started to brew on the streets of Vegas. Fat Nicky and his bosses were desperate for revenge against a rival mob family deeply connected yet staying under the radar of the Las Vegas Police Department.

CHAPTER 8

THE MEADES

I glanced at my watch continually as I paced around the back room of the church. The rhythm of my heart danced at a quick beat, anxious to get through the day. My mind drifted to a conversation Sadie and I had when we first decided on the wedding style. Pop anticipated splurging, but Sadie preferred the exact opposite.

"Tommy, talk to your pop. He wants us to have a lavish wedding. Given my fragile condition, I'd rather have a simple ceremony. You know my father probably can't afford to pay for a formal event. No announcements, either."

We compromised. No public declarations in local papers about our union were made. Pop insisted he invite his wide circle of friends and business associates, whereas the Meade side only consisted of the immediate family. We planned a simple yet elegant mass at St. Francis Church, complete with the standard vows, followed by a delicious meal prepared by the Montgomery's head chef in the large banquet hall with filet mignon and lobster tails to serve our guests.

I felt grateful she didn't want to broadcast my giving up the single life, but I was also curious why Sadie had been tight-lipped about her pregnancy before the wedding. "Did you tell your parents you're pregnant yet?" I asked her numerous times.

"Of course not," she'd reply matter-of-factly.

"What are you waiting for? They're going to find out soon enough. Pop will bust if he has to keep this secret much longer."

"*After* the wedding," she insisted.

"I think they'll figure out you weren't a virgin bride when they learn your due date."

I played by Sadie's rules and kept her pregnancy quiet from everyone except Pop and John.

Sadie was right about Fred, her father, who couldn't contribute a dime toward our wedding.

When Fred's career launched as our security manager, he offered keen insight into the development of processes for his team to ensure the safety of guests as well as profit increases. People cheated and conned casinos regularly. Fred installed beneficial plans to protect our business from swindlers. He attended conferences to learn surveillance techniques and educate the security team and pit bosses on detecting potential scams. I had to admit, the man was smart.

After a while, negative accounts and specific, adverse trends poured in from employees. Fred mistreated employees if they weren't white Catholics. We took recruitment and other accountabilities away from him to salvage our integrity.

Fred required a babysitter—me.

I began to pay more attention to his actions to verify employee complaints. Soon, I realized that Fred gave into temptation. He spent too much time losing at Blackjack. Little by little, Pop removed responsibilities from his plate. Unfortunately, that gave Fred more free time. Time he used to gamble.

Pop bailed Fred out of so many jams with the local loan sharks. Fred had already lost part of his foot in Korea, requiring a cane to balance his steps. You owed these sharks money, and they'd start snipping off fingers one by one until the debt was paid in full with a ton of interest. Loan sharks didn't care if their debtors were men, women, or handicapped. They'd prey on weaknesses and threaten family members. Whatever it took to get their money. Fred's golden hair grayed and thinned over time, most likely from stress.

I wondered if Pop felt sorry he hired this guy as much as I did. But Fred was under my father's protection, so I remained cautious with my criticisms. The history they shared as Army brothers bonded them in a way civilians couldn't understand. Pop had Fred's back.

Fred's gambling began to severely impact his marriage and the lifestyle he could have offered his family in Vegas.

Suzanne, Fred's wife, was always kind, pleasant, and gentle— an attractive woman with honey-blond hair and a shapely figure, displaying a delicate aura. In some ways, she reminded me of my mother, whom I missed terribly, especially on my wedding day. If Suzanne doted on me, I'd welcome it. Her genuine presence gave me the sense of a nurturing, motherly figure in my life. A sensation I craved.

Sadie's younger sister, Lisa, an introverted bookworm, kept her blue eyes set inside a book at all times. Her pretty features resembled Sadie's, but she had a touch of red highlights through her blond hair. She was also much taller than Sadie's mere five-foot height.

The youngest Meade sibling, Patrick, timidly spoke at a whisper. His father never paid him attention unless he screwed up. Once Patrick and I started talking regularly, he'd open up to me, exposing more confidence. We easily built trust and respect for each other.

Patrick spent time with me at the Montgomery, helping out at some events. I noticed he never checked out the dancers in their revealing wardrobes or any girl for that matter. The ladies flirted with him, but he'd only respond if a good-looking guy stopped to speak to him. Then he'd blush. Patrick's head, layered with thick golden waves, turned at the male performers, security guards, bellhops, and valets.

Given society's objections to homosexuality in the sixties, this was not a topic I'd bring up. But I assumed he was gay. I kept my thoughts to myself about Patrick. Sexual orientation wasn't something you spoke about openly unless you joined one of the many protests occurring.

A wide variety of demonstrations exhibited daily in the sixties. Rallies and marches against the war and the draft, people either for or against the women's liberation movement, and the brave people who fought for their right to love whomever they wanted in spite of race or same-sex relationships. Some men like Patrick wouldn't call attention to themselves. A dark secret that could turn the community against them if revealed. It was a tumultuous era for people needing to be heard or accepted for their beliefs if outside the horizon of society's views.

John and Sadie seemed to hit it off initially, but he wasn't overly thrilled about my marriage to a knocked-up bride. As my older brother, he worried. John might have been deaf, but his other senses were rather perceptive. Who knew where his sixth sense about Sadie originated? He insisted I look into her past. "Please, Tommy, reconsider this. You don't have to get married," he demanded in sign.

My friendship with Sadie developed in the fall of 1967. Sadie worked as a coat check girl at the hotel. Around that time was when I discovered Pop sold a large chunk of the business to the Toscanos—49 percent worth. I never liked sharing our business with outsiders, especially those thugs. Our association with the Toscanos felt like an anchor tied to my legs, drowning me into a deep, dark abyss.

I slammed back Jameson shots like water one day. Sadie noticed me drinking and joined me. She could hold her liquor. Kept up with me, in fact. My stress level and the buzz landed us in between the sheets in my private suite. I might have been plastered that afternoon, but she was something else in the sack. That afternoon led to her pregnancy.

Fate sucker-punched me in the gut.

Despite my pleading with Pop, he insisted I do right by Sadie and the baby. I heard the same lecture since I was a teenager about responsibility and becoming a family man. Pop wanted me to settle down to be prepared to take over the business someday.

Falling in love and having a family would have been part of my future at some point, but you'd think I could have had a say in the woman I married. My irresponsibility, having unprotected sex, initiated a significant diversion to my destiny. I couldn't accept the fact that marrying Sadie was my fate or a lousy joke designed by the universe.

Before a church filled with guests, Father Flanagan, and God, Sadie and I said, *I do*, legally binding us together as Pop wanted.

CHAPTER 9

THE RUSSO FAMILY

Because Sadie hated to fly, we stayed in town for our honeymoon at a suite at the Montgomery. I had planned a Hawaiian adventure for our vacation, but Sadie's nervous stomach couldn't tolerate the flight. Instead, I introduced her to a variety of Vegas attractions: exciting shows, gambling, fine meals, and a drive to the magnificent Grand Canyon.

One night, I brought Sadie to a local nightclub, Spritz, a hotspot for locals made popular by celebrities. President Kennedy supposedly showed his face in this joint a few times with his Rat Pack pals.

Vince Russo, the club's owner, was a business associate of Pop's. I introduced Sadie to Vince, a made man in the Italian Mafia, who climbed to the top position of boss. Vince proved to be intelligent with limited education, earning the nickname Brains by his superiors and peers. The organization was stitched within his genetics. He followed in his father's footsteps into this life of crime for men who could validate their full Italian heritage.

Frank Russo, Vince's brother, held the number two spot in the criminal family tree as underboss. I heard a lot of stories about Frank Russo, mob enforcer, nicknamed Madman. I wondered if it bothered him that his nickname labeled him a crazy lunatic, whereas Vince, the brains, was considered the smart brother.

Pop warned me if I ever saw Madman walking down the street, cross the road, and don't make eye contact. That psychopath loved to kill things and required no reasonable rationale to do so.

Vince knew how to make money while staying under the radar from the cops. He owned a couple of nightclubs in Vegas and Reno as a front for his racketeering franchise. He also owned several brothels. That was how he made the big bucks.

The brothels were legal businesses in some Nevada counties, but prostitution wasn't legal in Vegas. That didn't prevent pimps and streetwalkers from trolling the Strip.

Vince never got his hands dirty. He had business associates and close friends he relied upon. Big Sal Maroni, consigliere or counselor in the organization, held the number three position. Capos, Benny "the Blade" DeLeone and Angelo "Sweets" Francisco, controlled the pimps monopolizing the Strip to claim a piece of that action. If street pimps were taking money away from Vince's legal brothel businesses, they needed to pay a tax. Vince's capos and soldiers carried out his orders. They made a fortune over the years on hookers.

Rumor had it that Frank was responsible for the hits of at least thirty-five men and women. I had no clue if that number was accurate or who those victims were that he allegedly murdered in cold blood. The man had no soul, and his ruthless tactics bore no boundaries.

Vince might have been the boss and the brains, but Frank had Vince's ear and could persuade him on business matters.

In 1967, Frank got whacked in his own home. Who would have had the balls to execute Madman, and did the suspect live to talk about it? Vince must have had his cronies look into Frank's death since the cops weren't spending much time finding the murderer of a murderer.

I never divulged these details to Sadie. There was no reason for her to know anything about my knowledge of such crimes and affiliations.

CHAPTER 10

Pop's wedding gift to us was a beautiful English Tudor in Henderson with enough space and acreage for a large family to reside—the family my father expected me to have. Heirs to our family's fortune with business minds to take over the hotel in the future, maintaining its growth and protecting Pop's legacy long past his death.

I tried my best to prepare for the baby's arrival. The baby's bedroom was painted a pale-yellow color, stocked with the necessary furniture and supplies a newborn needed.

I added Sadie's name to my accounts at the local stores around town so she could pick out and purchase whatever she wanted for the baby. For some reason, she still hadn't told her family about the pregnancy, but she loved shopping at Sears and J. C. Penney. I enjoyed watching her eyes widen when the register reflected the money she spent, knowing I covered the charges.

Sadie had no problem spending my money, but she worried what her parents would say about becoming grandparents so soon. Hell, we were married at that point, so who cared when conception actually occurred?

Unfortunately, she never had the opportunity to tell her family about the baby, despite my constant hounding. Sadie tumbled down the patio steps in the backyard one afternoon. That fall caused a miscarriage. Her doctor called me, expressing the somber news.

"I don't know what happened, Tommy. If only I was able to prevent that terrible fall. I'm so sorry." Tears built up in her sad blue eyes.

"It's not your fault, Sadie. I know you'd never do anything to hurt the baby."

"We'll have another baby someday. I know it," she said with an ounce of excitement in her tone.

I couldn't be excited about a future baby. I wasn't sure how I felt about losing this one. I admit to feeling relief, but I grieved the loss of that baby more than I thought possible.

My emotions ran from sadness to anger to a sour numbness. I didn't quite know how to deal with the trauma. I started drinking a little more than usual to ease the stabbing blow to my heart. I might not have married Sadie for love, but I liked her—back then.

Pop felt devastated, hearing the tragic news. Becoming a grandfather had been a monumental event he dreamed about. He desperately wanted grandchildren to secure leadership of the family business and fortune for future generations.

Eventually, the Meades learned about Sadie's pregnancy and miscarriage. She never explained how far along she had been, feigning purity.

Since the baby didn't survive, why stay married? I asked myself this question every day. Sadie wasn't a bad wife. Smoking hot and phenomenal between the sheets. She looked good on my arm and could cook a good meal, but I didn't love her. I thought I could try for the baby's sake, but then there was no baby. I wasn't in a rush to get divorced, but continuing a marriage without love didn't seem right. I felt confident I could pay her off. Make her leave without regrets. I wished her no harm. We could have remained friends if we divorced amicably.

"How much should we pay Sadie to go away?" I asked my father.

"Cavallo men don't get divorced!" Pop shouted, reminding me of the commitment I made to my wife and marriage. "Grow up! Give marriage a chance," he demanded.

Pop loved Sadie and her family. He admired Sadie's strength and boldness, which he deemed as honest and direct. From the moment Fred's family moved to Vegas, we suddenly spent a lot of time with them for holidays, dinners, and business parties.

John didn't believe it was a coincidence that Sadie lost the baby after having access to a shitload of money. He implied she might not have been pregnant at all.

Her doctor and I spoke after the miscarriage. Sadie didn't create such a farce to marry me for my money. At that time, I had no reason to question her.

I entered a loveless marriage out of an obligation, and my father wouldn't consider the ugly term divorce.

I felt trapped.

CHAPTER 11

My buddy Jim fit the bill for an open security position. He and I had become friends when we lived in Utah. Jim was a couple of years older than me. We met at a function at John's school. Jim's cousin was hearing-impaired, so he knew some sign language. Once Jim and I discovered we both knew sign, our friendship grew, and he befriended John too.

Jim enlisted in the Marines while my family settled in Vegas. When Jim completed his tour, he contacted me in search of steady employment. Pop hired him on the spot because of his military background. Jim was a trustworthy man who understood discretion. Built like a freight train, he stood a good six feet, two inches.

I'd probably be a scrawny guy if Jim didn't teach me how to box in a ring and the proper techniques of weight training. Working out with Jim transformed my body into a toned, sculpted shape with six-pack abs.

If any customer stepped out of line at the Montgomery, Jim knew how to take them down. Normally, his demeanor appeared calm, but Jim didn't tolerate con artists or threats. He dished out some tough disciplinary actions against a few grifters who deserved a tune-up before handing them over to the police after the blood was wiped clean from their body parts. The less threatening thieves were kindly escorted out, blackballed from the premises or arrested, minus the beatdown approach.

Once Jim demonstrated his worth, he enlisted some of his Marine brothers to apply for employment in security.

Fred made preposterous remarks because a couple of these Marines were black. If they were qualified for the job, I didn't care about the color of their skin.

Fred's job hung in the balance, but he thought he had a solid hook—his daughter.

CHAPTER 12

With the Toscano crew taking advantage of the special privileges they procured, Fred, Jim, and the security team acted cautiously. They knew that this gang of felons shouldn't be hassled.

Pop realized he made a deal with the devil. But we were stuck with this unholy allegiance—engraved in legal forms, bolstered by coercion.

Fat Nicky and his associates ran the casino skim, annihilating the integrity of our business. Before the casino money was counted for the IRS to capture, these crooks robbed a chunk of it every night to line Carmine and Aniello's pockets. They were an entitled bunch, believing we owed them for their investment to support the renovations Pop envisioned.

Like I already stated, if the mob didn't get what they wanted, they'd destroy us.

I worked late many nights to keep an eye on Fat Nicky's thugs. Sadie probably thought I was having an affair. If only it were that simple. If these guys got carried away, I didn't want the police on our asses.

A few times, I had to tell Nicky that his boys were getting out of hand. He'd listen to my respectful argument and tell those idiots to tone it down. They would listen for a while, only to revert to bad behavior. They thought they were invincible and could get away with anything.

Sometimes I'd leave the noise of the crowded casino to return home to the noise that ached in my head. My subconscious screamed, warning me to run from this doomed marriage. Staying overnight at the hotel allowed me a better night's sleep with fewer nightmares.

Sadie complained when I didn't make it home at a reasonable hour to enjoy a meal she prepared. She loved to fight with me, adding an intense blaze to some erotic romps in our bed. The business consumed a lot of my time. My absence wasn't personal. Well, not really.

On one prosperous night for the Montgomery in 1969, I was summoned to take an urgent call. Pop had been admitted to the hospital. I called Sadie. Buck was notified to ensure John arrived at the hospital immediately.

The doctor and I reviewed the potential outcomes before John and Sadie arrived. Heart attack? Stroke? Pop's symptoms pointed toward stroke, but additional tests were needed to rule out other possibilities and to confirm the severity of his condition.

John and I recently discussed planning his fiftieth birthday party. Could men at this young age have a heart attack or a stroke? Apparently, if they maintained a stressful life, drank too much alcohol, and smoked, they were at risk. I could help Pop quit smoking those cigars he enjoyed and cut back on booze. However, running the Montgomery with undesirable business associates would never be stress-free.

Pop was alive, but he remained unconscious, attached to a web of wires that flowed to a machine beside his bed. I contacted our attorney, Len Stein. I knew Pop devised legal agreements in which I would take over the business in his absence or death. I couldn't come to terms with my father dying. I did my best to stay calm and positive, but I was scared of losing him.

A tough Army sergeant like Rocky Cavallo never looked so helpless and frail as he did in that grim hospital bed—pale, bleak, instantly aging twenty years. His rich brown hair seemed to turn silver with each passing second. Wrinkles around his lips and eyes became more pronounced.

He would want me to ensure there were no disruptions in the hotel operations while he recovered. My father had groomed me for this role since my teen years. No matter how much planning and grooming Pop concocted, I didn't feel ready. But I had to be.

CHAPTER 13

Len Stein, a brilliant and ambitious attorney, handled my father's legal documents. Pop had options when searching for a good legal mind. Something special clicked between Len and him, despite Len's youth. As our attorney, Len kept our details confidential and legally sound. Did he know the Toscano crew was robbing us blind? Possibly.

Carmine acted as the official owner of the Heavenly Tea Emporium. Len didn't represent Carmine personally. Len worked for the Montgomery and my family. He didn't have to deal with Carmine unless his silent partner status impacted the Montgomery.

I stepped through a haze of cigarette smoke when I entered Len's office, which otherwise appeared neat and orderly. The only paperwork on his desk was related to the discussion about to take place. The good news was Pop survived his health ordeal. His will would be useless unless he died. However, Len explained he encouraged my father to prepare a power of attorney in case Pop might be unavailable or incapacitated—like right now. Len said that Pop created an addendum to this POA shortly after my wedding.

The POA indicated that I was to have full control of the business and operate it as Pop would have, with some provisions.

I always appreciated Len's wealth of knowledge with legal matters. He ensured the legal paperwork, contracts, and taxes were legitimate and official.

Len offered me a smoke. I declined the Camel cigarette.

At a young age, Len's hairline receded tremendously. He sat back in his bulky chair behind his tidy desk and smoothed out his navy and gold plaid pants. He blew a puff of smoke into the air and said, "I can ensure the power of attorney is activated, Tommy. That means you'll have access to your father's assets and the legal right to run the Montgomery."

Relief washed over me. No one, including the Toscanos, could muscle in while Pop was ill. I automatically took over as the majority shareholder with 51 percent of the business. The Heavenly Tea Emporium owned 49 percent plus an added bonus—the skim. If I could find a way to be rid of my partners, I would—unless they had me killed.

Before I became too excited, Len's hazel eyes floated up to meet mine, blowing a ring of smoke through the air. "Regarding the addendum, your father established three stipulations that you must abide by to remain in charge. I discouraged him from adding the codicil, Tommy, but Rocky insisted upon it. Who knew a sudden health crisis would happen to him at fifty? Your tough father survived World War II and Korea when so many other soldiers gave their lives. These terms were meant to protect your family and the Montgomery's longevity."

"What are they?"

"The first one is to ensure John is taken care of, meaning his health, special needs, and financial livelihood."

"Done. I wouldn't have it any other way." I blew out a breath, exhaling a fair amount of anxiety.

"The second condition is meant to assure your ability to run the Montgomery, attaining lucrative outcomes. A role he claimed you were groomed for as his successor."

I acknowledged his statement with a hesitant nod, eager to understand the meaning of Len's words.

Len tapped his fingers across the desk, then flicked his cigarette ashes over a silver ceramic ashtray filled with stubs. "Your father wants you to show a profit. Be innovative. Visualize the future. The bottom line is, as long as the POA is in place, quarterly profits need to exceed the current financial report."

Beads of sweat glistened against my forehead. That sounded reasonable, but I'd need to review the last report to understand what I was up against. "Why would he challenge me to this degree, Len?"

"He's protecting the business he built, Tommy. If you can't run it properly, you're out. Maybe in a few weeks, Rocky's condition will improve. In which case, I'll speak with him about updating or terminating this paperwork. He wanted the business to remain in the family, but he didn't want it to fail, either."

My head nodded absently. "Believe me, I'd love to talk to him about this too. You said there were three stipulations."

Len cleared his throat and wiped his hand across the back of his head.

A bad feeling surfaced. Len was a terrible poker player. Stroking the back of his head was his *tell*. He had no clue everyone at the table knew he'd fold or bluff his way through that hand. The other players would win big, thanks to Len's signature quirk.

He lit another cigarette and took a deep drag, blowing smoke from his nose. "Your father was a family man. He was so proud of you for settling down and planning a family. I advised him to have your wife sign a prenuptial agreement, but he liked Sadie, and he believed she'd be good for you. You were finally showing signs of maturity and taking on more responsibility."

"At that time, I wasn't in a good frame of mind to think about a prenup. You realize why I married Sadie, right?"

"Yes, but unfortunately, she lost the baby. I'm sorry about that."

My head lowered, still anguished about that tragedy. The mere thought of my child dying inside her left a twinge of pain in my heart. "Pop wouldn't let me pay her off for an amicable divorce. I wanted to give Sadie something to leave the marriage peacefully. After all, she was carrying my child. Pop wanted me to stay married, but I had every intention of resurrecting the subject of divorce again."

"Yes, your father wanted your marriage to stay intact. The final stipulation is that you can't divorce Sadie or annul the marriage."

"What? He can't put that in a legal document! Can he?"

"Your father wrote the book on eccentricity. I disagreed with him, Tommy, but he felt very strongly that you needed to stay in this marriage and give it a chance. He didn't want you to run away from responsibility. Instead of acting like a playboy, chasing skirts, Rocky wanted you grounded and focused on maintaining the success of the business. He believed Sadie was the girl to settle you down and give you children. This addendum was legally filed, per his request."

I shook my head in disbelief, recognizing the foundation of my marriage wasn't love, but Sadie and I were okay at that moment. "I didn't plan to rush to divorce court, Len. I mean, this document is only valid while Pop is recuperating. When he recovers and takes the business back, he'll change these terms. He can't sentence me to a life I might not want forever in legal text."

"I understand. For now, this codicil is in effect until he is capable of making legal decisions, or…he dies."

My gray eyes met Len's, filled with sorrow at the thought. "I can't think about that, Len. He's my father."

"If Rocky dies, Tommy, his will would be legally binding and the POA branded irrelevant. You'd outright own his part of the Montgomery and all his assets. Whatever you do with the business would be your decision without the influential factors stipulated in this document."

"If I divorced Sadie tomorrow, Len, what exactly would happen? Could I challenge this addendum?"

"Legally, Carmine could take full control of the Montgomery because you'd be out. These are your father's wishes that he put in writing. You *can* get divorced, but your fifty-one percent would be up for grabs to an interested buyer, like Carmine. Although I never divulged your father's legal requisites to him."

My body shifted in my seat as my mind worked in overdrive, wondering how to get out of this. I prayed Pop would regain consciousness and recover quickly. Losing the family business to the Mafia would be unacceptable. They would destroy everything Pop built. John and I could lose our financial stability. It was my duty to protect the Montgomery and our economic future.

CHAPTER 14

Before formal announcements were issued to the staff about Pop's health crisis and the leadership change, I contacted Carmine in Philly to explain the situation as well as the power of attorney, confirming my new leadership role.

Carmine insisted he'd fly to Vegas.

Len arrived at my office before Carmine. I didn't want any problems with the Toscano crew working directly with me while Pop recovered. To ensure Carmine wouldn't dispute the change in leadership, Len brought a copy of the initial legal document that declared me in charge. He conveniently excluded the addendum with Pop's stipulations spelled out. Carmine didn't need to know about Pop's peculiar test, confirming my ability as a businessman and family man. If we sat in a court of law, Len would be more forthcoming. We chose not to disclose those details to Carmine, and I didn't want there to be any question about who was in charge of the Montgomery.

Carmine entered the room all decked out, wearing a black business suit with a striped silver tie and a dark cloud drifting over the fedora covering his bald spot, displaying agitation. He approached me, then kissed both of my cheeks before allowing a bright smile to show that suddenly decimated the shadowy cloud.

What concerned me to a moderate degree was something Pop used to say. *Beware of a mobster approaching you like he's your best friend, wearing a smile. No sooner will he stab you in the back or shoot you in the head.* Funny, the thoughts that entered your mind in a time of crisis.

Carmine could shake your essence with this intense eye glare as if he could read your mind and sense fear. He seemed to enjoy that intimidation tactic. Stare at somebody for several minutes without a blink or a sound uttered, which he did to me before his eyes swayed toward Len, who sat by my side.

"You need a lawyer to talk to me, Tommy? Should I be insulted?"

"Of course not, Carmine. Len can answer any questions you have about my father's power of attorney."

My introduction of the agenda triggered Len to ramble on about the legalities of the situation while Carmine's intense glare shot daggers through me.

Len broke up the wicked eye exchange between Carmine and me when he handed the document to Carmine.

Carmine breezed through the paperwork with only one question directed at me. "Tommy, there's not going to be any changes to the arrangement I had with Rocky, right?"

I wanted to ask if he'd sell me his shares, but I knew that would not go over well. "No, Carmine."

He displayed an uncertain grin, then nodded. "Is there anything else we need to discuss with Mr. Stein present?"

I shook my head, then glanced at Len. My continual, hardened stare forced Len to realize I was signaling him to leave, rolling my eyes toward the door.

After Len jumped to attention and left the room, Carmine spat out, "My son-in-law, Dominic Ricci, packed his bags. He's flying to Vegas to assist Fat Nicky. He's family and will help to look over my interests here."

Could my day have gone any worse? I didn't ask what Dominic's role would be. I knew precisely what Carmine meant.

CHAPTER 15

After numerous tests, the doctors concluded that Pop had a stroke, damaging part of the cerebrum. His initial prognosis was not favorable, especially since Pop suffered from that traumatic head injury in Exeter, which caused inflammation and tissue scarring. That wound might have done more damage than he realized. The doctor couldn't confirm with certainty that Pop's war injury was related.

Pop awoke in a confused state. The trauma to his brain impacted his speech and cognitive abilities. He experienced difficulties recognizing people—including me. Initially, he couldn't remember my name. Sometimes he didn't know where he was. His home became the institution where he resided with regular clinical care.

I demanded that Pop be brought home to recuperate. I'd hire a nurse to take care of him. His doctor didn't recommend it because he needed 'round-the-clock care. I was far too obstinate to heed their medical advice.

If only Mom still lived. She'd know what to do. I stared at the portrait of Mom that hung on the living room wall in my father's home, praying for some direction. "I hope I'm doing the right thing. I want what's best for Pop, Mom. He should be home in familiar surroundings."

Pop's house became equipped with clinical staff and all the medical necessities to help him function. Unfortunately, he took a tumble down a flight of stairs and suffered a knee injury and shoulder strain with significant bruising. He was lucky he didn't break any bones from that horrendous fall.

Perhaps I was selfish for keeping him home. Maybe this wasn't the best idea. My guilty conscience screamed at me to keep him in his luxurious mansion instead of locking him up in some psych ward as described in Ken Kesey's *One Flew Over the Cuckoo's Nest*. No abusive staff would torture my father or order a lobotomy.

When Pop slipped in the bathroom and whacked his head on the corner of the sink, causing a slight concussion, I was forced to accept defeat. A large black welt formed around his right eye. He looked like he sparred a few rounds with Muhammad Ali.

John and I anguished about the decision to put him in a convalescent home permanently. He needed help with normal, everyday tasks like dressing, eating, brushing his teeth, and using the bathroom. A very sad end to my father's young life. If he was in his right mind, he'd certainly want to die. There was nothing I could do for him except ensure he received proper care. No vicious nurse or overeager physician performing experimental treatments on my father.

I saw him regularly. John made arrangements with his driver to visit often too.

Pop had good days and bad days. I never knew the condition I'd find him in during my visits. Some days, his words sounded jumbled. He attempted to use sign language, but that method often failed. On good days, he tried to talk shop. I merely assured the Montgomery made loads of money to increase his bank account. Even on those few good days he had, Pop wasn't capable of updating the power of attorney in his state of mind. I had no choice but to remain married to Sadie and do my best to manage the Montgomery.

I reviewed policies and employee complaints. Improvements were necessary. The most worthwhile change was letting some dead weight go. My father-in-law was the first head on the chopping block. Pop might have owed this guy his life, but I owed Fred Meade shit. He morphed into an entitled, sloppy employee once his gambling habit soared out of control. I offered his job as security director to Jim, who accepted the promotion prior to my firing Fred.

Before I could tell Fred the good news, good news for me, anyway, the man had to be found. Fred was anywhere except where he should have been, at his desk or on the casino floor, performing security functions.

Jim and a couple of guards launched a manhunt on the premises to find Fred. I figured he had slipped a coin in a slot machine or placed chips down at a Blackjack table. Sure enough, he was found playing poker. I heard he had a good hand and won. Maybe he thought this was his lucky day. Not when I got through with him.

Jim stood outside the door as Fred entered my office. Pink, bumpy blotches freckled his cheeks, and his fingernails were chewed down to the stubs. I wondered if a loan shark threatened to snip off a finger or another important extremity. His suit jacket looked wrinkled, and his dark brown tie hung loosely from his neck.

"Sit down, Fred." I smiled and asked about Suzanne. I remembered my father's saying to beware of mobsters acting like your best friend wearing a smile. Except for the fact that I wasn't a wise guy, the rest of that statement was true once again, with Fred on the receiving end.

Once the pleasantries were out of the way, I got down to business. "Fred, I've been looking at your file. There are numerous complaints about your management style. Accusations that you discriminated against multiple staff members. We've talked about this before."

"Tommy, come on. You know me. People don't like that I lay down the law, so they start complaining. I'm sure your other managers have similar employees who act up."

I listened, although it was *because* I knew him that I didn't believe him. "Actually, Fred, I don't have these issues in other departments. My pop cut you a lot of slack against my better judgment. That's over now."

"What are you saying? You puttin' me on some kinda warning?" He snickered.

"No."

He looked relieved for five seconds until I sprung the news. "I'm letting you go, Fred." With a serious expression, I handed him an envelope. "This is your final paycheck that includes payment through the end of this week."

Fred laughed. "Cut the crap, Tommy."

I didn't flinch or show any kind of reaction.

Fred's blue eyes widened, suddenly understanding the seriousness of this meeting. "We're family." He stretched his arms out, animated and anxious. He needed the job to support his gambling habit, not his family.

"Family has nothing to do with the business."

"No, no, no! Family has *everything* to do with the business," he yelled loud enough for the walls to vibrate. "Your father would be the first person to point that out to you! You can't do this! You can't fire me! Give me a warning if you have to, but you're firing me over some complaints?"

"Where were you before you were escorted to my office, Fred?"

Beads of sweat filled the creases set in his forehead. "I was on the floor."

"Gambling *again*. During your work hours, you were sitting at a poker table. My father warned you that key employees should not gamble here. You took advantage of my father from the beginning. That's over!"

"I saved Rocky's life! The moment he's ill, you fire me! He won't be happy about this, Tommy."

"No need to play the *I saved your father's life* card, Fred. You cashed in that credit too many times. You were both soldiers, protecting your brothers in arms. Pop bailed you out of so many jams after giving you an incredible opportunity here in Vegas, but you blew it! Since you were away from your desk for so long playing poker, here are some personal items from your office." I stood from my leather chair and picked up a box with a few family photos, a necktie, and an empty money clip.

"What will my daughter think about this?"

"Sadie isn't involved in my business. She has no say in how I manage it." I quickly moved past his still body to open the office door while he remained seated as if the conversation weren't over.

Jim strolled in, approached Fred, and offered to escort him out politely. Jim was always polite.

CHAPTER 16

Desperate for a decent night's sleep, I took up residence in one of the spare bedrooms. So much animosity loomed between Sadie and me. Her demands were reasonable for an ordinary husband-and-wife relationship. Our situation was anything but ordinary. I felt imprisoned in the bed with Sadie, especially after learning about Pop's irrational lifestyle tests etched within formal documents.

My heavy thoughts were filled with worry about the hotel, my business partners, and Pop's health. A recurring, painful nightmare from my childhood often forced me awake, disrupting the opportunity for rest.

I wondered if Sadie's father would bend her ear, complaining about his termination. An ending to his career at the Montgomery that any normal person would have seen coming. As predicted, Fred called Sadie, desperate and discouraged about losing his job and income to satisfy his habit. Naturally, she wanted to help her father and bust my chops over it. I had every reason to fire Fred, and I made sure Sadie knew it.

Within no time, Fred and Suzanne left the state of Nevada. He had dug himself into a giant sinkhole. He lost the house, a perfectly nice house for his family that was outright handed to him. Fred didn't have the means to support the lifestyle my father offered, thanks to his gambling problem.

Sadie helped her parents pack up their belongings. None of their children followed them to Bakersfield, California—a few hours away by car.

I might sound like a hard ass, but as much money as I had, I wouldn't give Fred a penny. Not because I couldn't stand the man. He had a gambling problem he needed to tame. Fred couldn't be trusted with cash. Leaving Nevada was the best decision they could make. Living in an area where a casino dwelled a stone's throw away in every direction wasn't a healthy residential option.

Every time Sadie talked about visiting her father, I'd say, "Have a great time!" I had no desire to see Fred Meade again, especially on his turf in Bakersfield.

My life transitioned to a state of misery. I couldn't talk to anyone about Pop's stipulations. I wasn't arming people with pivotal details they could use against me. Exposing truth and secrets would give others the power to ruin me.

Sadie would definitely hold such potent knowledge over my head. Trust wasn't in my nature. Maybe I was paranoid. I was forced to remain tied to Sadie until Pop died, or I killed myself, whichever came first.

I met with Len again, anxious to find a way to work around this legal language. How the hell could I stay married to a woman I didn't love with the threat of losing the family business to gangsters? Len consulted with a legal advisor about my unique concerns. The language was clear, with no apparent loopholes.

Pop's mind wasn't well enough to perform everyday tasks, and his memory was shot. However, his other organs still functioned well. The doctor said he could live in his current state for years, stagnant in mind.

The more I stayed away from home, the more Sadie complained. My long hours, poor sleeping habits, and missing dinner were her top grievances. Trust me, she had others.

I had a 24-7 hotel operation to manage. I hired extra help to delegate responsibilities, but I still had work to do and clients to entertain. Making time to be home with a woman I didn't love didn't reach the top of my priority list.

At night, I'd crash at my suite at the Montgomery. I slept better there than at home. Fewer nightmares. But my wife demanded I slept at home every night. One evening, she threatened to leave me.

According to Len, I couldn't get divorced. That meant Sadie couldn't leave this marriage, either.

I had to kiss her ass sometimes, more times than I could count. Our arguments were daunting. I wanted to open the door and tell her to go, but I couldn't. If we divorced, I wouldn't be able to run the hotel, which would leave Carmine in charge. My father's blood, sweat, and tears formed this successful entity. Pop entrusted me with its longevity, despite his peculiar tests to prove my worth. Admittedly, I enjoyed financial security too.

So I returned home every night and ensured I was home every Christmas when Sadie's family visited for the holiday per her exasperating demands. Her father, thankfully, refused to visit our home in Henderson. If I had to endure a holiday meal with my in-laws, at least Fred wasn't glowering at the table across me. I liked the rest of the Meades.

Sadie commenced a tradition to drive to Bakersfield for New Year's to see her father since he wouldn't join us for Christmas. She had this far-fetched idea engraved in her thick skull that I'd take the trip with her. Every year, we fought the same battle. Another ritual she initiated.

On what planet was her request realistic? She knew Fred and I couldn't stand each other. It could be risky putting us in the same room together, never mind spending several days and nights stuck with the man.

Jesus, we had such a fight. Sadie threw a plant at me as I strode out the front door, ensuring we would spend New Year's separately.

However, for New Year's Eve in 1970, I wasn't completely alone. I had no idea my whole world was about to turn upside down.

"Angie"

CHAPTER 17

I found myself at Vince Russo's club, Spritz. Figured I'd have a drink and talk some business with Benny the blade. Because it was New Year's Eve, I'd expect him to show up.

Fat Nicky asked me to obtain the services of several ladies for a party he arranged for his crew. Vince and his capos were my father's connection for girls at some noteworthy events he hosted at the hotel. These affairs included politicians and law enforcement officials. Let's just say the girls were extremely friendly to these guests, but they didn't take a dime from the men. Technically, that wasn't illegal. Whatever Pop paid Vince for this action was unknown and might have been illegal, even if they were ladies from a brothel. Prostitution was not legal in Clark County. Nicky's request wasn't an expense to put on the ledger.

New Year's Eve alone in a crowded club wasn't my idea of a good time unless a lovely lady without a date sought companionship. Sometimes people felt lonely or sad around the holidays. Maybe I felt lonely too.

The air smelled like barbecue ribs, fries, and cigarettes. The bar was packed with customers ordering a variety of alcoholic beverages. I found myself an empty stool and ordered a shot of Jameson while waiting for Vince and his capos to arrive.

Vince secured live entertainment that night. Unfortunately, instead of listening to some rock 'n' roll I loved like the Rolling Stones or a tribute to the recently departed Janis Joplin, a crappy folk song with a familiar ring to it began to chime as a beautiful sound echoed over the music.

I spun around and observed a gorgeous brunette on the stage, belting out the Carpenter's "Close to You." If I didn't know any better, her eyes affixed to mine. Mesmerized by her beauty and the harmonious sounds strumming from her soul, I had to meet her.

For a moment, I forgot anyone else was in the club, tuning out soft-spoken conversations and a few couples dancing to the slow-paced beat.

When her song ended, I whistled and clapped as loudly as everyone else in the room who enjoyed her amazing performance. I watched her movements, wondering if a man stood nearby, waiting to kiss her.

She skipped to the opposite end of the bar alone and struck up a conversation with the bartender.

An introduction was in order, so I could tell her how much I loved her song, although I wasn't a Carpenters fan. I tapped her shoulder, feeling her soft, porcelain skin to gain her attention. When she turned, our eyes met, and an incredible, pulsating jolt hit me like a bolt of lightning to the skull. Her exquisite features dazzled me before knocking me on my ass. "Hi. You have a beautiful voice. Are you a professional singer or something?" Not the smoothest line, I admit. I couldn't think of what to say, distracted by her flawless face and shapely figure.

"Who, me? No. I mean, I'd love to be a professional singer someday." Her words sounded as soft and delicate as she looked.

"Well, you've got talent. What was your name again?"

"Angie."

"Hi, Angie. I'm Tommy. Tommy Cavallo." I took hold of her hand, not wanting to let go. "Can I buy you a drink?"

She held up a bottle of Pepsi. I was too absorbed, drowning in those beautiful brown eyes, to realize she already had a drink in hand.

We made some small talk. I had difficulty staying focused on the conversation, examining every inch of her face. Her delicate skin, the small bridge of her nose, and those painted pink lips, luscious and full. Something about her dark chocolate eyes drew me in.

Our discussion was instantly interrupted by Vince. The man had terrible timing. I was there to talk business, but my business needs suddenly seemed unimportant. He stood practically between Angie and me, towering over us at well over six feet. He asked about my father's health as he brushed his fingers through his shiny jet-black hair with several patches of protruding gray strands.

I didn't want Angie to walk away from our conversation. I might have been answering Vince's questions about Pop's current health status, but I couldn't take my eyes off of her as if frozen in a trance. To end the insufferable dialogue, I managed to change the subject. "I was just talking with Angie here. Where did you find such a talent?"

"She's my niece, Tommy. I'm her guardian."

A crash as loud as thunder struck my nerves. "Frank's daughter?" I asked with surprise to verify this beautiful woman was the infamous Madman Russo's daughter.

"You knew my father?" she questioned, confirming her relationship to a vicious yet dead mob underboss.

"I knew *of* him through your uncle." I raised my arm to pat Vince on the back as I uttered the sentence like we were old pals, of which we were anything but.

Again, Vince cut off our conversation. "Angie, I need to talk business with Tommy. Do me a favor and look for Katie. I lost sight of her."

Katie, I remembered, was Vince's daughter.

My ears were listening to Vince, but my eyes perused the bar area for Angie. I couldn't let Vince notice my interest in his niece, mainly because he knew I was married. Hell, he was invited to my wedding shortly after Frank's death. He sent Benny the blade to make an appearance in his place.

Sadie complicated my life enough. Could I allow my marital status to stop this immediate gravitational pull I felt toward Angie?

I told Vince my colleague wanted six youthful-looking ladies to attend an event he planned in Reno in a couple of weeks. Youthful, not underage, I clarified. We negotiated a price as the countdown to the New Year, 1971, began. I might have yielded a better deal if I dealt with Benny.

After a quick handshake with Vince, I left him with a tall, attractive strawberry blond he called Nancy to kiss at the stroke of midnight. She looked younger than him, but older than her years. Probably a brothel whore he had an exclusive arrangement with.

My head shifted around the room in search of Angie. The tables and booths were packed with guests in their party hats, tooting on noisemakers, and cheering. A couple kissed in front of a hundred-gallon sapphire-blue fish tank with pretty tropical fish dancing to "Auld Lang Syne."

Then I caught a glimpse of Angie's sparkly silver dress and long, black hair heading toward the back where the sign clearly read, EMPLOYEES ONLY.

I slipped behind the bar and found the soda bottles, grabbed a Pepsi, and removed the metal cap. The bartenders were too absorbed with their customers to notice me. I was practically out of breath when I raced in the back, hoping she hadn't left. "Angie!" I shouted. Maybe I overdid it a little by yelling out her name, but the noise in this place turned wicked. I offered her the bottle and received a lovely smile. "Happy New Year, Angie."

How I wanted to feel her lips against mine. She didn't strike me as the kind of girl who would welcome a kiss on the lips from a strange man, even though it was New Year's Eve. I acted like a gentleman and left a soft kiss against her cheek. Our lips were close enough to feel the warmth of her breath against my face. As much as I wanted more from her at that moment, I restrained myself, considering her notorious family. Thank God Madman was dead because he'd kill me for having vulgar thoughts about his stunning daughter. Vince, however, was very much alive.

Somehow, she was worth the risk. I never thought any woman was worth a risk before meeting Angie. I never had trouble getting a girl in the sack, and if I couldn't get her into bed, I'd move on.

I had to wonder if this was how Pop felt when he first met Mom. He always thought about that sweet Irish nurse who treated his sprained ankle. Something as corny as love at first sight suddenly seemed real.

It took me twenty-seven years to feel such an indescribable level of excitement, and I had just met this girl.

"Would you like to have dinner with me, Angie?"

She looked surprised, but she nodded in agreement.

That night, I got less sleep than normal, swearing that destiny led me to Angie. My eyes were glued to the clock, anxious for time to advance quickly, so I could see her beautiful face again.

CHAPTER 18

A married man planning a *date* with another woman. What was I doing? Although I wasn't married in my heart and mind, I couldn't divorce Sadie anytime soon.

I didn't think of Angie as a mere hookup to cheat on my wife. Something about this beautiful young woman excited me, and I wasn't thinking with my dick for once. Tight knots formed in my gut. A sleepless night with thoughts emerging only about Angie. Wonderful fantasies feeding a desolate soul.

Pop said this feeling was possible. The thought seemed too outrageous to believe. The way he talked about meeting Mom, not getting her out of his head. I finally understood that insatiable hunger.

But Angie was Frank Russo's daughter. Vince Russo's niece. How could I make this work without losing everything, thanks to that legal document Pop forced upon me?

I needed Len to find a way out of Pop's stipulations. Consult with different attorneys. Destroy the paperwork like it didn't exist. Never before did I have a reason to divorce Sadie. Since I met Angie, the pressure mounted to end my marriage.

Maybe this internal, chaotic craving I felt would die out in time. It was one night. One meeting that stirred my heart. Once Vince learned about my interest in Angie, he'd tell her I was married, and my chance with her would be finito.

Another strong possibility—Vince could have me killed.

The day dragged as I waited to see Angie again. To take my mind off our date, I kept busy. I drove to the office at the hotel to review contracts and budgets. My business never closed on holidays. Many people were still throwing coins into the slots on New Year's morning. As I dashed through the crowds, hearing the rattling of ka-ching sounds, my mind wandered to the perfect place to take Angie tonight. Palmieri's was a fabulous Italian restaurant off the beaten track. I had a good relationship with the manager there. I requested privacy in the back area near the fireplace. Privacy to get to know each other and to hide from the elements. The elements being anyone who knew me as a married man.

Random thoughts constantly distracted me the entire day, wondering how this night would go. I watched the hands of the clock move, wishing time would fly so I could see this woman again.

I drove to John's house for some brotherly advice and to pass the time. Between doctor appointments, friends who stopped by to visit him, and his job, I knew the best time to drop in. Since it was the New Year holiday, he had the day off. John continued to work at the post office. Although he was handicapped, he managed to perform on the production line, sorting outgoing mail by zones and stamping envelopes in preparation for delivery to their final destinations. He needed a purpose in life to feel useful without our father controlling his future—the way he controlled mine.

My brother proved his disabilities wouldn't hold him back, words our mother drilled into him. He was smart and could learn anything as long as someone had the patience to train him, allowing him to read their lips to communicate. Reading lips was John's superpower. He could write down his thoughts to those who didn't understand sign language or use his muffled voice when he attempted to speak.

His manager said John was a hardworking employee. The wheelchair and his inability to hear were irrelevant to his boss.

From what I was told, several coworkers picked up some sign language to communicate with him directly. John always got invited to picnics or to join the guys after work for beers. Knowing that instilled a sense of pride and joy.

John never let his handicaps restrain him, even after the accident. The wheelchair didn't prevent him from having a solid work ethic or a social life. My brother got thrown a bucket of lemons in life, but he always came out on top.

I slipped my key into the lock of John's house and let myself inside. He wasn't expecting me, but he enjoyed having company. John stroked his black hair while sizing me up. He grinned. In sign language, he told me I looked happy. Happiness, a depleted emotion until recently. No one knew me better than John. I signed back, describing Angie and how we met. The first question John asked was, "What about Sadie?"

"I don't love her, John. Len is developing the divorce papers."

He nodded, seemingly relieved with my decision. "There's no baby. You should've divorced her already."

"Pop gave me a hard time about that. He wanted me to settle down. There are a lot of legalities tied to my marriage that I didn't realize. It'll take some time before I'm a free man."

As much as I trusted John, I didn't tell him about Pop's tests. He'd try to convince me to let the hotel and the money go. My decision impacted John's financial future too. His part-time job wouldn't support his lifestyle and special needs. Technically, I didn't lie to my brother, but I chose to omit Pop's version of emotional blackmail, binding me to Sadie.

"There's something about this girl, Angie. But if I tell her I'm married, she won't give me a chance. I didn't want to marry Sadie, not even because she was pregnant. Pop pulled my strings like always. I love Pop, but he controls me like a business deal."

John understood our father's domineering personality. A puppeteer and I was the clown tangled in strings. That was evident in the addendum to the power of attorney. Some might say I took after him. That could be true on some level. I was used to getting what I wanted—unless Pop's plans differed from mine.

"You have to be honest with her, Tommy. If you're getting divorced, tell her that. Take your time. You don't need to rush into anything with this new girl." He smiled that mischievous smile he often wore. "Keep it in your pants," he signed.

CHAPTER 19

ANGIE RUSSO

Reflecting on my life with Angie, our time together had been filled with so much love and adoration, mixed with a whirlwind of complexities. My marriage was only one obstacle. The dangerous lifestyle of her family posed a hazardous threat.

Angie had moved in with Vince after her father's gruesome murder. She didn't tell her uncle about our first date. If she had, one of his goons would've paid me a visit. Maybe I should have spoken to Vince man-to-man first. Explained my intentions to walk away from my marriage. He wouldn't have allowed me to see Angie socially until I was divorced—if at all.

The first moment I laid eyes on her on that stage, sparks flew like the Fourth of July. The beautiful image of Angie sashaying down the staircase captivated me when I picked her up for our first date on New Year's Day 1971. She wore a short orange dress that hugged her body and all its slight curves. Her raven hair dropped in waves to the middle of her back. She had long, shapely legs and large breasts. Gorgeous!

Vince mentioned a business deal going down the evening of January 1 when we spoke the night prior. It was perfect timing to see Angie without Vince obstructing my plans.

Angie seemed quiet yet inquisitive on our drive to Palmieri's. She asked a lot of questions, but she didn't say much about herself. I wanted to know everything about her. The fact that she lived with Vince told me either she had no immediate family left or she parted ways with them. I mean, I knew her father got whacked.

She blushed and lowered those dark, doe-like eyes when I inquired. Making her feel uncomfortable wasn't on my agenda. Instead, I shared my own family stories with her. In particular, she was curious about John's handicaps and speaking in sign.

Palmieri's displayed colorful Christmas lights stringing along the building and shrubs. An enormous blue spruce greeted us when we entered, dressed in red and gold ornaments and bows. A soft instrumental chorus of "Silent Night" played in the background. Christmas candles were lit in each window. Mistletoe hung from the row of chandeliers as we were escorted to our table near the glistening fireplace burning logs that snapped and crackled a warm blaze of heat. The perfect ambiance I sought for our date.

During our conversation over shrimp cocktail and prime rib, I learned an important fact about her. She had just turned eighteen. She looked to be at least twenty-one. I had nine years on her. That explained why she was still single and living with Vince.

Today, she was legally an adult. Our timing was nearly perfect. The situation would be perfect if I was single. I dreaded telling her the truth. My mind wandered, struggling to come up with the right words to explain my ominous marital status.

Later that evening, when I drove her back to Vince's mansion, I didn't want to say goodbye. This date and a potential future with Angie could be ruined once I exposed my secret. I had to tell her about Sadie before I kissed her. If I kissed her, I knew I'd never want to let her go. If she dumped me before I had a chance to feel her lips against mine, I'd never know what I was missing—my philosophy at that particularly stressful moment.

Those pink-glossed lips were close enough for me to taste. I squeezed her body against mine, but I released her, knowing I had to tell her the truth before Vince did. Somehow, I managed to say the words aloud, "I'm married."

The shock in her fragile expression was noticeable. Dead, lingering silence ensued.

I began to ramble, reassuring her that my marriage had been over for a while. That wasn't a lie. I just hadn't told Sadie yet. Sadie didn't love me, either. We both soared through the motions of acting like a married couple, but we weren't in love. Sadie didn't know about Pop's scheme to keep me connected to her. Not something I wanted her to know. Information I had no intention of divulging to anyone.

If I told Angie this crazy story, she might not give me a chance. I begged her to think about it overnight. I promised her my divorce was imminent, and I slept in a separate bedroom. That was true unless Sadie's family visited. We had to put on a show for the outside world. Sadie and I were very good at pretending and playing games when necessary, like sharing a bed to sleep if her mother stayed with us. Len had been consulting with more experienced colleagues to help release me from my tainted vows.

"I need some time to think," Angie mumbled, appearing confused, possibly hurt.

I kissed her cheek to comfort her and soothe the mixed emotions she expressed, but it didn't end there. I couldn't resist sampling those delectable pink lips against my better judgment.

She responded, teasing me with the rhythm of her fingers caressing my neck before running them through my thick brown waves.

My tongue parted her lips to explore hers.

Eventually, she forced my body back with her hands. Then she disappeared behind the closed door.

CHAPTER 20

Angie took a mammoth leap of faith and forged a friendship with me that rapidly grew, festered with intense passion. I wanted so much more of her than the easygoing hand-holding and good-night kisses. I struggled to keep my feelings subdued as any man with a healthy libido could. My marital status clouded her mind with doubt as much as it clobbered around in mine.

She began singing regularly at Spritz, earning a paycheck while I secured a front-row seat. What a fantastic voice she had. I'd attend her performances, then spend time with her afterward, sneaking in kisses before she returned home. Saying good night became more challenging each time we parted ways.

Angie had lived an extremely sheltered existence. Homeschooled with no friends except her cousin, Katie. Frank wouldn't let his beautiful daughter out of his sight. He might have been a maniac, but he wasn't a stupid one.

Frank lost his teen daughter, Connie, to heroin. That tragic event tortured him every moment of every waking day. He began monitoring Angie constantly, allowing her little freedom, which he saw as a means of protection.

After Frank died, Angie moved in with Vince and Katie. At that time, I didn't know where her mother lived or if she was alive. I was afraid to ask her. Angie clammed up whenever I mentioned her family. Some details I discovered through other sources. She didn't necessarily tell me a lot of information and not all at once.

I brought her to various casinos on the Strip and to see a couple of popular shows in town. She met John, and they quickly formed a tight bond. I was falling hard for Angie, unlike any other woman I met previously.

John understood why I was crazy about her. Her soul proved beautiful and as pure as her elegant looks. With softness in her tone and a radiating glow from her eyes, John sensed Angie's big heart that overflowed with sincerity.

Angie asked me to teach her sign language so she could communicate directly with my brother. Her interest in John told me a lot about her genuine character. She constantly surprised me.

I couldn't wait anymore. I planned to make my move on Angie. I finally brought her to the Montgomery. The hotel was a monumental part of me that I flaunted with pride. This was the first time I publicly brought a woman here who wasn't my wife since my wedding.

Some employees remembered Sadie from her days working in the coat check room. Most of the staff knew I had a wife, but Sadie no longer worked here, and I never wore my wedding ring. Firing Fred was the smartest move I had ever made. Not just for the business, but I couldn't openly parade my girlfriend in front of my father-in-law or any of the Meades.

As we stepped onto the red carpet outside and pushed through the revolving door, Angie's eyes glistened with wonder, witnessing the extreme renovations in the hotel lobby. "What a gorgeous hotel! I've never been to England before," she said as we stepped through the main lobby, viewing the décor that favored charming England. The traditional-looking red phone booths were set up as working payphones. We glided across the green and gray marbled tile, then beneath an enormous monument of the Tower Bridge to reach the path that led to the Westminster casino. Murals were painted across the walls that bordered the space, depicting Buckingham Palace and Windsor Castle.

Angie sat at a slot machine, winning at first. I loved watching her face light up as brightly as the casino lights, hoping for a matched set on the slots to win. Even when she lost, she pursed her lips in a sexy way.

I snuck away to ensure a chilled bottle of champagne had been sent to my private suite. Once my order was confirmed, I took Angie's hand and escorted her through the replica of Stonehenge, which wasn't true-to-life in size but a whimsical maze for guests to stroll through.

People would walk in off the streets to visit our fabulous hotel, lured by the extravagance, hoping to make a reservation when they returned to Vegas.

We rode the elevator up to the twentieth floor. A spurt of excitement moved my legs quickly to the entrance of my suite.

She couldn't sit still. Angie approached the balcony door, dazzled by the beautiful view of the Strip below, with blinking lights and thousands of tourists who roamed the streets.

"Are you all right?"

She nodded. "Your hotel is amazing! Your description didn't do it justice. I'd love to see the Ireland wing, especially the Cliffs of Moher model with the water fountain set below it as you described."

"I'll show you everything. I want you to know the real me, Angie. This hotel is only a part of who I am." I offered her a glass of champagne and a kiss. "And I want to know everything about you." Before I knew it, I told her I loved her, and I meant it. Those words weren't a ploy to get her into bed. I felt that magical emotion, overcome by desire, eager to express my feelings physically.

With Angie, my heart opened fully with a unique sensation of nerves thumping in sync with the rhythm of my heart. Pure, sweet, sentimental love.

Jim Morrison and the Doors song "Touch Me" rattled off in my head as that twitch between my legs became more prominent. I kissed her until extreme hesitation emerged. Did my marital status cause her to have second thoughts?

She looked visibly shaken, wrapping her hands around her arms, pulling away from me.

As my thoughts jumbled through my brain, it occurred to me that Angie was a girl who never got out much. Her father and uncle practically kept her under lock and key.

I suspected she could be a virgin, pure in body, mind, and spirit. Gently, I secured her body close to mine, explaining if she wasn't ready, I'd understand. Of course, I wanted her to be ready without pressure.

After careful consideration, she gave me the green light with a nod and a blink from her sultry eyes.

I knew to take things slowly, so her first time would be special, which made Angie more precious to me. The voice of Captain Kirk from *Star Trek* crept into my head: *to boldly go where no man has gone before*. I was rock-hard before swooping her off her feet, carrying her to the bed.

Her body tasted as delicious as it was beautiful. I took my time with her in a gentle manner, exploring every inch of her fair skin with my lips and tongue until she moaned with passion bursting as her first orgasm detonated.

I was ready to enter, but I didn't want to hurt her. I tried to hold back, not giving her all of me at once. I didn't want her first time to be painful, especially with the extra-large size tool I packed. Slow and steady movements until I was fully inside.

Then she was all mine.

My heart overflowed with immense love.

She gasped and kissed me long and passionately in response. Our bodies molded together as one. I didn't want to let her go. I wouldn't risk losing her to some other guy. Allow another man to encounter her untainted body like this?

That night with Angie changed my feelings about love and relationships forever. She was all I wanted. At the end of the evening, when I brought her home, she declared her love for me too.

Yet, I had to return home to the prison Pop locked me up in. Sadie hated it if I didn't come home every night. Before Angie, the "other woman" was this hotel. The Montgomery kept me too busy to have affairs.

If I didn't go home every night, Sadie threatened to leave and divorce me. I couldn't divorce her until Len had the ability to quash the power of attorney. I couldn't *let* Sadie leave me.

CHAPTER 21

Countless minutes and hours were spent thinking about Angie, triggering restless nights. I craved to spend time with her. There had to be a way to see her more often. Keep her in bed with me, all to myself, for an entire night. Pop's wild stipulations weighed on my mind. I needed to be innovative. Envision the future of the Montgomery. A future to secure its place in a competitive market, leading to an excessive profit margin.

The last quarterly financial report showed tremendous profits. I had to top that last report each quarter moving forward to maintain power and control. How could I leverage our auspicious reputation and hefty bank accounts? What had our competitors achieved to remain successful and profitable? The thought occurred to me as quick as a flash of lightning illuminating the evening sky.

With no time to waste, I contacted Aaron, my Realtor, and scheduled an immediate meeting at seven o'clock in the morning.

Pop had been approached by a hotel owner in Aruba before the stroke conquered his mind. The Caribbean hotel had been losing money, so its owner sought an investor. Pop maintained the financial records within his desk. I wasn't interested in another partnership, but I would be interested in completely taking the hotel off his hands if this facility demonstrated value.

Once Aaron jumped on board with my idea, I asked him to thoroughly check out the hotel, the property, the surrounding area, and any other pertinent information I needed to know before I made a decision.

Aruba was in the eastern time zone. Alberto Garcia, the owner of the Bay Breeze hotel, had been wide awake and at his office when I contacted him. He remembered Pop and the Montgomery name. He seemed elated to speak with me in person.

I called Sadie to tell her a business trip came up, and I'd be away for a few days. At first, I wondered if she'd want to join me when I told her my destination was Aruba, but I remembered she hated to fly. Between her fears and motion sickness, she wouldn't invite herself to tag along.

"Aruba? Why would you purchase a hotel so far away? Honestly, Tommy, you're never home as it is," she grumbled with irritation.

"This is business! Pop wanted to branch out and expand the hotel. I'll be away for several days," I said quickly, then hung up.

I kept Len in the loop with my activities. He thought I should discuss my idea with Carmine. He was right, but I hated to include Carmine. This was *my* plan. *My* brainstorm.

Carmine sounded thrilled with my proposal. He suggested I take Fat Nicky with me.

Hell no! Not that I answered him using those exact words. I recommended Nicky manage the casino with Dominic while I traveled. Maybe I could flush out other potential hotels to add to our family.

By the time eight o'clock rolled around, it felt like I had worked a full day. Seeing as I was running on little sleep and moving quickly, I had worked a full day.

My next call was to Angie. Vince planned to be out of town the entire week. Naturally, I had to take advantage of this opportunity to have my girl to myself.

When I first considered divorcing Sadie, Aaron began to scout properties in Vegas for me to buy. A new place to call home would be necessary when the divorce became final. Aaron had found this amazing house in the Paradise Palms area, not far from the Montgomery. The twenty-five-hundred-square-foot house appeared immaculate and quite private with a gated entrance.

Out of curiosity, I asked Aaron to check on that piece of land to see if it was still available. The company jet was fueled and waiting for me. So let the chips fall where they may.

CHAPTER 22

As the plane landed smoothly in Aruba, the warm sun sparkled against our skin from the purest of blue skies I'd ever witnessed. Every bit of fresh sea air breathed in soothed the familiar stresses that gnawed at my achy muscles.

Although Angie thought this trip would be about having fun and relaxing by the pool, I had to remind her this was a business trip for me. I hated to disappoint her. She expected we'd be joined at the hip on the white sandy beaches, swimming in the pristine turquoise water.

Numerous activities were available to keep her busy while I worked. I wanted her insight into the hotel's amenities. Alberto ensured I had a line of credit to use on the premises. Angie was included in this offer. She merely had to use my name.

I left her to unpack and indulge at the beauty parlor while I met with Alberto and his senior staff to show me the facilities and the surrounding area, followed by financial reports. They were losing money and didn't have the revenue to upgrade or properly market the facility. The competition was tough to attract guests from various countries. Alberto looked to be in his late seventies, itching to retire.

My brain flurried with visions of opportunity. Bring a taste of Vegas to the island to spruce the place up. Erect excitement and mystery within its foundation.

The trip was both productive and romantic, with Angie by my side. As promised, I spent our entire last day with her in the glistening sun at the tranquil beach a few paces from the hotel.

We visited an open market where many locals sold crafts and beaded jewelry they created by hand.

"Tommy, let's buy some items at these tables."

"Is there something you like?" The surprise in my voice was evident, considering the questionable quality of the merchandise.

"I want to purchase their crafts to help them. They can use the money," she said.

"I'll leave a donation."

"And hurt their pride? No." Angie bought items from every table, without bargaining, to help the locals earn income with dignity.

Later that evening, Angie slept peacefully. At around three in the morning, a cool breeze filled the room, waking me. I stood to close the window as thoughts of returning home and parting ways devastated me.

It was midnight in Nevada when I called Aaron. If he was sleeping, I couldn't tell. He followed up on the house in Paradise I had an interest in buying. My offer had been accepted.

Another sleepless night, orchestrating my next steps. One of those steps included an inevitable conversation with Angie's uncle, an essential discussion on which I procrastinated.

Our beautiful journey came to an end. On the flight home, Angie seemed exceptionally quiet. Her lovely figure positioned upon my lap, our arms and legs entwined. If she only knew about the surprise that awaited.

Aaron stuffed an envelope inside the glove compartment of my Camaro at the airport. Instead of taking Angie back to Vince's house, we took a detour to Paradise.

She looked utterly confused when I pulled into the gated driveway that led us to a lovely stucco ranch-style home. The lawn was a rich green color, trimmed perfectly. An array of plants lined the brick walkway to the front door. Soon the plants would burst with colors as the anticipated warmer weather was due.

The house appeared as I remembered. I envisioned the empty space furnished with exquisite luxuries.

Angie's eyes widened with surprise when I announced I had purchased this home for us. A place where I had her all to myself, out of Vince and Sadie's control. I prayed Len would soon find a way to cut me loose from those binding legal constraints.

She twisted her fingers, thinking about how she'd explain to her uncle that she was moving in with me. She expected pushback, to put it mildly. I offered to go with her and speak with Vince, but Angie thought that would only add tension and escalate the situation to a miserable degree. I listened and let her play this out her way.

Later that day, she arrived at our home with one suitcase in hand. My heart fluttered with ecstasy. She rushed into my arms and shed some tears. Her discussion with Vince went as badly as we both predicted. I suspected he'd try to make me out as a cheating husband who merely wanted to take advantage of Angie's good nature and innocence.

"Shh, it's okay, baby. I'll speak with Vince," I said, attempting to ease her crushed heart.

"That's not a good idea, Tommy. He's so angry."

"We'll figure it out together, honey. I'm so happy you're here. I promise, I'll take care of everything."

In time, our house became completely furnished with every amenity possible. But it wasn't the material possessions that made this structure a home. Despite my marital commitment to Sadie, my heart beat within Angie. Angie showed her love through the dazzling gaze of her dark eyes or a warm smile whenever she looked at me. Her hugs felt magical, and her kisses tasted scrumptious. She could tell when I needed a shot of Jameson, time to unwind, or a kind ear to listen about a whiny customer at the hotel. Angie paid attention to the cues I absently emitted. Together, we lived in our own world filled with beauty and wonder. Our love flourished, constructed within the walls of each room, and happiness cemented in the foundation.

"Flirtin' with Disaster"

CHAPTER 23

Time escaped me. A wife at home, demanding as ever. A girlfriend to spend time with. Managing an all-encompassing business with criminal partners.

Procrastination was inconveniently stitched into my nature, but I couldn't postpone the inevitable meeting with Vince any longer. I had to meet him on my terms. Take charge. Be in control. An impromptu visit with the element of surprise might work to my advantage. I'd explain that my love for his niece was real, and I'd divorce Sadie as soon as possible.

Deep down, I knew he wouldn't give his blessing.

In the brief time that Angie and I evolved as a couple, I quickly learned just how naïve she was. She had no clue about the business her uncle and father ran. I often had to remind myself she was only eighteen. A woman on the outside but still a youthful girl within. Angie had no idea I'd be coming face-to-face with the ruthless man she lovingly called uncle.

Jim drove us in his Lincoln Mark III, prepared to back me up if necessary.

The Beatles tune "Let it Be" reverberated through the car radio as we approached the Russo property on a crisp day in February 1971. The vast acreage seemed to spread in width and length for miles. The dark, gloomy mansion was set in the back of the ritzy Rancho Circle area of Las Vegas. To most eyes, this elaborate manor looked like a phenomenal piece of architecture, but I knew of the deadly viper who reigned.

A large, husky man with dark hair and pockmarks across his cheeks answered the door, presumably a bodyguard.

"I'd like to speak with Vince, please. Tell him Tommy Cavallo is here." My voice assured confidence despite the swishing of my stomach.

Vince's goon patted me down from top to bottom, then he turned toward Jim to repeat the process. He lifted a walkie-talkie from his belt, clicked the button, and said, "Vito, tell the boss he's got company—Tommy Cavallo."

While waiting, my mind flashed to witnessing Angie wearing that short orange dress, strolling down the stairwell. I had been too absorbed in her beauty that first night to notice the detail in the woodwork and the enormous chandelier glittering from the high ceiling. No average businessman owned a mansion like this without either an inheritance, a prosperous business like my family, or ties to organized crime.

Angie's cousin, Katie, was nowhere to be seen. I wished she were here. Vince wouldn't slash my throat in front of his daughter. The attractive solid oak floors beneath my feet left me praying this visit wouldn't end with blood from my veins seeping into its cracks.

Soon enough, the man presented himself. Usually, he greeted me with a pat on the back. Today, I received cold, dead eyes as a whirl of gray smoke from his Cuban cigar filled the space between us. Vince's tall, commanding presence displayed confidence infused with arrogance.

"You've got a lot of nerve. I'll give you that." He glanced at Jim. "He waits here with Sonny."

Vince signaled me to follow him into a dimly lit room with dark mahogany furniture and an overwhelmingly large desk. Hundreds of books lined the built-in shelves within the walls. This rustic office with an extraordinary library distracted my concerns briefly. I couldn't help but wonder if Vince read any of these books.

I wasn't standing over a rug he could roll my body up in, then toss into the lake or bury in the desert. A good sign.

"Vince, you know why I'm here," I started, then cleared my throat. "I love Angie. I'll take care of her. She'll never want for anything. I promise she's in good hands." By now, I felt as though I was rambling.

He sat silently in his colossal leather chair, listening yet studying my every move with a hardened gaze.

"I understand why you have concerns—"

He cut me off. "What about your wife? Your *wife*, Tommy! That adorable little blonde I met on your honeymoon. Did you get tired of her already? Want a cute little number to entertain you between the sheets for a while?"

I shook my head. "I *love* Angie. I plan to marry her, Vince."

"Marry her? A lot of things are legal in this state, but polygamy isn't one of them. Angie is *my* responsibility. I owe that to her father. Frank and I promised each other that our daughters would always be safe and protected, no matter what happened to us."

"She loves me, Vince."

"She's a kid! She doesn't know what love is or what loving you will cost her."

"There are legal issues tied in with my divorce. Once they're resolved, I'll be a free man."

"You have a reputation with the ladies. I was surprised to hear you settled down at all. And here you are, still chasing skirts." He poured bourbon into a crystal glass and swirled the liquid around before taking a generous sip from the rim. "What kind of man, who's married, takes advantage of an innocent girl? Not to mention your lack of *respect* for me. Do you have any idea how insulted I felt to learn about this farce of a relationship you started behind my back?"

"That wasn't my intention."

Vince stood to his feet and stepped dangerously close to me. "I will ruin you, and she'll be back under my roof very soon." His voice rang low and fierce, offering no indication of approving my relationship with Angie.

But I was still breathing.

CHAPTER 24

Feeling comfortable in our home, Angie attempted to cook regular meals. I loved this girl so much, I'd eat anything she made, even if it wasn't edible. Often the meal was surprisingly good. I'd rave about a dish when it tasted adequate, so she'd know to prepare it again with potential improvements.

She had been estranged from her mother for many years. No one taught her how to properly roast a chicken or broil chops. Over the years, with the various cookbooks I subtly bought, her skills as a chef would improve.

The majority of my days were spent at the Montgomery. My afternoons and evenings were spent with Angie at our home, the place I considered *home*.

I added a phone line in a spare room I had transformed into an office. I made business calls from the house and brought home paperwork that required my review or signature for approval. I'd always know if Angie stood near the door thanks to a severe creaking sound in one of the floorboards. I knew to be careful discussing anything related to the Toscanos or Sadie should Angie be close by.

Rob Lubitski, my second-in-command, was sharp as a tack and earned my trust with his hard work and dedication. I delegated overseeing the hotel operations directly to Rob, and he'd contact me as necessary for my input. Rob stood more than six feet tall with a stocky build, soft brown eyes, and a warm smile. Pleasant in nature but tough when warranted to keep staff in line and profits rocketing.

As my business grew with more hotels under my umbrella, I hired a "Rob Lubitski" at each location. These intelligent, loyal individuals were paid exceptionally well for their hard work and discretion about my personal life and business associates.

Sadie's rules about coming home every night were exhausting, but I had to keep her suspicions at bay. If she called the hotel to speak with me, Mrs. Arden, my secretary at the time, contacted me at my home with Angie. I'd return to Henderson nightly to accommodate Sadie's rules. We didn't share a bed anymore. My dependence upon sleeping pills began to rid my head of the constant noise for a few mere hours. Without them, my wired brain would remind me of the trouble the Toscano crew caused, Vince's threat of ruination, or how to free myself from my marriage.

One afternoon with Angie, a call chimed in to tend to a situation at the hotel. Angie insisted she tag along. I never wanted to involve her in the business, so she'd stay busy gambling or shopping while I worked.

Angie drove us in the white Cadillac I purchased for her. We left the car with the valet and entered the building, trailing across the red carpet, practically bumping into Carmine and Fat Nicky, who stood in the lobby, deep in conversation.

Normally, Carmine informed me when he visited. Since his daughter, Patty, Dominic's wife, moved to Vegas to live with her husband, Carmine's trips became more frequent.

Carmine had his wife, his mistress, Paula, and other women who flocked in his direction. The man was not much to look at, but he had money and power, which interested many women.

Angie understood some people who worked for me knew I was married. She didn't openly kiss me in the lobby, but when Carmine saw her by my side, his lips widened to the biggest smile he ever showed. That beaming grin always threw me. A smiling, happy gangster often held something up his sleeve.

He approached me with outstretched arms and a hearty back slap before gripping my cheeks with his extra-large hands. When Carmine's eyes shifted to Angie, I had no choice but to introduce him to her.

"Carmine, this is Angie. Angie, Carmine, my business partner."
Angie displayed a delightful smile.

"It's a pleasure." Carmine placed his arms around her.

She strained a bit uncomfortably in his grasp but welcomed his affectionate greeting. "It's nice to meet you," she replied.

"Excuse me for interrupting, Tommy, but we need to talk." His sharp direction was clear. "Would you excuse us, Miss..."

"Russo, but please call me Angie."

An unfamiliar expression prominently boasted across Carmine's face. He smiled at Angie, slightly perplexed. The wheels were turning in his head, but I wasn't certain why.

I turned toward Angie and said, "Drive yourself home. I'll be there as soon as I can." A smile was forced, trying to hide my discomfort.

With a simple nod, she took the valet ticket from me and left the building without an argument. Angie didn't fight with me like Sadie did.

Carmine's happy glance faded to a distressed smirk by the time we reached my office on the second floor. Fat Nicky staggered a few paces behind, then closed the office door for privacy.

"What's the deal with the Russo girl, Tommy?"

"Deal? There's no deal, Carmine. She's got nothing to do with the business."

His face stiffened further. "Madman Russo had a daughter. A daughter named Angela."

I wasn't sure how to answer him. It wasn't really a question, so I remained quiet.

"Is she Madman's daughter, Tommy?"

"What difference does it make?"

Carmine's nostrils flared. Steam blustered from his ears. His demented expression forced me to respond.

"Yes, Carmine. Angie is Madman's daughter."

His head lowered, pondering in stormy silence as he began to pace across the beige carpet. "What you do in your personal life is your business. I don't care who you choose to screw. It's nice to have a beautiful wife and another lovely girl in your bed. Madman may be departed, but his brother is very much alive."

"You're familiar with the Russo family, Carmine?"

He nodded. "We don't want to cross them. You are my partner. Part of my organization. This causes trouble for me, for all of us."

"No disrespect, Carmine, but we are partners in the hotel business only." His statement implicating me as a partner in his criminal enterprise confused me. I was only one-quarter Italian thanks to Grandpa Cavallo's genes. The Italian Mafia liked members of their organization to have nothing but Italian blood running through their veins, at least for the soldiers and capos. The British and Irish blood flowing within me prevented my true membership in the Toscano family.

"You're not listening, son. Sit down and be quiet!" he ordered.

I followed his direction at a cautious rate, forced to look up at him, feeling relatively small.

He spat out, "Our business association makes us family. You get yourself involved with the *Russo* girl? There are hundreds of women in town a good-looking boy like you can easily get into bed. You need to let this one go."

I stood and faced Carmine, man-to-man. "I *love* Angie. I *won't* lose her."

He chuckled as his large frame spun to face Nicky, who suddenly snickered, finding humor in my sentimental words.

"I thought you were smart, Tommy. You're thinking with your heart, and that could get you killed. I assure you, her uncle had you thoroughly checked out. He knows you're married, and he won't allow this affair to continue for long. If you don't walk away willingly, he'll take you out in his own style." Carmine turned toward Nicky. "What's Vincenzo Russo's preferred method?"

"Cars. He toys with the brakes," Nicky replied.

I pretended not to be intimidated, but I suddenly was. I didn't think Vince would tinker with my car. Angie could be in the car with me. He wouldn't risk *her* life.

The room grew silent, except for Carmine's continuous pacing, dragging the heels of his feet when he walked. "Has Vincenzo contacted you, Tommy?"

"I met with him face-to-face and explained my intentions."

"Which are?"

"Carmine, I love Angie."

His eyes widened, surprised brows showing as he stared through me, deep in thought. He looked at Nicky and said, "I want to meet Vincenzo Russo. Make it happen."

CHAPTER 25

Joey Briganti, a member of Nicky's crew, had met Vince previously through a mutual associate. Joey agreed to initiate a meeting between Carmine and Vince.

Two mob bosses never met on their own without a proper introduction from a mutual acquaintance. Bosses and made guys would know each other by reputation, but they'd never speak unless properly introduced.

The meeting had been scheduled at a neutral location. Lorenzi Park was the selected meeting spot early on a Tuesday morning in March 1971.

Much to my surprise, Carmine's cousin, Aniello Toscano, arrived in Vegas for this gathering. Something seemed off about his presence. Why would a powerful mob boss have an interest in the drama invading my life?

My nerves rattled at the mere thought of meeting Aniello, the head of the criminal enterprise I'd been adopted into. Black Sabbath's "Paranoid" echoed through my mind. Paranoid, an instinctive emotion, tearing apart my insides.

A mild breeze chilled my spine when I stood before the boss for the first time.

Aniello Toscano, a short, stocky bull of a man, wore a severe expression as if it pained him to leave his Philadelphia home. He sported a sharp-looking black Italian suit with shoes lavishly shined brightly enough to see your reflection. His thick salt-and-pepper hair was groomed to perfection above a clean-shaven face.

"Thank you for flying out here, Mr. Toscano," I said, grateful a man of his caliber had my back. The frickin' boss had *my* back.

Aniello said nothing, then raised his left hand, displaying his large gold pinky ring. I heard he was married, but he wore no wedding ring. La Cosa Nostra, the Italian phrase that meant "our thing" to Mafia affiliates, was a bigger commitment than marriage.

The soldiers accompanying us kissed his ring, a respectful gesture I complied with.

Carmine insisted I drive with Aniello and him to establish our association. I sat quietly as the two men spoke in Italian. I could make out a few words here and there but not enough to fully understand their conversation. They knew that. Otherwise, they would've spoken English.

Lorenzi Park appeared fairly empty when we arrived, except for a few health-conscious joggers and a couple of people walking their dogs.

Vince and a few of his thugs waited near a bench facing the lake. Vince stepped away from the black-painted bench, appearing less than thrilled to see me approaching behind Aniello Toscano.

Joey Briganti stood tall and solid when he formally introduced the two bosses.

My stomach rumbled with nausea. I'd never been invited to an official mob meeting before, and I had no desire to repeat the tense event. I simply wanted my freedom to be with Angie without Vince's interference or my demise.

Vince's cold black eyes stared me down, angered by my presence. As if it weren't enough that I was sleeping with his niece, he believed I joined forces with a rival mob family. Technically, I wasn't, but because Carmine had been my business partner, perhaps I was more enmeshed with organized crime than I cared to admit.

Joey stepped aside, allowing Aniello, Carmine, and Vince to share a traditional and respectful hug and kiss on the cheek. Their only other company was a family of swans waddling by to reach the water's edge.

The other soldiers crept about twenty paces away from the three wise guys, standing in a protective perimeter. I followed suit until

Carmine snapped his fingers crisply, signaling me to stand next to them while they squatted to sit upon the bench. My shoes sank into the small space in the ground behind Carmine.

"Tommy here tells me he's in love with your niece," Carmine said.

Vince's eyes remained on Aniello, although Carmine was speaking. It seemed Vince didn't want to talk to the underboss with the actual boss present.

"I mean no disrespect, Vincenzo. I met your niece. She's a lovely girl. Tommy means no disrespect, either." Carmine looked at me as though I was expected to say something.

"No disrespect at all," I repeated Carmine's words rather awkwardly.

"They're both young and in love. I realize Tommy's personal situation isn't *ideal*, but he assures me he's working on resolving that."

Vince spoke to Aniello, practically ignoring Carmine. "Don Toscano, I appreciate you wanting to meet with me in person. But you can't expect me to allow my niece, who is like my own daughter, to be made a fool of by this *married* man?"

Aniello composed himself, shifting his body to a more comfortable position on the park bench before replying, "What fool? She's no fool. She's in love. As much as we want to choose an appropriate mate for our children, it's their decision. I have three sons and two daughters. I understand your concerns. Tommy promised he'd take care of your niece, and Angela wants to be with him."

Vince grew silent. His eyes blinked a fair amount of bitterness.

Aniello tapped Carmine's shoulder to speak.

"We're vouching for Tommy as an associate of our family. He has our full protection."

"With all due respect, if I agree to these terms and don't retaliate for my niece's honor, how will *my* family benefit?" Vince asked.

Aniello gave his question some thought. "We shall have peace between our two families. This war cost too many lives. We both lost good men. You lost your brother. Frank killed my nephew and his pregnant wife. My sister's only child and grandchild are dead, and she'll live in hell for the rest of her days." Aniello paused, thinking about the loss his family suffered.

Carmine bowed his head in honor of their deceased family members.

Aniello continued. "I will offer you and your organization a peace treaty, Vincenzo. We won't interfere in your businesses, and you don't interfere with ours, including Tommy's relationship with your niece."

"My niece's reputation is on the line. He'll break her heart."

"If Tommy harms your niece, he will no longer be under our protection." Carmine looked directly into my gray eyes and added, "You understand?"

I nodded. I had no intention of hurting Angie. But what if we argued and she was pissed at me? Would that constitute personal injury or death? Mine?

"Cosa Nostra till we die," Aniello declared before they started to speak in Italian.

Carmine shooed me away to join Joey, who stood out of hearing range.

My heart pounded in my throat. Would this sit-down actually ease the tension between Vince and me? Would he leave Angie and me alone?

Did Aniello's people kill Frank because Frank killed his nephew? He mentioned a war between their families. So many questions I shouldn't know the answers to piqued my curiosity.

Ten minutes passed before the men stood from the bench and exchanged a respectful hug and kissed cheek.

As they approached me, Carmine smiled. "Everything is okay now, Tommy." He twisted his body to look Vince in the eye. "Right, Vincenzo?"

Vince gave a slow, firm nod. "As long as he treats my niece with *respect*."

Despite my trembling fingers, I held my hand out to Vince, and he returned the gesture, squeezing with tremendous force. Then I shook hands with Carmine and Aniello, offering my sincere gratitude.

CHAPTER 26

On the drive back to the Montgomery, I must have thanked Aniello and Carmine a dozen times for helping me soothe the tension with Vince. A feeling of security swept over me since I was under their protection.

"You're a good boy, Tommy. We're partners. We help you. You help us."

My smile faded while my brain worked in overdrive, wondering what Carmine meant, exactly. How much more could I help them? They embezzled money, skimming the casino against my will.

Carmine continued to stare into my eyes—that damn game of chicken he mastered. What would these men receive in exchange for this favor they awarded me? "Dominic is starting a loan business in town. You should find him a nice office at the Montgomery."

I knew what he meant. Sharks and bookies operating out of the Montgomery. After what they just did for me, getting Vince off my back, I didn't have a choice unless I preferred death.

"Does Dominic get a title? Is he on our payroll?"

Aniello chimed in, seemingly annoyed, speaking to me directly for the first time. "You ask too many questions, boy!"

"You let me and Nicky take care of everything, Tommy. There's nothing for you to worry about," Carmine said.

"Please don't take this the wrong way. I'm concerned about drawing attention. I wouldn't want the police coming down on us. We're partners. I should know what's going on."

Maybe it would have been better if Carmine didn't tell me anything. But he did. He included me in on more of his criminal activities. If I wanted to survive, I couldn't stop the Toscanos.

Aniello growled in irritation when he spoke. "Funny, you expect to know about our business. When were you going to tell us about the codicil to Rocky's power of attorney? You conveniently left out those terms your father put in writing."

The surprised look on my face confirmed what he already knew. Len was careful to keep that detail quiet. Hell, if Len and I were the only two people who knew about those terms, perhaps I could've divorced Sadie without anyone questioning it. Maybe that wasn't the legal thing to do, but a man could dream, right?

"It's good you're traveling and buying hotels. More profits earned and more money in my pocket. I want you to be successful. If you're not, I could squash you like a cockroach, and my people will run the *entire* Montgomery." Aniello smiled for the first time, showing severely crooked teeth. Then his head turned, staring out the car window, tapping his gold pinky ring against the glass like the rhythm of Morse code.

Perspiration lined the edge of my hairline.

Carmine was the chattier of the two. "We took care of your pop so he could keep his business. Today, we helped you out of a jam. Saved your life! You don't believe a powerful man like Vincenzo Russo would've allowed your relationship with his niece to continue, do you? We own half of the Montgomery, which is growing thanks to our investment. We're entitled to our cut, Tommy. Dominic's branch of the business begins effective immediately," Carmine insisted.

Technically, they owned 49 percent, but no need to split hairs. What choice did I have? The Toscanos knew what I was up against with Pop's irrational tests. Let's face it, if I got caught with Angie, Sadie could leave me, rendering them the opportunity to take over my family's business. They didn't help me out of this debacle with Vince for free. All along, the Toscanos had an agenda.

I sold my soul to the devil to be with Angie.

CHAPTER 27

I dialed Len's phone number at a frantic pace. How did Pop's codicil leak to Aniello? Because the papers were filed legally, the Toscanos' attorney had a variety of ways to discover the addendum. It was only a matter of time before this secret became exposed.

They knew if I couldn't properly manage the hotel operations and maintain a soaring profit margin, they could tap into my 51 percent. They also learned if I failed at my marriage, the same result applied.

Ideas crawled into my head with Angie as my muse. I wanted her all to myself, day and night. Since I couldn't do that while married to Sadie, I worked with my key executives to develop a strategy for buying more hotels under the Montgomery umbrella. I'd forage for prospects and take Angie along for the ride.

Carmine agreed with my plan. More investments meant more profits, which equaled more money lining his pockets too.

Within a short time, our investments paid off. We made millions, excluding Carmine's additional activities like loan sharking and skimming. There were two sets of books to manage: the real ones and the ones for the IRS, which appeared to show factual numbers.

The branch of the Toscanos' business that stayed far away from the Montgomery was drugs. If drug money got washed through the Montgomery, awareness could be heightened by local law enforcement and the gaming commission, who would shut us down. I worried Carmine's greed would force that connection. Luckily, he didn't allow anything to disrupt the profits pouring in. The Montgomery had to appear completely legitimate. Otherwise, our income would cease, and peering through a six by nine cell could be our future.

The pressure was on. My drug use increased. Pills to sleep at night. Other substances kept me awake during the day. Cocaine gave me an extra charge when I needed it. Later, I'd learn the hard way the damage this lifestyle would cause.

CHAPTER 28

A breathtaking tropical adventure topped my list for romance and relaxation. Angie and I flew to the stunning island of Oahu. A prime piece of real estate was available for me to explore in person after numerous legal discussions. Hawaii, a gorgeous location year-round. Serene beaches, smoking volcanos, and beautiful sunsets greeted us warmly.

After Len approved the legal paperwork and I signed on the dotted line, Angie and I celebrated at the bar lounge in the soon-to-be Montgomery Hawaiian Hotel.

I whisked Angie atop my lap and kissed her, just as a woman brought us the champagne on ice I ordered. "Mr. Cavallo, I'm Sandy Strickland, the bar manager."

I slid Angie off my lap and stood to shake her hand. "It's a pleasure to meet you, Sandy."

"I heard you'll be the new owner. Congratulations!"

"Thank you."

"Is this your wife?" she asked, approaching Angie.

"Oh, no," Angie replied, blushing a sweet shade of pink.

Sandy smirked and turned toward me, harshly saying, "I heard you were married."

I paused, digesting Sandy's callous tone. "My social status has nothing to do with running this hotel or signing paychecks, Sandy. Is that understood?"

"Yes, sir," she answered in a militant fashion.

My prickly-pitched message was received.

She faced Angie, sending a malicious look from her blue eyes before marching away.

I reached for Angie's hand, but she pulled away, suffering from Sandy's wrath.

"Listen, I don't care what she thinks. The next time someone asks if you're my wife, I'm going to say yes."

For added privacy, I bought a house near the Hawaiian hotel in Waikiki. The house I purchased on Hoakoa Drive was situated in the Diamond Head area near Waikiki Beach. We loved Hawaii and planned to return often.

"Tommy, this house is beautiful! The view of the beach is amazing! Is it really ours?" Angie asked as she bounced around what would be our kitchen.

"It's all ours, babe."

"This is too much. We can stay at the hotel when we visit. You didn't need to buy a separate house for us."

She was right. We could have stayed at the hotel, but I didn't want to be scrutinized by meddlesome employees like Sandy Strickland, who would act disrespectfully toward Angie. I also sought discretion. Would someone like Sandy seek out Sadie and reveal my affair?

I ensured Angie stayed busy when we traveled, and I worked, keeping her at arm's length from my business affiliations. Sometimes, she simply sat by the pool, looking gorgeous in a bikini.

At the end of a fantastic week of swimming and snorkeling along a coral reef to view unique plant life and vibrantly colored fish, we attended an evening show with fire dancers, hula girls, and a performance by Don Ho jamming on his ukulele.

When Angie spoke, I listened. After our Hawaiian adventure, she suggested we visit Europe—Italy and France, in particular. Aaron made it happen. He worked hard, locating superior hotels that met my specific criteria and price.

Angie and I enjoyed many trips overseas to expand my business. Throughout our entire relationship, we saw the world, creating a lifetime of spectacular memories that entwined our emotions and hearts in every spot we visited.

I never allowed Carmine's crew to tag along. I wasn't a fan of their tactics to secure a sale. Threats, mischief, and bullying might have been how La Cosa Nostra operated, but I wasn't a member. Every sale had to be legitimate.

Sadie hadn't seemed interested in me or my whereabouts. She had a couple of girlfriends, whom I met in passing once or twice. They took up a lot of her time. I didn't question how she spent her days and nights, and I didn't want her to ask me. We got along for the most part and lived like roommates.

I tried to be attentive and cordial with Sadie as much as possible. She couldn't find out about Angie. If she did, she might leave. If it weren't for the damn conditions Pop put on me, I wouldn't care. I'd even hold the door open for her. I didn't hate Sadie back then, but I despised being legally bound to her against my will.

CHAPTER 29

I became completely engrossed in my world with Angie. My taste for partying too much in the early seventies eventually caught up with me. The combination of cocaine and Jameson messed with my mind and my relationships. Drugs clouded my judgment, fueling a miserable temperament. I took too many risks that might have cost me my business, Angie, and my life.

After a year or better, Angie and I knew the time had come to stop the hardcore partying. I got introduced to rock bottom and smacked it hard. Initially, Angie never wanted any part of drugs after her sister, Connie, died from a heroin overdose. We never messed with heroin. Angie's first taste of cocaine was at my suggestion, not realizing the intoxicating power the effect of that drug would hold on her. I blamed myself for inducting her into an addictive culture, difficult to escape from.

Our affair with cocaine started in 1973 after Angie learned the devastating news that she was infertile. She wanted to have a child someday with me. God, she was crushed, and I missed her adoring smile and perky personality. She suffered through a period of depression. At that time, I didn't understand the constant mood swings and frequent shifts in her behavior. She was sad and angry often, shedding an abundance of tears. Depression wasn't commonly diagnosed then. No one openly talked about it, fearing the stigma associated with mental health disorders, even if the condition was temporary like Angie's, triggered by grief.

Some days, she wouldn't get out of bed. Other days, Angie had these wild ideas about things she wanted to accomplish in life, like earning a college degree and securing a career. She didn't want to get out of bed. How would she manage an education and a job?

Angie challenged the label of infertility by securing a second and third opinion. Her diagnosis had proven to be a severe case of endometriosis, which would prevent her from becoming pregnant.

Whether a baby could be created from my own flesh and blood or through a legal adoption didn't matter to me. I tried to tell her we'd adopt a baby after we were married. Her heart broke, dealing with sterility and the fact that the future she wanted required adjusting.

Her cousin Katie announced her second pregnancy shortly after Angie's dream of motherhood was decimated. Angie's misery amplified when she learned Katie's joyous news.

In an attempt to bring her out of the funk she was in, I convinced her to snort a line of coke with me. The powerful effect of cocaine brought her out of her despondent state, but it didn't solve her problems. We were constantly high that year, which prevented Angie from dealing with her fate.

Witnessing Angie's struggle with sobriety had been more difficult than tolerating my own potent appetite for Jameson. Withdrawal symptoms were tough to beat. Mapping out a path to lead us back to a state of normalcy was instrumental in handling the cravings we experienced.

Thankfully, Angie spoke with a doctor who gave her tips to handle our hunger for drugs. A vicious urge we'd have to cope with for the rest of our lives. As we desperately worked toward sobriety, we both had to face the destiny bestowed on us—a childless future unless we went the adoption route.

CHAPTER 30

All aspects of my life slid while Angie and I were recuperating. Once my head cleared from controlled substances, my ability to focus and work a full day resumed.

Rob managed everything while I had been incapacitated, including dealing with the individual hotel managers in the US and overseas. The only thing Rob wouldn't do was contend with Carmine's crew. They were my sole responsibility.

Carmine's guys were getting out of control more than usual because I wasn't available to intervene and restrict their criminal behaviors. Numerous robberies were reported by guests. Room safes were cracked. Because my security team knew the thieves were Carmine's boys, they couldn't stop it without retaliation.

The Las Vegas Police Department merged with the Clark County sheriff's office by this time, establishing themselves as the Las Vegas Metropolitan Police Department, commonly referred to as Metro by locals. Metro was brought in by a couple from Nebraska to investigate, which became problematic for everyone. I comped the rooms and meals for all guests who lost valuables, and promised security would investigate to prevent Metro from being called. But this couple from Nebraska couldn't be dissuaded.

Carmine wanted to deal with these Nebraskans in his own style.

I had to step in and control the situation. "If anything happens to that couple, Metro will investigate *everything* related to the Montgomery, Carmine. You gotta let this go. Somebody has to take responsibility for this, and your guys can't commit crimes on these premises. If Metro catches any scent of illegal activities happening here, we're finished!"

A gang member confessed to the theft ring, taking the fall. He was later sentenced to three years in prison.

The business was nearly back on track, and Carmine ended the crimewave his thugs launched inside the hotel.

My next thorough review included the finances of my home in Henderson. I evaluated my personal bank account. Studying the statements sobered me up real quick. Tens of thousands of dollars had been withdrawn over the last year. I wasn't making large sum withdrawals from that account.

Sadie hadn't spent the money on a new television or furniture. No new cars sat in the driveway. Where was the money going?

Then it occurred to me that Sadie became involved with a local Evangelical church. She found her calling as a community activist, launching *A New Beginning* program, which helped people find temporary shelter, jobs, or a permanent place to live. I never pegged her for a selfless volunteer, managing a shelter to save the homeless. However, it was *my* money she chose to be selfless with.

I started to pay more attention to her whereabouts, confirming precisely what she was doing with such a large portion of money.

A buddy of mine, Larry, started a private investigation business. Larry wanted to be a cop, but he never made it through the police academy. I never asked him why, but he had solid instincts and street smarts, and he learned enough from the academy about the justice system, as well as the use of the proper tools and resources for surveillance operations. The stories he told me about his time in the academy were pretty awesome!

Larry was hired to discover how Sadie spent her time while I had been partying throughout the US and Europe with Angie. It didn't take much time for Larry to present me with pictures of Sadie making out with some wannabe rock star in a second-rate band. My reaction wasn't triggered by jealousy. I shouldn't have been surprised, but I wasn't expecting to hear she was screwing around with some half-rate, penniless crooner.

Larry's next assignment was to check out this guy, Joel Sinclair. Who was this guy my wife had been spending time with, and would she leave me for him? I wanted to let her go. Let her live her life elsewhere with whomever she desired.

If Carmine knew Sadie left me, which would ultimately lead to a divorce, he could take over my entire business.

Shit, if Joel made Sadie happy, I'd pack her bags for her. But I couldn't let that happen. She couldn't leave. Sadie was as trapped in this marriage as I was. She just didn't know it.

Could I have come clean with Sadie? Shared this damning legal information with her—details she or anyone could use against me? If I trusted her, yes. But I didn't trust her. She could hold this over my head, turning me into a lapdog, obliged to do her bidding for the unforeseeable future. I refused to live like that.

According to Larry, Joel Sinclair had skills. Talented enough to entice him with a career change. The Montgomery in New York City had expanded its entertainment. I fronted the cash to expense a record deal, allowing a renowned record producer to keep the majority of the profits, except for a meager one percent if Sinclair had potential. If Joel didn't make it in the industry, I'd lose my investment entirely. I didn't care about the money. I needed Joel gone. I flew the producer to Nevada and encouraged him to listen to Joel's band, then offer the singer an opportunity of a lifetime to cut a record and secure steady work, singing at a luxury hotel in New York—my hotel. But Joel would have to leave his band and his life in Vegas behind.

Unless he really loved Sadie, he wouldn't pass up this kind of career move.

My suspicions were spot-on. He jumped at the deal, leaving my wife behind. I knew Sadie would never get on a plane to fly across the country, leaving me and my millions for this singer. Joel Sinclair took off to the big time. Surprisingly, he made me some decent money off that mere one percent as a successful pop artist.

CHAPTER 31

May 26, 1975, the date that altered my existence.

Sadie slept soundly in her bedroom.

Unable to sleep, I attempted to fix a wobbly kitchen cabinet door. When the phone chimed, I assumed the late-night call related to the hotel, but I was wrong.

A frenzied woman spoke in circles with an accent, preventing me from fully understanding her words. As I was about to hang up, thinking she had the wrong number, she stuttered, "I'm with John at the hospital."

"John? Who is this?"

"It's Cherry, Tommy."

Cherry, a girl John saw regularly. A professional. My brother had a penchant for the ladies. Throughout his life, John became involved with many women without disabilities. But John didn't love them. He'd let them go once the relationship ran its course.

Cherry was different. She spent a lot of time with John. So much so, I thought she'd quit her profession to be with my brother. Shivers ran up my spine when the unthinkable words left Cherry's lips, "He's gone. I'm so sorry. I tried to help him, but it was too late. It happened so fast."

"Gone?"

"John died, Tommy." Heartbreak resonated through her words.

I dropped the receiver and lost my balance. I bent to pick up the phone handle, despite my unwavering denial.

Cherry's gut-wrenching sobs led to hysterics as she described my brother's final gruesome moments, clutching his chest, turning blue, and waiting for the ambulance to arrive. Once she settled down, I offered to send a driver to take her home.

I contacted the Desert Springs Hospital and demanded to speak to someone about my brother.

With a heartfelt apology, a woman on the opposite end confirmed that the world lost a good man. John passed away very unexpectedly from a probable heart attack.

"Probable? You aren't sure how he died? Find out! Do an autopsy! I need to know exactly how my thirty-four-year-old brother died tonight!" Anguish swept through me. Pains in my chest combatted with the agony in my head.

Then I lost it! My heart burned like a bonfire. Anger rushed through my veins. My fist smashed the wall hard enough to leave an indentation. I sprained my wrist, but I didn't care. Pots and pans within my grasp were thrown across the kitchen. A warm, numbing sensation entombed my body as the tears began to fall.

He couldn't be gone. We just ate lunch at Amici's last week. I watched him eat almost a whole sausage and pepperoni pizza. Then I broke his chops about putting on a few pounds.

My breakdown must have woken Sadie, frightening her. She held onto an old baseball bat when she entered the kitchen. "Tommy? Oh my God! You scared the hell out of me. What are you doing?" Her blue eyes widened in surprise to see the kitchen in shambles.

"It's John." My heart suffered as I mumbled the words, "He's dead."

She dropped the bat to the floor. "John? No!" The look of distress worn upon her face was proof of her affection for my brother, despite John's suspicion of her.

What would I tell Pop? The stroke cost him his mind and independence. This news would break his heart. Could he comprehend losing his oldest son in his state of mind?

God, I wanted to see Angie and hold her in my arms. But it was the middle of the night, and I needed time to accept the fact that I lost my brother.

Sadie stayed up with me and let me ramble. Then I confided something I never spoke about with anyone outside the family and the few friends involved—witnesses to the unfortunate tragedy.

Most people believed John was born handicapped. He was born deaf, but his legs worked like any normal kid until age twelve. Painful nightmares resided in my head after that incident. I rarely slept well after such a horrendous day.

I never thought of my older brother as "disabled." We fought as most brothers did. We would cause quite a ruckus sometimes with our arguments. We even had a fistfight over a one-on-one basketball game once.

John acquired his own group of friends. Some of my friends were uncomfortable because they didn't understand John when he spoke, using his unique-sounding voice or sign language. I wanted to build a bridge between my brother and my friends. I'd include John when we played outside with the neighborhood kids at the basketball court, wiffleball in the field at the end of the block, and go-kart racing. Pop had taken apart a baby carriage, an old hope chest, and some other junk from the garage to help us build the fastest go-kart in town!

Mom was always concerned. She warned me to look after John because he couldn't hear.

One partially cloudy yet warm day, a group of us decided to play ball at our usual spot. Although we typically goofed around, the game turned serious. I acted as if we were playing in the major leagues, and I was Mickey Mantle, my idol.

John was stationed in left field. When at-bat, he could hit the ball pretty hard. He ran fast too—back then. He'd chase that ball and dance with pride whenever he made a good play. He was no different from the rest of us. I tried to tell the other guys that. They warmed up to him and picked up on some key phrases in sign language. John had formed a whole new circle of friends.

Suddenly, the sky grew wickedly dark. Drizzling flecks of rain turned to a steady stream through thickening black clouds. We were in the middle of the game. The other team just tied us. Two outs with a man on third. We needed to get this guy out, then clean up at the bottom of the ninth with some extra runs to win. The rain didn't stop us from finishing the game, despite the fierce bolt of lightning followed by a roar of thunder.

The batter positioned his body at the plate.

A curveball pitch was thrown.

He hit the ball far, and we argued if it was foul. As the captain of my team, I disputed with my opponents. My eyes left John for several seconds. Those few ever-important seconds haunted me to this day.

John raced to get the ball.

An ear-piercing screech of tires braking disrupted my argument. Thick skid marks from burnt rubber covered the street, filling my senses with an obnoxious, burning odor so vulgar I could taste it. When I turned to look toward the hideous sound, my brother lay in the middle of the street with a dark-colored Chevy parked over his body.

And I screamed. I screamed so loud, I nearly lost consciousness.

Everything seemed to move in slow motion from that moment on. The other kids ran to John first. My brain demanded my feet move, but several seconds passed before I could make myself move closer to witness the ugly scene.

The driver sprang from his car, shouting, "The kid came out of nowhere! I swear, I didn't see him!" He tried speaking to John and praying to God, wishing John would open his eyes, jump up, and race back to the field, as did I.

I knelt next to John and stared at his broken body, unconscious. I gently poked his shoulder, hoping the touch of my finger would magically waken him.

The rain continued to pour.

People who lived on that street raced outside. I vaguely remembered hearing a woman say she called for help.

Someone shouted, "Don't move him until help arrives!"

Between the thick splashes of rain soaking my hair and the ominous crash of thunder, the voices of others around me sounded muffled. Someone stood over us with an umbrella. I ensured John stayed dry. His body lay so still, I thought he was dead. I'd never been so scared or felt so helpless in my entire life.

My body sat frozen over John until a medic lifted me up and away from him. I squirmed from the man's grasp, kicking and screaming to let me go, not wanting to leave my brother's side.

A police officer kindly mumbled that John was alive, and these men had to rush him to the hospital.

Despite the anger that fueled my emotions, I watched the medical team strap braces around John's neck and body before carefully moving him onto a gurney.

I demanded to ride with John to the hospital while those blinding red lights blinked and shrieking sirens blared, but the patient policeman insisted I drove with him when he realized John was my brother. He needed me to take him to my parents so he could advise them about the accident.

Later that day, the doctor told Mom and Pop that John's spinal cord had been damaged. "Your son is lucky to be alive," he said with a stupid smile plastered across his face. This was good news, according to him. The injury cost John the use of his legs. There was nothing *lucky* about it.

I blamed myself. Visions of that car and shrilling brake sounds invaded my dreams for years. I was responsible for John that day. He must have been too excited and distracted to see that car driving around the corner. He wanted to fit in and play ball like a regular boy. To me, he was normal. Suddenly, he couldn't walk anymore.

I failed him.

As devastated as Mom and Pop were, they never blamed me. John never blamed me for that traumatic accident, either. With time and after physical therapy, John accepted his fate. He tolerated the fact that the wheelchair permanently acted as his legs.

I never accepted it, though. I let him down that day. Maybe that was why I grew up to be such a control freak. I couldn't control what happened to John, but I tried to influence every other aspect of my life to a painful degree, even with the numerous responsibilities Pop put on me since my youth.

CHAPTER 32

Angie had her own schedule to keep in the mornings while I worked. She achieved her dream, earning a college degree and launching a career in real estate. Her determination for success alleviated her depressed state and allowed her to defeat her addiction.

Usually, I wouldn't stop by to see her until later in the afternoon or sometimes for lunch, depending upon our schedules.

She planned to register for classes for the next semester at the University of Nevada on this gloomy morning. She liked proving that a woman could be useful in a man's career. At that time in the mid-seventies, progress for women was being made—slowly.

Telling her about John made my heart ache worse than it already felt.

Angie and John had become the closest of friends since I introduced them. I loved that she learned to speak sign language to enhance their friendship. She met John weekly for lunch or a cup of coffee and practiced signing with him.

John adored Angie.

Angie was sweet and genuine, one of the kindest people I ever knew. A tender soul with a powerful shoulder I leaned on. Angie, my rock, helped me to cope with the mountain of grief I suffered.

We spent the day talking about John and planning his funeral. She drove to the morgue with me, a heart-wrenching experience. It was hard to leave the vehicle and step inside the cold brick hospital building where my brother's body had been stored among the dead.

We were escorted to a private room with dim lighting. The temperature seemed to drop thirty degrees upon entering. Maybe this wasn't John. They could have John mixed up with someone else.

Angie's fingers clamped firmly around my hand when we saw the figure of a body lying on a table beneath a large white sheet. "Are you ready, Tommy? I mean, are you sure you want to see him like this?" she asked.

I nodded, unable to utter a word. Then I glanced at the hospital professional, signaling him to pull back the sheet. My eyelids were sealed, taking a moment before looking, promising God I'd be a better person if this wasn't my brother.

Seeing John's jet-black hair, his thick eyelashes concealing his green eyes, and his body resting on that flat table, cold to the touch, didn't seem real. The color of his complexion had washed away. My tears couldn't be contained. I reached for his hand to hold. His pale skin felt clammy and sticky as I held on tightly. "This wasn't supposed to happen to you, John. You weren't supposed to leave me."

Angie leaned in and kissed John's forehead.

"How can I say goodbye?" I muttered as tears streamed down my cheeks.

"No need for goodbyes, Tommy. John will always be with you. He's a part of you," she said.

"The *good* part," I stammered, wiping the puddles from my eyes, choking on the frothy sputum gathered in my throat.

She grabbed my cheeks, forcing me to face her. "Hey, you are a good man, Tommy Cavallo. John was so proud of you and all you've accomplished. He loved you unconditionally. So do I." She kissed me and said, "Lean on me, baby. I'm here for you."

Thank God Angie had been with me. She kept me sane and focused. In particular, she kept me sober. The immense temptation to slam back Jameson shots overwhelmed me. No better excuse to break sobriety than my brother's death. I always believed I failed John when we were kids. I wouldn't fail him now. He'd want me to stay sober.

I never shared the story about John losing the use of his legs as a young boy with Angie. Nor did I express the dread I felt, blaming myself or dealing with the insufferable nightmares. Angie had strength but a delicate soul. Most people thought John had been born without the ability to walk. It was easier to let others think that than admit to my failure as his protector when we were kids.

Sharing John's unfortunate accident with Sadie was difficult enough. Sadie and Angie were entirely different women. Their looks, styles, upbringing, and personalities prevailed on opposing ends of the spectrum. I felt incapable of talking about John's tragedy so soon after bringing it up the night prior. Discussing it, even thinking about that terrifying day, tore at my heart. Why put that kind of pain and misery on Angie?

With the vast amount of planning Angie and I coordinated to make John's funeral simple yet memorable, I had to break the news to her that she couldn't attend the ceremony with me. How could I pull that off? She knew Sadie would be there. I hated hurting her, forbidding her to go, but I had no choice.

Father Flanagan expressed kind words about John at the service, but my thoughts wandered with the breeze, unable to retain the lovely sentiments. Many people shook my hand with pity darting from somber eyes.

At the end of the solemn funeral, guests in attendance drove to my home in Henderson for a catered meal, followed by coffee and cake my mother-in-law prepared. I wasn't ready to join the others, listening to sympathy quotes as if they were pitching to Hallmark.

A minor tantrum erupted as I stood before John's casket. A final realization that I'd never see him again. Someone propped John's wheelchair with colorful flowers as if that stupid chair was a symbolic memento of his life. I knocked the wheelchair over with my foot, destroying the flowers. "This fucking chair! I hate that you needed this, John! It wasn't fair! It's my fault you needed this contraption!"

I kicked and punched the chair until Sadie gently tugged at my arm.

"Tommy, John's accident wasn't your fault. Not your cross to bear. Let it go."

Somehow, her words calmed my frenzied state.

Sadie and I visited Pop at the nursing home once the service concluded. I controlled my emotions to the best of my ability. It killed me inside to keep such pertinent information about John from him, but telling Pop he lost his firstborn son might destroy him. It was in my father's best interest to lie. Maybe Pop's fate, living in a swirl of confusion, protected him from such a gruesome reality.

At the end of this abysmal day, I tumbled into Angie's arms. Her love helped me survive the loss of my brother and to cope with the emotional turmoil.

"Highway to Hell"

CHAPTER 33

Spending New Year's Eve in Paris became an extraordinary ritual for Angie and me. Each year, we celebrated her birthday and our anniversary while welcoming in a brand-new year. Our magical trifecta of happiness, seeing the romantic sights of Paris. We were never bored. I didn't buy a hotel in France—not without trying. But we adored the Paris apartment I purchased in the early seventies, with a picture-perfect view of the magnificent Eiffel Tower.

Watching Angie in the moonlight with the grand Eiffel as the backdrop was one of the most spectacular views my eyes ever witnessed. We shopped along the elegant Champs Elysees, viewing the Place de la Concorde on one end and the astonishing Arc de Triomphe situated on the opposite end of the famous street. Dining in fine restaurants and browsing through the Musée du Louvre never got old.

In January 1976, we left Paris to spend time at our second favorite place in the world, Lake Como in northern Italy.

I purchased a penthouse atop an impressive structure that overlooked the colorful homes and luminously painted scenery. A wondrous place to stay while conducting business in Italy. Some days, we'd sit and stare into the beautiful crystal waters absorbing the rays of the sun, reflecting the charming village against the small waves as sailboats drifted by. My blood pressure dropped several points whenever we stayed at the lake. Harmony and relaxation saturated with every breath we took.

An important meeting had been scheduled at the Venice hotel with key staff. Since I was only a quick flight away, Captain Roy, the pilot of my private jet, flew me from Milan to Venice so I could attend the meeting in person. The Venice resort stood in a prime spot, a quick walk from the boat launches that transported tourists to St. Mark's Square.

Angie stayed behind to spend the day in Bellagio, a lovely nearby town, lined with colorful villas, gardens, and charming shops.

The meeting in Venice began on a productive note until a woman walked into the conference room and handed me a message from Angie. She signaled its importance with a nod of her head and a worrisome eye exchange.

Angie never disrupted my business meetings. I apologized to my associates and requested access to the nearest phone. My gut swirled. Jesus, I left her alone for a few hours. What could have happened in this short amount of time?

Her voice sounded panicked. Mrs. Arden called her, explaining that Sadie was in a car accident. Her Porsche was destroyed. Sadie sustained injuries and had been brought to the Desert Springs Hospital.

Angie was at the lake. Sadie had been hurt, lying in a hospital bed in Vegas. I had to make a painful choice.

Roy flew me directly from Venice to McCarran International. Before we departed the gate in Venice, I asked Angie to make arrangements to travel home and to close up the Como penthouse until we returned.

Sadie had been driving home from a visit with her parents in Bakersfield when her Porsche smacked into a large truck.

Some guilty feelings crept up. Sadie asked me to drive to Bakersfield with her. Fred and I hadn't spoken much since I fired him. She expected me to put off my Paris trip to make peace with her father. Under no circumstances would I have done that. Not only did I detest the man, but New Year's was my special time with Angie. Of course, Sadie didn't know that. I refused to join her, which led to a horrible fight before I picked up Angie for our annual holiday. That fight lingered in my thoughts. I said some nasty things I wasn't proud of. Sadie could be a pain in the ass sometimes, but I could be a prick too.

Leaving Angie alone for Christmas was a challenge in itself. She hated that I stayed home with Sadie and the Meades, pretending to have a happy marriage when in reality, we lived like roommates. These thoughts cluttered my mind the entire flight home. I might not have wanted to be married to Sadie, but I didn't want anything bad to happen to her.

When I arrived at the hospital, Sadie lay in bed, out cold, in and out of consciousness several times, but she was mostly out of it. I sat in the corner of the room, watching and waiting.

A few of her friends from the shelter she worked at stopped by. I greeted them warmly and allowed them some privacy with her. But she remained unconscious.

The doctor told me it could be a couple of days. Her brain was bruised. Tests were needed to determine the damage and recovery period.

When Sadie finally came to, she screamed at the sight of me. "Stay away from me!"

"What? Sadie, it's me. I flew home as soon as I could."

"No, you wanted this. You want me dead!"

Dead? She accused me of attempted murder. She lost her mind! We might have argued the last time we were together, but murder?

Her doctor advised she had a head injury, which added to her confusion.

It didn't take long before an officer probed her about the accident.

Suddenly, they dragged me down to the station, questioning my whereabouts and motive for murder. The only word that left my lips was, "Lawyer."

The one phone call Metro allowed me to make was to Len, who drove like a bat out of hell to the precinct. He arrived to find me sitting in a dimly lit room on a cold steel chair. They gave me nothing to drink and refused me access to a bathroom as if I were a criminal.

Time seemed to pass as slow as molasses before Len could confirm what evidence they had against me. I knew nothing about Sadie's accident and profusely denied the accusation. My mind drifted to Angie. Had she returned from Lake Como safely? She wasn't happy I chose to fly to Vegas without her.

My patience was depleted when this arrogant cop continued to drill me with the same damn questions. I stood to my feet, prepared to walk out, saying, "If you're not charging me, I'm done."

"Tommy, wait," Len calmly stated.

The officer put his hand on me to force me back in the seat.

Then I lost it. "Take your hands off me, you fucking prick!" When my hand mindlessly pushed the officer away, he grabbed me by the neck. The next thing I knew, my face pummeled against the cool metal table. I could taste the trickles of blood across my upper lip.

Then that egomaniac cop read me my rights, arresting me for assaulting a police officer. He found a reason to detain me.

As he cuffed my wrists, Len attempted to persuade the overzealous officer to take a moment and think about the amount of stress I had been under with my wife in the hospital. "Officer, Mrs. Cavallo has a head injury. She doesn't remember the events clearly."

During the chaos, the dark, demented face of Vince Russo popped into my thoughts. I recalled Fat Nicky rattling off about Vince's favorite method of revenge—tampering with cars.

Did Vince send me a message, plotting to remove Sadie from the picture to make an honest woman out of Angie? If he tampered with *my* car, Angie might get hurt. But Angie wouldn't be anywhere near Sadie's vehicle. His soldiers referred to him as Brains for a reason. I couldn't share this revelation with the cops. I'd be handing them a motive to kill my wife. Free myself from marriage to be with my girlfriend.

Len insisted he speak with his client alone.

The alleged assault against an officer deemed me too dangerous a threat to relieve me from the steel binds while speaking with my attorney. I wished I'd punched that asshole, seeing he arrested me for *assault* when all I did was tap his shoulder—a bit abruptly.

When Len and I were alone, I asked him to verify Angie's whereabouts. I began to worry about her since I abandoned her at the lake.

Not knowing where Angie was added to my stress level. I did what I thought was right. I needed to be here, despite Sadie's fabricated accusations, which led to a bogus arrest.

Eventually, Len managed to track Angie down, safe and sound. I could finally catch my breath in between tedious interviews with cops.

The officer validated my whereabouts in Italy. I had zero mechanical knowledge to pull off such a stunt. However, I had the means to hire someone to do the job. Of course, I didn't. I worried the cops might make a circumstantial case with that information.

They held me for hours because they could with the assault charge I faced. The monotonous, repetitive questions drained every ounce of my patience, but I calmly stuck to my story, word for word.

Sadie's Porsche was examined to determine the cause of the crash. Experts noted the brake line had been frayed—normal wear and tear of the car. There'd be no further investigation of attempted murder as alleged by a woman recovering from a concussion.

Len managed to get the ridiculous assault charge dropped, and I was finally free to go.

Once Sadie learned the details of her accident, and her memory returned, we managed to find a way to coexist again. Trust between us had never been established, but at least she didn't think I was capable of murder.

No matter how badly I wanted out of my marriage, I wasn't a killer, and I never wished Sadie dead.

CHAPTER 34

Vince wasn't off the hook as far as I was concerned. Would he have sought pleasure in tormenting me through my wife?

The streets of Vegas were hit hard in the seventies with various crimes like robberies, explosions, and murder. Many people lost their lives, and the police continuously investigated members from a Chicago mob family for those offenses. The criminals in question acted like celebrities, begging for media attention, making headlines, and egging on Metro, daring law enforcement to catch them in the cat-and-mouse game they instigated.

I wondered if the cops ever looked in Carmine or Vince's direction. Maybe they laid low enough, out of the public eye.

Carmine's tea business wasn't a majority owner of the Montgomery. Perhaps he was smarter than I gave him credit for, hiding behind the beard of a legitimate company that specialized in herbal teas. Carmine chose to use my clean record as the face of the Montgomery to their advantage.

I couldn't rule out Carmine as a suspect in Sadie's accident, either. However, keeping Sadie alive was more of a benefit to Carmine than a detriment. If the Toscanos wanted to take total control of the Montgomery, my divorcing Sadie influenced that outcome. Her death would prevent that opportunity.

I wasn't about to accuse Carmine, but I wanted his take on the situation.

"Wives are off-limits!" Carmine's voice rang with ferocity. "If Vincenzo had anything to do with that accident, he's broken our agreement. We don't attack wives or babies of family members—unless there was some type of betrayal they were personally responsible for."

The glorious feeling of relief ran through me when I heard the outrage in Carmine's tone.

Carmine sent Sadie a massive arrangement of colorful wildflowers. A sincere gesture, wishing her a speedy recovery.

CHAPTER 35

Ironically enough, Led Zeppelin's "Stairway to Heaven" wailed from the car radio when I started the BMW, headed to Vince's mansion in Rancho Circle. I wasn't about to let any superstitious thoughts cloud my judgment.

I planned to speak to Vince alone—without warning. Since Angie wasn't with me, I rang the doorbell. Usually, she would simply stroll inside, and I'd trail behind. Somehow, walking in unannounced and uninvited didn't seem appropriate, even though I had been attending Sunday dinners for the last five years.

Sonny, Vince's muscle, sent an abrasive glare when he found me on the other side of the door. Since I came alone to speak with Vince, I endured a generous pat-down before he escorted me into the rustic den to wait for the prince of darkness.

I never fancied Vince as a hunter, but several stuffed heads hung prominently from the dark-paneled walls. Twenty-five minutes, I waited, staring into the glass eyes of buffalo, elk, and deer. For a second, I envisioned *my* head mounted on the wall for his sick pleasure.

Vince loved toying with me, making me wait, but I didn't squirm. I sat patiently reading the *Chronicle* to catch up on the news of the day. He showed himself, wearing a dark-blue suit, sipping caffeine from an espresso cup. He inched his way with confidence toward the tall black leather chair across me. Slowly, he sat and crossed his legs. "What brings you by, Tommy?"

"You heard about Sadie's accident?" I asked.

He nodded, revealing no emotion. "Sounded like quite a collision."

"Seems her brake line was damaged," I lied to make him sweat. Why tell him that Metro confirmed the crash was an accident? "She could have been killed."

"You know, you don't sound like a man ready to divorce his wife. In fact, I had you pegged from the start. If only my niece saw through your act."

"Just because I want to divorce my wife doesn't mean I want her *dead*," I insisted.

"Why come to me? Are you looking for sympathy...from *me*?" Vince coolly tapped all ten of his fingers together incessantly, waiting for my reply.

"Maybe this wasn't an accident. According to Carmine, wives and children are off-limits."

"Off-limits? From what?" His tone sounded calm, but his flaring nostrils displayed outrage.

I hesitated to respond at first but showed my cards a bit prematurely. "Did you have anything to do with Sadie's accident?"

He sent me a sinister look as if I insulted him. "I'm a man of my word, Tommy. I made a deal with Don Toscano that I wouldn't interfere in your relationship with Angie. It hurts to know you lack faith in me." Vince paused momentarily and scratched his chin, thinking. "You came here in defense of your wife while you promised you'd get divorced and marry Angie. Maybe I'm old-fashioned about these things, I don't know, but *you're* the one not keeping his word." He rose from the leather chair and approached me, spewing venom between his words. "There are many ways to bring you down, son. I don't need to go through your wife to do it."

"If you come after my wife or me, there will be consequences, Vince. The Toscanos will see to that."

"You have big cojones coming into my home, making threats!" His tall, lean figure towered over me by four inches. He mumbled something in Italian I couldn't comprehend, but I understood the charming Italian curse words.

His dark, soulless eyes stared me down. "You piss me off any further, you fucking piece of shit, and you'll be at my mercy. I could kill you right here and now and toss your body out with the trash… in tiny pieces. I'd smooth things over with Toscano, and Angie would move on," he snarled, beaming with arrogance.

My ego and big mouth challenged him. "That may not be a wise move."

"You think the Toscanos have more power than me?"

I scoffed and shook my head in disagreement. "I learned some potent information about Angie's mother and what your brother put her through. Details you wouldn't want exposed."

The man flinched the moment I mentioned Betty Russo. I never saw Vince sweat before. I had struck a nerve and plucked it like a guitar chord.

At this time in our relationship, Angie didn't know if her mother was dead or alive. I didn't tell her because the truth would devastate her. She adored her father, well-deserving of the nickname Madman.

Vince didn't say another word, but those dark eyes suddenly softened. "Betty abandoned her daughters. Where she moved to, I don't know, and Angie doesn't care. She was a horrible mother. Why would you inflict pain on my niece, the woman you claim to love?"

"Angie is a grown woman. Not knowing why her mother abandoned her has been painful for her. Angie can handle the truth. Can *you* handle the exposure?"

"If Betty is still breathing, she's either lying in a ditch or on her knees, working for her next fix. Why should I care where she is or if Angie searched for her, other than worrying about the emotional toll this would take on Angie?"

"You know she's alive! You know exactly where Betty is. I know everything, Vince. And I haven't said a word to Angie…yet." I relayed the information I garnered about Betty and Frank's disastrous marriage to Vince, intimidating him with the knowledge I possessed. I knew enough about Betty's whereabouts to be dangerous.

Vince offered no facial expression, but I noticed a severe, uncontrollable twitch in his right eye.

"I've got evidence, Vince. Valid information. All I'm asking for is safety for Sadie and me, and I won't outright tell Angie the brutal truth about her father. If anything happens to either of us, the evidence I have will hit the media and the sheriff's office. No more *accidents* or the trigger I hold about Betty will be pulled. Once that bullet fires, it can't be undone."

Vince inched his way close to me. I worried he'd attempt to strangle me or threaten to seek revenge. Instead, he folded his arms and wearily nodded without saying a word.

I reestablished our arrangement and my protection. He'd never admit to tampering with Sadie's brakes. I had no viable proof of his involvement, but I wasn't a big believer in coincidences, no matter what Metro's investigation of Sadie's brakes revealed.

As a precaution, Fat Nicky added security guards around my house in Henderson and a personal bodyguard to act as my shadow in case Vince chose to break the pact he originally established with the Toscanos. The pact that protected me, including Sadie.

Perhaps I went too far, using Betty Russo as leverage.

CHAPTER 36

BETTY RUSSO

The year was 1979 when Angie reunited with her mother. Years had passed since she saw Betty. Angie held so much unhealthy bitterness toward her mother. She merely knew the information her father supplied. She believed her mother abandoned her at a young age, starving for her next fix only a dose of heroin could satisfy—a tumultuous piece of fiction.

My PI, Larry, had found Betty tucked away in a mental ward of a nursing home in New York. I kept that detail quiet until Angie was prepared to deal with the facts about her parents' relationship.

She blamed Betty for Connie's addiction. Angie dreaded conversations about her mother, her sister, and their wretched vices. The subject caused her agony and shame. I didn't want to add heartbreak to that list. Peace for her was my main goal.

Angie first asked Vince if he knew where her mother was or if he'd help find her. I overheard their argument behind closed doors.

"Angie, your mother had too many problems. Why would you welcome that into your life? She left. It's her loss. Leave it alone," Vince suggested.

"Uncle, I want to know where she is and face her. You have no clue how much anger I carry for her."

"This is Tommy's doing, isn't it? Tommy's words coming out of your mouth! He started this bullshit!"

"Tommy has nothing to do with this! This is *my* choice. I'm asking you to find her. Please do this…for me," she pleaded.

"Sweetheart, if your mother is alive, she's only going to disappoint you again."

"Stop trying to protect me! I'm a grown woman, and I'm ready."

Vince paused, assessing Angie's determination. "Okay, my dear. Against my better judgment, I'll see what I can do."

He lied. He allowed Angie to believe he'd help, but he did *nothing*. Vince wasn't acting difficult because Angie might have to deal with emotional scars. He worried Betty would share secrets, exposing Vince and Frank as ruthless gangsters who operated a criminal empire.

Memories of Betty haunted Angie since I introduced the idea, opening up old wounds and pouring salt. My only objective was that Angie made peace with her mother.

After several weeks with zero help from Vince, Angie asked me to use my resources to locate Betty. I agreed if she didn't tell her uncle. I didn't want Vince to know I found Betty for Angie. He'd take that as a declaration of war.

I waited a few weeks before giving Angie the information she desired to make it appear as if the task was more complicated than it actually was.

Although she learned where Betty lived, she suddenly procrastinated their reunion.

"Baby, I'll never force you to do something you aren't ready for. You're in complete control. It's your call if you ever want to see her. At least you know she's alive."

She lowered her head, thinking, and said, "She's in a nursing home. Maybe her health isn't good. What if I don't have much time left to speak to her. I love you for all you've done to locate her." She paused and tapped her finger against her lip, deep in thought. "Let's do this."

We visited her mother on one of the coldest days in February 1979. Living in the desert for my adult life didn't prepare me for the frigid East Coast winter temperatures that numbed my extremities and closed my airways.

The nursing facility Betty called home appeared gloomy. The grounds were snow-covered, and the air was gray and frosty with ambiance as endearing as Alcatraz. The inside looked clean and orderly. The staff exhibited equally sterile expressions.

Once she checked in, Angie insisted she see her mother alone. Watching her step within the clunky elevator triggered an uneasy feeling. I abided by her wishes and waited patiently in the lobby, reviewing the bulletin board accumulated with activities for the residents to enjoy.

I wandered about the lobby area and attempted to have a conversation with the woman managing the reception desk. I'd swear the middle-aged lady with a stunning afro cracked a smile when I winked at her.

I found my way to a plastic-covered sofa, uncomfortable for my backside. My legs crossed naturally, attempting to appear slick when I picked up the new *Sports Illustrated* edition with Christie Brinkley showcased on the cover to keep myself busy while I waited.

When Angie returned to the lobby after her visit, her face appeared visibly anguished. Vince's fear that Betty would be open and honest with Angie proved valid. I'd never know if Angie told me all the nasty, vivid details her mother revealed.

Betty left Angie with sufficient clues about the type of men who raised her. No matter what her mother told her, Angie never turned her back on her uncle or her father's memory. She loved them. However, she was left with many questions about her mother's addiction and her father's involvement in that.

Betty had described the grueling, inconceivable details to Angie, explaining that Frank shot her up with heroin against her will until the lethal addiction took hold of her. A ploy to keep her under his thumb, so she wouldn't humiliate him by walking out on their marriage.

Frank, the devious, controlling Madman, wouldn't let Betty divorce him, taking Connie and Angie away. Marrying a made man with Frank's nasty disposition meant the wife was expected to tolerate criminal behavior, a few black eyes, split lips, and habitual cheating. A wife leaving her powerful, wealthy husband in those days was a major embarrassment. She didn't get to leave unless Frank wanted her gone.

The possibility of Betty's story being true troubled Angie; it disturbed her to the point where I wouldn't validate anything I suspected because it would have hurt her more. I never confirmed the fact that I believed every secret Betty exposed. I also had an agreement with Vince that I wouldn't reveal such a detrimental family secret. Angie didn't hear this news from me, and I reacted to Betty's story like the notion was far-fetched and outlandish.

Angie didn't want to believe her mother's story about the terrible villain she had made Frank out to be. She considered Betty's mental incapacities diluted her memories. Yet Angie made peace with her mother and started to call her regularly, sending weekly packages to offer Betty a more luxurious, warm feeling of comfort. No one had taken care of Betty after Frank dumped her on that awful floor for mental patients years prior and across the country from her children.

The woman became dependent on methadone to rid her body of the heroin withdrawal Frank imposed on her. She suffered from suicidal tendencies. Who wouldn't want to off themselves after living through the nightmare Betty endured? Her doctors didn't want to release her or transfer her in such a fragile state. Ultimately, Angie's mission was to relocate Betty to a facility closer to her.

A drastic threat against Vince—moving Betty close to home.

We flew to New York again a few months after Angie had reconnected with Betty. Angie planned to introduce me to her mother this time. Believe it or not, I felt a little nervous about meeting the mother of the woman I adored.

The beautiful, balmy day unearthed blossoming plants and rich green grass, adding more charm to the facility compared to our first visit during the dead of winter. A staff member advised us to wait for the doctor before seeing Betty.

Upon greeting Betty's physician, we were sadly informed that Betty hung herself the night prior. As painful as this loss was for

Angie to deal with, at least she had the chance to reestablish their relationship as best as she could under the circumstances.

I considered all the details I had gained about Betty Russo from my PI, plus the insight Angie offered. Her sister, Connie, supposedly ransacked her mother's stash of heroin, quickly forming an addiction like many first-time users. If Frank launched that entire situation, having dope in his house to keep Betty in line, it was *his* fault his daughter died, not Betty's.

Frank might have attempted to murder his wife with a deadly dose of heroin, but it was a teenage Connie who lost her battle with addiction in a dark, lonely alley near the Tropicana, where she prostituted herself for every fix. Connie's body had been found lying near a group of stacked crates in an alley, wearing only a torn T-shirt and a needle in her arm.

Word on the street said Connie was targeted as Frank's weakness. Her dependency on heroin made her an easy mark for Frank's enemies to take advantage of. Her last high was laced with poison, not the standard OD Angie was erroneously informed about. Connie being found in such a devastating state was meant to further humiliate Frank and send a message.

Angie struggled to believe her father, her hero, could be accountable for any of this. She constructed emotional boundaries where Betty was concerned. It was much easier to believe the father who remained present in her life than her estranged, drug-addicted mother's tales that could destroy the perfect image held by her dear daddy.

She would never know the truth about her parents' marriage, but Angie felt satisfied that she made peace with Betty before she took her life.

My turbulent thoughts had me questioning if Betty really committed suicide or if someone made it look that way to keep her mouth shut. To kill herself the night before Angie and I were visiting never sat right with me.

Angie said Betty acted excited to meet me when they last spoke on the telephone. One of the nurses mentioned that Betty had been elated about her daughter's upcoming visit and spoke about it the entire week before her death.

Betty was happy Angie planned to see her. She had something to look forward to. She couldn't hold off her suicide mission one more day until she saw her daughter for the last time?

Angie told Vince about our travel plans. Moving Betty to Nevada, rekindling a mother-daughter bond, could have been perceived as a threat.

CHAPTER 37

Vince could have killed me for finding Betty, but eliminating the source would be a wiser, more constructive move. There was no evidence Betty had been murdered, but Vince had the means and motive to eradicate a problem.

Guilt washed over me. Maybe if I didn't plant that seed to reunite Angie with Betty, she'd still be alive. I might not own the responsibility of murdering the woman, but I antagonized a dangerous man, dangling my knowledge of his misdeeds right before his nose.

Vince got even with me for helping Angie find her mother—through my business.

I planned to expand my hotels in the Caribbean. My hotels in Aruba and the Bahamas netted significant profits. I sought to branch out further, looking at St. Kitts, Antigua, and St. Thomas to start. Unfortunately, my generous proposals were respectfully declined. It seemed like the Montgomery was not welcome on that island or any prime tropical spot.

Vince had opened several nightclubs in the Caribbean. He discussed it one Sunday afternoon after family dinner, a brief period after Betty's alleged suicide. Angie followed her family outside onto the patio while I was finishing my cup of cappuccino and enjoying the pizzelle cookies she baked.

Vince remained inside with me and began speaking before I could attempt to join Angie outside. "Ya know, Tommy, I have numerous connections in the Caribbean. They love the employment

opportunities my business brings to the islands. I also funded restoration plans for the citizens of Antigua after that hurricane destroyed
a good part of the beautiful island. They talk about building a statue
of me in their honor." He laughed, beaming with pride. "Ever consider a hotel in Antigua, Tommy?"

The way he asked the question in an annoyingly shrewd tone
made my skin crawl.

"That island is gorgeous! I've got a lot of pull there and in other
beautiful locations like St. Kitts and St. Thomas."

It couldn't be a coincidence that the three islands I attempted to
secure roots at were the three he mentioned in casual conversation.

"You're awfully quiet for some reason. For a change." His voice
turned to a low growl. "You think I don't know it was *you* who opened
your mouth and planted that thought about Angie searching for her
mother? Then you brought Angie to her!"

"Angie asked me to find Betty. It was her decision. I couldn't
turn her down."

"And with the snap of your fingers, you did it, knowing how
that meeting would hurt her. Especially after we made an agreement."

"We agreed on an exchange that served both our purposes. My
protection, including Sadie, in exchange for my silence, never to
divulge Frank's secrets about Betty to anyone."

"You allowed Angie to meet her!"

"She heard nothing from me directly, Vince. In fact, I told Angie
the whole story sounded far-fetched. I reminded her of Betty's mental state. You couldn't have stopped Angie from finding her mother.
Her mind was set. She wanted to make peace with her."

"Peace? Well, Betty's resting in peace now, isn't she," he snickered.

I said nothing. Vince admitted nothing. But I was more confident than ever that he had Betty killed, and he punished me by
eliminating my Caribbean opportunities.

Vince and his business carried a lot of weight. Not the good
kind—for me, anyway. I was fortunate to maintain what I had
already established in Aruba and the Bahamas. Launching my business on other Caribbean islands would be a waste of time now.

Two days after my antagonizing conversation with Vince, my Aruba hotel caught fire in the kitchen. The massive flames spread quickly. A few employees were injured, and the chaos frightened guests. Local law enforcement ruled it an accident. It was no accident. It was arson, but the authorities disagreed. Maybe they were on Vince's payroll.

Luckily, no one died, but I lost a ton of money and some valued employees who found employment with my competition. The insurance company delayed payment for the restoration. Maybe Vince controlled the insurance company too.

The following week, a bomb scare threatened my Bahamas hotel. The call filtered to the lobby while the police were simultaneously notified. The building had to be cleared. Guests were inconvenienced. These island cops didn't quite know how to handle a bomb threat. The place flew into a frenzy.

After a thorough investigation, no evidence of a bomb was found. The threat had been ruled a hoax. Guests checked out, fearing they might have missed a hidden bomb in the building. Employees quit, unwilling to work in an unsafe environment while being lured for other employment opportunities with my competition.

For protection, Carmine sent a few of his men to monitor our island investments and beef up security. I never told Carmine this was Vince's doing. I pissed Vince off enough. He hurt my business in retaliation for my leading Angie to Betty. But he let me live, believing my initial warning that if anything happened to me, the details about Betty's tortured life would leak to the press and the police.

Carmine would seek revenge if he knew Vince harmed our business, damaging the steady flow of income. If Carmine attacked Vince for retribution, innocent people could become casualties in the cross fire. I kept my mouth shut to keep the number of victims at a minimum.

Carmine's people, who protected our Caribbean investments, ended Vince's Chess game.

Vince had no pull in Europe. So I switched gears, forgot about expansions in the tropical Caribbean region, and focused on Ireland.

CHAPTER 38

Every year, I arranged an extravagant formal dinner party for my executive staff to meet with and entertain VIP clients. Usually, I'd hold this type of function at the Montgomery. However, Len wanted to add a few extra guests to the invitation list to promote his legal services. Because he wanted to add a personal touch to the event, he offered to use his beautiful mansion as the venue in June 1980.

The heat that night dampened my skin and parched my throat, constantly thirsting for club soda with lemon slices, my drink of choice at that time, seven years sober.

Len's wife, Wanda Sherman, and Angie coordinated the caterers, bar options, décor, and every other detail imaginable. Wanda and Angie were professional working women, but they agreed to take on the hefty tasks of organizing an extraordinary event.

Carmine and his crew sat out on these affairs. Their investment in my enterprise remained silent, hidden in the shadows, robbing my casino without drawing attention to their crimes. I had been labeled the front man, attending festivities to promote the Montgomery and its amenities to secure new business and maintain existing relationships.

The event was a black-tie affair. I drove my yellow Ferrari, wearing my white tuxedo jacket with black pants. Angie wore an elegant gown in the shade of lavender. Pastel colors always looked beautiful against her delicate skin and dark features, but I thought Angie looked spectacular in anything she wore.

We mingled throughout the night. Angie was so charming. Everyone loved her. I kept my eye on her, though. She was like a rare gem, turning the heads of every man she met. She never noticed or paid attention to their bedroom eyes overflowing with desire. I felt like the luckiest man in the world to have Angie on my arm.

I was not a fan of surprises, but Jim had a doozy of one. Sadie arrived unexpectedly. Instantly, it hit me. I left the invitation in my bedroom. I never spoke about this event with Sadie, but she must have seen the notice. This was Angie's baby. Angie planned it. How stupid of me to be so careless with that invitation!

One of these women would be disappointed and seriously angry with me. I hated to make such a grueling decision. Most people at the party knew Angie already. How could I convince Sadie to leave when other men brought their wives? As much as it killed me to send Angie home, I had no choice.

The hard slap felt across my face unveiled Angie's anger and disappointment. I deserved the prickly bite her fingers left on my cheek. I hurt her, but if Angie stayed, this lovely party would have turned into a brawl.

Sadie would have caused a scene, fighting with me, Angie, and anyone else within her petite reach. She might threaten me with divorce.

I hated to upset Angie, but I insisted Jim take her home and leave the party she helped arrange. Somehow, I would make it up to her. I convinced myself I could.

With Angie pulling a Houdini act out the kitchen door with Jim, I caught up with Sadie and soon introduced her to my guests. The looks I received from several women showcased their surprise. These people knew Angie as my girlfriend. Some believed Angie was my wife. Now, I escorted a completely different woman around the same party, presenting Sadie as my wife.

One woman asked her husband where the lovely brunette went. I prayed Sadie didn't overhear that remark and question me.

Sadie sensed my irritation with her sudden, unexpected visit. She admitted to seeing the invitation in my bedroom. Since the event was local, her determination to surprise me was an impulsive reaction.

A plot, in my opinion.

A New Beginning, the shelter she managed, took up the majority of her time. Somehow, I doubted she had an interest in my business affairs. I covered up my lies, explaining she'd been so entangled with her charity work, I didn't assume she'd put my business ahead of hers. We argued some, but we made the most of the night. She dressed appropriately and looked lovely in a sequined gold gown with a slit up the side that showed her shapely legs. Sadie was easy on the eyes.

While in deep conversation with one of my guests, Sadie returned from the bar and handed me a club soda. "Here you go, darling."

I forced a smile and sipped what was supposed to have been club soda. After a few slugs, I couldn't deny the fact that my glass had more than soda in it. I wasn't fond of vodka, a subtle grainy flavor that packed a punch. My brain sensed that buzzed feeling, absorbing every drop. Seven years of fighting that itch...until now.

As soon as my glass emptied, Sadie replenished it.

I accepted every drink she brought me, and I felt pretty damn amazing, enjoying the plastered road I was traveling down. I should've stopped instantly, spit it out, and rinsed my mouth. But that delicious, warm sensation against my throat felt like bumping into a dear old friend. One more wouldn't hurt, I thought. An alcoholic in remission could easily fall off the wagon, thirsting for inebriation. I lost control, slamming back those glasses, knowing very well what I was drinking. Honestly, I had no idea how many drinks she brought me. It eased my tension and mind at that moment. I shouldn't have lost control after seven years of sobriety.

I had no further recollections of that evening—the main reason why I stopped drinking. I often experienced blackouts, and I despised that miserable feeling of weakness brought on by intoxication.

When morning came, along with a throbbing hangover, I was beyond pissed that seven years of restraint ended. I awoke in bed naked with Sadie sleeping soundly by my side. Some flashes of the evening entered my foggy brain. My hands wrapped around my head, slowly remembering bits and pieces.

We had sex.

It had been a long time since Sadie and I connected in bed. If she didn't get me sloshed, I wouldn't have had the interest. I loved Angie.

Once my mind surged to sort out every detail, I expected to have it out with that blond barracuda I referred to as my wife. She annihilated my sobriety and manipulated my actions through my most intimate desires.

Ann and Nancy Wilson's popular Heart tune, "Barracuda," invaded my aching head. I popped some aspirin, then inserted the *Little Queen* cassette into the device in my car as I raced to my girl. I had a lot of apologizing to do.

CHAPTER 39

When I entered the house in Paradise, a suitcase sat in the foyer with clothes packed haphazardly. Angie considered leaving me. I couldn't let another incident like last night occur. I was teetering on a high wire, clinging on for dear life.

Jim informed me with a hardened gaze that Angie scrambled off early that day. Since it was Sunday, I knew she'd show up at Vince's house. She rarely missed those family meals.

I arrived at the gloomy mansion a little bit after one o'clock. Angie's car was parked out front. She wouldn't have shared the events from last night with her family, knowing that would escalate the tension between Vince and me.

Angie refused to make eye contact with me as I approached the dinner table. I was in the doghouse for sure. Hell, I wasn't sure if I'd be allowed on the same property as the doghouse.

She had every reason to be angry. When we found a private moment together, she requested space. I hated hearing that, but she didn't leave me much choice. My options were to give her the space she requested, or she'd move out of our home and in with her uncle.

The agony of our brief separation encouraged inebriation. Sadie instigated that wicked obsession. My nerves were on edge, requiring a fix to tame the sinful cravings I fought to control for seven years. I desperately grappled with the temptation. If Angie realized I started drinking again, that wouldn't fare well for me if I was to win her back.

I had a gorgeous engagement ring custom-designed for Angie, nearly three carats. The magnificent stone, shaped like a heart, sat upon a twenty-four-carat gold band. The band had been engraved with an inscription that read "Forever" because she would be in my heart forever. I held onto that ring for a while, waiting for the right time to propose.

When Angie finally decided to see me, my sincere apology and the ring I offered on bended knee with a heartfelt proposal prompted her forgiveness. She agreed to be my wife as soon as it was possible.

I desired Angie more than the Jameson my body demanded. I scooped her up into my arms and carried her to the bedroom to show her how much I loved her. We spent hours that day making up, our bodies gliding together as one. Loving Angie came as naturally to me as breathing.

There was no reason to tell her I had sex with Sadie.

When Vince saw the large diamond on Angie's finger, he became outraged.

Luckily, the Toscanos still protected me. Vince couldn't touch me without the threat of retaliation or a mob war ensuing.

The Midwest wise guys who ran scams, burglaries, and skims at other hotels were making a lot of noise. Bodies were piling up on the streets. The souring scent of death drifted from fields and wooded areas. Some people who were reported missing were never found. Numerous articles declared Vegas the stomping grounds for racketeering, violence, and murder. These guys were getting cocky and sloppy.

With the heat on them, Metro didn't hassle my partners or me. They were too busy chasing after the Midwest guys, who performed like celebrities in front of the cameras, in and out of courthouses, drawing mounds of attention to their families.

Carmine and Vince knew to keep a low volume on their felonious activities. The power of silence, the Mafia's code of omertà, worked to their advantage.

CHAPTER 40

Pop's health continued to deteriorate—a slow demise of his once dynamic existence. He might have controlled my life to some extent, but I still loved him. It was unbearable watching him struggle to hold a simple conversation. This once strong, brave soldier declined considerably, barely weighing 140 pounds. He refused to eat. If his health diminished further, the professionals predicted his suffering would end soon. I tried to talk to him when I visited. Either he wouldn't engage, or he'd bring up a painful subject.

"Where's John?"

"He's working today, Pop. He'll stop by later." I lied.

"Oh. I think he stopped by Friday." He smiled, tossing around jumbled thoughts, missing John as much as I did. If Pop's mind was as sharp as it once had been, he would hate to be stuck in this bed. He'd rather be dead than contend with the unspeakable reality of losing his son. No one deserved the crappy hand in life like the cards he was dealt, dying a slow, degrading death. All I could do for my father was to ensure he remained as comfortable as possible. I visited him regularly, so he didn't feel alone.

Knowing the impending moment was inevitable, I asked Len to finalize the paperwork for my divorce in preparation for my father's last breath. Pop's doctor didn't believe he'd survive to see Thanksgiving. My commitment to Angie would be fulfilled. Wedding plans occupied our minds. She understood we couldn't pick a date until my divorce was final. But she had no idea of the inner chaos that haunted me, realizing our future depended on Pop's death.

CHAPTER 41

A miserably hot summer day in 1980 altered the course of my future. Fate punched me in the gut—hard. Sadie called the hotel office several times, impatiently reminding me to come home early. I made an excuse to Angie, so I could drive to Henderson and determine what Sadie deemed as important.

The moment I stepped through the front door, Sadie set her sights on me with a suspicious expression displayed like I'd never seen. I wasn't sure what game she was playing, but I had to ask why she looked like she'd soon explode.

With a rush of excitement, she announced, "I'm pregnant!"

Pregnant? We had sex once a couple of months ago, after the night she slipped vodka into my drink. I didn't sleep with her consciously. I knew it happened, but when I drank too much, my memory often skewed reality to some degree. I indulged excessively. My recollection of that night proved utterly unreliable.

We argued, a typical event in our house. I accused her of having an affair, which sent her over the edge. "We didn't plan this. I didn't plan this. Having a baby now is not in the plan!" I shouted.

"What plan? People don't always plan a family. It just happens!" she hollered back.

"That's what got us into this marriage. Jesus Christ!"

The worst-case scenario, I considered, was that the baby turned out to be mine because of a sperm donation I left on one stupid, drunken night without wearing a condom—again. My future with

Angie was at stake. For years, she waited patiently for me to leave Sadie. This couldn't be happening!

I spoke with my doctor to inquire about a paternity test. Those tests weren't easily accessible in 1980, and I had to wait until the baby was born. Waiting nine months felt like an eternity.

Angie's heart had already been shattered because of her inability to conceive. She accepted that situation, but I couldn't break her spirit, telling her Sadie became pregnant after one night in an alcohol-induced state. When I proved the baby wasn't mine, there'd be no reason to tell Angie anything. Why hurt her, admitting I *might have* gotten Sadie pregnant? So I kept my mouth shut and prayed.

CHAPTER 42

Between Sadie's pregnancy and Pop's failing health, I had little free time. Angie understood my spending extra time with Pop in the convalescent home. She didn't know I spent more time helping Sadie cope with morning sickness that lasted all day.

I visited my father daily. Some days, I stayed only a few minutes because he typically slept for hours, weak and frail. I'd speak to the staff to assess his health and affirm he was comfortable.

Other days, Pop lay awake, still and quiet. He loved to reminisce about the past.

"Pop, remember when Jayne Mansfield sauntered into the Montgomery back in sixty-four, or was it sixty-five?"

"Nineteen sixty-five," he mumbled with confidence. His long-term memory seemed better than his short-term memory, especially since that meaningful moment was meeting a beauty like Jayne Mansfield.

"You were starstruck meeting her." I brought the photograph of Pop blushing next to gorgeous Jayne and flashed the memorable incident before his eyes.

He showed a hint of a smile, then said, "The rack on her, huh?"

I whistled, launching a chuckle from him. "Stars poured into your casino, Pop. Ursula Andress, Raquel Welch, Ann-Margret, Sophia Loren, Natalie Wood. I don't care what anyone says, Liz Taylor flirted with you relentlessly! You owned the swankiest hotel on the Strip!"

His brown eyes glistened. "Where's Mary? She was here last night." His mind shifted. He actually believed my mother still breathed and spent time with him. I wished his mind functioned to reclaim his life and meet Angie. As much as Pop loved Sadie, I knew he'd adore Angie, especially seeing how happy she made me.

Sadie's pregnancy weighed on my mind. Sex with Sadie didn't happen out of love. A carnal response to my drinking and the elements my father put in motion. He meant well in some strange way. If he knew I fell in love, Pop never would have bound me to Sadie without the threat of losing the business or my happiness.

CHAPTER 43

An evening in November 1980 changed the future I envisioned. The future I felt excited about—a life with Angie.

I had picked up chicken and broccoli, lo mein, and egg rolls from a nearby Chinese takeout place for Sadie and me. Despite nausea and cramping, she produced multiple cravings to be fulfilled regularly.

Sadie was petite, but between the pregnancy and an unhealthy diet, she was gaining weight fast. Her back and legs struggled to carry the excess pounds. I made myself available to help her more often than I normally would have, including spending dinners with her instead of Angie.

She awakened my desire to drink again, provoking bitter feelings. My emotions changed with the wind—angry with myself for losing control but loving the succulent taste of Jameson. I tried not to overdo it, but I couldn't resist a couple of drinks every night.

Sadie didn't understand why I had to stay sober.

If I spent more time with Angie, she'd recognize the signs, realizing I took a flying leap off the wagon. She wouldn't tolerate my occasional fling with alcohol. On the days my temptation won, I'd cancel plans with Angie, making up a variety of excuses. Instead, I sat at home, drowning my restless nerves and coarse indignation with Jameson.

After dinner that night, I opened the garbage pail to dispose of the Chinese food remnants. Sitting on top of an empty box of Wheaties was a business card I identified as Angie's realty card. How the hell would Angie's business card be in this house? I might have been sloshed once in a while, but I never kept anything related to Angie around for Sadie to find.

Angie earned respect in the real estate market, soaring in her career. I began using her services, dropping Aaron as my Realtor. I loved working exclusively with Angie. We spent more time together, and I gave her a lot of business. More time with the woman I loved and the business sustained profits for both of us.

I glanced at Sadie, attempting to hide the shock to my system, holding the card as I stuttered, "W-w-where'd you get this?"

"Some Realtor lady dropped by to see the house."

"What? Why would she come to see our house?"

"I don't know. She rang the doorbell and told me she was hoping to attract more clients. I probably should've told her you had a guy already."

Angie wouldn't have driven to Henderson—on my street. She came here to check up on me, meeting a very pregnant Sadie.

My head whirled with worry and frustration. Was I drinking too much to realize Angie might have been suspicious? I attempted to call Angie earlier, but she didn't answer the phone. At the time, I assumed she stepped out, perhaps to Sears or to visit Katie. Maybe she was avoiding me because she knew the truth. My *pregnant* wife— pure indisputable evidence of my betrayal.

I kept my cool in front of Sadie, encouraging her to rest while I cleaned the kitchen. My heart accelerated with the desire to consume the entire bottle of Jameson sitting atop the bar. That bottle of whiskey called to me like the enchanting sirens from Greek mythology. How I struggled to give in to the enticing song.

To hell with cleaning the kitchen. Once Sadie laid down in her room, I raced to the phone. I called Angie multiple times. Still no answer.

I gave into the tempting siren calls and slammed back shot after shot, unable to keep track of the number. It had been years since I faltered to this degree. Binge-drinking was a thing of the past, or so I thought.

Was Sadie asleep when I made the treacherous decision to hop into my car and drive to Angie's house completely plastered? I didn't know because I stopped thinking rationally.

Somehow, I made it in one piece to Paradise. Angie's car was parked in the driveway, and the lights indoors shone brightly. I vaguely remembered trying to enter, but the chain on the front door prevented that. I couldn't recall exactly how I got inside, but we argued at first sight.

Vivid recollections of the tears streaming from her dark eyes, trailing along her beautiful face, incited an achy wound in my bruised heart. I desperately explained that Sadie's baby might not be mine, but Angie wouldn't listen.

Her suitcases were packed, and the bedroom appeared messy with clothes tossed about. We were so close to having it all. I prepared to sit her down and tell her everything about Pop's power of attorney—the conditions he forced upon me against my personal wants and desires.

Sadie worked against me most of the time, but she didn't understand the chaos swirling in my head, either. My brain was locked and loaded, ready to explode when I saw Angie's suitcases packed, yet in my drunken state, I struggled to properly articulate a logical conversation.

I held Angie, trying to calm her. If I could explain everything, I knew we would work it out. We always worked things out. Our love was pure, timeless, eternal. After a brief dispute, she calmed, and I managed to get through to her amid slurred words.

We made love. She told me she loved me. That part of the evening was clear.

Losing her wasn't an option. I'd explain all the painful parts, like the night Sadie got me drunk, which might have resulted in this unplanned pregnancy.

I needed to sober up before we had such a meaningful conversation. Witnessing me in this messy state upset her. I broke my promise to remain sober and faithful all on one miserable night back in June. I had to stop drinking. This time for good!

Leaving Angie that evening and the drive back to Henderson was an absolute blur.

CHAPTER 44

Damn, was I hungover! Let's face it, I had a lot of nasty hangovers in my life, but last night, I overdid it.

Forced recollections presented, enlightening me with the trauma I caused. Angie met Sadie in person, witnessing the home where I lived with my pregnant wife. She knew I could be the baby's father. At this point, she might not believe Sadie got me drunk that night after seven years of sobriety. Until last night, I managed to control my drinking, enough so that Angie never noticed I slipped.

Angie would have left me if I hadn't convinced her to stay. I lost my mind with worry, and I overindulged.

Not only did I need to restore love and trust, I had to stop drinking—completely.

The grandfather clock chimed seven o'clock.

Sadie slept peacefully. Pregnancy discomforts interrupted her rest, so she'd often sleep late in the mornings.

On the way to see Angie, I stopped by a local florist and picked out the biggest, brightest bouquet. We were so close to sharing a life. Close enough for Angie to become my *wife*.

Scattered visions from the previous night hazily flashed at random as I approached the main entrance. Broken glass from the window covered the diamond-pattern tile floor.

I'd make arrangements to have the window replaced immediately, then clean this mess up properly.

"Angie! Baby, where are you?" My voice echoed inside the large, seemingly empty home. I staggered about, calling for her. My gut suddenly tightened. Anxiously, I raced through the kitchen and out the sliding glass door, stepping into the backyard by the pool and gardens.

No sign of Angie, but her Oldsmobile remained parked in the driveway.

My heart pumped excessively as the sound of footsteps and a door closing inside the house was detected. Then that creak in the floorboard told me Angie had to be home. I charged inside, longing to see her lovely face. Instead, my relief turned to unsettled confusion when Vince and four large snarling goons stared me down.

CHAPTER 45

"Vince? Where's Angie?" I asked, acting nonchalant as if nothing were wrong.

He flicked a cigarette lighter incessantly. "She's gone, Tommy. You'll never see her again." The guttural tone in his voice rang more harshly than usual. His eyes looked hungry. Hungry for blood. Mine.

Angie must have told him Sadie was pregnant, I thought.

"Where is she, Vince? I need to talk to her."

"After what you did to my niece last night, why should I let you *live?*" Bitterness and hostility emanated through his deep, raspy tone.

Vince took small yet commanding strides toward me.

I staggered backward in sync with each step Vince took, saying, "I can explain."

"I found my niece crying and trembling with bruises all over her arms and legs. Her dress torn."

"Bruises? What happened to her?" My concern rose, hearing about injuries she somehow sustained.

"My niece made a huge mistake being loyal to you, putting up with your constant lies and bullshit for years. Her devotion to you got her a broken heart! What kind of man holds down the woman he loves and *rapes* her?"

Hearing those words made no sense. I knew I hurt her on an emotional level because of Sadie's pregnancy, but rape? "No, no, no, I would never do that to her, Vince!" My fingers ran through my brown hair, desperately trying to recall the instrumental details from the previous night, thanks to the sinful love affair with Jameson I suffered from.

"You'd never do that. Never take her body against her will." He punched my jaw hard, forcing my body back and into the arms of two of his men, Aldo and Max. Aldo wore a jagged scar across his cheek that resembled an old knife wound. Max never uttered a sound or cracked a smile anytime I walked past him at Vince's home.

The flowers I held flew across the room in utter disarray, sending petals, leaves, and stems high in the air, landing across the floor and furniture.

Vince signaled the other pair of thugs, whom I never saw before. They grabbed my feet, despite my kicking. As strong a man as I was, I couldn't fight these four gargantuan men by myself. There was no escape. One of them struck me hard in the nose, gaining control. The weight of their bodies secured me to the floor. A knee slammed into my kidney while the force of a hand crushed my face that burned against the beige, shag carpet.

"What are you doing, Vince?" I screamed. This crappy day in November could be my last day alive. My carcass might be found in twenty years, buried beneath a prickly cactus somewhere in the desert after vicious little prairie dogs gnawed the flesh from my bones.

I'd never be able to make amends to Angie. She'd never learn the truth. I'd never know if Sadie's baby was mine.

I tried to wrestle from their grasp. Even if I escaped, they'd find me. I managed to get in a few good licks at one of their faces, but the torture began, beating my chest, back, and gut until I couldn't move without fierce agony exuding from every muscle and cracked rib.

"Having fun yet, Tom? We're not quite finished. No one touches my niece like that! You *destroyed* her!"

"Angie will never forgive you if you kill me!"

He laughed. "I've got other plans *before* I kill you." He turned to his thugs and nodded. Vince dropped to one knee, pulled my head up, grasping a handful of roots from my brown strands, and whispered into my ear, "An eye for an eye, Tommy." Vince used my face as a tool to help him stand over me. He snapped his fingers crisply. "Get him ready, boys!"

Shit! As much as I squirmed, they secured my hands with rope, then tore off my pants and boxers. My shirt was soaked with sweat. They beat me with their fists and feet, conjuring welts and deep lacerations across my side and legs.

That bastard, Vince, sat calmly and patiently in the corner chair as one of those fuckers grabbed some object I couldn't see and rammed it straight up my ass, hard and deep. I screamed bloody murder as I felt the tearing of my flesh from behind.

"I think he likes it. Give him some more," Vince said, enjoying my humiliation and pain as much as I hated it.

I wanted to threaten to kill them all! I had connections too. But threatening a made man would only prolong their fun and bury me sooner. I took the abuse and tried not to give them any more satisfaction from my wincing and screaming.

They tortured me for a while, perhaps hours, between beating me near unconsciousness and the agonizing sodomy.

At some point, his men released me.

My body tensed, then fell limp. I attempted to roll over to see where they stood. Tears filled my sockets, but I refused to acknowledge the stream by wiping the puddles. After a few blinks, a blur of Vince's figure came into view, smirking with contempt. My fingers bent, attempting to loosen the rope from my wrists.

Vince's eyes grew darker than his black soul. "That's for hurting my niece, you bastard!" Vince grabbed a gun from his waistband and squatted to my level.

I was too weak to move, and the rope still secured my hands.

He pulled my cheeks open forcibly with the muzzle of the gun rammed down my throat, choking me. "You're gonna eat a bullet next, you fucking punk!" His finger clicked the trigger.

My eyes squeezed shut, waiting for the impending moment when my brains splattered across the walls, but I was still breathing. He shoved the barrel further into my mouth. I thought I'd vomit. My body trembled as sweat fell like a rain shower, dripping down my face. I felt a molar crack from chewing on his pistol. Vince's finger clicked the trigger again—a game of Russian roulette.

Still alive, Vince withdrew his gun and stood to his feet. "You're one lucky bastard. I don't need any problems with the Toscanos, but I can assure you, Aniello and Carmine won't protect you from me anymore. Not after what you've done. If you go near Angie for any reason, I will *kill* you!" He tossed something at my head, triggering me to hit it away with the back of my constrained hands.

Liquid continued to build up in my eyes, preventing me from seeing clearly. When I blinked, they were gone. The hard slam of the front door was heard.

The unbearable pain forced me to lay still. It hurt to move, but my fingers worked at the poorly knotted rope to free my hands. I knew I wouldn't be able to sit. If I didn't get help or stand on my own, I'd die in the fetal position. I pulled myself up with limited strength in my arms. Blood clung to the carpet. I wiped my eyes to gain a clear view. Splashes of blood led to a large screwdriver with pieces of my flesh in the grooves of its handle. I hated that son of a bitch!

Then I realized what Vince flung at me—Angie's engagement ring. She removed my ring from her finger, and naturally, Vince took pleasure throwing it in my face.

Jesus, did she think I raped her? I desperately tried to remember the events from last night. I knew she packed her clothes, prepared to leave me. I couldn't let her go that easily. I remembered we made love. Yeah, I was drunk, but I told her how much I loved her. Too much alcohol and sometimes I lost control of myself.

The only person I could call was Jim. As humiliating as this was, I needed help.

My mind instantly raced to devise a plan to talk to Angie. First, I had to put the pieces together about last night. It destroyed me, thinking she believed I raped her.

Exacting revenge on Vince became my new hobby.

CHAPTER 46

After my brief, agonizing stint in the hospital, I resumed my routine visits with Pop. With each depressing visit, he seemed thinner and less coherent. He developed a fever and was brought to the hospital for extra care to battle the infection his body had been fighting.

He lived a bit longer than the doctor anticipated. We lost my father on December 1, 1980.

Pop had opened his eyes wide and peaceful. He glanced toward the corner of the ceiling and shed a tear. "Mary?" he whispered. Pop saw the vision of his greatest love, my mother, who came for him.

My heart practically tore out of my chest when I swear Pop mumbled, "Johnny? My boy."

I clenched Pop's hand and whispered, "It's okay to join them, Pop. You don't have to worry about me."

Mom and John had been waiting for Pop's time to come to walk him through those pearly gates.

Following a lingering flutter, his eyes closed and the hand I held went limp. Finally, my father moved to a more peaceful existence. He lived in a deep, ominous fog for too many years. Wherever his spirit rested now, he had no more memory issues and was back to being as sharp as a tack.

I laid my head upon his shoulder and sobbed. I felt a little jealous he got to see Mom and John. I'd see them all again someday, but I had too much left to accomplish in this world. I had to see Sadie through this pregnancy, determine if the baby was mine, seek out

Angie to ensure she was okay, and execute vengeance on her miserable, piece-of-shit uncle.

I had been recovering from Vince's sneak attack. My chest was wrapped daily to support two broken ribs. Three teeth needed crowns after tasting Vince's .38 Special. I wore long sleeves to hide the mountain of bruises painted across my arms and torso. Worst of all, my backside required stitches. I lied to Sadie, telling her I got in the middle of a dispute at the casino to explain the bruises and broken ribs.

Sadie took care of my wounded parts and worked overtime to interest me in the baby. She always reminded me of the life we created, growing inside her. She grabbed my hand and placed it against her stomach. "Do you feel that, Tommy?"

"Was that a kick?" I asked, surprised by the hearty blow I felt.

"Our baby is very active. Maybe he'll be a football player. If she's a girl, an Olympic gold medalist!"

I smiled, thinking this wasn't something she could've predicted to tear at my heart. Maybe this energetic baby was mine. He or she would soon be part of our lives. Something different to fantasize about while arranging Pop's services.

Pop received a formal military ceremony to honor his life and his service to our great country. He'd be thrilled to know I planned such an extravagant event. A glorious party with Pop as the center of attention. I was proud to give him a proper send-off. The traditional honor guards masterfully folding the American flag, the beating rhythm of drums, and a three-volley rifle salute carried out in his honor. Announcements about his death were beautifully written in every local paper.

Carmine and his soldiers were in attendance. Staff from the Montgomery stopped by. Veterans and former Army buddies made a point to attend, including Fred Meade.

I hoped Angie would have come to pay her respects. No one from the Russo clan showed.

In addition to a traditional wake, the room was filled with old pictures and colorful floral arrangements. I hired a violinist to play some of Pop's favorite classical pieces.

Pop's death initiated my freedom. Freedom to divorce Sadie and marry Angie. My plan was far from perfect. Too many holes that grew bigger as the years passed.

Len shared the divorce papers he finalized with me to present to Sadie. She was due in a few months. After the funeral, I stared at the legal language, unable to comprehend the content as if written in a foreign language. The words looked blurred to my remorseful eyes. I wasn't in the right frame of mind to review the details and hand them over to her.

My head spun chaotically with numerous thoughts about my future. What if this baby was mine? I resisted the idea at first. It seemed incomprehensible that one drunken night would have led to her pregnancy after all the years we were married.

Had my wife been truthful and faithful? Sadie indulged in numerous affairs that I knew of while I was involved with Angie. If this baby proved to be mine, he or she was my responsibility. I had the divorce papers ready to go, but in that moment of profound thought, I chose to put them aside.

CHAPTER 47

I tried everything to contact Angie, except knocking on Vince's front door. I did a lot of stupid things in my day, but I wasn't that dumb. I knew what that man was capable of, and I wouldn't test him further.

Carmine couldn't help me. "Angie left you, Tommy. That's her choice. Vincenzo is claiming rape. Did you hurt that girl?"

Anguish clung to my words. "No, Carmine. Of course, I didn't rape her. Sadie's pregnant. Angie found out. I need to speak to Angie without Vince's interference."

Carmine nodded. "He let you live, Tommy. Be grateful. I can't retaliate if he harms you. Il nostro accordo. That was our agreement. You hurt her. She left. I have to step aside. Walk away if you know what's good for you." He turned to leave my office and said, "Congratulations on the baby! Children are a blessing."

Without Carmine's backing, Vince could murder me without the threat of retaliation. So I found another avenue to pursue—Vince's daughter, Katie Russo-Maroni.

Katie understood my love for Angie. Her husband, Louis, and I respected each other. Their three sons, Michael, Louie, and David, meant the world to Angie. I watched them grow up. I loved those boys like they were my own family.

When Katie opened her front door and saw me standing before her, an expression showing both surprise and dread flashed from her brown eyes. Her father was a mob boss, and her uncle was an enforcer and underboss, and she acted like she feared me.

"Why are you here, Tommy?"

"Katie, is Angie okay? I'd like to talk to her."

"How the hell do you think she is after what you did to her? You lied about your marriage. You were so desperate to keep her, you *raped* her? How could you do that?"

I shook my head in disbelief. "I'd never hurt Angie like that."

Katie's eyes drifted down, displaying sadness. "She said that."

"She said what? She *said* I didn't rape her? Why don't you and your father believe her? You don't believe me, fine, but believe Angie."

"You two had a twisted relationship I'll never understand. I heard her side of the story, defending you because you were drunk. She merely appeased you and allowed you to—well, I think you took her body. Although she has some crazy obligation to protect you."

Angie didn't label our last night together as "rape." Her uncle spread that insidious word like wildfire through her family.

"Katie, you weren't there. I was drinking, I admit, but you know how much I love her. Tell her I'm sorry. I just want to talk to her."

She ordered me to leave after throwing my marriage to Sadie up in my face with a baby on the way.

Showing up at Vince's daughter's door was not the smartest move on my part. An old thought crept into my mind as I inched my way from her home. Something I hadn't thought about in years. Katie's oldest son, Michael, was not Louis Maroni's biological child. Katie got knocked up by Brett Corbyn, a high school senior with aspirations to be a pro basketball player for the NBA. He was a hot-shot player, earning a full ride to Duke on a basketball scholarship. I never met the kid, yet I remembered his name clearly. The hot-shot ballplayer made local headlines and not for his skill in shooting hoops.

According to the media, one night walking home after scoring forty points and winning the game against the school's biggest rival, Brett got mugged. His wallet had been stolen. The brutes beat his legs with baseball bats, tearing his tendons and breaking numerous bones so badly that he couldn't finish the last few weeks of his senior year. He spent weeks in the hospital, enduring years of physical therapy.

The actions of a group of psychopathic muggers changed the course of his destiny. He lost his college scholarship since he was incapable of playing basketball. He never played the game he loved again. His injuries were too severe to walk at a regular pace, never mind running up and down a court, dribbling a basketball.

The kid had to retrain his body to walk normally again. The teen superhero who had it all—popularity, money, and a good chance at fame—lost everything that night. No one ever heard his name again after the media attention to his injuries died down. Was a young man like Brett singled out to be mugged to the degree of near death? Bailing on a pregnant mob princess was not his brightest move.

Vince wouldn't have allowed Brett to live his life with a successful career, while Katie raised Brett's son with another man through an arranged marriage to Louis Maroni at the tender age of eighteen.

Brett survived the ordeal. Vince had stolen a vital part of his life. He took away what that kid loved most, shattering his future.

Vince allowed me to keep breathing too, but he took away the one precious piece of my life—the woman I truly loved.

After I left Katie's home, thinking about such a horrid memory, I contacted Jim and asked that he secure several of his biggest, strongest ex-military detail to follow me around. I had no idea if Vince would kill me the next time our paths crossed. He had the means and motive to carry out that mission if he wanted to, and Carmine wouldn't stand in his way.

I had a billion-dollar business to run, a criminal partner to manage, a mob boss for an enemy, and a pregnant wife to cater to. A heart attack might be imminent. Vince wouldn't have to send his goons after me if Katie told him I showed up at her door. Thanks to my bubbling blood pressure, I could drop dead at any moment—the same demise my brother faced. My only shred of hope was the fact that Angie said I didn't rape her. That sinister word launched from Vince's hatred of me.

Learning Sadie was pregnant must have sent Angie over the edge since she couldn't have a baby of her own. I feared honesty, convinced Angie would leave me without a second thought or another chance. Any shred of hope to win her back was deteriorating.

CHAPTER 48

Larry, the best PI on the West Coast, couldn't locate Angie. If she was living with her uncle, she never left his home. She wouldn't remain imprisoned at that eerie estate forever. He moved her somewhere out of my reach. I couldn't believe she'd leave her home, her family, and a career she loved to avoid me.

Larry conducted several searches through a contact he established at Metro. He checked the airports, train and bus stations. No one could validate that she left town. Her Oldsmobile remained parked at our house in Paradise.

Feeling hopeless, the fragile state of my emotions triggered my drinking habit—heavily. I scored coke to take the edge off. My mood was irregular, and my eyes were the color of tomatoes. I gave up whiskey and cocaine for Angie. Since she left, sobriety seemed unimportant.

Rob got on my back because I couldn't pull my weight, overseeing the needs of the hotels. I left him to handle all accountabilities.

Jim hassled me, and he never hassled me, saying, "If Angie comes back, she'll turn around and run!"

He was right. She'd walk out because I transformed into a blatant, slobbering mess.

"You're going to be a father. That baby needs you, Tommy," Jim added.

I didn't have proof the baby was mine, but Jim was right. This baby *could be* mine. My days of getting high had to end.

Sadie knew I started to drink regularly. After she slipped the booze in my drink at that party in June, I never stopped drinking completely. I tried but failed, a brutal cycle many addicts endured. I needed Sadie on my side if I were to beat these relentless cravings.

She was in the mood for pasta one night. I picked up a manicotti order with garlic bread from Gaetano's and joined her for dinner. The last remaining bottle of Jameson in the house sat on the kitchen counter, daring me to open it. My eyes swayed in its direction, thirsting for a taste. I approached the bottle, stared at the label for a moment, then poured the contents down the kitchen sink, listening to the liquid glug, absorbing that scent I desired. "I have to stop. No more whiskey or any alcohol. Not with a baby on the way."

Sadie's blue eyes popped in surprise.

"No more laced drinks, understand?" I said with a frigid tone.

"Tommy, I'm sorry. I didn't realize you hadn't had a drink in so long. You never said…well, we never used to talk. We have to communicate better now. Our baby needs us. You have my full support." Her words sounded sincere, and I believed her.

Her belly grew by the second. Sadie was petite, weighing about a hundred pounds soaking wet before she became pregnant. Toward the end of her pregnancy, walking took extra effort, and she needed help getting out of bed each morning.

At night, I left my bedroom door open a crack in case I heard her groaning or calling me. As much as I didn't think it would happen, I became anxious, in a good way, about this baby's arrival. If he or she wasn't mine, divorcing Sadie would become a priority.

I stayed married to her for the sake of the baby. When Pop died in December, I could've left scot-free and inherited everything. I didn't need Sadie anymore. The power of attorney had zero value. Because Angie was gone and the baby could be mine, I remained in this loveless marriage.

"Peace of Mind"

CHAPTER 49

DANIEL JOHN CAVALLO

The painted black sky shimmered with sparkling stars and a bright crescent moon. Sleep, an unattainable fantasy of late. Sadness. Cravings. Withdrawal symptoms. I leaned against the windowsill, staring at the luminous moon, wondering if Angie had a similar view from wherever she lived. Thinking about seeing Angie again helped me battle my dark and desperate demons.

Sadie started grumbling. She needed to use the bathroom again, I thought. I hurried across the hall to help her out of bed, but she sat upright, grabbing onto her stomach as if it were going to explode, moaning wildly.

"Sadie! Is this it?"

"I think so. God, I hope so!"

Suddenly, I turned into a complete wreck, watching her grunt and pant as I called her doctor. "How the hell do I know how far apart her contractions are? Isn't that your job?" I shouted. I wasn't timing her contractions, then calling him back. He needed to get his ass to the hospital. What the hell did I know about birthing babies? She couldn't deliver the baby at home or in my Ferrari that blocked the end of the driveway. I neglected to move it to its rightful spot in the garage earlier.

Thankfully, it was the middle of the night. No traffic on the roads. No cops flashed their bright red lights to pull me over for speeding.

"Tommy, slow down," she said with a chillingly calm demeanor. She started to breathe with a quick rhythm, causing me to involuntarily breathe at her pace.

I took a sharp inside turn, barely touching the brake.

"You're making me nauseous! Slow down, damn it!" she shouted between breaths.

I decelerated slightly. One really couldn't drive slow in a Ferrari.

Daniel John arrived shortly after twelve o'clock on March 19, 1981, on St. Joseph's Day, after several painful hours of Sadie pushing in the delivery room.

He weighed in at eight pounds, twelve ounces, and measured twenty-one inches long. His wailing sounded like a soulful melody. Everything about him felt precious, nearly magical with excitement enriching my emotions.

Sadie held onto Danny as protectively as a mother bear. I almost didn't recognize her. This special baby showered her aura with peace. She smiled with a look of pure, genuine affection. She never showed nurturing qualities to this degree.

I watched as the tiny bundle of joy snuggled in her arms. I didn't know what to do with this rush of unexpected feelings.

Could he be *my* son? What if he wasn't? I couldn't tell by looking at him if he was mine. My eyes observed every inch of him, in awe of his movements. Then it occurred to me that I really could have created him.

"This is your pop," Sadie said as she attempted to hand his tiny figure to me.

I stepped back a few paces. I couldn't hold him, ill-prepared for the emotional roller coaster I suddenly rode. What wasn't I ready for? Falling in love with a baby who might not be mine. Taking responsibility for this new life laying atop his mother's breast. I watched him from afar, but I couldn't touch him.

Sadie's parents drove in from Bakersfield the moment they heard Sadie went into labor. For the first week of Danny's life, Suzanne stayed with us. That meant I slept in Sadie's room. Our entire family dynamic had changed. Everything in our lives revolved around Danny, but I welcomed that.

Suzanne proved to be a tremendous help. She demonstrated changing his diaper, burping him, and how to instinctively tell what each cry meant.

For a little person less than nine pounds, Danny had a set of powerful lungs. I couldn't figure out the hungry cry from the gassy cry or the sleepy cry. After a while, we could assess his needs. Suzanne was right. With patience, practice, and some time to get to know him, we uncovered Danny's unique personality.

Sadie was exhausted, yet Suzanne decided she would stay at Sadie's sister Lisa's house with her husband Al before returning to California. She encouraged the three of us to bond as a family without her help. We had to navigate parenting ourselves.

That first night on our own, I slept in Sadie's room. I wasn't sure why. I had my bedroom back with her mother gone. Danny started to cry, his habitual performance around midnight. For the first time, I manned up and stammered out of bed to see him. My eyes set on his little figure lying in his cradle, weeping from hunger. His arms swayed as his legs kicked about in his bassinet.

I observed the way others had picked him up and held him close to their chests. My fear of holding him released—slightly. Carefully, I positioned my arm beneath him, resting his small head in the palm of my hand, then I scooped him up, placing him close to my heart.

His wailing curbed to wee whimpers.

My eyes absorbed every ounce of him in the crook of my arm. I kissed his forehead, my senses taking in that fresh baby scent.

As he gazed up at me, I caught a glimpse of a smile. He trusted me. He had to. The most important reason for me to stay sober stared at me with love and hope.

From that moment on, I declared Danny my son, no matter what any test might reveal.

He began to fuss, but I held him securely.

"Shh, your pop is here. Everything is okay. Do you want your mama? Are you hungry? Let me take you to see her."

When I brought him to Sadie, she sat upright with a towel draped over her shoulder and chest. She smiled at me and said, "Thanks for getting him."

Danny went straight for her breast. As she nursed him, I remembered her pretty blue eyes focused on me as I watched Danny drink his midnight snack.

This little guy was amazing! I loved watching him at the cusp of falling asleep, but he'd always try to force his eyes to remain open.

I went under the assumption that Danny was my flesh and blood. Then I prayed he was my son. This helpless little person relied on us to give him everything he needed. I felt completely attached and in love.

As much as I said his paternity didn't matter, I wanted to know. My curiosity had nothing to do with the love I felt for Danny. It was about trusting Sadie. I couldn't recall a time when trust had been established. Maybe before we were married, when we were mere friends, I trusted her on some level.

So much happened between us through the years. Her first pregnancy and miscarriage, my love for Angie, and Sadie's affairs with other men. She wrecked my sobriety. I held numerous doubts, but we were suddenly connecting. Even if our connection was generated from our love for Danny, something felt right about this family unit.

I told Sadie I had planned a father-son afternoon one day. She packed a diaper bag with everything I'd need. A couple of hours to herself made her happy.

I brought Danny with me to my doctor, a woman I trusted, for a blood test. After several exasperatingly long weeks, the results were in, proving that I was Danny's biological father.

Sadie didn't lie.

And I felt…relieved.

CHAPTER 50

FATHERHOOD

In a blink of an eye, my life greatly improved after my son entered the world. Danny was a smart, funny kid. Handsome too. I must say, he looked exactly like me when I was his age. I threw Sadie a bone, telling her that Danny had her nose. Every feature this kid had resembled *me*. Old baby photos of me proved he was 100 percent Cavallo in the looks department.

Sadie spent more time at home as a mother than at the shelter she supported. Her hands were still in our bank account to help her cause—but within reason. Her priorities shifted after Danny's birth. She genuinely was a good mother, and Danny adored her.

Sleeping in Sadie's room became habitual. Within no time, we resumed a normal sex life. I couldn't explain how it happened. We weren't fighting about anything except maybe whose turn it was to change a dirty diaper. We laughed together more often too.

Angie was gone, so Sadie and Danny became entwined in my life. Sadie and I reinvented the friendship we once shared. Sex came naturally thereafter. Sadie had an erotic way about her. She knew how to get to me, wearing sexy lingerie to bed and caressing my hungry flesh with her fingertips and soft thighs. The fights we had when we were first married were ridiculous! Too young, perhaps, for the responsibility of marriage, lacking sentiments of love. My feelings for Sadie couldn't compare to the emotions tattooed in my heart for Angie. But I liked her better, and I enjoyed our family. Danny's existence brought us closer as parents. Our family life blossomed.

That didn't mean I stopped trying to find Angie. Larry was on retainer to keep searching. He watched Vince's house to see if she visited. Vince had major security measures in place. The six-foot-tall, two-hundred-fifty-pound-of-muscle type surveilling his house.

I hoped for a chance to talk to Angie. I couldn't bear the thought of her hating me or thinking I *chose* to have a child with Sadie. Our home in Paradise contained a wealth of memories I wasn't ready to part with. I'd walk through the front door and imagine Angie greeting me, wearing a big bright smile. Her gorgeous dark-chocolate eyes used to gleam in my direction, happy to see me. The fragrance of her sweet perfume lingered. She left most of her things behind.

Could I let her go? She knew how to find me if she wanted to. If I left Sadie, I might not see Danny every day. My love for my son outweighed the love I could have for any woman.

CHAPTER 51

I hired a vice president to handle my international businesses, while Rob maintained a VP status overseeing the US hotels. Additional management positions were filled because I wanted to spend more time at home with Danny. I delegated a lot of my work, and Rob appreciated the relief. Significant responsibilities to the business landed on my plate, but my family was equally important.

The competition among hotels and casinos on the Strip grew incredibly wicked. Owners like me would check out the layout, shows, and all the bells and whistles occurring at rival locations to see if they measured above par.

I hired an entertainment director. This time someone who knew what he was doing, and not some jamoke Fat Nicky hired, who spent more time skimming the casino than actually developing acts for our guests.

The Montgomery secured incredible magicians, exceeding the abilities of Siegfried & Roy, minus the tigers, at the Frontier Hotel and Casino. We beefed up our musical artists and variety shows as well. Each night, we offered entertainment that brought in crowds.

The Dunes added a new tower, which ultimately led to new shows and a fundamental facelift to the place. Out of pure curiosity, I wanted to check out their new entertainers.

After I lost a few hundred at Blackjack, I headed toward the theater. Along the way, I recognized a man squashed between two lovely blondes, wearing sparkly, skimpy attire that displayed their youth as well as their assets. I knew the man well—Louis Maroni, Katie's husband. At that time, he was also known as Senator Maroni.

A married senator with beautiful girls wrapped around his thin body seemed to age his boyish look. I couldn't resist bumping into him.

"Louis, how've ya been?" My eyes wavered to the women.

He smiled that infamous politician's grin in my direction until he recognized me. His hand had already presented for a shake, so I grabbed it firmly. His abrasive facial response and weak handshake contributed to this awkward moment. "Tommy. It's been a while," he said with a chill in his tone.

"Yes, it has, Louis. How's your wife and sons?" Again, my eyes wandered to the ladies, clinging tightly to his arms. If they didn't know he was married, they knew now.

"Everyone is good." Louis managed a trace of a smile. He'd never allow me the satisfaction of believing I put a damper on his evening with those girls.

"How's Angie?" I asked with no subtlety.

He turned toward his femme fatales and mumbled, "Go have a drink, girls."

The seductresses promenaded to the bar with the fifty-dollar bill he handed them, as Louis's dark eyes focused on me like daggers plunging for the kill. "Angie is great, Tommy. She's moved on. Forgot all about you. She's got a great boyfriend now."

I snickered to disguise the sharp pain stabbing my chest. "Your entire family made me feel like an outcast when I was with Angie. And here you are, out in the open with women other than your wife. Does Vince know you're two-timing his daughter?"

"I'm a senator. My constituents follow me around. That doesn't mean I'm unfaithful."

"Would Katie agree?"

"What do you want, Tommy?"

"I saw you and thought I'd ask about Angie."

He scoffed. "You think I'm gonna fuckin' tell you anything about Angie after what you did to her?" His tone sounded wicked. "Forget Angie. She doesn't think about you anymore."

My mouth rambled before my brain considered the ramifications. "You can tell me how to find Angie, or I may have to tell your wife about your evening out with those two ladies."

"You got a set of balls on you, punk, threatening me." His thin body pulsed closer in a hostile manner, as intimidating as a slight one-hundred-sixty-five-pound politician could be, although he was backed by the weight of Vince's organization.

Punching out a senator wouldn't fare well for me, as much as I'd enjoy it.

"I'm not telling you shit about Angie." He pushed me aside so he could slither by, clearly unafraid of my threat. The blondes witnessed him pass by swiftly and chased after him.

I hoped to get some information out of him, even with a bogus threat. The truth was, I had no intention of hurting Katie. I liked her. Katie was sweet, like Angie.

No one would call me a saint. I betrayed my wife for years with Angie. Who was I to judge Louis or anyone else for stepping out on their spouse?

Did Angie have a boyfriend, or did Louis intentionally gouge a knife through my heart?

My life had moved on between Danny, my business, and a surprisingly better relationship with Sadie, but Angie still held a big chunk of my heart.

CHAPTER 52

The temperature outdoors had turned a scorching 110 degrees by midafternoon one summer day in 1986. Danny, Sadie, and I played in the pool together, tossing around a beachball when the telephone rang. The beads of water against my skin dried instantly from the immense heat the moment I stepped out of the pool to answer the phone.

When I heard Larry's voice on the other end of the line, I quickly stepped inside the house and closed the sliding glass door behind me.

"I found her, Tommy."

I paused for a moment, thinking. Larry had a few assignments he was working on for me, but when he said *her*, my mind raced to one possibility. My heart thumped at a wildly strong beat. "Angie?" I whispered, glancing at my family through the pale blue sheers that decorated the picture window.

"Yeah, Tommy. Can you talk?"

"For a minute. What did you find?" I watched Sadie and Danny in the pool, happily splashing about as Larry spoke.

"She changed her last name. That's why we couldn't locate her. You were right about her uncle having connections. The paperwork must have been buried deep enough not to be found. I never would've found her if I kept looking for Angela *Russo*."

Sly Vince. Since I learned where Angie lived and the different last name she used, my next move played out in my head.

After careful consideration, Larry and I discussed the best method to proceed. I sent him to her locale and asked that he discreetly monitor her movement. I didn't want to spook her if she noticed someone was watching her. So much time had passed. The thought of standing in her presence again lit a fire within me. My eyes closed, remembering her laugh, gentle touch, and the fresh scent of her hair.

I also recalled Louis telling me she had a boyfriend—an important question to have answered in advance. As anxious as I felt to see her, the last thing I wanted to do was knock on her door and have some man call her *honey*, then wrap his arms around her. The pit in my stomach filled with bile at that thought.

Danny's voice shouted with a giggle, "Pop, come back in the pool!"

Larry understood his next steps.

CHAPTER 53

Nearly six years had passed after the night I got drunk and lost control with Angie. It seemed like a lifetime since I held her in my arms. Most guys would have moved on quickly, but Angie was the special one who got away. The woman I never stopped loving and longing for. Clear memories of her and the life I cherished were permanently engraved in my soul.

Larry confirmed there was no man in her life. Louis Maroni messed with my mind.

The day I flew out of McCarren International, my relief about Angie's single status was immediately taken over by pure anxiety. I rented a Mercury sedan, using a map to find her home, and unfortunately lost my way for a brief moment. Usually, my sense of direction was excellent, but my nerves shook like a rattlesnake's tail.

I parked a block from her residence with a good view of her yard and gardens with the lovely ocean scenery in the backdrop. I watched her from a safe distance, not to spook her. My heart melted, seeing her from afar. She cut her hair to the tips of her shoulders. Her black waves were full and wavy with some curls at the end. Still gorgeous and seemingly well. She remained in the realty business. Judging by the quaint cottage she owned and her striking sense of style, her business must be thriving.

My typical confident self feared rejection. Somehow, knocking on her cottage door felt inappropriate. The last time I saw Angie, I frightened her in my drunken state. I didn't have it in me to show up unexpectedly at her home and possibly witness an expression of distress.

Angie was far more independent than she realized. Maybe that's why I latched onto her so tightly. She loved me with her whole heart. I also recognized a woman like Angie didn't *need* me. She went to school and started a career on her own without my help.

Deep down, I always knew it was *me* who needed *her*. Maybe that was why I went crazy whenever another man looked at her with interest. A single man could give her a real marriage and a family, an imminent threat that shook my core. I knew I could lose her outright to another man, one without the obligations I bore.

She didn't care about my money. Unfortunately, I did. The one thing Angie wanted from me was 100 percent of a commitment and a marriage. Because of the power of attorney, I couldn't recite marriage vows before Pop's death. Well, not without losing everything else in my life.

I sat, lurking in the shadows, following her around throughout the day, observing her movements. I had no idea how she felt about me after that hazy night. My memory still failed me regarding the complete details of that evening—the night Vince accused me of rape.

Angie stopped by her office for a while before showing a house to a young couple. I couldn't speak with her in front of an audience of her colleagues or clients. My anxiety bubbled. I was ready for a face-to-face conversation. I practiced my speech in my head as I followed her sporty-looking Toyota.

I hoped for an opportunity to speak privately without spooking her, but I had no clue what her day looked like.

Her vehicle turned abruptly into the parking lot of the town library.

I drove a safe distance from her car and parked on the side of the building. I needed a minute to consider the viability of approaching her in a safe, public place. Seeing her in public might be a better idea to gauge her reaction than knocking on her front door. Once I found the strength to leave the vehicle, I peered around the corner of the building. My eyes caught sight of her entering through the back.

Slowly, I strolled to the back entrance of the library to keep my eyes on her. I didn't want to miss her leaving and speeding off in her car. She had quite a lead foot.

The door swung open, causing me to leap backward and instinctively cover my eyes with the ball cap placed atop my head.

Luckily, a mother with her toddler trod quickly out the door. She mumbled an apology for startling me when I turned to catch my breath.

As I stepped through the entrance for a closer look to observe where Angie wandered off to, I noticed her classy, sensual movements, standing about twenty feet from me.

In an instant, I realized I'd been made. Our eye contact was immediate. The moment I longed for had finally arrived. There was no turning back. My stomach rumbled, thinking I should start with an apology or ease my way into a sterile conversation about life. The speech I had rehearsed became jumbled in my head. My feet felt like they were trapped in quicksand. Somehow, I managed to follow her into a private, closed-door room after her head cocked to her right as if signaling me.

Excitement beamed from within as I took a closer look at her beautiful face and figure. I barely paid attention to the clues she tried to display.

She seemed strangely quiet. Was she speechless by my presence? Angie faced me with a beautiful yet serious grin, showing no fear of me. A heavy weight lifted off my shoulders.

As I attempted to speak, she kissed me hard on the mouth with intense passion. God, I missed those lips. My hands traced along the edges of her delicate frame. A fire ignited between my legs. That unexpected kiss was hot. She distracted me enough to realize she was using sign language instead of her voice to communicate.

My brain muddied between the desire her sensuous kiss instigated and comprehending her signs. I hadn't used sign since John's death, but I understood her message.

"The FBI is listening to us. Don't say a word."

This alert sharpened my senses instantaneously. "FBI?" I signed back.

She unbuttoned her blouse and displayed a wire taped to those full, luscious breasts.

It was a trap. A setup. And I fell for it. The Feds played me like a violin, using Angie as a weapon against me. Everything changed at that moment. Rather than charming her back into my arms, I had to pay close attention to her serious pleas through sign.

She might have told the Feds she'd wear a wire to entrap and incriminate me, but these motherfuckers didn't realize Angie and I were fluent in sign language.

Within seconds, she explained the FBI could show up at any time. "They're investigating your business associations."

I knew that meant Carmine. That fucking thorn in my gut who pressured his way into my family's business through Pop.

"I'm sorry you got involved in all of this. I had to see you. It's been so long. I tried to see you sooner, but I couldn't find you. I'm so sorry about everything that happened. It's all my fault. You know I never wanted to hurt you. My marriage. Sadie's pregnancy. It wasn't what you were thinking that day you found out. I never had a chance to explain everything to you."

Although my mind spun viciously, thinking about how to get out of this situation, Angie threw another wrench my way. Sadie knew about the FBI surveillance. Angie witnessed Sadie speaking with the FBI with her own eyes. Since Sadie never told me the FBI was watching me, she must be their mole.

The surprised expression I wore gave Angie the impression that I didn't believe her. Of course, I believed Angie. I trusted her with my life. Hearing my wife betrayed me while we had been acting like a real family since Danny's birth was incomprehensible!

Shit, I could've left Sadie the day after Pop died, but I chose to stay and act like some version of a husband to her. I was never a good husband, but it seemed like we had been trying for Danny's sake.

We rebuilt the friendship we once constructed. To work against me and possibly send me to jail, keeping me from my son, was an unforgivable trap! My back suffered from the knife Sadie wedged deep between my shoulder blades.

With Angie standing before me, I had to clear the air with her. I signed, "Your uncle told people I raped you."

"I never said that. I never thought that. You were drunk, and my heart was pretty beat up. That one night doesn't define what we had. We had our chance, but it had to end."

"I started drinking again, yes. Scared to lose you. You're so beautiful. I don't want to let you go again." A tear shed from my eye.

"You have to let me go. The FBI could see us together. Please, Tommy, walk away. I have a new life here. I'm happy."

"I never loved anyone the way I love you," I signed as my dreams washed away with the tide. As much as I hated to leave her again, I had to say goodbye before the Feds arrived and witnessed our silent discussion. The last thing I wanted to do was hurt her further. They threatened her, thinking she had inside information about the Toscanos infiltrating what was supposed to be a perfectly legitimate business. She knew nothing about my illicit affiliations, and I wouldn't allow the Feds to continue bullying her.

She didn't flinch when she first saw me. No sign of fear. And that incredible kiss! I wanted to tell her the whole story about Sadie and Pop's stipulations, but there was no time.

Angie insisted I return home and free my business from any evidence the FBI had been hunting for.

A shadow of a memory, envisioning strength through her sad eyes, settled in my heart when I cautiously walked out of the library and out of Angie's life—again.

CHAPTER 54

Carmine needed to learn about the FBI's surveillance. If they were following me, they must be monitoring Carmine and his crew. Our offices and phones could be bugged. Shit, that was how the Midwest families were recently indicted—through wiretapping.

I warned Carmine months previously when the media broadcasted the law planning to take Vegas back, shutting down organized crime. The Feds busted some heavy hitters from powerful families. Either these wise guys turned up dead, or they went to prison. Some entered the witness protection program in exchange for ratting out their bosses.

The code of omertà crumbled.

Carmine could be as arrogant as hell. He never thought he'd get caught, ending this moneymaking venture. He ensured his soldiers didn't make the same level of noise these other families made that drew attention. With the Midwest guys defeated, we were next on the FBI's hit list.

Paranoia suddenly set in with Van Halen's "Runnin' with the Devil" playing in my head. Since I was being watched, I thought of a way to send a message to Carmine. Instead of flying directly home after seeing Angie, my plane landed in Los Angeles to drop in on Rob's brother Jack.

Jack Lubitski established his own successful business in the food industry in California. We chatted about working together in the near future. My friendship with Rob and Jack was genuine, but my ulterior motive included using a safe phone.

From Jack's home, I called Gayle, Carmine's latest mistress. I developed a few trigger phrases to use if trouble seemed imminent. "Gayle, tell Carmine I read my son that *Chicken Little* book he gave him." The *Chicken Little* reference meant the sky was falling.

Gayle had been trained to keep her mouth shut. She also knew to whisper messages of this nature in the old man's ear or turn up the volume on the stereo in the room. We required assurance that a planted bug couldn't pick up our voices, just in case wires were hidden at any location where we spent a lot of time.

An hour later, Carmine called me at Jack's house. He drove out of town and hopped in a taxi before stopping at a random Holiday Inn he'd never frequented to return my call. We spoke about family and bullshit topics at first to be safe. After a few minutes, if the FBI had been listening, legally, they were obligated to discontinue surveillance unless we discussed anything illegal.

My words certainly sounded as rattled as I felt, belting out, "I'm being followed by the Feds. I confirmed with a friend of mine we're being watched."

"What friend?" he asked with irritation because I disrupted time with his mistress.

"It's a credible source," I responded confidently without bringing Angie into the conversation. "Carmine, we could be risking our lives or prison time like the Midwest bosses. They were too greedy to stop, and they knew they were being watched! They played a dangerous game, always thinking they'd outsmart the Feds. You know how that turned out for them."

Complete silence on the other end. His greed desperately tried to outweigh the obvious. Giving up a gold mine like the Montgomery wouldn't be a hasty decision.

"Look, we've got good books if we're investigated or audited, but we gotta clean up now. Get rid of any paper trail that can be used against us, and you need to sell your shares of the business back to me. The tea business can't be affiliated anymore. Hell, you could lose that too."

"Who the fuck are you to tell me what I need to do?" Carmine growled. The old man still scared the crap out of me, even though I sat across the country, out of his reach at that moment.

"Look, you made a shitload of money for years off the Montgomery. You have a choice now. You could walk away clean with the money for the shares of the hotel I will buy back from you. Or you could wind up in prison and live out the rest of your life there, for Christ's sake! I'm not being a smart ass or telling you what to fucking do. I'm a realist, Carmine. This is happening! The other families cared more about the money than their freedom. Their soldiers ratted them out. They got beat. They *failed!* Do you want to take that risk or save yourself?"

"I wanna talk to this friend of yours. Who tipped you off about these sons of bitches watching us?"

"Carmine, I saw with my own eyes that I'm being followed. My source is a cop. He took a big risk coming to me with this information to help us. He can't risk his career." I lied through my teeth. "If you don't believe me, confirm with your own sources that we're being monitored. You got ears in high places. We can't talk about this at our homes, offices, or any place they know where we hang out. Wires could be everywhere!"

"I'll look into it," he said before sharply hanging up on me.

My heart beat wildly, and my head felt dizzy, causing me to drop the phone. Anxiety rose as high as my raging blood pressure. Jack helped me to sit before an unexpected panic attack caused me to collapse.

CHAPTER 55

The moment I returned home, exhausted and stressed, I scrubbed everything.

A valuable recommendation Pop had taught me was to separate all data related to the Toscano family. "Tommy, you know how they got Al Capone? Tax evasion. The cops couldn't arrest Capone for being a criminal mastermind, so they found another way to destroy him. We gotta be smart with our financial records."

Pop walked me to a five-drawer file cabinet in his office and pointed to the bottom two drawers. "This is where I keep information about the transactions with the Toscanos. I won't mix our legitimate business with Carmine's scams. If the two worlds collide, I'll have to make a choice which drawer to choose. When in doubt, choose the bottom drawers."

Since I followed Pop's philosophy, I knew exactly where information had been stored that could hurt me if I were served with a warrant to search the premises. My life hung on the line.

I shredded then burned every scrap of paper related to the skim for years, including correspondence exchanged with people from the Heavenly Tea Emporium that wasn't about tea orders or the partnership. I believed Carmine's tea business was legit, but I couldn't validate my theory. If the FBI could prove the tea company was crooked, my freedom would be on the line.

I had the capital to buy out Carmine, but Rob suggested I consider another option. He wanted in on a partnership. Rob was a tremendous asset and a good friend for years. As much as I didn't like to have partners, I had faith in Rob. Because his brother, Jack, made a fortune on his fast-food chain, Scooters, they wanted to combine their assets and join forces to own a piece of the Montgomery.

I'd split Carmine's shares between Rob and Jack if they came up with the funds to invest under the Scooters name. Scooters was a legitimate, untainted entity. We might have to add a Scooters restaurant to our dining options. I could live with that if it meant Carmine, Nicky, and their gang hit the pavement.

Once Carmine confirmed through his sources the reality of an FBI investigation, he was smart enough to cut his losses and walk away with Aniello's blessing. They had no intention of rotting in a prison cell like the bosses from several Midwest states. They chose freedom over greed.

Carmine ordered Fat Nicky and Dominic out, and the Heavenly Tea Emporium sold their shares legitimately.

Rob and Jack became my new business partners. Len ensured the exchange in ownership was on the level. For the first time in twenty years, the Montgomery chain leaned toward the horizon of legitimacy.

Months passed before I erased my association with the mob entirely. If any rat wanted to squeal, or if Carmine held evidence of crimes affiliated with my hotel enterprise, I was screwed. For months I worried the Feds might find *something* to charge me with. Carmine shared generous kickbacks from his scams with me throughout the years. Funds I stashed in a safe, secure location outside the US.

Cleaning up the paper trail was merely one headache resolved. If the Feds brought me in for questioning, I'd become a walking bull's-eye.

People romanticized about the glamorous life of gangsters—money, women, power. In all actuality, they were thieves, bullies, and murderers. You didn't become a soldier without making your bones, meaning ending someone's life upon an order. They'd kill their best friend if ordered.

If the FBI questioned me, I'd be dead before I uttered a syllable. Carmine wouldn't risk me spilling my guts to the Feds.

Was that my wife's plan? Did she realize I might not do time because my former partners would whack me first? What was Sadie thinking, cooperating with the law and not warning me? Several times, I caught Sadie rifling through my desk at home, her nose scanning through documents. She always had an excuse to be snooping around my home office—dusting, cleaning, organizing. I didn't question her actions.

A sick feeling gnawed at my insides. I had a rat in my house that required squashing. Once all of my books appeared clean, I left a trail of bread crumbs for Sadie. All legit documents to see what she'd do with them—if anything. I hoped I had been wrong about her. My gut told me I wasn't, but I needed hard evidence of her possible betrayal. I wanted to know everything she did and everywhere she went while Larry remained out of sight, observing her movements. I couldn't risk the FBI knowing I caught wind of their mission.

Larry showed me photos of Sadie meeting with agents at a diner, the park, and even the grocery store. Every document I purposely left for her to find proved nothing except that I ran a squeaky-clean business.

Besides the sting operation I commanded, I tasked Larry with a full investigation of Sadie. In all the years we were married, I didn't know much about her before hiring her at the Montgomery back in 1967. I provided Larry with sufficient information to check her out. And what he learned was the biggest surprise ever!

The Toscanos couldn't learn that Sadie betrayed us. She'd be dead! As much as I loathed her since discovering her betrayal, Danny loved his mother. I wouldn't be responsible for her death. Telling Carmine my wife fucked me over by working with the Feds would be a death sentence for her. He once said that wives were off-limits in this business, insinuating, *unless they betrayed the family.*

I couldn't possibly get Angie involved, especially since she saved our asses. If she hadn't given me this lead, I'd be dead or locked behind bars, away from my son.

Now, what would I do with my disloyal wife?

CHAPTER 56

Sadie thought I had been traveling out of town on business in November 1986. Len and I revisited my divorce settlement while I crashed at my suite at the Montgomery. I struggled to smile whenever Sadie and I made eye contact. If I continued to live under the same roof with her, I'd explode! My anger festered, bubbling like boiling water at two hundred twelve degrees.

We'd been married for eighteen years. As much as I paid out of my ass being married to her for so long, if I didn't give her a decent deal, she might fight me in court. I couldn't lose my son. His future with me was far more critical than revenge against his mother.

Len advised me not to fight for full custody. Threatening a well-known woman in the community, popular for her philanthropic efforts with the Evangelical church and shelter, wouldn't be wise. I'd appear like a spoiled, rich bully in court, taking away her child. A judge might not like that type of behavior.

Sadie's love for Danny, a positive attribute, was the main reason why I chose not to destroy her in court. From the moment he was born, she transformed into a loving, nurturing mom. Despite all I had learned about her shady past, my son loved her. I couldn't take his mother away from him completely, and a fight in court wouldn't be good for Danny.

If my connection to the Toscanos and Sadie's knowledge about an FBI investigation came up in court, which it would, my odds of losing were as good as hers. So I created an agreement that would suit us both while putting Danny's needs first.

I caught Sadie snooping in my office at the Montgomery when I was supposedly out of town. Her nose planted firmly in my safe as I snuck up behind her. I played it cool as if it were no big deal to witness her ransacking my safe. Why wouldn't I find her actions suspicious?

She'd never come clean to me about anything if I played a game of Q&A, and I grew tired of her bullshit.

Danny was at her sister's house. Fighting with her about divorce and custody wasn't a show to put on in front of our five-year-old.

Either she was shocked or she was one hell of an actress when she reviewed the divorce papers I tossed her way, ending this farce of a marriage.

"I don't understand. After all these years, *now* you want a divorce?" The high pitch in her tone exposed her surprise.

"I tried to make this as simple as possible. This agreement spells out everything crystal-clear. It's a pretty sweet deal for you."

"Deal?"

"If you sign this agreement, you can keep the house and the Cadillac. I'll give you sufficient alimony to cover the household expenses with a generous amount left for yourself. You'll get child support because I basically have no choice in that matter. I'll always take care of my son. Danny will *never* want for anything.

"If the amount doesn't work for you, you can find a job. One that pays a salary instead of all the volunteering you do."

Finally, I divulged my vision of shared custody. Neither of us maintained a perfect reputation to display in court in order to win full custody.

Then she brought Angie's name into our argument. She confirmed knowing the truth about my affair, validating my infidelity. She had affairs too, but she bitterly called me out on mine.

Maybe Angie was right about the way the FBI got to Sadie. She forewarned me, mentioning that the FBI acquired intimate knowledge about our relationship, complete with descriptive pictures. They had to be monitoring me for years.

Sadie didn't understand that my affair with Angie ended six years prior. Maybe if she realized I had been faithful to her since

Danny's birth, she wouldn't have turned on me. She got played, and instead of asking me about it, she chose revenge accompanied by a jail cell.

That was when I threw up her past as a *prostitute*. I married a former brothel whore. Some juicy information I could hold over her head. Larry discovered concrete evidence of her time working at the Belle Maiden Ranch in the late sixties, a cathouse owned by the Russo brothers.

I had to wonder if Vince knew Sadie was one of his girls. Did he screw my wife? If so, he must have been laughing behind my back for years!

Admittedly, I went ballistic! She lived in a brothel for several months. With her history, John could have been right. Maybe that baby we lost in 1968 wasn't mine.

Sadie looked surprised when I brought up the secret she managed to keep locked tight for years. We could one-up each other all day long. Neither of us was perfect.

If we were assigned a straitlaced judge, Danny might end up as a ward of the court because of our histories. I wasn't willing to risk my son's future like a chronic gambler rolling the dice.

I expected her to challenge me when I confronted her about her betrayal to our family. Fighting came naturally to her, but I was armed for a bitter fight. Since I cleaned up the books and got rid of the Mafia, my business sparkled with legitimacy. The Feds had no hard evidence to arrest me, so my future could soar with credibility.

The fact that she turned on me, willing to send me to prison or execution by the Toscano family, was inexcusable! I'd never forgive her for that.

I gave her seventy-two hours to sign the agreement I laid out for her, or I'd sue her for full custody. I hoped she'd sign it quickly and not risk losing Danny. Naturally, to yank my chain, she waited until the last minute on the clock before she personally threw the signed agreement on my desk without saying a word.

Within a day, I crammed my belongings into boxes and bags, prepared to leave the lovely English Tudor house in Henderson. I also packed a bag for Danny to begin the agreed-upon weekends he was to spend in my care. I wanted to explain to him why I'd no longer be living with him and his mommy.

Sadie didn't argue with me. She kissed Danny goodbye and said she'd see him Sunday night.

I didn't want to take Danny to the hotel for the weekend. My personal life was no one's business. Until I found us a house to live in, I brought him to the sanctuary I shared with Angie.

Everything looked the same, right down to the carpeting and dusty furniture. The place needed a facelift and a good cleaning.

Many framed photos of Angie and me together in this home stirred my heart. Pictures Danny wouldn't have understood. As he raced through the rooms to check the place out, I removed the frames with Angie's face in them from the walls and shelves, then stored them in the hall closet for the time being.

Having Danny with me felt less lonely, but the environment forced memories of Angie to shine through. It wasn't good for my peace of mind and restless heart to live here permanently.

Upon my calling, my energetic five-year-old charged to the cream-colored sofa and tackled me.

"Danny boy, I have to tell you something important."

He nodded, rolling his bright red truck across a layer of dust on the table.

"This house is where I have to live right now," I explained, choking on each syllable.

"Here? Why?"

"Mommy and I aren't going to live together anymore. This has nothing to do with how much we love you. You mean everything to us. Do you understand?"

"Okay." He shrugged his little shoulders.

"You're gonna live with Mommy, but you'll see me all the time. Even though I won't be living with your mom, I'll call you every day, and you can contact me anytime." I removed my pager from my pocket. "Remember, I showed you how to reach me when I'm at work."

"I know, Pop." His voice sounded grown up in that instant. He didn't flinch.

"That's not going to change. You and I are pals. No matter what, if you need me, I'll be there...like Batman!" I joked, forcing a chuckle out of him. "This pager is like the bat signal. You signal me, and I'll call you every time."

"Cool. I'm hungry. Can we eat?"

Somehow, this conversation was harder on me than on him. Next on my agenda was to find a new home for Danny and me after we grabbed burgers and fries.

"Go Your Own Way"

CHAPTER 57

Danny launched a meltdown one night with his mother when he couldn't sleep. Reality set in. He grew angry because I moved out. My heart cracked when I heard his cries. I managed to soothe his pain and drove to Henderson. His temper eased, realizing the bat signal worked. He tested me several times during the adjustment period we both had to adapt to. Even when entertaining a lady friend, I always responded to the bat signal.

I wasn't alone too often. I was single again! Nothing would prevent the divorce from becoming official, although the process seemed strenuous and more time-consuming than I anticipated. I started banging any woman who showed me her flirty eyes. Only brunettes and redheads. Blondes reminded me of Sadie.

Eventually, I picked out a spectacular five-thousand-square-foot house in Paradise on a different neighborhood block than where I lived with Angie. I filled the house with furniture and knickknacks, so the place resembled a home. I had a lot on my plate with Danny, women, traveling, and my hotels.

Sadie started to date her cop friend, Hank, a black man I met when she was in that car accident years ago. He volunteered at her shelter. I had him checked out, not because of Hank's skin color or that he and Sadie became a couple. I cared about Danny and his safety.

Danny had nothing but nice things to say about Hank. Larry confirmed Hank was a decent man, a good cop, and recently divorced. That information offered me a sense of relief.

CHAPTER 58

Danny traveled with me fairly often, as long as his education wasn't disrupted. We flew all over the world together to places like Italy, England, and Spain. Some spots were more memorable than others. One of Danny's favorite vacation spots was mystical Ireland. I explained his Irish heritage from his late grandmother and his McGee ancestors.

The Montgomery established a home in Cork, outside the industrialized region of the city.

I rented a Mercedes, so Danny and I could see this amazing country at our leisure. We drove through Kinsale, the seaside hometown of my maternal grandparents, witnessing the boats that sailed along the calm water. The town appeared lively with colorful buildings as we strode along the cobblestone walkways. A few houses wore vintage thatched roofs, a classic Irish look.

Sean Reilly, the Cork hotel's operations director, recommended dinner at Kitty O'se's in the heart of Kinsale. Your typical Irish pub with bubbly, Celtic folk music that could perk up any cranky old soul who sauntered into the joint. You couldn't help but feel happy, hearing tunes like "The Wild Rover." A few young girls dressed in plaid skirts eagerly stepped up to the band to show the crowd a few Irish step dancing moves. The impromptu entertainment was top-notch, and the cottage pie at Kitty's was delicious!

Danny became enthralled with Sean's whimsical tales of fairies and leprechauns. Sean suggested we visit an out of the way place outside of Cork, Saint Gobnait's Holy Well in Ballyvourney.

"The trees at the holy well are loaded with mischievous fairies. You don't want to upset them, Danny," Sean said with a heavy brogue.

I signaled my colleague with a firm shake of my head to tone it down a notch. Danny was only seven.

Finding this holy well proved challenging. When we arrived, a small tour group of nine American family members paced themselves through the tranquil country area. We overheard them talking about a beautiful wedding they recently attended in Kildare.

The tour guide stepped off the bus and signaled me with a welcoming high-pitched brogue. "Good day, sir!"

"Hello. How are you, sir?" I cheerfully replied.

"Ah, American, are ya?"

"That's right."

"Ever been to the well before?"

"First time."

He winked at Danny and said, "Be mindful of the fairy tree. Those little rascals love to play pranks on young boys." The friendly Irishman pointed in the direction of the well.

We walked a short distance through the woods along the worn path to arrive at a small serene spot surrounded by tall, thick trees. Numerous trinkets and holy figurines dangled from the branches of the fairy trees, left by people seeking healing from the properties of the still water within the ancient stone well.

I motioned Danny to bow his head and say a prayer out of respect for Saint Gobnait and in honor of my mother. Then we stepped a few paces down the stone stairway, leading to the well's entrance.

Sean had advised the well water was safe to drink if you held your cup down deep in the water below the inedible properties that floated at the top. I dropped a few pounds in a metal box labeled DONATIONS to use the paper cups available for guests to taste the holy water.

Danny watched me crouch through the small opening of the blessed stone structure. As I popped my head inside, I noticed a spider's web and a few tiny water bugs swimming atop the dark water. I felt lighthearted at the moment I plunged the cup beneath the water's rim, nearly an elbow's length, to ensure what we were about to taste would be safe to drink.

As I backed out, my eyes adjusted to the sunlight. The water appeared clean within the cup, and I enjoyed the refreshing taste. Danny turned his nose up at it.

I packed a small candle to light and leave at the well in my mother's memory to honor her family's history in this beautiful, scenic country.

We were nearly at the car when Danny stopped suddenly. "What if the candle starts a fire?" His concern was valid.

Perhaps I acted carelessly, leaving a burning wick near fairy trees. We treaded back to the well to blow out the flame.

We circled the well twice, then squatted at its base, staring into the shadowy well. The candle had vanished! The simple white candle we lit mere minutes ago disappeared in the few moments our backs were turned. I distinctly remembered setting it along the top of the stone wall next to a framed photo of the Virgin Mary that another believer left behind. It was a flat, sturdy place to ensure the candle didn't fall or roll off the ledge.

"The fairies took it, Pop! Maybe you shouldn't have lit the candle. Maybe they were afraid their trees would burn."

I nodded in agreement, scratching my head because I had no logical explanation for what happened to that lit candle. No other people were around to have moved it. The American tour group drove off before I had lit the match. A lit candle wouldn't evaporate like a tacky magic trick. Could it have rolled off the wall, falling down deep within the dark water? I took a moment to stare inside the mysterious opening of the holy well, contemplating. Seemed like a more logical revelation than a trickster fairy messing with our minds. I recalled my mother's superstitious nature and the fanciful stories she shared with me in my youth.

A shiver flew up my body. "Let's get out of here, Dan. Tomorrow we'll drive to Blarney Castle and kiss the famous Blarney Stone."

Danny stopped, deep in thought. He pulled out a red Match Box car from his jacket pocket and stared at the toy momentarily.

Gingerly, he stepped toward the stone well and said, "Here ya go, fairies. Sorry about lighting the candle." He carefully placed his favorite toy car atop the well and left it behind.

I had zero explanation for the whereabouts of that missing candle. But I stuck with my theory that it fell from the stone wall, rolled down the steps, and landed into the well water, never to be seen again, although the air was too calm to knock it over and the candle had a square base.

The Irish and their superstitions.

CHAPTER 59

Larry continually kept tabs on Angie for me since he found her in her new location with a new identity and life. I often wondered how receptive she'd be if I knocked on her door to see if the natural chemistry between us surfaced. That lightning bolt I felt the first time I laid eyes on her still sparked when we were face-to-face in the library.

My divorce didn't become official as quickly as I had hoped. Not that Sadie fought me. The legalities and administrative work took more than a year to finalize.

The FBI never stormed inside any of my buildings with search warrants, dragging me out in cuffs. Twenty years of crooked affiliations, records, and tax returns could come back to bite me. Thankfully, they must not have had sufficient evidence to proceed with their investigation.

Angie had a small group of friends she spent time with. She worked for a well-established real-estate agency. She enjoyed jogging along the ocean, swimming laps in her pool, and she joined a book club. Plus, she told me outright that she was happy—without me.

My ego deflated, having difficulty accepting such rejection.

The more I thought about seeing her again, the more I couldn't wait. I reminisced about Lake Como and Paris. Since I was divorced, sober, and maintained a legitimate business, all the promises I made to her years ago could be fulfilled if she'd take me back.

Danny would love Angie. We could have a real marriage and a family. I could offer her myself completely without secrets. I'd have to deal with Vince, the bane of my existence, but I'd figure out how to cope with him later. He must be pretty pleased with himself, keeping Angie and me apart for so long.

Just as my hope and heart lifted, Larry offered a dose of reality. Angie had been dating someone, and it was serious.

Had I been so selfish and ignorant to think she'd stay single forever, waiting for me to get my life in order? Because she was single two years ago when I had found where she moved to didn't mean she'd be available now.

The man in Angie's life was a widower with two young daughters. Any shred of hope I held in my heart faded. Larry didn't have to add that her boyfriend was a good-looking, wealthy businessman, but he did, rubbing salt into my widening wounds.

My buddy Larry knew me well. Before I could ask him to research this guy, he already checked him out. This man's reputation seemed as clean as a whistle. If Angie found love again with the chance of being a mother, I had to let her go.

The house in Paradise where I lived with Angie appeared dark and dreary when I pulled into the driveway as if a large, menacing black cloud suddenly hovered. I opened the closet where the pictures and memories shared with Angie were stored. I removed the photos from the frames and placed the pictures inside a large envelope. I couldn't part with them. The memories of our relationship were important, but I couldn't look at any reminders of the love I had decimated through sheer stupidity.

Then I lost my temper and released the pent-up anger in a wild fury. Without thinking, I smashed the frames against the walls. Glass shattered into the thick living room carpet. My fist smacked against the closet door, leaving a dent, a tingling sensation in my wrist, and a crick in my back. I fell to my knees, feeling the puncture of glass bits scraping my legs.

Losing Angie was my fault. I should have told her long ago what had been happening in my life and my marriage. I feared she wouldn't understand my rationale for staying tied to Sadie, even after Pop's death, which was all about Danny.

CHAPTER 60

Every few months, Larry provided an update on Angie's life, citing, "No change, Tommy."

I expected him to keep his distance. Angie never met Larry, and I wouldn't want her to worry, catching someone spying on her. She wouldn't understand there was no harm. No danger. It was me, unable to put her in the past and relinquish the feelings I still carried.

Larry snapped some photographs of her with her boyfriend, but I never looked at them. I told Larry to keep them to himself. I wanted Angie to be happy, but I didn't need an excruciating visual effect.

Time passed, and my wounded heart slowly healed, but I hadn't felt that chemical reaction and excitement with another woman that Angie stimulated.

Finding female companionship in Vegas wasn't difficult. But Angie was more than a lover. My love for her, an unsurmountable wave of emotions, inspired me to become a better man. I wished I could have given her more.

Then the day I had been dreading arrived. The day Larry called to say those devastatingly painful four words: "Angie is getting married."

It didn't take too long for her relationship to progress. Why not? She was a hell of a catch. This guy knew he had a great woman. He gave her what I couldn't—a commitment.

After sulking about her upcoming nuptials, I decided it was time to move on. As hard as this felt, I wanted to face her one more time. I never said goodbye to her. Vince wouldn't allow it. I convinced myself I needed closure. I made arrangements with my pilot to secure a flight path on a Monday in June 1989. How would I do this? Knock on her door? Casually approach her somewhere publicly like in the library a few years ago? The illustrious fantasy I held onto featured Angie's brown eyes connecting with mine from afar. Then she'd race to me, saying some cheesy line like, *I could never love anyone as much as you!* That silly melodramatic vision played out in my head constantly. I knew it wouldn't be that easy.

I rented a small Volkswagen at the airport terminal late in the afternoon—the type of car Angie would never suspect me to rent.

Her charming white cottage with red shutters looked empty. No vehicles were parked in the driveway. The lawn and gardens appeared neat.

I sat outside in the beetle for an hour across the street from her house like a chump. She could be with her boyfriend, Steve. Larry provided me with Steve's address.

Before the neighbors became suspicious of a potential prowler sitting outside in a tiny VW, I hit the road to find this guy's house.

I was pretty good with a map and directions, but I had difficulty finding his street. Eventually, I found the road and the white colonial house. Admittedly, it looked like a nice home. Not as nice as our home in Paradise, though. I parked the VW up the block on a slight incline. This gave me a clear view of the property before dark.

A big swimming pool, swing set, and what appeared to be a child's playhouse were situated in the backyard. This man had daughters, which explained the pink trim of the mini structure.

The front door opened, and out jumped a little girl with light brown pigtails on the oversize porch. She was younger than Danny's eight years. I'd guess she was five or six. She wore a turquoise shirt with a pink design and jean shorts with ruffles along the edges.

Then I spotted her. Angie followed the young girl outside, carrying another little girl on her hip, maybe three years old, dressed all in pink. The little one held onto Angie tightly.

Angie looked really good in a pair of white shorts, a royal blue tank top, and barefoot. She looked at home and comfortable.

It wasn't long before a man with black hair and a slim build stepped outside, holding a small bicycle with streamers dangling from the handlebars and a horn he beeped a few times. This was the widower who stole Angie's heart.

The older girl jumped up and down as her father positioned the purple and silver bike on the sidewalk for her to hop onto. He raced alongside her after giving her a gentle push. She called out to Angie, referring to her as "Mommy" as she peddled past them at a mild pace, thanks to the training wheels that kept her balance.

Angie cheered while entertaining the little one who wouldn't leave her hip. The younger daughter gave Angie a big kiss on her cheek and placed her small head into the crook of her neck.

I watched intently as Angie rocked the girl lovingly in her arms.

Soon enough, the little girl wanted to get down. They sat on the front porch and blew bubbles together, watching the older girl move along with more exuberance on her bike. They waved and cheered as she raced by, pumping her little legs.

When they all met on the front porch, I witnessed the loving way Steve looked at Angie. They exchanged a soft kiss.

My heart throbbed a wounded beat.

She looked happy and settled. She was loved, and she loved this family back. This was her home now. A place where she could be a mom. Her long-time wish finally converted to reality. She looked beautiful, and she blended into this life perfectly.

I didn't have to say goodbye to Angie directly. I mumbled a heartfelt "Goodbye" under my breath.

When I returned to Vegas, I told Larry to discontinue his surveillance of her. It was time I moved on. Hearing about her life with another man only allowed me to think about her more often and miss her. That had to stop.

I had to accept that destiny couldn't be planned or controlled. I succumbed to whatever fate had in store for me next.

CHAPTER 61

Most of Carmine's soldiers fled Vegas after our partnership dissolved. Marty still ran the drug operation. I'd bump into him on the street from time to time. He always told a good dirty joke with impeccable timing. Although I was always pleasant, I didn't want him hanging around the Montgomery, nor did I want to associate with him regularly in case the Feds still kept tabs on me. Marty understood that.

After a run-in with Marty outside a murder mystery dinner show, he told me Aniello Toscano had disappeared and was presumed dead. No one had seen or heard from him since he flew to Florida to meet his family for a vacation. He was last seen getting into a taxi at the Orlando airport.

As underboss, Carmine immediately claimed the top spot to lead the family.

Fat Nicky was suspected of murder in the early nineties. He offed some guy who owed him money. According to Marty, he didn't mean to kill the man. If the mob killed the people who owed them money, they'd never get repaid. Break body parts—yes. Kill them—no.

Before Nicky was arrested, he got popped in his house. Bullet to the back of his head while frying meatballs. Carmine must have ordered that hit. Bosses wouldn't want any heat brought down on them. They couldn't count on a soldier's loyalty if he faced hard prison time. Giving up the boss for a lighter sentence or starting a new life in the cushy witness protection program was a sweeter deal than death.

I never pegged Nicky for a rat, but someone did.

In the olden days, no one would dare rat out a boss. They'd do their time in prison and respect the family. The code of silence, omertà, kept many guys breathing. But some couldn't handle doing time.

Six months after Nicky's demise, Carmine died in the bed of his mistress. The woman called for an ambulance, but it was too late.

Carmine's children demanded an autopsy to determine the cause of death. The foam spewing from his mouth was a clue that the old man had been poisoned.

Because he died in the bed of a woman, his sons accused her of slipping him the toxin. A rival Philly family might have persuaded her, they thought.

Carmine's son, Gino, avenged his father's death. Allegedly, Gino viciously beat and strangled this woman, then dumped her body in the river where it washed up three days later. Her face was bloated and unrecognizable to be claimed by her family because of the torture she experienced. At least that was the story Marty told me.

Carmine's mistress might have been innocent. If she poisoned Carmine, she did it on someone else's orders.

Gino Toscano climbed up the ranks in the organization. It became clear to most people he wanted the top spot as boss someday to follow in his father's corrupt footsteps.

As long as their business ventures stayed on the East Coast, I didn't care what they did, but Marty's stories always fascinated me.

CHAPTER 62

Sadie and I rarely spoke a word to each other. The arrangement I devised sent her alimony and child support through an account my financial advisor, Chris, controlled.

We maintained a regular schedule with Danny throughout his childhood. Sometimes I'd send him home with a note for Sadie if I needed to alter the schedule. I didn't want to talk to her—ever.

Out of the blue, she called me at my office one day in 1992. She happened to catch me in between meetings. When I heard her voice, I worried something was wrong with Danny. Without so much as a hello, I immediately asked, "Is Danny okay?"

"Yes, Danny's fine."

I said nothing, waiting for her to tell me why she was disrupting my day.

"It's Patrick. He's ill. I thought you'd want to know."

Instantly, I stopped what I was doing and paid closer attention. "What do you mean, *ill?*" I sensed anxiety through her shaky voice, so I braced myself for bad news. I mean, she wouldn't have called to tell me her brother had the flu.

"We're not telling the family yet, Tommy. He doesn't know I'm calling you, but—"

"What's wrong with him?"

I detected a whimper as she caught her breath. "Patrick has HIV."

"HIV?" I paused momentarily, absorbing this painful detail. "Is he sure?"

This illness had taken many lives. An HIV diagnosis would eventually advance to AIDS if not identified and treated. Patrick was like a kid brother to me. In spite of the anger I held for Sadie, I never wanted to hear such tragic news about Patrick.

"With all the hype about this disease in the news, Patrick willingly got himself tested. There is a treatment regimen that could save his life until a cure is found, Tommy. For now, with treatment, there's a chance to prevent the progression to AIDS."

"What is the treatment?"

"The treatment isn't the issue. It's the expense that insurance doesn't cover. I could help him financially, but it's not enough."

"I'll take care of it," I said without a thought about the cost. Then I hung up on her. I didn't need to help Patrick through my ex-wife. I called him directly and made plans to meet him face-to-face on his turf in LA.

After a quick flight, I met him at a diner along the busy Hollywood Boulevard. The street was flocked with tourists, heads lowered, reading celebrity names in the star-shaped plaques along the path, instead of watching where they were walking. I dodged past Superman, Chewbacca, and Zorro wanting money in exchange for a photograph.

I recognized Patrick sitting nervously at a booth in the back. At first glance, Patrick didn't appear sick. His color looked good, but he seemed thinner since I last saw him.

Patrick and I always maintained a good rhythm when we spoke. Sometimes, we could sit quietly without saying a word. Other times, we couldn't keep quiet.

"My sister shouldn't have involved you," he said.

"My divorcing your sister doesn't affect our friendship, Pattie. I care what happens to you, and I've got the means to help."

His thin body stirred in the booth as his fingers combed through his golden hair.

"I'm gonna do whatever is necessary for you, and I'm not taking *no* for an answer."

He nodded. "Thank you, Tommy."

A memory struck, leading to a positive analogy. "Remember when I brought you to the gym to teach you how to box and strengthen your confidence? What did I tell you?"

He smirked, offering no response.

"Come on, what did I say?"

He thought momentarily. "You said, *Tune out all the noise in your head and stay focused on the here and now. Battle one demon at a time.*"

"Yeah, and right now, you've got me in your corner just like at the gym. You've got a pretty ruthless demon to tackle. Fight for your life, Pattie. I've got your back, always."

My message to Patrick years ago wasn't necessarily implied to fight the college campus homophobic bullies he dealt with. Sure, he needed to defend himself. But he had issues with his father, relationship struggles, and a tremendous fear of harsh criticisms from society since he was part of a misunderstood culture. A lifestyle profusely rejected by the majority of citizens at the time when he came out in the late sixties.

Patrick desperately craved acceptance to live his life peacefully with a partner he loved. I didn't want him to feel like he should take on every ugly obstacle at once when in that ring, facing an opponent. Challenge one issue or demon at a time.

I made arrangements to set up a payment plan to fully cover any out-of-pocket expenses for Patrick's health care. If my money could facilitate saving his life, I'd help him until the day came when he was officially cured.

Coming to terms with the fact that Patrick could lose this battle wasn't a thought I could process. The last thing I wanted was to lose someone else I cared about.

CHAPTER 63

The Montgomery won the diamond award in 1993, which signified overall excellence in cleanliness, staff friendliness, and quality. Rob, Jack, and I attended the black-tie ceremony to accept the honor.

I had arranged for a stretch limo to drive us to the venue. Bright lights. Red carpet. Photographers snapped numerous pictures. Was this a hotel awards ceremony or the Oscars?

Danny, at age twelve, was my plus one at the formal event. He was my mini-me, and like me, half way through the night, he'd become restless and tug at his bowtie or fling his jacket recklessly over the back of his chair.

The reception hall looked elegantly decorated with sleek yet simple props in blue and silver that shimmered like diamonds. We enjoyed a delicious five-course meal and an open bar. Sparkling cider for Danny and me, always.

From the corner of my eye, I spotted a cute young blonde approaching with a microphone in hand.

She nearly tumbled in her heels as she advanced toward me. "Mr. Cavallo, may I have a moment of your time, please? Olivia Crane from the *Chronicle*," she introduced herself, then awkwardly crammed the mic in my face.

I detested interviews, but I felt bad for this young woman with shaky hands and quivering lips. I knew many reporters from the *Chronicle*, but I never heard of Olivia Crane.

Some of her questions were good, solid, and professional when her teeth weren't chattering. I loved that Danny stood by my side, listening to our discussion about Pop's visions and my taking hold of the reins, managing the business, and building an empire—an international billion-dollar hotel enterprise.

The interview had gone well until this young novice turned into a viper. "How significant was Carmine Toscano's role with your success? The late Mr. Toscano was allegedly the head of a Philadelphia crime syndicate. Any comment about his murder?"

"No comment. Thank you." I displayed a mechanical smile as I escaped, nudging Danny along with me.

She sure had me fooled with her schoolgirl looks and nervous animations. I hoped her article wouldn't include her perceptions of the Toscano's roots, which were once entangled in my hotel.

We had just won a prestigious award. I couldn't afford the media slandering my name and reputation. I could only hope my former dealings with Carmine wouldn't come back to bite me.

CHAPTER 64

When Danny entered his teen years, he developed his own interests and hobbies, devising the agenda for our vacations. Together, Danny and I enjoyed tropical adventures and antiquated attractions overseas on other continents. As he grew up, I allowed him the freedom to choose our destinations. However, one area I had no interest in returning to was the French Riviera.

A girl Danny liked in school spent a good chunk of her summer vacation in Nice, which made him curious. He wanted to witness the breathtaking scenery and extraordinary culture of southern France he heard this girl rave about.

I had my reasons for not wanting to return to Nice. Nineteen seventy-three was a blur, the period when my cocaine/whiskey combo phase heightened, turning problematic.

I didn't consider myself an addict back then. I loved the energy experienced after a bump. That extra kick was needed, considering all that I had on my plate. The high felt good too.

A prime hotel in Nice hit the market at an exceptionally reasonable rate. The owners reeked of desperation to sell. Angie and I went clubbing in town to celebrate my win. Specific details remain unknown because my brain was utterly fried that year. Between the drugs and alcohol, I suffered from periods of blackouts.

I remembered meeting a blond woman who had set her sights on Angie. I thought it would be a good time to invite her back to our hotel room. In my right mind, I never would have allowed that. If anyone looked at Angie inappropriately, I'd lose my mind. We were so high that night, thanks to a cocktail of cocaine and shots of Jameson. We had quite a wild party. Sex, drugs, and rock and roll—all night long.

The next afternoon, I stumbled from the bed, disoriented. Flashes of images surfaced. Few precise details, but I witnessed this woman kissing Angie in the shower. That shower scene, I vividly recalled. My fury took hold, pissed at Angie for being alone with this wild temptress.

When high, drunk, or needing to be high or drunk, I could lose my temper quickly. I became enraged and violent. I threw the woman out of our room, spitting fire from every orifice. I scared Angie so badly that day in Nice, she considered leaving me and presented an ultimatum—drugs or her.

The Nice ménage à trois mortified Angie. The time had come to sober up. Angie refused to return to Nice, avoiding toxic thoughts about that blonde and my uncontrolled anger. That one stupid evening blew the hotel deal and almost cost me my girl. Of course, I chose Angie over my love for drugs and alcohol, as difficult as it was to give up.

Maintaining sobriety had been the most formidable challenge of my life. Giving up cocaine wasn't as difficult for me as breaking off my affair with alcohol.

Angie's withdrawal symptoms were more severe than mine. Some days I just held her, allowing her to weep away the pain and nausea. She had lost so much weight, her bones showed prominently through her skin. It took several months before we felt normal and looked like our true selves.

John had been worried about us. I saw him regularly back then. He could tell I was using too much, and he broke my chops about it for months before I sobered up completely.

The business, my marriage, Carmine—nothing mattered to me except helping Angie get clean and controlling my own sobriety.

Carmine screamed at me for walking away from the Nice hotel. What a hypocrite! Carmine wanted to make money in drug sales, but I got a lecture about abusing the drugs that made me "squirrely in the head."

I promised Carmine I'd make it up to him with other financial investments. I needed Carmine's protection from Vince at that time, but his protection always came with a price.

Angie couldn't face her family in her state, battling withdrawal. I never encouraged her to visit Vince because he'd figure out the demon she combatted, and he'd blame me.

Several months after Angie and I fought our cravings, Vince arrived unannounced and uninvited at the Montgomery. He barged into my office with a bull of a guy resembling Andre the Giant. I nearly jumped out of my skin, but I tried to act calmly. I felt anything but calm, staring at the hulk of a man approaching me with arms the size of a side of beef. His enormous hands lifted me out of my chair.

"Where is my niece, Tommy?" Vince asked, exposing a snarling temper.

"Hi, Vince. How've ya been?" I responded while my heartbeat thumped at an incredulous rate.

"I asked you a question! Where the hell is Angie? What have you done to her, you lousy piece of shit!"

The giant man's hands were as large as catcher's mitts. He pinned me against the office wall, destroying an oil painting I used to enjoy looking at. The force felt like a Mack truck crushing my chest.

"She's...probably...at...school," I struggled to say with a squashed windpipe.

"School? You think I don't know she dropped out? I see the signs. My brother went through this bullshit with Connie and his wife! This stinks of you and your kind of partying, Tommy!" Vince's voice shook the walls and raised the roof. He was rightfully concerned about Angie, but I couldn't tell him that.

Mrs. Arden heard the commotion. She made a call that saved my life that day.

Within seconds, Fat Nicky busted into my office with a baseball bat he pointed at Vince's head, warning him to back off.

Dominic rushed in behind Nicky with a Winchester rifle pointed at Vince's seven-foot mound of muscle.

Vince took a moment to compose himself. With a cool manner, he slowly showed his hands then straightened out his suit jacket. He stood tall and still, raising his chin. Vince turned toward Fat Nicky, an inch from his aluminum bat, and adjusted his tie, stating with a relaxed voice, "Gentlemen, this isn't necessary."

Despite his peaceful words, Nicky and Dominic didn't budge or utter a sound.

Vince slowly twisted his head in my direction, still crammed against the wall, my throat in the palm of the Incredible Hulk. "Tommy, I want to talk to Angie. If I don't hear from her *today*, we're going to have a problem. Understand?"

His thug released me from the wall, allowing my feet to touch the ground and catch my breath.

My voice cracked through a coughing fit as I replied, "I'll give her the message."

The two angry men left the room with their hands up to prevent getting shot or bludgeoned by my partners.

After thanking Nicky and Dominic, I immediately called Angie at home and begged her to contact Vince that afternoon. She had to convince him that she was okay.

Surprisingly, I didn't wind up in cement shoes, floating at the bottom of Lake Mead with bass and bluegills nibbling at specks of my flesh. Also, I evaded the wicked temptation to drink.

To sum up this remembrance, I never took Danny to the French Riviera. Too many painful memories I didn't want to relive. I explained to my teenage son that Nice was a romantic place to take a girl when he was older.

Instead, we visited Sicily, home of my favorite Italian pastry, cannoli. We stayed at a quaint inn in the picturesque village of Taormina. We awoke each morning to spectacular views of the sea. Danny's favorite attraction was Mount Etna, the active volcano. We trekked across the black mountainous terrain, stepping down deep within craters that looked like massive sinkholes. I felt like we were on an episode of *Battlestar Galactica*. We enjoyed a wonderful vacation that year. He didn't give France a second thought.

CHAPTER 65

Sadie pulled together a charity benefit with her church and other community activists, seeking donations to find a cure for AIDS.

I never went out of my way to speak to my ex-wife, but she would contact me if the topic concerned Danny or Patrick. Often, I would donate to her causes, but Danny wanted me to attend this particular event in person. He loved his uncle Patrick. I couldn't say no to this kid, especially if Patrick benefited.

Needless to say, I put on a suit and attended the event but not without a date. I brought Hillary Polk, a former dancer at the Montgomery. Tall, thin, graceful, with light brown hair and turquoise eyes—she was a knockout, and she had class. Hillary moved onto a popular cabaret along the Strip. We started spending time together after she left the Montgomery. Nothing too serious in my mind at first, but we had fun, and I cared about her. Hillary became a steady friend I spent time with, and we discussed keeping our friendship monogamous.

The media invaded the room as if President Clinton were attending this event to raise money that helped people like Patrick live contentedly with a deadly disease.

Eventually, Patrick told the rest of his family about his HIV diagnosis. He couldn't keep it quiet anymore. His treatment, which I paid for, kept AIDS at bay, and the virus was barely detectable in his system.

Sadie was determined to save her brother. I gave her credit for always supporting her family financially and emotionally.

When I sauntered into the banquet hall, I noticed a large rectangular table with the entire Meade family surrounding it. I knew I had to approach and say hello, despite my desire to run in the opposite direction.

Danny was the first to greet me with a bro hug. He had already met Hillary, who was dressed elegantly in a floor-length midnight-blue dress with silver trim and a low-cut neckline to highlight her magnificent breasts that I couldn't wait to see later. My son, much like his old man, eyed her shapely physique up and down, paying particular attention to her firm dancer legs through the lengthy slit in her gown.

Sadie took one glance at Hillary and left the table without saying a word to me.

I made the rounds to introduce my date, starting with Patrick and his boyfriend, Will. Patrick looked well despite his illness. Lisa and Al were quite cordial. Abby, their daughter, grew into a lovely young lady. Lisa's son, Jason, shook my hand. My ex-mother-in-law, Suzanne, flashed her blue eyes, charming as ever. I gave her a hug and kiss before introducing Hillary. Fred turned his head away from me, so I shuffled past him to shake Hank's hand. I liked Sadie's boyfriend. He was always pleasant when we saw each other, and he treated Danny well. That was all that mattered.

Hillary and I moved a few yards over to table number four. Danny walked back and forth between my table and the Meades' table. I never wanted Danny to choose between us, so I suggested he spend time with Hillary and me after his mother's speech ended.

Kudos to Sadie for coordinating the event and inviting heavy hitters with deep pockets to help with the cause. Once the soulful jazz music began and my pockets were emptied from the donation I made, I kissed the top of Hillary's hand. Time to take her home and tuck her in. I brushed the top of Danny's head before planting a kiss there. We were nearly out the main door when my quick getaway was suddenly interrupted.

"Mr. Cavallo! Olivia Crane from the *Chronicle*. What did you think of the event your ex-wife chaired?"

"Hello, Olivia." I attempted to be cordial, but I wanted to leave. "I'm sure the evening was successful. I'm delighted to help with worthwhile causes like this."

"Any comment about Sadie's nomination for Philanthropic Activist of the Year?"

Miss Crane must have recognized the look of surprise on my face, but I attempted to conceal it. "I think Sadie works hard for the community, and if she's recognized with such an honor, that's an incredible achievement for her, as well as the other nominees."

"I would love to get a photo with you and Sadie together."

"I'm sorry, Olivia, but I need to leave."

"Who's your date this evening?"

This was how gossip started. "This is my friend, Hillary."

"How long have you been dating?"

"Good night, Olivia." I blocked her mic and escaped with Hillary close to my side.

I understood the way the press operated. Olivia Crane liked to focus on personal bullshit like the tabloids. Readers of the *Chronicle* didn't care about my personal life or my relationship with my ex-wife. This was Las Vegas! She shouldn't have difficulty finding a scandalous narrative for her audience to devour.

CHAPTER 66

Jack planned his wedding in 1996 to his long-time girlfriend, Marisa. He had the funds to arrange a spectacular wedding, complete with all the bells and whistles imaginable. The reception would take place in the Royal Mile banquet hall in the Montgomery's Scotland wing. Champagne fountains, ice sculptures, large floral centerpieces at each table. Nothing but the best for the woman he loved.

As the best man for his brother, Rob organized the bachelor party. Gambling in a private room at our casino, a comedian for entertainment, and a barbecue buffet with lots of beer.

The guys had a blast, especially when dessert was served. Dessert being the strippers Rob hired from a club downtown near Freemont Street.

I opened the door to let the girls inside, anxiously awaiting to use my dollar bills. The sexy ladies sauntered in, escorted by a massive bodybuilder and a woman with a mass of strawberry blond curls whose face I recognized beneath sprays of lines around her eyes and lips. I hadn't seen Nancy Garrett in years—Vince Russo's ex-girlfriend.

Back in the day when Angie and I were together, I spent many Sunday afternoons breaking bread with the Russo family, including Nancy. I couldn't recall exactly when it happened, but Nancy stopped showing up for Sunday dinners. We knew she and Vince had split, but we never heard why.

Nancy's blue eyes widened in surprise when she saw me, but she soon sent me a friendly smile.

"Nancy, how are you?" I moved in closer and left a kiss on her cheek.

The man accompanying her sent me a chilling look. Presumably, his presence assured the ladies' safety. The muscles trailing along this guy's arms had muscles. He resembled a pro wrestler who just lost the match of his life.

"It's nice to see you, Tommy. I knew you still owned the Montgomery, but I had no idea you'd be at this bachelor party," she responded with a flirtatious wink.

"Jack is my buddy and one of my partners."

Nancy and the tall block of steel with her stood in the back of the room when the show began. Somehow, my desire to throw away dollar bills depleted with Nancy standing nearby. Between the loud music and the guys whooping it up, engaging in small talk seemed impossible.

The bachelor party went on until about midnight when Jack decided to call it quits. He needed his beauty sleep before his big day in the morning.

The party officially broke when the music stopped, and the girls picked up their clothes from the floor to dress. I offered to buy Nancy breakfast, so we could catch up.

Indeed, I had an ulterior motive.

Nancy and I sat at a booth in the back of the café. No other guests were seated in that section, and I requested it stay that way. She was always pleasantly social at those Sunday dinners and holidays at Vince's house. I used to wonder if Nancy was a prostitute whom Vince took a shining to at one of the brothels he owned. Maybe he wanted her exclusively and set her up nicely. Not the type of question you'd ask a lady at Sunday dinner. My suspicions were valid, considering this man made his mark in the prostitution business.

Nancy and I engaged in some small talk. I spoke highly of my enterprise and my son. She told me she managed the Gentleman's Club where we requested the dancers for Jack's party.

The waitress hurried to our table and poured two cups of coffee. I ordered a vegetable omelet. Nancy ordered cottage cheese with fresh fruit.

While we waited for our food to arrive, I brought up a memory from one of the many Sunday dinners with the Russos. When she didn't engage, I started to ramble. "Angie left me, but you may have known that."

"I'm sorry to hear that. I thought you two had something special. It took guts dating Vince Russo's niece. Especially when she was promised to the Maronis to be Louis's wife."

I nearly choked when I slugged down the steaming java from my mug. "What?"

She giggled at my shock and evident lack of knowledge. "Oh yeah, Vince and Big Sal tried to unite Angie and Louis, but you had already captured her heart." She sighed with a romantic rhythm, then shot me a clever smile.

Dumfounded, I was, that Vince attempted to bargain with Angie's heart.

"Vince was upset to hear Angie had no interest in Louis. When she told Vince she loved you and planned to live with you, he *freaked!* I don't know how you smoothed things over, but I worried you'd see an early grave." She raised her brows, leaving me to wonder if she was joking.

I suspected she wasn't.

"I suppose that worked out for Katie. She got to marry a soon-to-be senator and found a father for her unborn child," I managed to say, despite learning this shocking revelation. Angie never told me any of this. Her discretion had to be intentional. I probably would've been pissed anytime I saw Louis near her. Angie knew my jealous streak ran ten miles long.

Nancy shrugged, then sipped her coffee. "Personally, I think Louis was disappointed. Don't get me wrong, Katie was a lovely girl, but Louis wanted Angie." Her grin lit up the room as she spoke. "But yes, Vince found a good man, in his eyes, for his pregnant, single daughter."

Our food arrived. When the waitress left us, I subtly drilled Nancy for information from one ex-in-law of the Russo clan to another. "You know when you stopped showing up for Sunday dinners, no one talked about it. What happened?"

She stared at me at first, brushing the reddish curls from her face as she chewed on a small chunk of melon from her fruit cup. "Vince found a younger woman for his bed. I simply wasn't needed any longer."

I pretended to be surprised. "Really? He never brought a different woman around the house for us to meet. At least not while I was still welcome there." I snickered.

"She was a girl from Reno who stayed at his cabin up there."

"Cabin? I never knew Vince had a place in Reno. Angie never mentioned it."

"Angie wouldn't have gone there. It was used for special meetings near his Reno club. He brought me there to keep his bed warm only. That's what I was around for." Her apprehension to continue seemed obvious by the way she instantly clammed up.

"I wanted to make amends with Angie, but he sent her away. He changed her name and had her relocated, so I wouldn't find her. Anything you say against Vince is safe with me."

"It's not that I don't trust you, Tommy. I kind of like breathing, ya know."

I canned the conversation about her relationship with Vince to drive down a different path. "Did you know I met Angie's mother, Betty?"

The fork toppled from Nancy's fingers. "I didn't think she was alive."

Of course, I never actually met Betty. Nancy didn't need to know that Betty hung herself the day Angie planned to introduce us, or at least the incident was ruled as a suicide.

"Betty claimed Frank shot her up with heroin—a ploy to control her in their marriage. Angie had difficulty believing her mother's tale, but I heard stories about the Madman. Her mother was on medication and way out there in outer space, mentally, but I believed her."

"I knew Frank rather well." She displayed an awkward gleam in her eye as a smirk twinkled across her face.

My mind burst into overdrive, wondering how well she knew Frank. Were they intimate?

"Could Frank be capable of such a heinous act? Absolutely!" Anger emitted when she spoke. "Frank's temper was worse than Vince's, yet he could fool a lot of people with his charm. Vince acted like the sweetest man too. But if anyone crossed him or left him… well, like I said, I like breathing. I wanted to leave Vince for months. There was no leaving him. *He* had to be done with *me*. When I finally overstayed my welcome, he had my bags packed, called me a cab, and told me to get out. He expected me to grovel. I wanted to dance and do cartwheels! I had nowhere to go, but I was free and escaped unscathed. That's all I wanted."

"Between us, who do you think killed Frank? I know he had a beef with a rival family."

She paused, spooned the last morsel of cottage cheese into her mouth, then wiped her lips gently with a napkin, leaving a pink lipstick stain. "Frank started plenty of problems, and he had a lot of enemies, Tommy. He was such a hothead! His temper intensified after his daughter died. When Connie's body was found, dirty and broken with a needle in her arm, he turned into a soulless monster. Frank wanted blood. He started whacking the dealers selling drugs to Connie and anyone associated with them. Vince couldn't control him. Frank was bloodthirsty for revenge, and it got him killed."

"I used to do business with members connected to another family. I had a feeling they took Frank out."

She released a brief laugh and shook her head. "Frank's hit was much closer to home than you realize, Tommy."

My eyes locked with hers, hoping for mental telepathy to kick in, so I could read her mind—the thoughts she wasn't verbalizing. "Close to home? Are you saying Vince had his own brother knocked off?" I whispered so quietly, I wasn't sure she heard me.

"I'm not confirming anything," she said quietly, then peered over her shoulder, assuring no one else was nearby. "When Frank started that drug war, a number of casualties got caught in the cross fire. His actions attracted police attention to the family business. Someone had to put a stop to his madness, or the rest of the Russo family would suffer."

She daintily took a final sip of her coffee then picked up her purse. "Thanks for the snack, Tommy. It was nice seeing you again. And if you like breathing as much as I do, you won't tell anyone about our reconnecting tonight." She stood from the booth, gently tapped my shoulder with a serious expression on her face, and sauntered off.

I sat alone at the table, devouring the outrageous details I learned.

CHAPTER 67

"Do you love me, Tommy?" Hillary asked while her warm, toned body lay beside me in bed one cool January morning in 1998.

The sun began to rise, blinding my gray eyes momentarily. I hadn't had my first cup of coffee to engage in this in-depth discussion. "What? Well—" I was unable to respond. That question came out of nowhere, catching me completely off guard.

"That's what I thought." She flipped the ivory-colored sheet off her body and onto me before catapulting from the bed in search of her clothes scattered across the bedroom floor.

"Where is this coming from?" I wondered if she had some type of bad dream because we enjoyed a nice dinner, and we were never boring between the sheets.

"We've been seeing each other exclusively for a while now. At least I think it's exclusive." Her tone sounded suspicious.

I nodded as I stood from the bed, watching her scramble about the bedroom for her skirt. "I'm not seeing anyone else, Hil. We talked about that. But we never talked about *love*."

"Love isn't something you talk about, Tommy. It's what you feel. It's what's in your heart. I want a husband and a family someday. My biological clock is ticking."

I let out a breath and scratched my head. Danny began prepping for college. Having another child at this time in my life wasn't something I itched for. Not that I'd rule it out. I felt a bit mature to start all over again, having another baby in my fifties. Maybe ten years ago, I'd be more inclined. I had to be honest with Hillary.

And boy, was she honest with me. An old boyfriend wanted her back.

I enjoyed my relationship with Hillary and cared about her very much. I didn't want her to ride off into the sunset on a white stallion with another man, but I couldn't say the words she longed to hear. And kids? If she wanted children, I wasn't her guy.

I experienced the magical feeling of love only once in my life with Angie. And then there was my marriage to a woman I didn't love. Love and a real marriage didn't seem to be in the cards for me.

Hillary walked out of my door that day, and I never heard from her again.

Her wedding was announced in the *Chronicle* about six months later. I wished her a nice life, and I hoped she'd get everything she longed for from her husband, including children.

CHAPTER 68

Danny invited his new girlfriend to my house for dinner and an introduction. The only time I ever met girls my son liked was before he learned to drive. He had several girlfriends in high school. I'd pick them up and take them to school sporting events, dances, and movies—the types of activities kids typically enjoyed. He hadn't introduced me to girls he met in college until Bianca Warner in 2002.

Bianca had been working toward a degree in education—a pretty young woman with red hair, freckles across the bridge of her nose, and large round blue eyes. Irish looks that reminded me of my grandmother, Maureen McGee.

As I watched these two young kids interact, my mind wandered, thinking I should plan another excursion to Ireland with Danny. It had been a while since I'd taken him with me to view the patchwork of the rolling terrain. I'd been contemplating another Ireland hotel location to explore. Somewhere near the spirited streets of Killarney lined with exuberant pubs, shops, and street performers. Dublin was rich in history with attractions like St. Patrick's Cathedral and Dublin Castle. The energetic Temple Bar district near the River Liffey was another prime location to consider.

Danny pursued a business degree, but he had an interest in law. Hank, Sadie's boyfriend, endured a lifelong career with Metro. I wondered if he influenced Danny somehow, but Danny didn't plan to join the police academy.

I assured my son had the luxury of making his own life choices. Danny understood the hotel business, observing me throughout his entire life. We discussed the stress, long hours, and commitment, as well as overall pride.

His mother whispered in his ear about the financial benefits. I built an empire, based on my father's visions, with one son who'd inherit everything when I retired or died. His interests were half-hearted, and I wouldn't push my lifestyle onto my son.

I grilled marinated sirloin tips and corn on the cob for dinner, serving the savory meal with potato salad my housekeeper, Terri, made for us. Terri emigrated from Vietnam. I helped her legally bring her family members into the US, and for that, she respected my privacy. She was a decent cook and enjoyed Danny's visits. She loved taking care of my house and me, and I paid her exceptionally well for her efforts and discretion.

My son behaved like a perfect gentleman. He looked at this girl with such devotion. I knew he had it bad. I recognized the signs. This wasn't some fly-by-night romance. Danny loved Bianca.

He spent a lot of time with this lovely young lady. He asked me if he could rent an apartment off-campus with her. I didn't say no to the idea, but I reminded him that he had to study and do well in school.

I reverted momentarily to my partying college days. Fortunately, Danny acted more mature and responsible than I was at his age.

Sadie disagreed and contacted me the moment she heard their plan.

My eyes rolled as her name flashed across my cell. "Hello."

"Tommy, you agreed to finance an apartment so Danny and Bianca could live together? He needs to focus on his education, not play house! This is something you should have discussed with me first." She continued to ramble, but I pulled the phone from my ear as her shrilling voice forced the hair on the back of my neck to stand erect.

I interrupted her, saying, "Danny never gave us a reason not to trust him. He needs some independence."

"Independence? When *you're* funding this venture?" she shouted.

"You need to loosen the strings, Sadie. He's an adult. Let him find his way. I made a deal with him. If his grades drop, he's back in the dorm."

I learned through the years to speak calmly to Sadie. Raising my voice only added fuel to her anger. Once I rationalized my plan, she caved.

The next summer, when the kids finished school and Danny made the dean's list, I treated him and Bianca to a week along the French Riviera, the area Danny wanted to explore years ago. Since he had a love interest, I wanted him to visit the beautifully romantic scene suited for lovers.

Danny had grown accustomed to my generosity.

Bianca's widened blue eyes displayed shock. Then she kissed my cheek and gave me a warm bear hug, grateful for my thoughtfulness.

They enjoyed their incredible trip, seeing the wondrous sites of Nice, Monaco, and Monte Carlo.

"Sweet Emotion"

CHAPTER 69

The Nevada heat never deterred tourists from visiting Vegas. The hotel was fully air-conditioned, and the casino kept cool to accommodate the numerous people packed in with hopes and dreams of winning big. For some, that hope kept people going—praying to win a fortune to improve their lives or increase their wallets to lighten financial burdens. Others got carried away by the thrill of the casino, risking financial ruin or relationships for one more lucky instinct.

As the owner, I wouldn't want my guests to wander off to another casino or show in town. We offered numerous exciting options for guests to experience and spend their money without leaving the premises.

During the summer months, I hired additional barmaids to keep the drinks flowing, so the gamblers kept gambling, especially the high rollers, also known as *whales*. Those elite, wealthy guests dropped hundreds of thousands of dollars a night at the tables. My casino hosts ensured the whales spent their money at *my* casino, without the desire to visit Mandalay Bay or the Venetian, comping rooms, meals, tickets to shows—whatever made them happy to continue gambling on the premises.

The Montgomery expanded with renovations, adding a shopping section and a full food court, offering our guests various selections to tempt their palettes. As a restaurant entrepreneur, Jack produced multiple ideas with the help of Rob's keen insight.

Rob decided to add several fine-dining options to please our guests. Rob married an Italian chef named Lucia, who recruited other top-notch chefs to build sophisticated menus for our Italian, French, and Spanish restaurants. Tourists staying at other hotels made reservations to taste the variety of delicacies on the menu. For people on a budget, Scooters, a buffet, and our café offered meals at a lower cost.

The competition among the hotels on the Strip remained wicked and kept me on my toes. Without innovative thinking in every aspect, from food to entertainment to hotel amenities and the casino, the risk of failure was imminent.

I stopped for my daily afternoon caffeine jolt with a high-octane brew at the café. My attention instantly diverted to a woman with long dark hair, wearing a deep-red dress that showed off shapely legs. My eyes wavered to her sexy hips. From the back, those long raven locks reminded me of Angie, who still popped into my brain once in a while.

My curious thoughts and bewildered feelings carried me toward the woman several paces in front of me, moving fairly quickly. I wanted to see her face, but the crowd swelled, blocking me. I carefully pushed my way through a rowdy bunch until I practically stumbled on top of her. "Oh! Excuse me."

She turned reluctantly, straight-faced. A beautiful woman with a similar silhouette and long dark hair, but she wasn't Angie.

"I don't think I've ever seen someone look so *disappointed* to meet me before," she said. When she smiled, these adorable dimples formed, lightening the moment.

"I'm sorry, I thought you were someone else." Mesmerized by her dark almond-shaped eyes, I was. I noticed a small round beauty mark set below her incredible dimple on the right.

"She must be a lucky woman," she said with a tilt of her head, practically flirtatious.

"Who?"

"Whoever you *hoped* to see." Her eyes gave my body a once-over before sashaying away, taunting me with the sway of her luscious hips.

I stood breathless, watching the lovely woman in the crimson dress vanish through a mass of casino guests.

CHAPTER 70

A meeting with department heads was scheduled to review budgets and the semiannual report in the small conference room on the ninth floor in the Scotland wing. The year 2005 demonstrated significant financial growth to date.

Phyllis Santore, my latest assistant, stepped off the elevator with me as we strolled to the meeting room.

Since Mrs. Arden retired in the eighties, I had trouble keeping a decent assistant. Mrs. Arden's talents were tough to beat. Even at her older age, she proved to be a dedicated employee, sharp as a tack, and eager to learn about the computers I introduced back when they were considered a luxury to own.

Phyllis emitted youthful, bright energy, but anyone under forty seemed young to me. She acquired a solid knowledge of technology and computer programs. She kept me on my toes and tried to convince me to purchase the newest software and cell phones.

"Oh my God! It's her!" Phyllis radiated with elation, yet her voice was but a whisper.

"Who, Phyllis?" I asked, looking in the direction of her gaze.

"That woman at the end of the hall. That's her hotel room! She must be staying here under an alias." Phyllis beamed, wiping her puffy white-blond bangs from her brown eyes.

As I peeked down the long hallway in the direction Phyllis pointed, I realized she was speaking about the same gorgeous woman I thought was Angie. "Who is she? How do you know her?" I asked with sudden curiosity.

"That's Victoria Ursini!"

My face must have given away my cluelessness.

"Victoria Ursini, the actress." She rolled her eyes, annoyed by my sheer ignorance.

"Never heard of her." My ears clung to Phyllis's narration while my eyes absorbed the lovely lady searching for her key card in her purse.

"I read she was filming a new TV series here in Vegas. When I heard she'd be in town, her name wasn't listed with reservations. But she *is* staying here at the Montgomery!"

Victoria Ursini located her key to access her room. I watched her figure move through the door until I heard the loud thump of it closing.

"Phyllis, slow down. If she's staying here under an alias, then we have an obligation to protect her privacy. I see you're a fan, but you can't tell anyone."

"But—"

I interrupted her. "When I hired you, I advised discretion was key around here. If she realizes people know where she's staying, she could check out and go to another hotel."

"Do you think I can take a picture with her?"

I pondered a host of concepts. Who was this beautiful actress? "Let me see what I can do, but please keep this quiet."

She released a disappointing huff and folded her arms like a frustrated teenager.

My interest overflowed. "Tell me, what's she been in?"

Excitement conveyed across Phyllis's round face. Suddenly, her features glowed, oozing euphoria through every syllable. "Well, my favorite movie is *The Rings of Saturn*, but *Martians on Earth* is a close second."

"I had no idea you were a science-fiction fan, Phyllis."

"Oh, I love sci-fi! You need to watch her movies. She's as talented as she is lovely."

I had watched the original *Star Trek* and the *Star Wars* trilogy back in the day. That was the extent of my science-fiction habit. Suddenly, I craved watching an eerie, scientific plot.

CHAPTER 71

VICTORIA URSINI

Whenever high-profile guests dwelled at the Montgomery, my staff ensured their needs were fulfilled. That included privacy. Rock stars, actors, athletes, and politicians expected discretion, so added security would be in place to handle crowd control. Certain floors in the hotel couldn't be accessed without a particular key card, keeping celebrities contained to specific areas where they wouldn't be hassled by fans.

The reservation for room 918 was under the name Karen Jones. Ms. Ursini expected her identity to remain concealed. As the hotel owner, I learned her business manager arranged with my guest services manager to keep her name classified. I found it somewhat humorous because, typically, people with a large fan base hide out, using a nom de plume. I hadn't heard of her. Perhaps I was out of touch with the *who's who* in show business.

We were transforming the ninth floor in the Scotland wing into a technology center for our guests traveling on business to access state-of-the-art technology or hold business meetings. Several guest rooms were still available on this floor, but those suites would become meeting rooms in several months. If Ms. Ursini requested seclusion, this would be a reasonable floor to maintain privacy but not as isolated as the secured suites.

I requested our staff create an extravagant basket with high-end body lotion, hair supplies, chocolates, a bottle of champagne, and a key card for use in our VIP casino for private gambling. Added to the welcome wagon was a generously sized bouquet to brighten her room.

The cart overflowed with freebies, items I wanted to personally deliver to apologize for the confusion when I first met her. Maybe she thought I was a weird, geek fan of her sci-fi movies. Maybe I wanted to make her smile so I could catch a glimpse of those dimples.

I knocked hard on the outer door of room 918.

"One minute!" she hollered from the other side.

My head and body were practically hidden behind the cart carrying the luxurious treats. As I heard her footsteps approach the door, my fingers smoothed my hair to ensure each dark strand was in place. The sound of the heavy door slid open. I heard her gasp at the sight.

"Hello." I popped my head out from behind the flower arrangement, startling her.

It took her a moment to recognize me. "Oh, the man I *deeply* disappointed." Her smile exposed those delightful dimples.

I knew she was teasing me and returned the infamous smirk I had been known for. "No, it's not like that, and I wasn't disappointed. I'm Tommy Cavallo." I held my hand out.

She accepted my hand then stared at the basket, bursting with fragrant comforts. "Well, this is quite a gesture, Tommy. Why would you go through all this trouble?"

"This basket is to thank you for your business, Ms. Jones, or should I say, Ms. Ursini?" I whispered to conceal her identity to anyone within earshot. "I own the Montgomery."

Her head bobbed slowly, realizing I had made her, or maybe she was surprised I owned the hotel.

"I hope I'm not intruding on your privacy."

"Intrude? With such a lovely gift?" Her smile grew. "It's no intrusion, but why would the owner of this spectacular hotel deliver such a beautiful package personally?"

"I want my high-profile guests to know I appreciate their business. You could've selected another hotel on the Strip."

She held the door open, welcoming me and my cart into her room.

"You know, Ms. Jones…or should I call you Ms. Ursini?"

"Please, call me Vicki," she said, blushing.

"Vicki." I nodded and felt a large grin sprout upon my face. "I reviewed your registration. You've been with us a while. I can upgrade you to one of the suites on the top floor. The view of the Strip is remarkable at night. The floor upstairs is more secure for celebrities who require extra security."

She smirked as she shrugged, seemingly disinterested in my offer to upgrade her. "So you've heard of me? Seen some of my work?" She was flirting with me now, with those dimples highlighting a breath-taking smile, taunting me. Her hands seductively caressed the vase with the flowers while her beautiful brown eyes admired the red roses, white lilies, and pale pink alstroemeria.

I nodded, saying, "I've heard of you."

"Really? Which of my movies have you seen?"

"I'm not too good with names. Something about Saturn?" I tried to remember the names Phyllis rattled off to me.

"*The Rings of Saturn*, you mean?"

"Yeah, that's it!"

She giggled.

"Why are you laughing?"

"You don't look like one of my sci-fi fans."

"Who do I look like?" I stepped near her, seeing how close she'd allow me to get. She took a couple of paces backward, acknowledging I'd come close enough without actually saying the words. I respected her personal space and cemented my position. But I wanted to get closer.

She sized me up with those dark eyes. "Armani suit, so you've got class. Sharp haircut. Very stylish. Confidence blended with slight charisma." She paused and tapped her finger against her lower lip painted with cherry lip gloss. "I've got it! Alex Trebek."

"A game show host?"

"*Jeopardy* is an intellectually riveting show."

"*Slight* charisma? I must be doing something wrong."

A burst of laughter released. "I'm kidding. Thank you for this nice surprise, Tommy. You shouldn't have gone to the trouble."

"You're welcome. Are you sure you don't want to be moved to a suite?"

"This floor is rather quiet, but maybe next time."

"Well, it's nice to know you'll stay with us again."

"This hotel is amazing! Halle Berry recommended it to me. I have a few more weeks left in town."

Since the conversation flourished, I went for it. "Would you like to have dinner with me? I mean, if you'd be interested in dining with a man with *slight* charisma who'll make you answer questions in the form of a question."

She laughed. She had a great, bubbly kind of laugh. After a pause that lasted at least five seconds, she added casually, "Dinner is doable," and displayed those playful dimples.

CHAPTER 72

I barely knew this woman, but my desire to learn about her grew. Before our dinner date, I searched for Vicki's movies in the few spare moments I had. They weren't premium movies, judging by the lighting and quality of the script. Vicki's leading role seemed to require a loud, menacing scream. She had quite a set of lungs on her, and her scream was pretty intense too. Her acting skills were good, but she was no Meryl Streep.

Phyllis looked ecstatic when she learned I met Vicki and expected to check in on her again. That was the hospitality industry, after all. I didn't tell her I arranged a dinner date with Vicki. She'd drive me crazy, asking a million questions about the date and begging me for a photo op. Obtaining an autograph would be a warm gesture to reward Phyllis for her hard work.

I wore a slick, gray suit with a pale-blue Dolce & Gabbana shirt. Reservations were made at a steak house off the Strip. Considering she might desire privacy from fans or the media, this trendy restaurant resided off the beaten path. We could enter through the back door without being spotted. Then again, apart from using an alias at the hotel, she didn't request security or a suite on a private, more secure floor like other celebrities. Her movies were entertaining but not Oscar-worthy to warrant a swarm of fans circling her.

Feeling a tad anxious, I swept my fingers through my brown hair with frays of silver blended in before knocking on room 918.

She opened the door wearing a black silk jumper, slightly more casual than my attire, but the style illustrated a combination of class and fun. Vicki looked much younger than me. Maybe early fifties at best. It was hard to embrace my age at sixty-two. Many people would retire at this age, although I wasn't like most people, bursting with a bundle of energy to sit still for very long. Retirement seemed to be miles away.

A kiss on the cheek was left beside her dimple when I entered her room. "I made reservations at—"

"Oh. Reservations?"

"It's best to have reservations in Vegas," I replied with a brief chuckle.

"Your room service menu is pretty impressive. That is, if you don't mind."

A feeling of uncertainty loomed. She preferred eating in her hotel room. An internal instinct screamed that something was off, but I shut down my intuition. "Okay. Is there a reason you don't want to eat out? Are you afraid of a little publicity?"

"It's best to keep my private life private."

I smirked. "Oh, so I'm part of your *private* life now?"

Those dimples displayed prominently with her spectacular smile. "You're the one who called this a dinner *date*. And yes, a date should be private without any interruptions or chaos."

"Hmm, an actress without the need for drama."

She giggled.

"Actually, I have a much better idea." Frankly, I liked to show off in front of a woman I took an interest in. I made a call to the new steak house, Prime, that my partners recently opened on-site. They hired a first-rate chef with a succulent menu that would make Bobby Flay drool. Normally, this place didn't deliver, but I had connections.

Vicki said she didn't eat meat, so she selected the shrimp scampi dish off the menu. I was in the mood for the porterhouse. She preferred white wine to red. They added a bottle of Pinot Grigio and two slices of New York cheesecake with strawberries for dessert. My card was accepted, but it would take an hour or better before dinner would arrive.

There we stood in her small room, a couple of feet from her bed, waiting patiently for our meal, and making small talk.

Her eyes focused on the replica of a Claude Monet painting on the wall in her room. "Not a bad Monet copy. I love impressionism."

"Do you know this piece?" I asked.

"Yes, *Water Lilies*. One of his many adaptations of the pond outside his home in France." She smiled widely as she spoke passionately about impressionist art.

"I like Monet's work. Have you been to his house in Giverny?" I asked, contributing my personal experience to the conversation.

"Not yet, but I imagine it's lovely to witness in person."

"A beautiful place with colorful gardens, a serene lake, and the Japanese bridge he often resurrects in his work. Such a tranquil area to relax and become mesmerized by the numerous paths and archways smothered by hundreds of flowers, plants, and vines. I went there with…an old friend of mine many years ago." Suddenly, Angie cluttered my thoughts. I hated to bring memories of Angie on dates.

"C'est magnifique. Maybe someday I'll get there." She moved to the mini-fridge, removing the bottle of champagne I provided in her welcome package. She held the bottle up to my eye level, suggesting we open it.

"I don't drink anymore, but I'd be happy to open this for you." I attempted to grab the bottle from her delicate grasp.

She stopped me from taking the bottle and stepped backward. "Oh, I'm sorry." Her eyes squinted, seemingly uncomfortable.

Maybe I overshared prematurely by adding, "I stopped drinking years ago. Alcohol and I don't mix. I can't stop at one glass or a shot of anything."

She placed the bottle down without saying a word.

"Don't let me stop you."

"I'll wait for the wine you ordered with dinner."

My eyes wandered to a framed photo on the nightstand. As I approached, the picture of Elvis Presley made me smile. "You're a fan? Did you ever meet him?"

She giggled like a schoolgirl. "Meet him? I wish! I *love* him. Oh, how I cried when he went into hiding."

My head shook, confused. "Hiding? Honey, he died in seventy-seven, nearly thirty years ago."

She rolled her eyes. You and all the naysayers can believe what you want, but I don't believe he's dead. People who live in the limelight as he did need a break sometimes."

"A few decades is a long break, even for someone as famous as Elvis." I couldn't help but tease her. She was positively adorable, swooning over the star she admired.

"Didn't you hear the Mafia was after him? My mother and I wonder if he's in the witness protection program, hiding out in some suburban neighborhood in Idaho."

We both laughed.

"Elvis performed right here in my hotel back in the late sixties."

"No way!" she shrieked.

"Yeah, I spent a few minutes with him too. He was an unbelievable performer and amazingly kind and cordial to the staff, seeing he was the king of rock 'n' roll. But he's gone and at peace. Elvis Presley couldn't stay in hiding without someone spotting him, Vicki."

She moved her petite body before me, smiling. "You can make fun of me all you want, but when he comes out of hiding, I'll be sure to tell you, *I told you so!*"

"Come here." My arms gently nudged her shoulders as I brought her in for a deep, lingering kiss. Something I wanted to do since the first time I laid eyes on her in the casino.

She responded with fierce impatience, parting her lips, allowing our tongues to dance.

I pulled away, despite that familiar twitch between my legs. Dinner hadn't arrived, yet we rushed to dessert.

She kept me tight in her grasp as her sparkling brown eyes raised to meet mine. "Maybe we'll work up an appetite by the time the food arrives," she said.

And with that cue from her, I took hold of her slight frame, lifted her off her feet, and carried her a few paces forward, diving into the king-size bed.

Her cell buzzed. Thankfully she ignored it. When I realized she wasn't going to answer it, I flung the device off the nightstand across the room. This wasn't the time for any distractions.

CHAPTER 73

Vicki laid peacefully in my arms, stroking her fingers through a few hairs on my chest. A vision of beauty, seemingly deep in thought. Quiet. Satisfied.

A knock was heard at the door. I hated to move, feeling comfortable. I scooted her off to the side of me, stood from the bed, and grabbed my pants from the floor to greet the delivery boy, who barely looked sixteen.

I took the packages from his arms and asked him to wait at the door while I searched through my wallet for a tip. I had nothing less than a twenty, so a twenty was what he got.

He beamed with glee as I closed the door.

"You were right. I think we worked up an appetite, don't you?" I teased as she stood from the bed and inched her way toward the sofa to sit beside me. I loved that she didn't put on a stitch of clothing while I arranged our takeout containers and plastic silverware on the glass coffee table.

I poured her a glass of Pinot and grabbed a bottled water from the minibar for myself.

Her behavior gradually shifted to a serene, quiet nature, so I rambled about Danny and some of our overseas adventures. I asked her if she had any children, to which she quietly responded no.

Her silence was killing me. "You're suddenly very quiet."

She smiled, teasing, "You wore me out." Then she gently kissed my lips.

My senses heightened with wonder. Victoria Ursini, a mysterious enchantress I wanted to decipher. Most people liked to talk about themselves. Since my business focused on hospitality and sales, I learned over the years how to interact with people to discover more about them. I recently spent some time watching Vicki's movies, so I pummeled her with questions about her career. Questions like how she started in show business and her first big break.

She opened up, telling me about a friend who helped launch her acting career, and I recognized her from one of her first TV commercials for Tide.

I nearly forgot to ask for an autographed picture. She said she'd be delighted to sign a photo for Phyllis and suggested I introduce her to one of her biggest fans before she left town.

Around midnight, I began to collect my clothing tossed about the room.

"Where are you going?" she asked with those delicious dimples flirting with me.

"It's getting late. I'm sure you need to sleep."

"Can you stay the night?" She positioned her gorgeous figure on the bed, offering a generous view of her full breasts and fiery sweet spot.

Her playful invitation coaxed me to drop my clothes to the floor and join her.

CHAPTER 74

A couple of weeks passed since my night with Vicki. She had a busy schedule to keep, filming in town for her pilot series, *Rising 51*. She told me she needed this TV show to be successful in increasing her fan base, but the emotions behind her words sounded less than convincing.

Her movies were meant for TV, not the big screen. She secured fans like Phyllis, but she hadn't encountered a mass of sci-fi fanatics to warrant constant security.

Our paths hadn't crossed since our brief interlude—an evening I couldn't forget.

An unfortunate incident occurred at the New York hotel. A bomb threat. I flew into the city to ensure the hotel security measures were aboveboard and that my staff and guests were okay. It proved to be an intense business trip, to say the least. The event was benign, but the situation gave my team quite a scare.

Nothing had been the same in New York or anywhere in the world after the September 11 terror attack. Many of my New York staff lost family members and friends. We tapped into our employee assistance program resources, offering to counsel all associates who'd benefit from the service. The use of this program quadrupled after that terrifying tragedy.

That traumatic incident became stapled into the hearts and souls of all Americans, to be etched with blood in schoolbooks. Any threat since September 11 was taken seriously by law enforcement and, in many cases, considered an act of terrorism.

Despite my busy schedule and the menacing situation I handled in New York, an attempt was made to call Vicki, but she didn't respond. I wasn't the kind of guy who gave up easily.

She typically ordered room service late at night, which meant she worked long days on the set.

The manager of room service happily notified me when she ordered dinner for one in her room. I hoped she intended to stay in for the night—a night in which I had no immediate plans.

I dialed a number that cost me a small fortune before knocking on her door.

She greeted me with those dimples, indicating my dropping by unexpectedly was welcome. "Hi. Sorry I didn't return your call. My schedule is insane. I've been reviewing a contract," she explained, confirming she had a busy, job-related evening planned.

I stood in the doorjamb with no expectations of entering. "I understand. I just had to stop by and tell you something in person."

She nodded, waiting for me to continue.

"You were right. Absolutely right."

"Wait a minute. Have we known each other long enough for you to admit I'm *always* right?" she teased.

"Uh…yeah, I believe so."

"So what was I absolutely right about?"

My arm stretched around the corner of the doorway, signaling a tall man with black hair and long sideburns, wearing a high-collared white polyester jumpsuit, loaded with bright-colored beads and fringe along the arms of his outfit.

She screamed with excitement when he displayed his famous lip snarl and hip shake. She screeched loud enough like she was performing in one of her movies. But a happy squeal, not a wild, terrified scream like in her film, *Robots from Space.*

"Elvis *is* alive, and he came out of hiding to meet you!"

The best Elvis impersonator on the Strip went into his rendition of "Suspicious Minds," followed by "Viva Las Vegas," "All Shook Up," and "Don't Be Cruel," upon Vicki's request.

Spectators opened their doors to hear his performance, clapping, dancing in the hall, and yelling out song suggestions like "Return to

Sender" and "Jailhouse Rock." Quite a party ignited in the hallway on floor nine.

How I loved seeing Vicki's eyes sparkle with the biggest smile, accentuating the lovely beauty mark set in the crease of her dimple.

I slipped Elvis an extra C-note for the spur-of-the-moment performance before he left to jump on stage in front of a larger live audience than this hall.

Some of the guests gathered together, laughing about the impromptu show, while others returned to their rooms.

"That was amazing! I can't believe you brought me Elvis. Thank you, Tommy. Why would you do that?"

"Maybe I like seeing those dimples." I brushed a few strands of hair from her face to catch a better glimpse of those delightful indentations.

She blushed then kissed me softly on the lips, tugging my willing body inside her room.

We couldn't stop our desire to rip off our clothes and make our way to the bed.

CHAPTER 75

When morning came, I sat up in bed watching Vicki sleep soundly. A few little snores escaped as she began to wake ever so slowly.

I needed to start my day and head to my suite to change. I kept a couple of suits at the hotel if I crashed overnight. My home wasn't far from the Strip, but hotel operations never slept. Sometimes, neither did I.

"Good morning," she mumbled before resting her delicate arm across my waist beneath the white sheets. "What time is it?"

"About six fifteen."

Her eyes remained closed, but a smile formed as I played with the dark, wispy bangs across her forehead. "I have an hour or so before I should get up."

"A whole hour, huh? That gives me plenty of time." My hands wandered around her body, exploring every velvety inch with my fingers until the chime of her cell rang, interrupting the magic moment.

She jumped to answer it, leaving me hanging and in overdrive.

I waited patiently for her to finish her robotic-sounding conversation. She made excuses to the person on the other end of the phone, speaking cryptically. I sat silently, trying not to eavesdrop, but in this small space, there was no place for me to go where I wouldn't hear her side of the discussion.

As she spoke, she began to toss her shirt over her head. A clue that screamed it was time for me to leave.

I stood from the bed and staggered to the bathroom while she finished her call. When I returned, Vicki sat quietly on the sofa. I picked up my clothing from the floor and started to dress. "Is everything okay?"

She didn't flinch at my question, staring at an empty wall.

"Vicki?"

She jumped. "I'm sorry, what?"

"What's wrong? You were fine until you got that call."

She didn't respond.

"I guess I'm overstepping and overstaying my welcome." I slipped on my socks and shoes.

"Wait. It's not you. I'm sorry. Honestly, I had a great time last night." She attempted to smile with a touch of sadness casting from eyes that resembled drops of chocolate.

"You know, you can talk to me."

"You're such a nice guy, Tommy."

"Something upset you."

She shook her head. "I'm headed home today."

I nodded, concealing my disappointment. "Oh? Where's home, Vicki?"

"Fernley."

"That's not too far. Maybe I'll surprise you sometime."

"No!" She sprang from the sofa.

"What's going on? One minute you act like you want to see me, but I can't visit you?"

"This *thing* between us can't continue."

I was disheartened to hear her say that but annoyed with this push and pull game she played. "Have a safe trip to Fernley." I turned my back on her and headed toward the door.

"Tommy."

I stopped dead in my tracks when she called out to me.

"I'm...married."

My body swung around furiously. "You're what?"

Her movements were jittery, rocking from side to side. "I'm sorry, I didn't tell you. After that first night we spent together, I didn't expect to hear from you. Then again last night—and Elvis."

At that moment, I understood how Angie felt for many years. I became the "other man." However, I told Angie I was married before

I ever kissed her. I didn't take her to bed without telling her I had been in an unstable marriage, seeking a divorce. Was I a hypocrite for feeling really pissed off?

"I don't blame you for being angry. And I'm sorry if I gave you the impression that this would be anything more than a couple of really nice nights together."

"Forget it. I already have." Anger fueled my movements to storm out of her room. But the cold, hard truth was, I couldn't get that woman out of my head.

CHAPTER 76

Later that morning, Phyllis and I reviewed the edits needed for a report she generated each month. The autographed oak-framed photo of Vicki I gave her sat at the corner of her walnut desk. I couldn't help but glance at those dimples in the picture throughout my conversation with Phyllis, still ticked off that Vicki had strings.

My back faced the entrance of the office when Phyllis suddenly showed a blank expression while I spoke. She stopped listening to a word I said about updating a calculation in a field of her Excel spreadsheet.

I turned to see what stole her attention from me and noticed Vicki standing before us, wearing a scarf around her head and a pair of Coach sunglasses as if incognito.

"Ms. Ursini, this is s-s-such a p-p-pleasure," Phyllis stuttered, then jumped to her feet.

Vicki approached and shook Phyllis's hand, but her eyes were set on me. "You must be Phyllis. Tommy says you're my biggest fan."

"Yes! I loved *The Rings of Saturn* best, but I've seen all your movies! I can't believe you're standing here in my office. Well, his office." Phyllis pointed her thumb at me as she rambled, acting like a two-year-old being introduced to ice cream.

"How about a picture?" I suggested.

Phyllis yearned for a photo op. She scrambled through her purse and pulled out her cell.

I grabbed it from her, worried her trembling fingers would drop it.

Vicki removed her sunglasses and stood close to Phyllis, placing an arm around her shoulder. No trace of a wedding band as I glanced at her left hand. I would've caught that had she worn one.

"Say cheese!" I snapped a few shots of the two of them together, making my assistant extremely happy.

"Thank you so much, Ms. Ursini."

"Please, Phyllis, call me Vicki. I appreciate you keeping my staying here a secret."

Phyllis glanced at me with an anxious smile, absently releasing a hearty giggle. She realized the importance of her discretion. The reward for her silence was more than she had hoped.

Vicki's bedroom eyes gazed in my direction, tilting her head in that sexy way she mastered. "May I speak with you in your office?"

What did she want to say here that she couldn't express in her room earlier? I opened my office door for her to enter before I followed, closing the door behind me, elevating Phyllis's curiosity. I flipped the blinds closed so Phyllis couldn't peek inside as we spoke. That must have made her insane!

"I'm sorry, Tommy. I wasn't sure how to tell you or if I should say anything about my personal life."

"Your *personal* life? You mean the fact that you have a *husband?*"

"I keep my personal life quiet and separate from my career. My husband is a powerful man. He can't find out what happened between us."

It occurred to me why she wouldn't go out in public with me to have dinner. She ordered room service instead of potentially being caught on the arm of another man. My gut screamed that something wasn't right that first night, but I ignored those ear-piercing sirens.

"We wrapped up filming in Vegas early. My husband caught wind of that and expects me home."

I merely nodded. "Well, he's your husband. I suppose you should go."

Her head cocked to the side. A bit of awkwardness displayed through melancholic eyes. She allowed me a final look at those gorgeous dimples before leaving my office, my hotel, and my town.

CHAPTER 77

Danny turned twenty-five on March 19, 2006. He succeeded in a robust education in the law field, which made me proud. He went to school for exactly what he wanted to do with his life without any pressure. Law school kept him busy, but we talked and saw each other often.

I met Danny and Bianca at his favorite eating establishment, Kimono's Japanese Hibachi. Danny ate healthily, and he exercised faithfully. We'd spar at the gym. Seeing I had a lot more years on him, he was quicker and pretty strong. He could wipe the floor with me if I let him. Thankfully, my body was still in good shape.

Bianca taught the second grade at a public elementary school in town. With a big heart and warm soul, she spoke with adoration about the children in her classroom.

Dinner was both entertaining and delicious. It astounded me the way the chefs tossed knives around, chopping up the meat and vegetables at a brisk beat without losing any fingers. I examined my dinner plate to ensure no blood or extremities were mixed in with the shrimp.

I could tell something appeared off with these two, who seemed quieter than normal. My instinctive fatherly radar screamed a warning siren as I studied Danny's face. "What's wrong?"

In response, Danny lowered his head and stared at the white rice in his dish. Bianca wiggled in her chair, making no eye contact.

I dropped my fork to the right of my plate. "Okay, you two. What's going on?"

No answer.

"Do I have to guess? Come on, Danny. What's up?"

His gray eyes wafted toward Bianca before responding, "We need to talk, Pop."

"I'm all ears."

The two kids glanced at each other, then Danny's fingers swept through his brown hair.

Bianca calmly placed her fork and knife into her plate of fried rice and chimed in, rescuing Danny from the uncomfortable moment. "I'm pregnant. The baby is due in October."

Sure, I was taken aback. At that instant, I didn't understand *their* thoughts about this event, seeing that it took more than an hour to bring it up. "Are you happy?" I asked.

"Yes," they responded simultaneously as their eyes finally connected with mine.

I examined both of their faces. Bianca's fair skin shimmered. Danny wore a smile.

"If you're both happy, I'm thrilled for you! Wow, you're making me a poppy, son. That's fantastic!" I let out an enthusiastic snicker.

"You're cool about this, Pop?" Danny asked, seeking confirmation of my reaction.

"All I want is for you to be happy. If you're happy, then I'm thrilled!"

Relief washed across Danny's face as his color returned.

"Why would you think otherwise?" I asked.

Bianca excused herself to use the ladies' room.

I waited for her to step away before launching a heart-to-heart talk with my son. "You can tell me anything, Dan. No judgments here."

"Mom doesn't know yet. I love Bianca, but I'm not ready for *marriage*, Pop."

"Does *she* want to get married?"

"She hasn't pushed. She knows how I feel about marriage."

"Son, look at me." I paused, waiting for his eyes to meet mine. "You love her, and you're having a baby together. You have to do right by them. But there's no law or societal demands to become legally bound. In your own time and when you're both ready. You're living together. That was a serious step."

"Not as serious as a baby, Pop."

"Believe me, I know. When your mother and I got married in the sixties, times were different. She couldn't have the baby without a husband." When that last sentence left my lips, I realized Danny never knew why Sadie and I initially married, and his face displayed his surprise.

"Mom was pregnant when you got married?"

I sucked in a deep breath, then let it out with vigor. "Yeah, but we weren't in love like you and Bianca. We were pressured into marriage. Then she had a miscarriage." I shrugged. Thinking about that loss still hurt. "I don't want the pressure of a fast, forced marriage for you and Bianca like your mother and I had. It's up to the two of you to decide when you're ready for marriage. Pay attention because she might want a wedding at some point. And if you still don't want that, you have to be honest."

"You and Mom were so angry at each other. I guess it makes sense now that I know why you got married."

Jesus, my failed marriage affected my son more than I realized. "Danny, your mother and I are *not* you and Bianca. I'm sorry we couldn't make it work for you. Please don't use me as some type of role model for marriage. I am no expert on relationships. Hell, I'm still single."

"Pop, I always knew you and Mom loved *me*. I never wanted for anything. I had both parents in my life. Marriage is a huge legal commitment, and we have so much going on right now. I am committed to Bianca and this baby. I just don't feel I need to be *married*."

Between his childhood, being raised by divorced parents, and the legal ramifications he learned at law school, my life and failed relationships acted as a cautionary tale, urging him to take things slowly.

When Bianca returned to the table, we ordered dessert and discussed baby names.

CHAPTER 78

Although golf wasn't my best sport, I was invited to play eighteen holes at the country club with Rob, Jack, and one of our whales in town from Colorado. Rather than admitting my failure as a golfer, I blamed my poor game on the extreme 107 degrees of heat and sunshine that spring day in 2006.

After a much-needed shower, I headed to the office to return calls and emails before the day escaped me.

Phyllis jumped up at the sight of my presence and dashed toward me. "You really need to check your phone more often," she stated, obviously irritated with me.

I patted my pockets in search of my Blackberry.

"That's right, you don't have it on you." She handed me my phone with an annoying eye roll.

"Sorry. Was there an emergency?"

"Not an emergency, per se. Someone's waiting for you in your office." She twisted her head in the direction of my office door. The blinds were partially closed, but I detected movement inside.

"Who is it?"

"Vicki Ursini. She's back in town!" Phyllis grabbed my arm and shoved me to take a few steps despite my resisting her pushes.

"What does she want?" Curious was an understatement to describe my feelings as Phyllis continued to nudge me toward my office with great force. Her upper body strength surprised me.

"I don't know. I asked, but she merely said she'd wait for you. Ask her yourself."

Why was she in my office? When she left town last year, I didn't expect her to return, although I thought about her once in a while. Our brief time together was too premature to classify ambiguous emotions as anything but lust. However, I contacted Larry to investigate Vicki and her marriage to satisfy my curiosity. Not a typical request I'd make regarding a woman I spent a couple of nights with.

Since the internet was born, Larry's tasks became easier to perform. I could look up general information myself, but Larry accessed records I couldn't find. I didn't have the luxury of free time to search for a marriage certificate of a woman I barely knew. Larry's prime detective skills continued to be a highly valuable resource. He found Vicki's marriage certificate to a man whose name was familiar, but I couldn't place him immediately—Jeffrey Atkins. Larry connected the dots for me. Jeffrey Atkins was the mayor of Fernley with high ambitions to run for the governor of Nevada.

I usually voted conservatively on Election Day.

After opening my office door, Vicki's silhouette appeared before a painting that hung on the beige wall opposite my desk.

I slammed the door hard behind me, gaining her attention rather abruptly.

She released a gasp then smiled when she saw me. Those dimples possessed me. "Great piece! Where do you get your copies?"

"I'd have to check with my facilities team. You know it?"

"Sure, *Venus and Adonis* by Peter Paul Rubens. The original hangs at the Met in New York. I love Greek mythology, don't you?"

I shrugged. "How do you know so much about this stuff?"

"I majored in art history. I could get lost in a museum for days, studying every detail of a piece."

Her knowledge of such culture sounded impressive. I wanted not to give a crap. I'd love to say I was busy, and she needed to leave. Deep down, that wasn't what I wanted. "I suggest you travel to France and Italy. Remarkable museums to explore." I paused, carefully pondering what else to say. "What brings you back?"

"*Rising 51* got picked up for another season. A lot of scenes are filmed here or in Death Valley National Park. We have minimal access to the border of Area 51 for filming."

Area 51, a government base rumored to house confidential information about government aircraft, UFOs, and alien life. I understood why officials might not want recording equipment filming the area, drawing in a circus of fans who'd attempt to cross the border, warranting arrests.

Watching Vicki's sci-fi series proved bittersweet. Seeing those dimples and sexy bedroom eyes on-screen piqued my desire for her. She played Lexi Thorpe, a seasoned CIA agent—older, wiser, tough as nails, and incredibly hot.

"Are you staying in town long?"

"Several months. I hoped to stay at the Montgomery again."

"I don't get involved with reservations."

Her head slowly bobbed, probably understanding my abrasive response. "Tommy, I wanted to ensure you'd be okay with this."

"Me? I don't have a problem with it, Vicki." I forced a smile. "So are you using the name Karen Jones again?"

"No, I wanted something more French-sounding this time—Monique Trudeau."

"Well, you can't get much more French than that." My mind suddenly wandered, thinking about taking her to the Louvre in Paris and shopping along the Champs Elysees with lunch at Le Fouquet across from the Louis Vuitton store. Remembering the small fact that she had a husband came to mind, so I shook off those overzealous thoughts. I moved toward my desk and sat in the leatherback chair, continuously clicking a pen.

"I suppose I should let you get back to your busy day. Maybe I'll see you around." She smiled before making a hasty exit.

When her frame left my sight, I threw the pen across the room, splitting it in half as it smacked against the wall. Not only was she back in town, she chose to stay at my hotel again. So close to me yet off-limits. Still, I contacted reservations and advised them when Monique Trudeau checked in to upgrade her to an available private suite on the secure floor.

CHAPTER 79

In between an ordinary stressful day of meetings, contract reviews, and budget evaluations, a voice mail message grabbed my attention. Vicki asked me to return her call. By the time I listened to her message, the day had escaped me.

I let her stew for a while, but the truth was, I wanted to see her. Because hours passed since she left the message, I decided to knock on the door of her suite and take a chance she'd be in. Room service confirmed they sent up a salad with grilled scallops an hour earlier.

How I enjoyed being greeted by those magnificent dimples when her door flung open.

"I had a pretty busy day and didn't have a chance to call you back to see what you needed. Something, I assume, my staff couldn't accommodate for you?"

She took a step back, allowing me to enter her suite.

Cautiously, I stepped inside.

"I wanted to thank you for the upgrade."

I nodded, attempting to play it cool, but I wanted to kiss her.

"I'm sure it wasn't a coincidence I was selected *at random* to use this suite for several months. And I insist on paying the appropriate rate."

"You can discuss that with the guest services manager. I'm glad you're happy with the accommodations."

"The Ireland wing is gorgeous! The Cliffs of Moher simulation is stunning! But there's one thing you can modify in this room for the health of your guests."

"What's that?" My concern was valid since this was the second-best suite we offered. Matt Damon booked our best suite while in town filming *Ocean's Thirteen*.

She stepped toward the TV, pointed to a piece of art on the wall, and laughed at the absurdity. "This is an awful painting."

I admit, it wasn't a classic. Looked more like a child's drawing describing what a migraine felt like. I cracked a smile. "Would you prefer another Monet replica?"

"Monet, Picasso, or Rembrandt, please." She shook her head with a smile, giggling. "I'm joking. The décor is fine. Unless, of course, you have a suggestion."

"I do have a favorite piece."

"Wait! Let me guess. *Dogs Playing Poker*."

She made me laugh, even with a corny gambling analogy. "*Dogs Playing Poker* is a classic, especially at a casino, but it's not my favorite."

She waited patiently for me to tell her, looking beautiful with her long brown waves flowing past her shoulders. A small piece of her hair fell out of place against her sweet lower lip that I longed to taste.

"Are you familiar with the Italian artist Giulio Romano?"

Her brows raised. "He created several Madonna-and-child pieces. I didn't realize you favored Renaissance art."

"Well, I'm not familiar with his Virgin Mary collection. A piece caught my eye at the Hermitage Museum in St. Petersburg, *Love Scene*. Do you know it?"

She shook her head but appeared intrigued, listening intently.

I closed my eyes, thinking about this painting that left me breathless. "It's a sixteenth-century picture of lovers laying naked in bed, entwined in each other's arms and legs, tangled in a web of sheets. They come from wealth, judging by the ornate bed they shared, adorned with rich green and gold drapes, demanding privacy. He's captivated by her beauty."

I opened my eyes and focused directly on Vicki's dark-brown pupils, inching slowly toward her, getting as close to her as she'd allow. "The beautiful woman has her lover under some kind of hypnotic spell. Her left hand teases him, as if she wants to remove the delicate swath of sheet away from his waist, driving him crazy with desire." I stood mere inches from Vicki.

Her lips approached mine, seducing me. I wasn't a strong enough man to resist, even though I should have been. After several seconds of toying with each other's wants and needs, I let myself go and kissed her hard.

She responded, tantalizing my tongue with delightful strokes.

I dreamed the momentum would last. Keeping her with me in this instant, just the two of us, having her all to myself. Wasting no time, I scooped her body into my arms and carried her to the light-blue sofa.

She quickly tossed her candy-apple-colored sundress over her head, sending it across the room as my eyes absorbed her beauty. I didn't want to rush her, enjoying the view of her tan complexion and soft, delicate curves.

She unbuttoned my blue-striped Ralph Lauren shirt. I allowed her complete freedom and control, unfastening my belt, dropping my pants to my ankles. Her fingers sent me reeling when she grasped for me, using precise movements. I loved watching her luscious lips and expert tongue work their magic on my flesh.

My hands drifted between her firm, silky thighs. When I entered, I knew she was mine, even if only for a brief interlude. I took my time loving her, wanting every treasured moment to last.

CHAPTER 80

Vicki's body stayed glued to mine on the sofa. Neither of us said a word for what seemed like an hour. My left arm fell asleep, but I hated to move despite the prickly, tingling sensation.

She turned her body to face me, freeing my arm, allowing blood to flow again. Her fingers caressed the stubble on my cheek. "What are you thinking about?"

"I don't want to think about anything right now," I responded, unable to take my eyes off her sweet face.

"We have to talk about—"

I interrupted her, saying, "Don't ruin this moment."

She placed her head tenderly against my chest before we both drifted off.

My Blackberry began to vibrate from my pants pocket on the floor. I hated to disturb Vicki's peaceful sleep, but it was rare for my phone to ring late at night unless a hotel emergency arose.

As I lifted myself from beneath her warm well-sculpted body, she sat up, rubbing her eyes.

A missed call from an unknown phone number displayed. No voice mail message. I tossed the phone back on the floor after discovering it was one o'clock in the morning.

"Do you have to go?"

"Not unless you want me to leave."

She moved her body closer to me, leaning against my shoulder.

"Why don't we go to bed?" I suggested.

"I think we should talk, Tommy."

I waited for her to remind me about her marriage and that this friendship we had was going nowhere, in spite of the mind-blowing sex we both thoroughly enjoyed. "Okay, talk."

She took her time, cautiously contemplating her words. "I don't quite understand what happens to me when I'm around you. I can't explain it. When I left last year, it was hard to get you out of my mind." Her voice sounded rattled.

"You could've stayed at any hotel in Vegas, yet you chose *my* hotel. We might not have run into each other since our schedules are so busy, but you made a point to see me in my office. You wanted me to know you were back."

She nodded. "I wanted to see you again. I thought you'd still be angry with me. You could've thrown me out of your office the other day. Instead, you upgraded me to this lovely suite." Her smile grew.

"Tell me about your husband and marriage to Mayor Atkins."

She grinned, realizing I had checked up on her.

"I think I have a right to ask."

Vicki became quiet, pondering my question.

"I assume he believes you're staying here only to shoot your series. So what's your story? Are you in an unhappy relationship? Did you marry him for reasons outside of love? Are you divorcing him?" I tried to stay calm, but my sour temper flourished.

"Jeffrey and I have been married for twelve years. I loved him… once."

Once. Past tense. A promising sign.

"He wanted to make a difference in the community. I stood by his side when he first ran for mayor. He's been in office ever since. The people in the Fernley community love him. He pulled some strings to start my acting career. He has a few connections in the industry. I probably wouldn't have had many film opportunities if it weren't for him."

"You owe him?"

"I *did* love him, but being married to a politician isn't easy. Now he's making a run for governor with an ambitious goal leading to the White House. If I leave him, it could hurt his chances of winning."

"You've considered leaving him?"

"It's complicated."

"Uncomplicate it for me. Explain to me why whenever we're together, it feels right. You can't tell me you don't sense this connection."

A tear plopped from her eye as she nodded in agreement. "We hardly know each other. I have history with Jeffrey. He needs me to stay married to him through the race for governor. I can't walk away."

"Having you on his arm means you're in this election with him."

"That's how it has to be."

"And us?"

"It's not fair of me to expect anything from you, Tommy."

"Your entire life will be scrutinized. What's complicated is *me* being a part of your life and your bed."

She placed her hands upon my chest and slid her head up toward my face. She kissed my cheek tenderly. "I'll let you go if that's what you want, but it's not what I want. Maybe it's selfish of me to want you in my life."

Oh, the irony! The obvious parallels between Vicki and me and Angie and me—in reversed roles—were staggering. I loved Angie with everything I had. I wasn't looking to get married again or have more children at this stage in life. I wanted to be with Vicki, even if we were hiding away in our own world here at the Montgomery.

Sharing a woman I cared for with another man was a different story. Jealousy ran rampant through my veins. Could I handle such a complex relationship without losing my mind?

I chose to try, making no promises.

CHAPTER 81

One of the most meaningful moments in my life was Danny's birth in 1981. On this day, September 27, 2006, twenty-five years later, my granddaughter, Emma, was born. She entered this world pretty quickly and two weeks earlier than expected.

Danny had been on edge throughout Bianca's entire pregnancy. The pressure mounted with passing the bar exam, while guilty thoughts resonated about his single status. They might not have planned a wedding, but they planned a life.

They found a lovely house they liked in Summerlin with a lot of land for added privacy. They managed to move in and become settled before the baby arrived.

Seeing Sadie at the same hospital where Danny was born brought back memories. Mostly good memories, thinking about Danny's birth and how he improved my life.

I sometimes recalled the good times with Sadie. We had our moments, and we tried to make our marriage work toward the end. We both dished out a laundry list of betrayals. The one good thing we did together was create Danny. A grandchild, another common bond we shared, despite the disdain we felt for each other.

Normally, I didn't say much to my ex, but since we stood alone in the waiting room for a while, talking seemed better than awkward silence.

"Is Bianca's family coming?" I asked Sadie, hoping for others to arrive to have conversations with.

"No. They couldn't get a flight today. She's two weeks early. They purchased tickets to fly out closer to her due date."

"Should I have my pilot pick them up in North Carolina? Charlotte, right?"

"That would be great. I'm sure they'd love that." She smiled at me. "Can you believe we're going to be grandparents? The years flew by, didn't they?"

I nodded in agreement, followed by prickly silence. This might be the most words Sadie and I exchanged in years. Fortunately, I brought my Blackberry to check messages and make phone calls while Sadie thumbed through a magazine. I couldn't sit still. Relaxing, a trait in which I never excelled. I needed to work and have a purpose. I'd be working for as long as my mind and body allowed me to.

Sadie's parents called her every thirty minutes for an update.

After a solid four hours, Danny flew toward us with a nurse pushing a cart that held the best-looking baby in the hospital.

"Mom! Pop!" Danny yelled, grabbing our attention. He peeled off blue scrubs from his body, revealing black lounge pants and a Lakers T-shirt, grinning from ear to ear.

Sadie and I jumped to greet him and took a peek at our precious granddaughter, Emma, six pounds, five ounces.

"Danny, she looks so tiny. Much smaller than you were!" I laughed, remembering my boy weighed nearly nine pounds at birth.

"Where are you taking her?" Sadie asked.

"They need to run some general tests since she arrived early, and the cord was wrapped around her neck."

"Is she okay?" I asked, suddenly concerned.

"Yes, the tests are only a precaution, Pop."

"How's Bianca?" Sadie asked.

"Exhausted but good." He stood erect, clearly proud of this major life event that would alter his world in a beautiful way.

After a half-hour wait, we were allowed to see Bianca. I told her I sent my plane to fly in her parents. She smiled happily, surprised and grateful.

Danny returned with Emma.

A nurse prepared a bottle for Bianca to feed her, while Sadie attempted to convince Bianca to breastfeed.

I wanted to tell Sadie to leave the girl alone. If she wanted to feed her baby formula, that was her decision. But I kept my trap shut without taking my eyes off this sweet little one, who worked up quite an appetite after delivery.

Once Emma had enough to eat, Danny held her with warm devotion and some apparent jitters. He soon allowed his mother the opportunity to hold his beautiful baby girl.

Memories of Danny's birth registered again as Sadie showed the kids how to burp the baby and change a diaper. She reminded me more of her mother at that moment. Suzanne had shown us how to perform the same tasks as new parents when Danny was an infant.

When Sadie faced me to hand over this beloved bundle, a warm tear drizzled from my eye. Looking at this innocent little face, I absorbed all her sweet features.

This angelic girl became the light of my life.

CHAPTER 82

Many nights, Vicki and I met in her suite after a day of filming her show. Once in a while, to escape the monotony of the same four walls, she'd visit my home in Paradise. She'd drive my Lincoln MKS and park inside my garage. My property spread out wide enough for her to come and go without neighbors identifying her. People might recognize her from her TV series filmed locally or as the wife of a politician.

Atkins's campaign for governor began. Vicki's face exploded over ads and in the media, tying *Rising 51* to the upcoming election.

Radio and TV ads depicted the mayor as a Sunday school-teacher compared to his competitors. He promoted the importance of family values, yet he had a wife who fell out of love with him and no children. He took care of his elderly mother, scoring points as a wonderful son while showcasing advocacy of Medicare, prescription drugs, access to healthcare, and senior housing.

Vicki was forced to change her schedule a few times for him. Showing off his trophy wife at certain political functions became a necessity. She was educated, cultured, and refined with a killer smile. Her smile and those dimples lit up a room. Seeing Vicki on the campaign trail with him reminded me of Jackie Kennedy in support of her husband. But this guy, Atkins, was no JFK. It wasn't that I didn't agree with some of his views. I hated that he had a hold over Vicki. And I despised having no control of a situation.

Danny and Bianca dropped off Emma while they enjoyed some quiet time. I understood the importance of a couple needing privacy, and I was eager to spend quality time with my granddaughter.

Seeing that Emma couldn't speak or remember things, Vicki would drop by to hang out with us if her schedule allowed. I loved showing off my pride and joy to Vicki. Maybe I loved showing off Vicki to Emma, especially since no one else in my life could know about our affair. Well, Jim and my security detail knew, as did Terri, my housekeeper.

Soon, Vicki would return to Fernley. *Rising 51* filming was close to wrapping for the season. Atkins expected her home, glued to his side for the rest of his campaign. It would be seven months before she'd return to Vegas.

The emotional roller coaster I rode began to derail. But I didn't want to start a fight with Vicki so close to her leaving. Many questions filled my brain. Questions I might not want the answers to. Did she share a bed with her husband? Vicki never discussed her home life with me. Despite my curiosity, I never asked the questions that weighed on my mind.

Angie used to ask me about my living arrangement with Sadie. I hated when she'd ask me questions because I'd often have to lie. I didn't want to hurt Angie or lose her. Angie was the woman I loved with all my heart.

If I asked Vicki personal questions, I might not receive an honest answer. So what would be the point?

CHAPTER 83

Mayor Atkins traveled through the state in 2007, seeking supporters, volunteers, and contributors for his campaign. His lovely wife, Victoria Ursini, stood by his side.

Vicki and I kept in touch after she left Vegas, using private email addresses. No one would associate either of us with those emails. She kept a separate cell phone, a phone I paid for, so no bill would be in her name or traced to her. We tried to communicate daily. I missed her soft touch, the fruity scent of her hair, and her adorable laugh.

When Atkins brought his circus to Vegas in the form of a campaign event, I had to attend to see Vicki. I watched her on his TV ads that portrayed them as some kind of super couple. She told me she'd be in town, but Jeffrey would be with her constantly. She couldn't escape from her security detail for even a brief moment.

I needed to assess their relationship with my own eyes. Did she go out of her way to touch him the way she touched me? How did she look at him? If I didn't like what I saw, I'd probably chalk it up to her being a hell of an actress in front of an audience, executing the performance of her life.

Why torture myself attending this event?

Atkins booked a large banquet room at the Bellagio. The lobby ceiling at this magnificent hotel was famous for its stunning, colorful bouquet of glass flowers. The beautiful modern hotel was also known for its spectacular water fountains facing the Strip. The water danced to a variety of music. In the evening, a light show highlighted the fountains, enchanting guests to stop and watch the performance of whimsical leaping water. Every hotel on the Strip had its niche, like the Montgomery's unique theme representing England, Ireland, and Scotland.

When I entered the conference room, streamers, balloons, and posters filled the space. People were packed in tight. A lot of hand-shaking, big smiles, false promises, and greased palms were expected.

I dressed casually for this event, hiding any shred of wealth. I wore a 49-ers T-shirt, black jeans, sneakers, and a baseball cap to conceal my identity. I didn't want to stand out or alert Vicki that I was there, observing her life.

The last thing I wanted was Atkins's minions expecting me to donate to his campaign. If he won, Vicki could be tied to him for a four-year term. Selfishly, I hoped he'd lose.

I walked around the vast space with a smile coating my face—an attempt to display interest. In reality, my eyes scanned the room for Vicki.

Upon the stage next to the podium stood Senator Louis Maroni and his wife, Katie. I didn't want them to spot me, but things just got more interesting. Louis maintained his political position for years, bought and paid for by the criminal family he was born into. His character had been called into question by opponents, but the people in this state loved Louis, showering him with votes, allowing him to maintain power.

Off to the side of the room sat none other than Vince Russo himself. For a man in his late seventies who, I heard, fought off cancer, he looked pretty good. His head glistened with pure white strands, but I could sense his wicked soul like a psychic perceived death.

Louis's father, Big Sal, stood proudly beside him. Deep pockets in attendance, surely wanting a governor they could control in office.

I approached a large table in the back corner, enticing guests to sample a variety of sliced vegetables, several types of cheese, crackers, and something resembling sliced meat, served with eight-ounce water bottles, coffee, and tea. I moved to the opposite side of the room, away from the crowded table, to ensure a clear view of the

Russo/Maroni clan, waiting for Atkins to present a powerful, heartfelt speech to the enthusiastic group of supporters.

Senator Maroni approached the microphone, receiving a thunderous round of applause from the crowd—except me. He rambled on, describing the accolades of Mayor Atkins while in office. He beamed with excitement to promote a man like Jeffrey Atkins to be the next governor of the great state of Nevada.

Following a rowdy ovation, Atkins took to center stage with confidence. He held the delicate hand of his lovely wife, wearing the same shade of deep bubblegum pink Jackie Kennedy wore on the day our beloved former president was assassinated.

Someone dressed Vicki. She hated the color pink. But her lovely features and dark hair might remind people of Jackie. Atkins's campaign manager might have noticed certain similarities between Vicki and our former first lady to make this kind of public, political statement.

Vicki started to wear her wedding band with a glittering diamond enormous enough to blind the audience.

When Atkins spoke, he had a way to insult his competition without trying to make his comments sound insulting. A good bullshitter. Arrogant too.

My ears listened to his speech, but my eyes monitored Vicki. A bright smile cemented firmly across her face. She knew proper etiquette, living in the limelight of cameras and spontaneous interviews. Her hands clapped, encouraging the audience to applaud for every word that left her husband's lips. I knew she didn't love him, but I couldn't watch her support him.

I darted from the room through the busy lobby, then stepped outside the hotel for a breath of fresh air to calm my frazzled nerves. I felt like punching something. The Bellagio fountains entertained me for a while, easing my ferocious mood.

Seeing Vicki on this man's arm, wearing his ring, disturbed me to the core. I didn't want to let this woman go, but living in the shadows as a secret wasn't going to fly for much longer.

Two black stretch limos with dark-tinted windows pulled up close to where I stood.

Atkins's speech and games must have concluded. His flock of followers fled the Bellagio outside the main entrance. The media trailed behind, trying to capture a statement from Atkins as he and Vicki raced outside to quickly escape the masses.

He planned for the fanfare and publicity. Atkins demanded attention.

Security guards scurried the couple into the vehicle. Before Vicki stepped inside, her eyes drifted in my direction. She stopped and stared momentarily, revealing her dimples—just for me.

CHAPTER 84

My phone rang around eleven that night, playing Vicki's tune, Springsteen's "Born to Run." I often thought about what it would take to run away with Vicki, taking her from her husband, the spotlight, and all the noise in her life. I always took Vicki's calls because it wasn't easy for her to contact me. Being a celebrity and political champion didn't allow for privacy.

"You were at the Bellagio today."

"I wanted to see you. Nice suit."

She scoffed.

"Who picked it out?" I asked.

"What makes you say that?"

"You hate pink."

She chuckled. "You know me very well. Hey, I'm sorry." Her tone dimmed.

"For what, baby?"

"I don't want you to see me like that. You know, in public with Jeffrey, playing the part of a devoted wife. The whole thing is a lie." She paused.

Maybe she expected me to say something, but no words came to mind.

"I need to see you," she whispered, desperation captured in her voice.

"If you can make it happen, I'll be there."

A sigh formed. "He has me stuck to him and his schedule, but I may be able to see you on the eleventh in Fallon. I have the whole day open."

"It's a date," I confirmed.

"I miss you." The tone of her words sounded terribly lonely.

"Ditto."

I never thought it would happen to me twice in a lifetime, but I fell in love. I hadn't said the expression aloud, but I was determined to make this love last, even if I had to wait for her to let go of her marriage to Jeffrey Atkins.

"Take It to the Limit"

CHAPTER 85

Vicki's plane landed at McCarran. She arranged for a driver to bring her straight to the Montgomery, where I waited in her suite, nibbling on strawberries from a fruit platter. The room had been set up with candles flickering and the Beatles' "Something" playing softly while the Jacuzzi filled with warm water.

As long as she stayed at my hotel in a secure suite, no one would question my presence. I handpicked her security detail at the hotel. Men who were loyal to me.

Jeffrey insisted she use her real name and not hide from the public, but she refused to comply, claiming she wanted privacy.

This time, she used the alias Leslie Walters. She would be recognized by fans, the media, and voters if she stood in the lobby, using traditional methods to check in. I suggested she enter through the back of the building where a security officer would greet her and quickly escort her to her suite.

I played out every scenario in my head. If our affair was exposed, the media would damage Vicki's reputation and possibly end her marriage. The only person who'd benefit would be me. I spent most of my life acting selfishly in relationships.

Her marriage. Her mess. I could help her clean it up, but I couldn't control Vicki or the situation.

Vicki raced into my arms the moment she flew inside the room. Her sensual, heated kisses ignited a throbbing passion. She tore my red-striped dress shirt open. Buttons flung through the air. Her fingers danced along my brawny arms. Clothing quickly scattered across the floor.

My eyes fused to hers as I lifted her body, charging to the over-size bed, beneath a maroon-shaded canopy, for some much-needed TLC.

* * *

I ordered Thai for lunch, following our steamy tryst in the Jacuzzi. We worked up a healthy appetite.

She had a business meeting at four, and I had a conference call at four thirty. Having her here with me rejuvenated my heart. How could I let her go again in a few months to be with another man, even if she loved me?

Her phone chimed, breaking up my ominous thoughts. She wore that "oh crap" reaction on her face, telling me it was Jeffrey.

"I have to take this. Sorry."

I didn't leave the room, and she didn't walk away for privacy. Anytime she spoke to Jeffrey, her tone sounded methodical. No provocative or loving gestures were declared. Their marriage behind closed doors seemed more like a business partnership.

CHAPTER 86

The summer of 2007 was in my rear-view mirror. Thrilled to have Vicki with me, but I knew the time would come for her to leave again. I tried to make the most of our time together, seeing her daily.

I installed a privacy fence around the grounds of my house. I owned a lot of land, and the neighbors never bothered me. With Vicki spending time here, I couldn't risk her being seen frequently. We couldn't travel together or eat in a public restaurant like a normal couple. The paparazzi would follow her and snap photographs to share with the public or extort us to keep our affair a secret.

When Angie and I were together, cell phones and video devices didn't exist to publicly out our relationship. Times had changed thanks to modern technology and social media. Vicki shined in the Nevada limelight, easily recognizable. My love for her had to remain concealed.

The inground pool in my backyard had been transformed into an exceptionally tranquil venue. I added a rocky terrain on one side with a visually appealing waterfall. The soft, soothing sound of water drizzling like rain showering into the pool often put me to sleep when lounging. At night, the waterfall lit up with gleaming rays bouncing off the crystal-clear water. Tiki torches surrounded the corners, glowing in the moonlight. I added a sound system to play various music we desired, preferably my favorite classic rock songs by the Eagles, Boston, and Queen, and Elvis for Vicki.

The first time I said those magical words of love to Vicki, we were spread out on top of colorful floating lounge chairs on a steamy summer day, soaking in the bright sun.

She looked amazing in a turquoise strapless bikini. I held her hand and tugged her closer to me. Vicki reached over to kiss me and inadvertently slipped off the lounge chair, falling into the pool, taking me with her into the deep end.

The cool water felt refreshing on my warm, tan skin, but her shriek caught my attention. My head whipped back and forth. I couldn't see Vicki above water.

I dove under and noticed her arms waving, but her feet weren't kicking. Vicki was sinking into the twelve-foot depths. I kicked my feet fast to reach her, secured my arm around her waist, and guided her to the surface.

Vicki's arms thrashed erratically, coughing like she swallowed some chlorinated water. She wrapped her arms tightly around my neck, attempting to catch her breath.

"I've got you. You're okay."

She nodded, taking in deep breaths.

"You can't swim?"

"W-w-what gave you that idea?" She chuckled awkwardly through a panicked expression.

"Maybe that's something we'll work on this summer."

Her grip around my neck tightened.

"Trust me. I won't let you go," I said, swimming to the edge of the shallow end with her body in my grasp before pinning her to the wall.

She calmed herself, breathing steadily now, feeling safe. Her feet could touch the bottom if I let her go. Instead, I kissed her sweet lips and said, "I'm not letting you go. I love you."

She responded with a deep, lingering kiss, declaring her love for me in return.

I slipped my hand inside her bikini bottom, fondling and teasing. She reciprocated, perfecting the art of seduction, releasing a mass of wild energy from within. I freed her from her bikini and thoroughly enjoyed our blazing, rhythmic dance in the cool water.

CHAPTER 87

Jeffrey called, interrupting our breakfast in Vicki's suite, demanding she meet him for several speaking engagements in the northern region of the state. That would take her away from me for two weeks. Away from me and her schedule to shoot *Rising 51*. I eavesdropped on their call. The conversation fired up, fueling a shouting match. Vicki's hands rose over her head, wildly animated, then settled on her hips, caving.

Her contract with the production company to complete filming and promote her show would be disrupted, throwing off her entire schedule.

He expected her to change everything solely for his benefit. Atkins was concerned about the polls. His rival turned out to be a viable competitor.

She let out a powerful huff. "I'm sorry. I have to pack and travel with him for a couple of weeks. There are some public events he needs me to attend."

"Whether he wins or loses the election in November, you're leaving him, right?"

Eye contact became as nil as her words.

"Vicki? We can't go on like this. You said you owed him and had to help him become governor. Come Election Day, either way, what's next for us?"

"I haven't thought that far ahead, Tommy."

"It's not that far off, babe."

"I have to wait and see how things go."

I nearly lost it with her vague responses. "Don't. Don't fucking lie to me!" I barked.

"Lie?"

I shook my head and walked in a circle, contemplating. "I never told you about Angie."

"Who's Angie?" she asked, irritated that I changed the subject, bringing up another woman.

"Angie was an old flame. I never thought of her as a *mistress*, but…she was."

Vicki's brows raised with surprise, but she remained quiet.

"I told you about my sham of a marriage. I had every intention of divorcing Sadie and marrying Angie."

"You loved this…Angie?"

"Very much, but I wasn't honest with her. I didn't tell her what was happening in my marriage. Maybe if I was honest, we could've made it work. Ten years we were together. I loved her more than anything."

"Do you think I'd make you wait ten years?"

"Oh, I *won't* wait ten years. Two have been hard enough. And if you won't leave him to be with me, you either don't love me or you're not being honest with me about your marriage. Which is it?" I shouted.

"I love you, Tommy." She shed a tear as she approached me, arms open.

I stopped her from stepping closer. "If you love me, then leave him, or give me a reasonable explanation why you're not divorced yet."

She struggled to say her next sentence. "If I leave him, I could go to jail."

"Jail? What the hell, Vicki? Does he have something on you?"

"It's a long story." She shook her head and paced.

I stood before her, stopping her movement, gently taking hold of her arm. "Talk to me."

After a few seconds, attempting to find the right words, she sucked in a deep, lamenting breath before speaking. "I came into possession of a stolen piece of art."

"Stolen art? This is about a frickin' painting?"

"Do you realize how much art theft occurs in the world? Billions of dollars lost, destroyed, or stolen. The FBI has a special division charged to find missing pieces. The criminal justice system takes robbing famous artwork seriously, Tommy." She cleared her throat and took a sip from her mug of coffee, stalling.

With the extreme amount of violence and drug dealing in this country, I never considered pilfering a painting to be a serious crime.

"During World War II, the Nazis stole numerous paintings and sculptures from museums and the Jewish families they destroyed. Hitler envisioned creating a fuhrer museum in Germany with the art he robbed. He fantasized this museum would become the greatest in all of Europe. Many pieces were recouped and returned to the precise museums or rightful owners after Germany was defeated.

"Hitler didn't want any other country to get their hands on the collection he had hidden. The Americans were closing in on him with their mission to salvage and preserve works of art. Hitler ordered the destruction of the pieces to prevent his enemies, like the US, from locating his hiding places, taking back what he considered his prized possessions. If he couldn't keep his treasures, he'd prefer it if they were destroyed than taken from him. What wasn't ruined or recovered by the Americans or the Russians was stolen, and in some cases, sold on the black market."

"And you came across one of these paintings?"

"My grandfather did. He acquired a painting by Camille Pissarro, *The Boulevard Montmartre at Twilight, 1897,* in the early forties. Pissarro, a Danish-French impressionist, created beautiful masterpieces in the nineteenth century." She paused momentarily, collecting her thoughts.

"Grandpa loved to talk about the first time he saw Pissarro's painting. How his eyes lit up at the sight, gleaming. An internal swirl of energy swept up within him. His excitement never faltered, especially after he learned of its value when the notorious history of the painting had been highlighted on a televised documentary, proving that very painting was once in Hitler's hands. Perhaps the risk of being caught with it intensified his enthusiasm."

"How are *you* going to be arrested for artwork your grandfather obtained, legally or not?"

"Grandpa taught me about art since I was a little girl, which led to my studying art history in college. My love for art bonded us. He was a strong, positive role model for me throughout my childhood. He wanted *me* to have that painting. It has sentimental value and keeps me connected to him. God rest his soul.

"Years ago, my grandfather owned a market in Whitney with a partner, Russ Lombard. Growing up, I spent a lot of time at the market with him. Grandpa and Russ had a bitter dispute about finances that destroyed their friendship and partnership. Grandpa swore Russ was embezzling money. He threatened Russ with a lawsuit unless he cut their fiscal ties.

"One day, the painting disappeared, stripped from its place on Grandpa's living room wall. It wasn't some random burglary. No average burglar would've known the value of that painting. The thief didn't take anything else—no jewelry or Grandma's silver.

"Russ knew of Grandpa's obsession with it, and he knew its origin. Grandpa swore Russ stole it for revenge because of their failed partnership. He couldn't call the police because he worried he might get in some legal trouble for harboring a stolen piece of art from World War II. My grandfather vowed to get that painting back. He wouldn't allow Russ to take it away from him without consequence. Their feud was reenergized.

"It took years, but we found where Russ kept the painting. And I...kind of...stole it back." She stopped speaking, shrugged, and turned her back on me as if that were the end of her tale.

"How'd you do it?"

She tossed me a look as if she wasn't prepared to reveal those details, despite my curiosity.

"Vicki?"

She let out a huff. "Tommy, I don't want you involved. This is *my* problem."

"If Atkins is holding this over your head, this impacts our future, so I'm invested. I want to help, but you have to tell me the whole story."

Vicki blew out a breath of irritation, then continued. "My grandfather battled congestive heart failure but neglected to tell me about his health problems. I watched his energy level decrease, and his breathing became labored. I hoped by seeing that painting again, he'd magically heal.

"I remember the day I showed it to him, proof I had found it. I held the magnificent piece at his bedside. Happiness radiated from his smile! Although he was delighted to see it again, his health continued to deteriorate. Then he received threatening messages on the phone. Dead rats were left in his car. A black snake was curled inside his mailbox. That's when Jeffrey intervened."

A sudden taste of revulsion crept up, hearing the lengths someone went to just to hurt Vicki's grandfather over a painting. Rats and snakes? "So Jeffrey knows you stole the painting, triggering this animosity with Russ Lombard?"

"Not only does he know I stole it, Jeffrey stashed it away to prevent anyone from taking it or threatening my grandfather and me. At the time, I thought he was a wonderful man who helped me out of a bad jam, protecting me and the art. Later, I learned he *recorded* me describing the hoops I jumped through to steal it. If I leave him—"

"That's extortion. He's blackmailing you about this stupid painting?"

"This is a painting stolen by the Nazis during the war. It's worth a fortune today! The recording Jeffrey holds confirms my knowledge of its value, where it's kept, and the mere fact that I stole it from someone's home. I could do time.

"If I help him win this election, he claims he'll let me go. He cares more about power, money, and status than me. He's not popular with the voters in the eighteen-to-twenty-nine age range. He hopes my young sci-fi fans will vote for him. A divorce during an election year may damage his reputation as a *family values* man."

"Sweetheart, if he wins, you mentioned he wanted the presidency. He won't go through a divorce on that journey, either. This blackmail could go on for years! Call his bluff and leave him!"

She crossed her arms and sat at the edge of the sofa. "I don't trust Jeffrey. I tried to leave him peacefully years ago. That was the first time he threatened me with the tape. I was stunned when he played it! He had me trapped. Insurance to prevent a divorce from tarnishing his perfect record."

Vicki stood, then walked to the balcony glass door, staring at the Strip below, softly saying, "He turned into a different person after he became mayor. His aspirations to become governor and a future presidential candidate outweigh his humanity. He's on a power trip, and he isn't afraid of using that tape against me if I left him." She turned to face me. "If I walk away from the marriage, he'll have no reason to protect me. He'll *destroy* me for spite and make himself look like a victim who did the right thing—turning his wife, the thief, into the police. He scares me."

I pulled her into a warm embrace. "Get rid of it! Ship it to the Met in New York."

"Jeffrey's got it locked up tight with an alarm system. He convinced me we shouldn't keep that painting out in the open. Besides, shipping it across the country wouldn't take away from Jeffrey's blackmail, and his security camera would catch me stealing it *again*. I don't want to stay in this marriage, Tommy, but I don't want to go to prison! Jeffrey has Russ's whole family in his pocket. There's no question they'd verify the accuracy of that tape with my confession after what I did. It's all of their words against mine."

"Vicki, what exactly did you do? Is there more to the story?"

Vicki's bare feet wore a permanent path along the plush gray carpet with her continuous pacing. Her chattering teeth gnawed at her painted red nails. "I don't want you anywhere near this, Tommy. And I don't want to discuss it anymore. It's my problem."

Standing before her petite body, I firmly grasped her arms. "We're not going to be that kind of couple. The kind with secrets. Not anymore. If you can't trust me, what are we doing?" My temper flared.

Her fingers twirled her long, dark hair as a tear splashed down her cheek, running over the dark, dotted birthmark I adored.

I hated it when a woman cried. I took a breath and softened my tone. "All I want to do is help you get out of this mess, sweetheart."

She nodded while wiping away the puddles from her eyes. "Russ didn't keep Pissarro's painting out in the open for spectators like my grandfather did." She paused, thinking. Her eyes shifted to the left, stalling.

Jeffrey betrayed her. Perhaps she didn't completely trust me.

"Vicki, I'll do whatever I can to protect you. I may be able to help."

"Russ has an illegitimate son—Matthew Winters, a secret he shared with Grandpa when they were still friends. Russ never legally claimed Matthew as his child, but he supported him financially while he grew up in Illinois. I got the impression Russ sent his lover and her son out of Vegas so his wife wouldn't learn of his infidelity.

"Trusted friends of Grandpa's participated in the search to reclaim the piece, but it wasn't in Matthew's home in Chicago. We caught another potential lead. Matthew had a son of his own named Trey, who was set up in an apartment in Evanston. Trey Winters, Russ Lombard's illegitimate grandson, is my age and a major loser of a human being. Unless Russ destroyed the painting or sold it, Trey was our last hope—the only other family member we needed to check out. If Trey didn't have it, the whereabouts of Pissarro's masterpiece would be unknown.

"If Russ wanted to maintain the art in a pristine state, he wouldn't have allowed his drug-addicted grandson to keep it. If Trey knew how much that painting was worth, he would've bartered it for drugs. Luckily, Trey had it, and I stole it from him." Vicki casually shrugged, ending the story, clearly glossing over some details.

"How did you steal it?"

She squirmed, replying, "Trey had a penchant for pretty girls and hardcore drugs."

My brows raised.

"Trey's apartment was quite secure, so accessing it without his knowledge wasn't possible. I tailed Trey to a bar he frequented, and I hit on him, assuming he'd invite me back to his place. I played the part of a strung-out tramp, leading him to think he'd get lucky.

"When I followed him home, I discovered why his place was locked up tighter than Fort Knox with several locks securing the entrance. Jeez, his apartment looked like a bomb went off! Dirty. Drugs everywhere. A powerful odor came from one of the rooms down the hallway, causing a severe gag reflex until I plugged my nose for several seconds. Immediate fear overwhelmed me, unsure if he had a decaying body back there. I asked him to open a window, but he ignored me and laid out a line of coke on the kitchen table.

"I requested some scotch from a bottle sitting on the countertop. He jumped up and poured us each a glass. He mumbled something incoherently and walked back to his stash while I sort of... roofied his drink when his back was turned."

Now, I was surprised. My girl knew how to incapacitate someone with an illegal substance.

"My goal wasn't to hurt him," she insisted, remorse detected in her tone. "I didn't want him to remember me. Believe me, he was no stranger to drug use. I figured when he woke up in the morning, he'd think he passed out after a wild night of partying.

"The addict I *pretended* to be would've pounced at his stash. Instead, I sipped at the scotch, making him suspicious. Trey was very paranoid."

"Drugs will do that to you," I said, recalling my personal battle with addiction.

"He held the drink I laced, then pulled a gun on me, questioning who I really was and why I was there if I wasn't going to party."

"Jesus, he had a gun, Vicki?"

"Pointed right at my forehead! I had no interest in drugs, but getting high was better than getting shot. I positioned myself near the table about to ingest the coke, when he finally guzzled his drink. The mickey I slipped him kicked in. He started to lose his balance. As he staggered, he dropped the pistol. Trey's body hit the floor next. He might have killed me, otherwise! After he collapsed, I slid on gloves, then removed his pants and shirt so it would appear like he had a good time. I tossed the gun beneath a recliner in the living room.

"I had to open the windows so I could breathe fresh air over the rotten smell inside. His place wasn't very big as I raced around in search of the art. I found the masterpiece carelessly hanging crooked on the wall of his bedroom. It appeared dusty but in good condition, overall.

"Seeing that painting again sent chills up my spine. I took a moment to drink in its beauty before climbing atop his mattress to stretch my fingers, carefully reaching for the bottom of the frame. It easily glided off its mounted base and into my hands. With no time to waste, I covered the painting with a sheet from his bed, feeling grateful that the terrible scent throughout his home didn't seem to damage the paint or the colors.

"To satisfy my curiosity, I opened the door where the obnoxious odor derived, unsure what I'd find. Thankfully, it wasn't a dead body, but it looked like a chemistry lab. Beakers, bottles, and powder smeared across tables. I didn't know at that time what he was cooking, but I learned afterward it was meth. I closed the door of his lab to contain the powerful chemical aroma. I needed to get out of there!"

Vicki slumped into the armchair. Her palms continuously smoothed her tan slacks. "I kept a forgery of the painting in the trunk of my car. I planned to replace the original with the fake. I tried to ensure the frame matched. It was slightly different from the original frame, a rookie mistake. Unfortunately, I didn't have a chance to replace it. He would've never known the original went missing if I could've gone back inside to hang up the replica.

"After I carefully placed the painting in the trunk, three police cruisers parked directly outside the building near my car. I thought they were going to arrest me! Instead, they drew guns and slowly maneuvered toward the building's entrance. I overheard they were looking for a man wearing a dark-colored hoodie. One of the officers suggested I get inside my vehicle for safety. He approached my car and peeked inside, I assume, to check if their suspect was hiding in it. Their presence had nothing to do with me, but they interfered with my plan.

"I sped off since I couldn't get back inside Trey's apartment to hang the Pissarro copy with the police there or sit in my car, waiting for the commotion to end. I felt a little concerned because I left his door unlocked so I could get back in. But I couldn't risk being spotted by the cops.

"Because his apartment reeked of drugs with a potent smell, I didn't think he'd report the painting stolen. He wouldn't invite the police inside to investigate a theft about an inconsequential piece of art because it might send him to jail for running some kind of drug factory."

"This guy sounded dangerous. Drug dealers could be unpredictable and ruthless. I can't believe you put yourself in harm's way, Vicki. He had a gun!"

"I didn't know all the dangerous facts about Trey back then. At the time, my initial plan made sense, as crazy as that sounds."

"How did all of this come out?"

"The accusations didn't happen overnight. Maybe Trey didn't immediately tell his family the painting went missing. He didn't understand its origin or value. Drugs were all Trey cared about. At some point, he must have remembered me or described me to his family when they learned the painting vanished.

"Naturally, I denied having it. Trey was so spaced out that night, he couldn't be a credible witness. No one had *any* hard evidence until Jeffrey taped what wound up being my confession. Everything I told you is on that tape." She shook her head, angry she allowed him to deceive her.

I knelt beside her chair. "How did Jeffrey defuse the situation? You said he intervened."

"Trey's lifestyle caught up with him. He did a stint in prison for cooking meth, drug possession, and dealing. To stop the threats against my grandfather and me, Jeffrey had powerful associations he used as a bargaining tool. Connections that ultimately got Trey out of jail and into a good rehab facility. Matthew Winters still wanted blood, accusing me of seducing his son into drugs. Trey already had a serious problem before I slipped Rohypnol in his drink.

"In spite of my denial to the Winters family about taking back the Pissarro painting, Jeffrey needed their accusations to go away before his reputation became stained. He appeased their plot for revenge by keeping his word, setting Trey up in rehab. A monetary bribe was part of the package too. If I leave Jeffrey, he could easily have them corroborate my taped confession. Again, all of them against me. I believed he wanted to help me then. I made a terrible mistake trusting him. The man I loved and married taped our private conversation."

"You know, I wouldn't do that to you, honey." I stood before her and playfully lifted my shirt, exposing my midsection. "No wires."

Her eyes met mine when she rose from the chair, exhausted from spilling her guts. "I trust you, Tommy. If it weren't for that damn tape, there'd be no evidence against me at all. I could box up the painting and ship it to a museum like you suggested if I could access it without being seen."

"Somehow, I'll get you out of this. Win or lose in November, I want you here with me."

CHAPTER 88

Learning about Jeffrey Atkins became a tedious, draining pastime. I didn't care about all the wonderful things the internet had to say about his political career. I wanted to know more about Jeffrey Atkins, the man. He married an art connoisseur, yet the photo of him on his mayoral page showed him standing before one of the ugliest paintings I'd ever seen.

Vicki shared all that she knew about him. His family background, recreational activities, friends, colleagues, habits. Anything and everything she could think of, she made me a list.

She knew where Jeffrey kept the painting, but she didn't know where he stored her taped confession—the tape of her voice admitting to stealing the art from Trey's apartment. If we could find that, she'd be free. No other evidence existed. The credibility of a drug addict was less than meaningful without hard evidence.

The odds of Jeffrey keeping that tape anywhere Vicki could access it was slim to none. When she returned to Fernley, she paid closer attention to his routine and always rummaged through his belongings. If he had a safe deposit box, she never found a key. Unfortunately, Vicki couldn't find anything remotely tied to this tape for her freedom.

Larry was my next call. Bringing down a politician heightened his interest in this case. He'd do some digging and follow Atkins around, within reason. He also hired a sharp young kid—a hacker. This kid had the ability to access Atkins's computer files to ensure there wasn't a digital recording.

According to Vicki, Jeffrey barely got by using a cell phone. Modern technology wasn't a talent he possessed, but he had people working for him who might have helped.

Vicki provided Larry with lengthy details about Jeffrey's security measures. If Larry followed too closely or got caught, our mission could be blown.

CHAPTER 89

My time with Vicki in 2007 felt short-lived. Atkins had her running back and forth from her film set to wherever he needed his trophy wife on his arm. She used that time to pay closer attention to his habits. Regrettably, she still found no clues of the hidden tape's location.

His phone and computers maintained no recorded conversations, according to Larry's hacker colleague. Atkins's personal computers were simple for this genius to hack. I'd never ask how he broke through the Fernley Town Hall's firewall.

Vicki agreed to discuss the case with my attorney. As Vicki's legal representative, Len would keep the information he learned confidential. The statute of limitations for robbery might be a sound legal defense tactic, depending upon the circumstances.

But Vicki added more stress to an already difficult situation. She omitted an important detail when she told me this story. The drug she laced Trey's drink with might have interacted with other substances in his system. He nearly died on the night in question.

She had opened the windows in Trey's basement apartment to reduce the powerful odor from the drugs he cooked. The cops on the premises, who had been searching for that suspect in a dark hoodie, smelled the fumes from Trey's meth lab. They assessed the danger and entered the unlocked apartment to find Trey lying on the floor, unresponsive.

CPR saved Trey's life. His stomach got pumped, which proved that someone slipped him Rohypnol. At what point he remembered Vicki, she didn't know.

"They can charge you with attempted murder, Vicki. This was a premeditated act. You went to his apartment with Rohypnol, which medical records will prove was in his bloodstream the same night you confessed on tape to stealing a priceless painting. Your confession will link you to incapacitating Trey," Len said with concern.

"I didn't mean to cause him harm, and I certainly didn't want to kill him." Mounds of regret poured through her words.

"If I were the prosecutor, I could create a long list of charges against you. There is no statute of limitations on attempted murder."

"Len, if she's charged, could you get the charges reduced or dropped?"

"Possibly, Tommy. It depends on the evidence presented. But Vicki would still go through the motions of the legal system. An attempted murder charge would be the worst-case scenario. Her life would be scrutinized. She's married to a sitting mayor who's running for governor. The publicity would be damaging, whether she's indicted or not."

Both Trey and Vicki got caught up in some crazy cat-and-mouse game launched by their grandfathers. I had no idea how to help her without getting my hands on her confession.

After some investigating, we learned Russ Lombard died an old man in a convalescent home, but Matthew and Trey Winters remained viable threats. The Winters clan appeared clean, except for Trey's drug issues. If this family didn't want to press charges against Vicki, she'd have a good chance of getting off. Trey had escaped a few near-death experiences, overdosing on his product, which showcased a continual theme brought on by his perpetual addiction. The night Vicki slipped him Rohypnol wasn't his first or last brush with death.

Len would attain a medical professional to review the toxicology report to see if the Rohypnol Vicki gave him caused his health crisis that night or if the cocktail of drugs and alcohol he consumed could have killed him.

If Atkins gave the Winters family the green light to take Vicki down and press charges, I had no idea how they'd retaliate, knowing she drugged Trey to steal that painting. They had a right to press charges, and Jeffrey had the ammunition.

Without that cassette tape, the Winters clan couldn't validate they owned the Pissarro masterpiece at all since they stole it themselves. Nor had they filed a police report at the time of the theft. If they were devastated about their stolen painting, why didn't they notify the police? If they knew Vicki drugged Trey, why hadn't they pressed charges sooner? Their story appeared flimsy with as many holes as a slice of Swiss cheese, so I didn't necessarily fear the Winters. I feared Jeffrey's blackmail.

Len concurred with my assessment that the missing tape would be vital to the prosecutor's case. Without it, there was no case.

Wherever Jeffrey hid the tape, we weren't looking in the right spot. Larry did everything from jimmying the padlock of Atkins's locker at the gym to breaking into his car. Nothing!

Because Atkins took care of his aging mother, Larry cautiously searched her house for as long as he possibly could without getting caught. His efforts were unsuccessful.

The one place we couldn't physically enter without being noticed was the mayor's office at Fernley Town Hall. The possibility existed that the evidence could be hiding in Jeffrey's office. With Vicki working the political scene, she searched his office at the Town Hall for the tape or a random key. A key that could lead to the missing cassette.

Finding this tape was as challenging as looking for a needle in a haystack. For months, we attempted with valiant effort to find the smoking gun, but we came up empty-handed.

∗ ∗ ∗

Mayor Jeffrey Atkins became the governor-elect of Nevada in November 2007. He would officially take office in January for the next four years. And he wasn't letting Vicki go anytime soon.

CHAPTER 90

My mind and body yearned for Vicki. She transformed into the governor's wife and maintained certain accountabilities in that role.

Vicki envisioned creating several enhancements for the community. As the mayor's wife previously, she sustained legitimate connections. For instance, she met with clinical specialists to discuss her thoughts about developing wellness programs throughout major cities within the state to help improve the health of Nevada citizens.

Reports reflected concerns in some school districts about the inaccessibility of art and music classes due to budget cuts. With her love for art, she pushed for budget increases so students could enjoy those cultural programs.

Her visions emphasized making a difference in the state with areas of concern that hadn't been addressed. As angry as I was that she stayed away from me, the pride in my heart for her dedication to the public overflowed.

She had so much work to do, but when filming for her TV series resumed, she'd be back in Vegas for her career—and me.

For a change of scenery, I made my way to Duffy's Irish pub for dinner and a nonalcoholic beverage. I laughed, driving by Spritz, Vince's club. Still a mob-ruled business but a popular place for entertainment—standing room only every weekend.

When I entered the pub, I took a seat at the end and watched CNN on the overhead tube discussing politics. Thankfully, Governor Atkins wasn't the topic of conversation. I sipped iced tea and ordered buffalo wings with curly fries. I was in the mood for something greasy for a change instead of my typical, healthy fare.

Anthony, the bartender, placed a shot of something alcoholic before me. The familiar scent of Jameson filled my senses. I glanced up at Anthony and said, "I didn't order this."

He pointed to a table in the back.

My eyes caught sight of the reporter Olivia Crane sitting alone, raising her glass filled with a colorful, fruity-looking drink with a small umbrella set atop the rim.

I missed the smooth flavor of Jameson sliding down my throat, but I knew all too well how alcohol controlled me. I picked up my iced tea glass and the Jameson, then strolled to her table. "Hello, Olivia. Jeez, it's been a while since I saw you around town." I twisted my head, thinking momentarily. "In fact, I haven't seen any articles by you lately."

"Should I feel hurt you didn't notice I left town a few years ago?"

My eyes lifted in surprise. I guess I hadn't noticed, but no need to rub it in. I placed the Jameson in front of her. "I don't drink anymore, but I appreciate the gesture."

She nodded, then slammed back the shot herself. "Why waste it?" Her blue eyes winced hard, the after-effect of the whiskey she gulped.

I never paid attention to the color of her eyes before. "So where did you go?" I asked.

"I got married and moved to California. Had a column in the *Los Angeles Daily News.*"

"And you're back in Vegas for a visit?"

"The marriage didn't last. Vegas is home. News 5 hired me but not necessarily for the type of journalism I want to do."

"Which is?"

"Investigative reporting. I either missed out on opportunities, or they hired journalists with more experience instead of taking a chance on a woman with light society-type reports under her belt."

I chuckled, remembering how she got on my nerves, question-ing me about my business or women I dated. She reported mostly fluff pieces, but she had good instincts and ambition.

Anthony approached the table and refilled her glass.

I watched as she continued to hammer away pretty heavily. "You okay?"

"I felt like being a little *bad* tonight." She threw me a wink.

Don't get me wrong, Olivia was a good-looking woman. Even if I wasn't committed to Vicki, Olivia was half my age and already pretty drunk. I sat with her to ensure her safety from a rowdy bunch of suits who walked in, bragging about big bonuses and climbing the corporate ladder.

She swiped a couple of fries from my plate. I ordered another helping so she'd have some food in her. Not sure if the food would resurface later, considering the amount of booze in her. I insisted she stop with the alcohol, then requested Anthony bring a carafe of black coffee.

She was quite funny and entertaining when buzzed. I wasn't looking at her as an annoying media personality that night. She was an intelligent woman, working toward career goals. I respected that.

I wished her a good night and called her a cab before I left. The cabdriver said he'd ensure she got home safely. I offered him suffi-cient fare, including a generous tip, to do just that.

CHAPTER 91

Two Weddings and a Baby

On June 14, 2008, Danny and Bianca officially tied the knot. A lovely church ceremony was held at St. Francis with a reception at the Montgomery. Nearly two hundred guests in attendance. Many were out-of-towners in need of a hotel room. Having the reception at my hotel made sense.

Bianca's entire family flew in from North Carolina. They booked rooms so they could enjoy themselves at the phenomenal event I threw for my son. Good food, gambling, and a murder mystery wedding-themed show during the rehearsal dinner was a great time for all.

Las Vegas had been known as one of the most entertaining cities in the world! I felt thrilled to introduce Bianca's family to the exciting world I called home.

Sadie's parents were still alive and kicking. They enjoyed the parties and ceremonies to celebrate Danny and Bianca legally binding their relationship. The Meades must have good genes. My parents and grandparents all died young from a variety of health issues. I thought about John every day and how young he was to die from a heart attack. My health proved well. My life choices, however, could do damage.

Bianca's folks, Elliot and Pam Warner, were always pleasant to spend time with. Pam was a high school English teacher. Elliot sold life insurance. He consistently tried to sell me a policy. They were at least ten years younger than me, but I enjoyed their company.

Patrick and Will usually sat with me at any Meade occasion. Lisa and Al would chat with me for a while. Suzanne was her usual, cheerful self. Fred barely looked at me, even after all these years. Sadie avoided me. I kept my disgruntled feelings for Fred and Sadie hidden from Danny and Emma. We dealt with our contention during wedding photos.

Bianca was pregnant at the time of their wedding. With a second baby on the way and Danny working at a local law office, he proposed.

Sadie acknowledged her happiness about the wedding. As for me, I didn't think it mattered. Nowadays, couples had families and lived together without the legality of marriage. All I ever wanted was for Danny to live his life to the fullest, without limits.

My beautiful granddaughter, Emma, stole the show, bouncing down the white-carpeted aisle in a cream-colored gown, carrying a basket with red satin rose petals. She threw the rose petals like she was throwing a softball. She had quite an arm. I told Danny he should sign her up for softball.

"Poppy! Poppy!" Emma always screamed with excitement when she saw me. I'd pick her up high in the air and zoom her around like an airplane. She loved that! The kids would bring Emma over often for a swim and a cookout in the yard. They kept me company as well as sane whenever I missed Vicki. Sometimes, Danny would ask me if I had anyone special in my life. It sucked that I couldn't be honest with my son. I told him he didn't have to worry about me.

* * *

Two weeks after Danny's nuptials, Patrick and Will planned their wedding on Sunday, June 29. Same-sex weddings had recently become legal in California, following the lead of East Coast states like Massachusetts that legalized same-sex marriage in 2004. They didn't want to wait another minute to celebrate with an impromptu ceremony in Los Angeles. The timing was perfect because Danny and Bianca had returned from their honeymoon in time to attend the service.

Will came from a supportive family who wore smiles throughout the event.

The Meades showed their support. Fred sat quietly the entire day, wearing a hint of a smile. Better he stayed quiet than open his mouth, risking prejudicial slurs escaping. Suzanne and Sadie must have warned him to be on his best behavior among Patrick and his friends. He made a point to shake both Patrick's and Will's hands when the ceremony concluded without saying much.

Not only was I invited to their wedding, Patrick asked me to be his best man. I felt deeply honored. Patrick had numerous friends he could have asked. The fact that my marriage to his sister ended yet he still considered me a friend and brother meant a lot.

Patrick marched along a difficult path in life against all obstacles, standing up for his rights and living life based on his happiness, despite society's malicious backlash. He was a hell of a man, determined, passionate, smart, and genuine. I felt proud to stand by him.

* * *

On November 11, 2008, Danny and Bianca welcomed their second daughter, Kristina, into the world. Another perfect bundle of joy.

Emma favored Bianca with her strawberry blond hair and freckles. But Kristina looked more like Danny. I recognized the resemblance instantly.

This little girl had a mess of dark hair. She resembled more of the Italian side of my family with an olive complexion. Kristina looked like a Cavallo with gray eyes inherited from me.

My family was growing, and I loved it! I adored being their Poppy.

The year 2008 was fantastic!

CHAPTER 92

The ratings for Vicki's series, *Rising 51*, dropped from last season. She had valid concerns the network would pull the plug. If her show was canceled, she'd have no legitimate reason to stay in town for a prolonged period. Jeffrey would expect her to act as a full-time governor's wife, living in Carson City. She seemed jittery, but she worked hard to convince me otherwise, always flashing a lovely smile highlighted by those dimples.

The thought of not having her here with me fueled my fire to do whatever it took to free her from her marriage without the threat that lingered over her head. What stone did we leave unturned? I promised her I wouldn't let Atkins blackmail her further. Unfortunately, I was failing her and the future we envisioned.

Vicki promoted her show more often, which meant more travel. On the plus side, when she traveled out of state to market the series on daytime and primetime talk shows, I'd fly wherever she landed to be with her. This show allowed her to see me regularly for seven months out of the year. The rest of the year, I took any opportunity possible.

Atkins gave her a difficult time about her travel schedule. His wife residing at a Vegas hotel while he lived at the governor's mansion didn't seem proper.

But she stood her ground. Her career was important to her. Of course, I knew I was important to her too.

Because she sustained the courage to confront him, and he was busy running the state, he stopped challenging her about her acting career or where she stayed while she filmed.

Vicki assured me she had her own bedroom, separate from her husband for many months before she met me. Any passion they once shared died years ago. Their marriage, a mere sham behind closed doors.

Maybe I wanted to hear her say those words. I needed to know she didn't share a bed with him.

She believed he had a mistress. Women flocked to powerful men in suits. If she wasn't having sex with him, some other woman fulfilled that role, but she didn't know who, nor did she care.

However, revealing a mistress might harm the "family values" image he portrayed publicly.

CHAPTER 93

Two weeks before Christmas in 2009, Vicki had been scheduled to speak at a charity function to sponsor after-school art and music programs for children living in impoverished neighborhoods. The venue was an elegant Sheraton Hotel in northern Nevada. She booked a room overnight and arranged to fly home the next afternoon.

I couldn't miss out on an opportunity to see my girl. I flew up north and booked a room at the Sheraton to spend some much-needed time with her.

Atkins had traveled to Washington, DC. He expected Vicki to join him, but she chose to speak at this specific event, knowing her husband would be occupied elsewhere.

For me, it wasn't a problem to reschedule a few meetings or delegate a couple of tasks. Whatever it took to see Vicki was well worth it.

We seldom benefited from opportunities to see each other, especially around Christmas. Since she moved into the governor's mansion, spending time together outside of filming in Vegas continued to be a barrier.

She wore her Christmas present for me. A very skimpy red lace nightie with a black velvet ribbon tied around her midsection. The type of gift I loved to unwrap slowly and with extra TLC.

After I ordered a chicken club for myself and a Caesar salad for Vicki from room service, I presented my Christmas gift to her. Knowing her love of art, I had a small replica of my favorite oil painting, *Love Scene,* created for her, wrapped in red-and-green checkered paper with a giant red bow and spiral ribbons swirling down. The original painting was an enormous size of approximately five by eleven feet. The irony of this masterpiece hit home for Vicki and me. The couple in the painting was in love, passion igniting through mystical gazes in the bed they shared. The woman, however, was married to another man. In the corner of the portrait stood an old woman opening the bedroom door, warning the lady of the house that her husband had returned home.

Frankly, I had no idea how good a fake it was, but Vicki had an eye for authenticity. She loved it! Anytime her eyes glanced in its direction, she'd think of me, our love, and our desire to be together.

Larry continued to monitor Atkins's every move in search of the tape of Vicki's confession.

Sneaking around was not how I intended to spend the next two years, hoping Atkins wouldn't win a second term as governor. Until she returned to film in Vegas, these rare moments we had together were priceless.

CHAPTER 94

Olivia Crane's pretty face and quirky mannerisms flaunted across my TV screen one morning. News 5 took advantage of her talent, reporting on an exclusive story. Perhaps she was finally climbing the media ladder. I'd never seen her report on subjects outside of society events, bridal fairs, and charity functions.

The morning newscast showed her standing on South Bruce near Freemont Street. Flashing police car lights, ambulances, and fire trucks were sporadically parked in the background. A fire broke out at a strip club during the night after closing. The same strip club Nancy Garrett managed.

I turned up the volume. My mind wandered to the conversation I had with Nancy in the café years back. The story she told, without actually saying that Vince ordered the hit on Angie's father. How could Vince live with murdering his brother? I hadn't said a word about that conversation to anyone.

"If you're just tuning in to this broadcast, two people were fatally wounded in a fire at the Gentleman's Club on South Bruce late last night. No other injuries were reported. The victims have been identified as Priscilla Cohen, a dancer at the club, and Nancy Garrett, the club's manager. The fire chief told News 5 an investigation is underway to determine the cause of the fire. Police are encouraging witnesses to come forward."

Jesus, Nancy died!

If Vince knew Nancy talked about anything related to him or his business, he'd want her eliminated. Hopefully, she never brought up such a delicate subject with anyone else. I never knew Vince to be an arsonist, but he had a lot of hired help. If Vince whacked her, why would he have waited all these years to do it? Maybe word circled back to him about Nancy's loose lips where he was concerned.

One thing about Vince, he desperately attempted to hide from the limelight, avoiding any attention that could potentially bust him. If he were capable of maliciously offing his own brother without consequence, anyone who crossed him might wind up dead.

Including me.

CHAPTER 95

This February day in 2010 seemed as bright as the sun that burst from the bluest of skies. Not a cloud in sight. I heard from Vicki first thing this morning when she had a moment to call me. Tonight, I looked forward to seeing my granddaughters for dinner. I stopped at the hotel café for my habitual jolt of high-octane coffee.

Someone called my name. The familiar voice wasn't loud, but the sound generated higher than a whisper. I turned my head to see Marty. Using the merchandise this drug hustler sold over the years did a number on his ticking biological clock. His leathery face held many wrinkles, and he hobbled around with the use of a cane.

The food court could be accessed by people off the street. As much as I didn't want anything to do with Marty's drugs, I wasn't stupid. I showed him respect since he held a powerful position in the Toscano family tree.

He signaled me over to the table where he sat next to a thin man with a dark goatee, a youthful olive complexion, large inset eyes displaying sleep deprivation, and a crewcut that highlighted dark brown specks of stubble.

"Hello, Marty. How ya doing?" I shook his hand.

"Good, Tommy. I wanna introduce you to somebody." He guided me to his friend, who stood from the chair, taller than me by at least five inches. "Tommy Cavallo, meet Gino Toscano, Carmine's son."

I searched for the family resemblance but didn't see it. I forced a smile and shook his hand. "How's your family?" I asked merely out of respect. Not because I cared.

"Everyone's good. I heard a lot about you and the famous Montgomery." His head slid to the right, absorbing the magnificent surroundings outside the café that led to the casino.

Here I stood, meeting another wise guy. I got rid of the mob more than two decades ago.

Marty did a few years in the nineties for drug trafficking. He must have kept his mouth shut, seeing that he was still breathing.

I wanted to get away from these men—and fast. "I'm sorry, but I've got an early morning meeting I'm late for."

"This will only take a minute of your time," Gino said as he sat, holding a dark expression that flowed from sinister eyes. Then he kicked out a chair at their table for four. My invitation to join them at Gino's insistence.

I sat as he requested, carefully sipping my coffee, attempting to hide my nervousness.

"My father liked you. Said you were smart, innovative. You also knew when enough was enough. He told me you probably saved him from doing time."

"Ancient history, Gino."

"Marty here tells me you're clever, discreet, trustworthy."

I said nothing, but Marty appeared pleased with himself, searching for recognition from a high-ranking gangster.

"We've got a situation. I thought you could help me out. It would be a personal favor to me. Out of respect, ya know, for my father's memory."

Suddenly, I heard Marlon Brando as Vito Corleone saying, *I'm gonna make him an offer he can't refuse.* I remained silent and listened as if I had a choice.

"We got a lot of money right now stored somewhere safe, but I gotta move it, Tom. I need your help."

I knew exactly where he was going with this conversation. Money laundering.

Carmine and Fat Nicky managed that angle years ago. Since Marty sat in this triangle, whispering criminal intentions, the money Gino wanted dry-cleaned must be from Marty's drug business.

If I agreed to help Gino, what would come next? More skimming? Loan sharking? I wasn't doing that again. The law was all over that type of shit now. I had to say no but respectfully decline without making waves. "Gino, with all due respect, the FBI still keeps tabs on me. This is too risky. Risky for you too. I'm afraid I can't help you. I can't jeopardize my business."

He paused and stared through me, thinking momentarily. "That's too bad, Tommy. I thought you'd help me out in memory of my father." He nodded, a little disappointed. Then he tapped Marty's shoulder, indicating it was time to go.

I exchanged a handshake with them. Marty didn't look happy, but Gino demonstratively showed an energetic smile. The family resemblance, instantly recognizable through the same suspicious smile Carmine wore.

Then Pop's voice rang through my head again, warning me about smiling gangsters.

CHAPTER 96

The hotel operations manager in Venice called me to discuss a security issue. During our discussion, some commotion could be heard outside my office door. I peeked through the blinds to see who was speaking to Phyllis in such a curt, demanding manner.

Nothing surprised me more than observing Governor Jeffrey Atkins, alongside his security detail, talking with my perky assistant. I couldn't hear the dialogue, but no public official ever dropped by my office unannounced for a casual conversation or a business discussion.

I ended the Venice call abruptly. Damn, could I go for a Jameson shot! Instead, I released a breath, smoothed my crisp white dress shirt with my palms, and wiped the sweat from my brow before stepping outside my office to greet my nemesis, a man I hadn't formally met— Vicki's husband.

"Governor Atkins. This is a surprise." My eyes met Phyllis's, indicating his presence was acceptable, although my body language lied like hell.

Phyllis clicked her black heels against the laminated floor and bit her lip rather aggressively.

Atkins approached me and shook my hand with a smile that made me think of Carmine. A fake smile, exposing whitened teeth and a slight overbite.

Maybe I had become programmed not to trust people who smiled so wide with narrow brows—like the Mafia and politicians.

"It's nice to meet you, Mr. Cavallo. I heard good things about the Montgomery," he said in a low, leisurely tone.

"Thank you."

"My wife stays here when she's filming."

"I make it a point to be aware of celebrities or public officials who are my guests."

He ran his fingers through his salt-and-pepper hair. "Could we speak in your office, Tommy? May I call you *Tommy*?" Another large smile appeared across his reddened face.

I opened my door, allowing his tall, thin body to stride through, wearing a dark-blue Versace suit fitted perfectly to his slim shape.

"What brings you to my hotel, Governor?"

"I wanted to check out the hotel my wife seems to spend all her time at. I mean, there are many luxury resorts along the Strip. Why the Montgomery? What's the draw to this place?"

"The amenities are fabulous, great shows, and an amazing food court."

He snickered. "Somehow, I doubt those activities are her...*passion*." He lurked around my office, observing the autographed memorabilia I had collected over the years. He stopped suddenly, appearing starstruck by my autographed basketball enclosed in a glass case. "Is that Wilt Chamberlain's autograph?"

I nodded. "It's one of my most cherished items."

"You keep it locked up tight."

"It wouldn't be valuable if everyone touched it," I replied.

"You know, I don't like anyone touching what belongs to me, either." His fake grin transitioned to a scowl.

Let the games begin!

"You've got a nice business here for yourself, Tom. I have a proposition for you, seeing that you're a businessman and all." He wandered around my office, spending an inordinate amount of time viewing my collection. Then he turned toward me and said, "From now on, you're going to stay away from my wife."

I offered him nothing except a stern facial expression. Not even a flinch, despite the gnawing ache that quickly ruptured in my belly.

"That stupid bitch thought I wouldn't know. She thinks she's going to make a fool out of *me*. In *my* position?"

"I've not heard your proposition." I tried with everything in me to remain calm, fighting the need to pop him hard in the jaw. Twenty years ago, this guy would have been knocked out cold without a second thought. Nevertheless, knocking out the governor wouldn't fare well for me. I could get arrested, which would make his life happier.

"You stay away from my wife, and your business will remain intact."

I chuckled. "You may run the state, Governor, but you don't run my business. You're not a partner or an investor."

"Oh, I promise, I *will* ruin you. You will lose *everything*, including my wife." Then he strutted out of my office, nose high in the air.

The moment the outer door slammed behind him, I attempted to contact Vicki. Her private cell was no longer in service. Her email address returned an undeliverable message.

"Damn it!"

Phyllis cautiously stepped inside my office, eager to learn why the governor stopped by unannounced. She was a smart cookie with keen senses.

I offered Phyllis a bullshit story about a campaign donation. I doubted she believed me, witnessing the distraught nutcase I instantly turned into, flinging my phone and papers across my desk.

She waited patiently, folding her arms and tapping her heel. She handed me a series of notes she'd taken from callers. "It's interesting the governor dropped in today. Vicki called the office to leave you a message literally seconds before her husband arrived."

My body jumped up from my chair and rushed toward her haphazardly. "You didn't put her through?"

"You were on that Venice call and didn't want to be disturbed."

Phyllis was a highly intelligent, organized assistant. I never elaborated that I'd always take Vicki's calls, exposing my love for a married woman. "Well, what did she say?"

She tugged on her burgundy suit jacket and fiddled with the printed silk scarf tied at the side of her neck, then explained, "Vicki said, *Tell Tommy I'll cherish the memories from our own love scene.*"

Vicki brought up the *Love Scene* painting I gave her, framing her message as if it were goodbye. "What? Is that all?"

"Yes, and she didn't give me a moment to respond. She quickly hung up." Phyllis must know about our affair now. Maybe she figured it out long before Vicki left that message. Her flustered facial expression said plenty. She turned her heels with a distressed blink of her brown eyes, then slowly inched back to her desk.

CHAPTER 97

Atkins made good on his threats. The IRS demanded an audit. That came out of left field. The Gaming Commission hassled me. The Nevada Division of Public and Behavioral Health was on my back, citing numerous allegations by patrons. The health inspector made a surprise visit to the restaurants in the food court.

I received a thorough colonoscopy.

Atkins proved his point. He could ruin my reputation and the Montgomery name. It cost me a ton of money in repairs and upgrades to get through those bogus inspections that otherwise would have shown favorable results.

I'd been forced to stay away from Vicki merely because I couldn't locate her. Maybe he'd back off if I stopped trying. But I wasn't about to give up.

Rising 51 got canceled. That meant Vicki had no reason to spend months at a time in Vegas with me. Did Atkins have power over the station airing the series, or did the show finally run its course?

Atkins knew she didn't love him. She loved me, and he couldn't handle it.

Larry had been digging into this guy's past. I waited for a bargaining chip that would force him to let Vicki go. Atkins had no idea who he was messing with. I had no plans of giving up altogether. It might take time, but I wasn't walking away without a damn good fight.

I lost Angie because of my business, my marriage, and the choices I made. I wasn't going to make the same mistake twice, losing another woman I loved.

Larry informed me that Vicki was heavily guarded and most likely monitored. If Atkins knew about our affair, someone had been watching her. Maybe he found the cell phone I bought her. One of her security guards, whom I paid handsomely for discretion, might have given us up.

My radar was turned on high alert related to any announcements about our governor's whereabouts and schedule. Vicki planned to meet with a woman's group to support wounded veterans at the state's capitol in Carson City.

After a brief flight, I watched Vicki from afar. She looked lovely in a sapphire-blue suit with black-beaded trim. I called out to her in between several large men escorting her from a private limo inside the guarded government building. She heard me, pausing momentarily at the sound of my desperate voice, but she wouldn't respond or glance in my direction. Or she *couldn't* respond.

Her security detail nudged her to continue walking away from me.

Loneliness possessed me.

The Montgomery had been legitimately clean and operating by the book for decades. I managed to clear up any threats or questions from those governing bodies' rectal exams. I hired an external accounting firm to clear up the unbearable tax audit. *Bring it on, Atkins. You can't hurt me!* I thought.

Then the death threats began in April. Intimidating messages, the car bomb, and the threat against my son. *My son?* If anything happened to Danny or his family, I wouldn't be able to live with myself.

The stench of defeat oozed through the air I breathed.

CHAPTER 98

At the end of May 2010, Larry discovered a remarkable bargaining tool—evidence of a straw donor scam. Granted, he broke into Atkins's mother's home to find it.

The woman was nearly deaf and slept soundly. She had no idea anyone broke into her house. Larry never would have hurt her, but he didn't want to frighten her or get caught.

A hideous black oil painting concealed a wall safe. He honed his skills working for me, adding safecracking to his resume, among other talents. I paid him double his usual rate since he risked a breaking and entering charge.

Atkins's campaign records indicated that funds were received by people who exceeded the legal limits of contributions. They associated other people's names with their donations, so the funds appeared legit. Filtering money to a political campaign under another person's name was a crime.

Larry found a paper trail with names and large dollar amounts. Guess whose names were on the list. Vince Russo, Big Sal Maroni, and Louis Maroni. It wasn't even my birthday.

Imagine the damage Atkins could do as President of the United States with the mob in his pocket. Visualize the damage someone like Vince Russo could do with a president who owed him a favor. Corruption at its worst.

As Larry observed Atkins's whereabouts, he managed to take some interesting photos. It seemed Atkins spent a lot of time in Reno with associates of the Russo family. Larry set up the exterior of Vince's cabin in Reno with surveillance cameras stationed in several trees of the heavily wooded area. This place was locked up tight, surrounded by strong-looking, solid men and a security system. A variety of men strolled in and out daily.

Brothels weren't legal in Reno.

Pictures were taken of Atkins visiting that secluded Reno cabin often. A few images were captured of him sitting outside, conversing with gangsters and prostitutes.

Vicki suspected he had another woman in his life. Perhaps this information could buy her freedom. A "family values" governor consorting with prostitutes and gangsters wouldn't be a good look for him amongst his constituents. Certainly, this was something to keep in my back pocket.

Accepting illegal funds to keep himself in office might be the icing on the cake.

CHAPTER 99

The clock told me it was nearly midnight on the first of June 2010 when my cell chimed. The caller ID displayed "Unknown Caller." Because I lay awake, sleep-deprived, I answered, expecting to hear an automated voice telling me I won a vacation to the Bahamas.

"Tommy, it's me."

My heartbeat jolted as if caffeine had been intravenously pumped through my veins. My body sprang from the bed, hearing Vicki's voice. "Are you okay? I've tried to contact you."

"I know. You have to stop."

"Is he threatening you?"

She grew abruptly quiet. So quiet, I thought she hung up.

"Vicki?"

"You need to let me go. I'll be okay as long as you stop trying to contact me. This is for your own good." Her voice sounded shaken.

"My own good?"

"Please, Tommy. If you love me, let me go. Otherwise, he'll keep coming after you. I can't handle the idea of him hurting you." Sadness drizzled through her words.

"I can take it. You can't let him win, Vicki."

"You still don't understand how powerful Jeffrey is and the strong ties he has. I'm begging you to stop." Some loud background noise and people shouting in the distance resonated as if a party ensued at the location she had called me from. "I'm sorry. I have to go. Goodbye, Tommy."

The phone disconnected.

CHAPTER 100

With so much uneasiness in my life, I had to prepare for the worst. I met with Len to update my will. The threats against me needed to be taken seriously. For a fun twist, I created a video at the outdoor pool at the Montgomery that outlined my wishes.

I couldn't give up on securing a future with Vicki, although I hadn't devised a solid plan to reunite us and protect her at the same time.

The clues related to a straw donor scam weren't concrete enough, according to Len. Atkins's reputation could be tarnished, but it wasn't enough to blow him out of the water and out of the governor's mansion. Nor was it a viable trade for him to divorce his wife because he still held the tape with her confession.

We tipped off the Reno cops about a potential brothel in their jurisdiction. I practically drew them a map, but no vice raids made the news. Did Vince have the Reno police in his pocket?

Atkins was responsible for the health inspections and tax audit I endured. Would he have gone as far as to blow up my car and threaten my son? If not him, someone else had it out for me.

Danny, Bianca, and the girls came by for lunch one afternoon. I wanted Danny to know where I kept certain papers should anything happen to me. I didn't want to present it like that, but I was getting older, and he should know these details.

The girls were merrily playing with new toys I picked up for them. Emma loved Barbies. Kristina adored baby dolls. Their eyes lit up big and bright at the sight like Christmas morning.

Once the girls were settled and playing nicely, Danny followed me into my office. Behind a piece of art hanging on the wall was my safe. I told him the combination before writing it down on a piece of paper for him to hold onto.

"Pop, what's this about?"

"Listen to me. If anything happens to me, you and your daughters are my heirs. You need to know where I keep certain legal papers." I opened the safe and showed him some money, safe deposit box keys, and various legal paperwork. "Len has duplicate copies of these documents, but I want you to have everything in this safe and the contents of the safe deposit boxes these keys access. Don't forget, my office is filled with autographed memorabilia. Phyllis will make sure you collect all of it. The value is substantial."

"Pop, stop! I can't think about your death. You talk like you're gonna die soon."

I shook my head. "When our time is up, it's up. I'm merely preparing for the inevitable. There's nothing for you to worry about. You know how much you and those girls mean to me."

"Yeah, Pop. We love you too. Although—"

"What?"

"I wish you weren't alone. You never bring any women around us. I'm sure you have dates, but I worry you might get lonely."

"Lonely? Me? Danny boy, you don't have to worry about me."

He smiled, pacifying me. Then he released a breath and said, "Bianca's pregnant again."

I grinned from ear to ear. "Wow, another baby."

"Maybe we'll have a boy this time."

"That would be nice. As long as he or she is healthy, that's all that matters." I reached out and brought my boy in for a hug. "I'm so proud of you, son. I love you."

As I moved to hang the painting back on the wall to conceal the safe, it slipped from my fingers and dropped to the floor.

Danny picked it up. "I had no idea you hid your valuables behind this painting."

Vicki had purchased the Monet replica for me, highlighting a serene tapestry of plants and flowers. The frame cracked slightly from the fall, I noticed.

Suddenly, a thought occurred to me. I stared behind the painting at the canvas and fractured wooden frame. Danny's comment about hiding my valuables behind a painting struck a nerve.

Vicki and her knowledge of priceless art versus fakes came to mind. But Vicki was always on my mind.

I replayed the day Vicki told me she was married, based on memory. The first time I looked up Atkins online, he stood before a horrible-looking piece of art.

Vicki talked about the dark energy and menacing aura of that oil painting. To me, it looked like an ugly black painting with a bunch of scribbles sketched throughout. Emma could've drawn nicer squiggly lines.

When Atkins became governor, he hung that painting inside the governor's mansion.

Vicki hated it. The sight of it felt heavy, and the darkness of the piece annoyed her. She believed he hung it in the mansion to intentionally irritate her. She attempted to get rid of it, but he caught her standing on a stepladder, taking the painting down.

They argued about where to hang it. Because he claimed to have loved that painting, he promised he'd move it to his office where she didn't have to look at it. He was surprisingly generous, going out of his way to make her happy.

She thought his conciliatory behavior was odd.

Then it disappeared from the mansion entirely. I doubted she cared where he hung it, as long as she didn't have to view it.

Larry once described an ugly black painting when he found the wall safe at Atkins's mother's home. The safe that contained information about his illegal campaign funds.

Something didn't sit right with me. I wanted to see that painting.

When Danny and his family left, I contacted Larry and offered to triple his rate if he could swipe that painting from Mrs. Atkins's wall covertly.

CHAPTER 101

On June 5, Larry managed to snatch the painting, replacing it with another dark portrait speckled with scribbles throughout.

Atkins's mother might not have realized the painting looked different in her current unhealthy mental state. However, Atkins would have noticed the disparities the next time he visited his mother. The backup image appeared equally obnoxious, but there were evident discrepancies we hoped his mother wouldn't detect.

I wasn't an artist, but viewing the painting Larry brought me proved Atkins had terrible taste. Ugly to view online in a photo but up close, his painting looked ridiculously cheap for someone with his wealth and power to own and enjoy.

I flipped it over, laying it across the dining room table. My fingers felt around the frame. Nothing seemed unusual. Then I massaged the canvas, starting at the top left corner and around the back, carefully sweeping my hands. That was when I felt a small bubble. Toward the bottom right corner, an envelope was tucked into the frame, creating a slight gap. Larry took out his pocket knife to carefully ease out the contents.

And there it was. The most beautiful thing I ever saw behind the ugliest painting I'd ever seen—a microcassette.

I raced to the attic entrance, tugged on the lever to pull the ladder down, and climbed into the musty-smelling area where I hoarded various antiquities related to technology over the years. I had an old eight-track player sitting in the corner as well as a phonograph, record player, and a vintage collection of 78 vinyl records.

I finally discovered the recorder beneath some old signs I had saved, promoting Ronald Reagan for president.

I slipped the cassette inside the dusty device. When I pressed play, no sound emitted. The tape needed to rewind. Impatiently, I waited until the tape spiraled to the beginning.

This time when I clicked play, I heard Vicki's voice speaking about the night she drugged Trey Winters and collected the priceless painting. Her voice crackled while confessing her sins as if she were sitting in a confessional box across from Father O'Brien. She broke down, confiding her darkest secret to a man she loved, not knowing he was taping her as insurance to extort her down the road. Atkins's voice sounded soft, encouraging her to provide him with more details. The snake!

The key to Vicki's freedom had been stored in a repulsive piece of art, hiding in plain sight. Atkins taunted her, forcing her to look at an awful painting she hated. But he got too cocky. When he found her touching it, wanting to move it, he brought this monstrosity to his mother's home for safekeeping. He couldn't let Vicki find his bargaining chip, knowing she'd leave their marriage without repercussion.

Len acted as her attorney for a brief stint when we discussed the potential use of this tape against her in court, should Jeffrey turn it over to the police. I considered smashing it to bits, but I thought Vicki should hear it for herself. Verification that I found it. We could finally be together. She should be the one to destroy the evidence.

I left Atkins's blackmail with Len.

Larry returned the painting to its rightful spot on Atkins's mother's wall.

My next move—to devise a plan to bring my girl home to me, even if I had to break into the governor's mansion to do it.

CHAPTER 102

I pissed off a lot of people throughout my life. I made my share of enemies. Vince Russo, Jeffrey Atkins, Gino Toscano, and Louis Maroni topped the list of those who wanted to exact revenge on me.

Vince loved messing with cars. Bombs and brake damage were his trademarks. His face flashed through my mind after my brand-new Aston Martin was blown to bits. So many years passed since Angie left me. If Vince wanted me dead, he would've killed me that torturous night his goons sodomized me with a screwdriver. He let me live then. Why would he attempt to murder me now?

I had valuable information on Vince, like the brothel in Reno. And if he found out that I knew he had Frank whacked, he'd want that knowledge buried along with me in a six-foot hole in the ground.

Perhaps he took care of Nancy for the same reason. The fire at her club was still under investigation, and Metro had been tight-lipped on the subject. Either she spoke about her relationship with Vince to someone other than me, or she had other illicit relationships in her life I didn't know about. Of course, a slight chance existed that the fire could have been an accident.

The information I kept close to me about Betty Russo's alleged suicide and traumatic marriage were added motives. With Betty's history of suicide attempts, the cops didn't rule her death as suspicious. Vince believed me when I lied, saying I secured hard evidence to use against him if he hurt Sadie or me. The Mafia did not like exposure. That bluff probably saved my life—more than once.

Let's not forget the evidence I had against Vince and his family in the straw donor scam, supporting Jeffrey Atkins.

Atkins hated that Vicki loved me. My involvement with her could jeopardize his reelection for governor. He desperately wanted a second term to make a name for himself. Positive credibility that could lead him to the White House. But I knew of his secret dealings with the Mafia and prostitutes—ammunition to ignite a wildfire of bad press, threatening his candidacy.

Gino wouldn't have made my list if Marty didn't recently introduce us. I declined the mob's request to launder money through my business. Not many people said no to gangsters and lived to talk about it. Had this been 1970, I'd be swimming with the fishes in Lake Mead already, or the Montgomery would have been burnt to a crisp or infested with rats to ruin me.

Louis Maroni, a mere puppet who did what he was told, as ordered by his father and father-in-law. Louis never acted on his own merit or had an original idea to pursue. It came as a complete surprise to me that he wanted Angie for himself. I stood in his way years ago. More recently, his ties to organized crime and Atkins's campaign could hurt his political career. If I brought down Atkins with the straw donor scam, Louis's career could be blown out of the water.

* * *

This is the end of Tommy's memoirs and life as he knew it.

"Knockin' on Heaven's Door"

CHAPTER 103

June 7, 2010

Tommy awoke earlier than usual, not feeling himself. "Old age or stress," he muttered with a laugh. He called his doctor, who made time to see him that morning.

He intended to seek out Vicki and tell her the fantastic news—that she was finally free. But his plans changed when a sharp pain pierced his chest.

After the doctor examined Tommy and took his vitals, his blood pressure surpassed his usual elevated results. She called for an ambulance, concerned about his symptoms, knowing his family's health history. Before help arrived, Tommy convulsed before her. Then he stopped breathing.

The doctor desperately tried to revive him to no avail. She pounced atop his body, thumping her steady hands into his chest in a rhythmic fashion until she accepted the horrible truth.

No movement. No breath. No sound.

Tommy's emergency contact was listed as his friend, Jim, so the doctor notified him first. The inconceivable shock hit the man hard, but Jim agreed to relay the painful news to Tommy's family in person.

Jim drove erratically to Danny's home, wondering how he could explain such a tragedy. The words weren't easily emerging.

Danny was surrounded by his pregnant wife, daughters, his mother, and Hank when Jim announced the devastating truth.

Jim explained that the doctor believed a heart attack killed Tommy, despite her efforts to save him. Jim reminded them about John's premature death by a heart attack, as well as the stroke that left Rocky without a mind for many years before his passing. None of the Cavallo men had healthy genes. Perhaps Tommy's history of alcohol abuse and drug use damaged his heart more than anyone realized.

Danny felt traumatized, in denial of his pop's fated ending. He walked around the grounds of his home before the tears poured like rain. Danny never had a chance to tell Tommy that Bianca was carrying twin boys, Tommy's first grandsons, who would carry on the Cavallo name. His pop would have been thrilled.

No matter how much hurt and anger loomed between Sadie and Tommy, she felt sad to hear of his passing. She reached out to Hank for a supportive embrace. Tommy was a good father to Danny. This loss would impact her son more than anyone.

Sadie believed Tommy knew about her torrid secrets now that he drifted to the other side. He must be cursing her, especially if he knew she manipulated her way into their marriage. There was no pregnancy back in 1967. A fake miscarriage in 1968, shortly after their wedding. A baby he grieved for years never existed. Marrying Tommy had been a means to an end, given the dangerous situation she put herself in, antagonizing a dangerous pimp when she got involved with prostitution in the late sixties.

Sadie's head turned upward toward the sky. She mumbled a heartfelt apology for the bad blood between them. Danny was the best thing that came out of her legal union to Tommy, and she vowed to help him through his grief.

CHAPTER 104

As his attorney, Len engaged in numerous discussions with Tommy about his will. Tommy wished to be cremated with no calling hours. He desired a simple service at St. Francis Church, followed by a party at the Montgomery with his loved ones and friends to talk about nothing but good memories and funny stories.

He hated wakes, staring down at a dead body in the traditional manner like he was obligated to do at the funerals for his parents and John. He didn't want to torture Danny, having to see his remains. Remembering Tommy for the man he was, full of zest and passion, would be a more meaningful sendoff than witnessing an immobile mound of flesh, dressed in a suit, morbidly wearing makeup to hide decaying parts.

Len organized a reading of the will, using the video Tommy had created to dispense his cherished possessions and money to friends and family. He outlined specific instructions, noting who should attend the reading in person. People who might want to see him again in a good, healthy state. Not the traumatized shell of a body his spirit once dominated.

Angie and Sadie in the same room for the will reading might be an interesting scene. Tommy had Len pull together the deeds to all the homes he purchased from when he and Angie were a happy couple. He never parted with the places he bought for them to hide away from his reality and loveless marriage. Tommy bequeathed to Angie those properties, the photos that highlighted the blissful moments they shared, and the engagement ring Vince threw at Tommy after

Angie walked out on him. He knew Jim would attend the will reading and intervene as necessary. Angie wasn't the type to harbor ill feelings, but Sadie could be unpredictable, especially when she'd discover he left her nothing but pocket change.

Sadie bled him dry with alimony for decades. Tommy wondered if Sadie never married her partner, Hank, solely for the purpose of collecting a regular monthly allowance from him. If she remarried, he wouldn't have had to support her anymore. Tommy didn't care what Sadie thought about the mere coins he bequeathed to her. After her betrayal, working with the FBI against him, he owed her no additional money or sympathy.

Tommy protected Sadie from the wrath of the Mafia. The Toscanos would've targeted her for working with the FBI. He believed Vince plotted to kill Sadie in that car accident years ago, so he'd be free to marry Angie. Sadie might not realize the hoops Tommy jumped through to spare her life.

Tommy never forgave Sadie for the night she got him drunk after seven years of sobriety—the night Danny was conceived. He bore no regrets for Danny's existence, but he hated that she lured him back to the bottle.

Naturally, Tommy ensured Danny and his children would be set for life. If Danny wanted to buy a chunk of his enterprise, he bestowed sufficient funds for Danny to invest. Tommy gave him a choice, wishing nothing but happiness for his only son.

Tommy hoped Angie would remember him fondly, reflecting on the many good times they shared. He was grateful to see her in person and look her in the eye when he saw her that day in 1986. The day she saved him from the FBI investigation and possible prison time.

On the day Angie heard from Len about Tommy's death, she cried after the shock faded. No matter what happened between them, Tommy was special to her once. He rescued her from the sheltered life in which she was raised. Although she came from an affluent family, her sister's death caused her father to be overly protective. Tommy took a lonely girl out of her shell and showed her the world. She mourned him as she reminisced about their intense, passionate history.

CHAPTER 105

Tommy left other instructions for Len to carry out, like ensuring his book became published after his death. Publishing his life's story prior to his death wouldn't be wise. Calling out his enemies might trigger retaliation.

Len sent a package confidentially and anonymously to Tommy's cunning acquaintance, Olivia Crane. Tommy had collected numerous documents and photographs that could bring down some ruthless people. Evidence that Governor Jeffrey Atkins had been corrupted by organized crime. Information for the ambitious reporter to explore that Vince Russo was responsible for the death of his brother, Frank.

Tommy's word and his evidence might not be sufficient to present in a court of law, but with Olivia following up on his anonymous tips, his memoirs could navigate her exploration. Olivia ran with the alleged story and finally caught her big break into investigative journalism. She started to be taken more seriously by her peers and superiors.

Governor Jeffrey Atkins disputed the prostitution claims and alleged ties to organized crime that Olivia exposed. The governor suddenly became shunned by most of society, labeled an outcast because of his suspected abuse of power. His name in the state of Nevada and any power he yielded steadily diminished.

Although he maintained an entourage of loyal followers, he lost the election to continue as the governor for a second term. His dream of becoming the president of the United States, the most powerful position in the country, was abolished.

With the exorbitant amount of heat Olivia put on Vince Russo, Vince couldn't allow Angie to believe he had anything to do with her father's death. Angelo "Sweets" Francisco, a capo in Vince's organization, suffered from chronic obstructive pulmonary disorder. He was dying, and he knew it. Soon after Olivia's accusations were released publicly, Angelo surprisingly confessed to Frank "Madman" Russo's murder, giving no implication anyone else had been involved, nor was he under any orders to commit murder.

Angelo's official statement cited that Frank felt outraged and inherently damaged by the death of his daughter, Connie. He was on the warpath to kill anyone involved in the drug business who could have sold his daughter the heroin that caused her untimely death.

Because Frank started a war on the streets, Angelo claimed he attempted to calm Frank down and reason with him. Many people lost their lives. Some innocent, others—not so much. The carnage had to end. Frank had transformed into a more deadly psychopath than he already was. Angelo never publicly stated that Frank's death protected the Russo crime family.

Angelo had little time left to live. His quality of life rapidly declined. He couldn't go anywhere without an oxygen tank and a wheelchair. He was indicted for manslaughter while receiving life-saving medical care. He died before his sentencing and never served any jail time. Good soldiers always protected their bosses. Angelo was a good soldier in the end.

Vince hadn't been charged or convicted of crimes committed through his brothel businesses. Cancer eventually caught up to Vince, and he died at the age of eighty-five in 2012. His criminal enterprise and brothels were taken over by his son-in-law, Louis. Ultimately, Vince expected his grandsons to run the family business someday.

Louis Maroni's association with Governor Atkins caused him to lose the next senate election. His long-term political career ended abruptly with mountains of allegations splashed across newspaper headlines. Louis was shocked that his lifelong career faded through a smokescreen of hypocrisy. He remained married to Katie and spent more time with his sons and grandchildren, grooming them to operate the Russo crime family.

CHAPTER 106

The emotional turmoil Vicki felt when learning about Tommy's death ranged from denial, anger, anxiety, and emptiness. She wished she had the strength to leave Jeffrey sooner so she could be with the man she loved, even if their time together would have been brief. She stayed away from Tommy to protect him and the empire he created. If she didn't, Jeffrey would have demolished his business and his bank account.

Len met with Vicki privately. Tommy didn't want their affair outed in front of a room full of people if she participated in the will reading. The envelope Tommy left for her included several legal documents, a seven-figure check, and the microcassette. Tommy solidified her freedom financially and emotionally.

A tear splashed down her cheek, listening to her taped confession that Tommy managed to obtain. No evidence of a digital copy had been discovered, although a slim chance existed that a copy could be out there somewhere.

Len handed Vicki a hammer. She held the base firmly and slammed the head down upon the tape that jeopardized her freedom. A slight grin appeared, showing off her dimples, knowing she shattered the threat against her.

She discovered an autographed photo of Elvis Presley from his early years in the package Tommy left her. A picture she'd never seen before and most likely rare. Len assured her of the authenticity of the signature. On the back of the photo, Tommy placed a note saying,

"He's dead, sweetheart. Get over it." She chuckled, thinking Tommy united her with Elvis again.

She wasted too much time under the thumb of a crooked politician. One of the legal documents Len reviewed was a divorce agreement. Tommy provided for her freedom and her future with the money he left her.

Vicki signed the paperwork immediately. Len coordinated a police escort for her to Jeffrey's mansion. She gathered together her personal belongings, prized artwork, and Elvis memorabilia safely.

Jeffrey interfered with her taking the paintings she cherished, insisting he should keep the art.

The only painting she kept out of Jeffrey's sight was *Love Scene*, the piece to remind her of the love she and Tommy shared. The replica Tommy had created for her. As much as she hated leaving her other paintings behind, fighting with Jeffrey wasn't worth her trouble. He never cared about the art. He only wanted to hurt her, something he'd done since his political career began. She didn't recognize the man she had married and once loved anymore. Now, she was free of him—thanks to Tommy.

Jeffrey Atkins lives alone in his mansion with only his money and an art collection to keep him company.

CHAPTER 107

Tommy's Memoirs Release

The world was introduced to a platform of bliss, fortune, and tribulations through Tommy's profound reflections. The media promoted his memoirs in January 2011 as if he was a celebrity, owning a star on the Hollywood Walk of Fame.

Sadie made headlines for her dramatic role as Tommy's wife. Her past came back to haunt her at a time when her life overflowed with happiness and security. Scorching secrets revealed from the voice of a bitter ex-husband.

Thankfully, Tommy never found out she wasn't pregnant when he felt pressured to propose marriage in 1967. Her ingenious scheme with her doctor to forge medical records, aiding and abetting her lie, was never exposed.

Knowing Tommy had her followed throughout their marriage shouldn't have surprised her. She always knew he was a control freak. Learning that her affair with Joel Sinclair ended because Tommy schemed to launch his music career in New York shocked her. Instead of divorcing her, he bribed a man she cared about to leave town, keeping her chained in an unhealthy marriage.

She wondered if Joel knew that Tommy was behind that arrangement. She had no regrets about their passionate affair. Maybe he wouldn't have hit the big time if it weren't for Tommy. Joel created several albums that reached gold and platinum statuses. Today, he lived in Rhode Island with his wife, four children, and some grandkids.

Sadie's parents, brother, and sister now understood where she went when she left home in 1967 after a horrible fight with her father. More than forty years had passed. Her family exhibited no adverse feelings toward her. Deep down, they were saddened to discover what she must have gone through, working in a brothel, catering to the lust of random men.

Sadie wanted her voice heard on her own terms. Patrick, a journalist for the *LA Times*, assisted her in developing a statement for the public. She had no desire to appear on talk shows or risk being ambushed during a one-on-one interview. Sadie trusted her brother to express the feelings she struggled to script. Patrick released the following statement on behalf of Sadie.

My family and I are deeply saddened by the loss of my ex-husband. Tommy Cavallo was more than an entrepreneur. He was a good father to our son, a man his friends could count on, and a generous employer. My marriage to Tommy will not be the feature presentation of this commentary.

I never shared my past personal experiences working at the Belle Maiden Ranch with anyone, not even with Tommy. It's ancient history from long before Tommy and I married.

What people should know is that brief period in my young life had changed me in an immensely positive way. I sought to generate more assistance to secure optimistic outcomes for women. My mission was accomplished.

Through decades of hard work and benevolence, I evolved into a strong activist, founding *A New Beginning* program. A cause that not only helps to free women from a life of prostitution— it also assists adults and children in escaping the depraved streets of Las Vegas. The program has proven its value, reducing homelessness, aiding people to find a place to live, and procuring legitimate employment to support a typical environment. Tommy was proud of these achievements, advocating for its mission financially and passionately.

Additionally, Tommy supported another worthwhile cause close to my heart—AIDS research. Medical professionals have made astounding advancements to save lives and to prevent HIV's progression to AIDS. Through hard work and perseverance, I'm committed to supporting this cause that will lead to greater triumphs!

Tommy would want us to continue honoring these life-changing programs. Please allow my family, especially my son, to grieve this tremendous loss privately.

The paparazzi stalked Sadie, but she refused to speak to anyone in the media after this statement released. The article was meant to divert attention about her past and shine on her community successes, a tribute to her altruistic work.

Mostly, she worried about Danny's state of mind.

The tales in Tommy's book disturbed Danny. Learning about his mother's past, working in a brothel, was difficult to digest. He understood his parents were far from perfect. His father should not have judged his mother so harshly when he engaged in a long-term affair and contributed to illegal activities associated with organized crime, of which he clearly got away with. Still, he loved and missed his pop.

Danny and Bianca would raise their four children with fond recollections of their poppy. Danny planned to keep his father's memory alive in their minds.

Sadie didn't care if the public considered her as a conniving, vindictive woman—the way Tommy portrayed her in his memoirs. In no time, the press would find a bigger, more malignant story to follow.

More than two decades had passed since Tommy divorced her and shunned her from his life. She couldn't blame him after all that had happened between them. The lies she told, schemes she devised, and affairs of the heart were bound to catch up with her. She married Tommy with the hope of love developing. They didn't have a chance with her deceptions and his love for Angie Russo.

The press harassed Sadie terribly, and Angie's name kept popping up into conversations. The media had no idea where to find Angie because Tommy did not reveal the current name she used or her location in his memoirs. Reporters attempted to obtain details from the Russo family, but they refused to comment about Tommy's story or where Angie lived.

But Sadie knew. She knew Angie's last name since the will reading. Tommy's book captured Sadie as some kind of villain while his mistress sat upon a pedestal of high morality and righteousness.

Sadie sent an anonymous tip to several journalists, handing them a map directly to Angie's doorstep—another secret she would take to the grave.

CHAPTER 108

When the press caught up with Angie, they campaigned outside her home and the Morgan Realty office. Unlike Sadie, Angie never put anything in writing, nor did she comment to the press about her affair with Tommy. She worried her business would suffer, but the opposite effect occurred.

People became intrigued by the woman who stole a wealthy entrepreneur's heart. The commotion of the press promoted her business favorably, even if she was labeled a mistress and homewrecker—names her uncle warned her about.

She had informed her husband, Steve, about her past affair with Tommy long before they married. Tommy left a copy of his manuscript in a safe deposit box he bequeathed to her before it was released. Angie was one of the few people who received advanced notice about his memoirs. Somehow, she found the words to explain her dramatic past with Tommy to her daughters.

Her daughters seemed understanding, but Angie imagined Alicia would be embarrassed if she read some of the details Tommy shared with the world. Alicia could be considered straitlaced, whereas Samantha would probably think her mother was cool. That notion scared Angie a little bit. Samantha had a mischievous side.

Angie didn't want her girls to think that some of her choices were proper. Having an affair with a married man was heart-wrenching for everyone involved, as much as she relished the memories of her love for Tommy. Her daughters heard her side of the story in advance of her life being critiqued publicly. She explained the wild love she had for an older, wealthy man and her brief battle with depression that led to drug abuse. She hoped they could forgive the decisions she made as a naïve, gullible young woman who thought with her heart instead of her head.

Explaining the accusation that her beloved father and uncle headed a criminal empire through a chain of clubs and brothels was more challenging. Frankly, she didn't understand that allegation. Tommy's story described them as vicious criminals. His depictions of them altered the perfect images of the men she adored. Anger was her first reaction, annoyed with Tommy for revealing such deplorable information.

Betty, Angie's mother, tried to warn her that Frank and Vince were not the wonderful men she loved and admired. The idea of them attempting to murder their wives and other people was difficult to absorb.

Her father wasn't murdered by a burglar, the fantasy that was drilled into her head as an innocent teenager. Tommy believed her uncle took her father's life. However, a member of her extended family confessed to killing him. Angie enjoyed more Sunday dinners with Angelo Francisco than she could count. How could he look at her, knowing he took her father away from her in such a hideous manner? She breathed a sigh of relief, believing Vince had no knowledge that Angelo betrayed them both by murdering her father.

The torturous incident Tommy claimed that Vince commenced after she left him in 1980 was beyond disturbing to read. She recalled begging her uncle not to go after Tommy. Angie assumed he'd interfere with his business or pick a fight with Tommy. Even if the story Tommy wrote was true, she couldn't hate her uncle or her father. Feeling conflicted, she never saw the callous, vengeful side of the men that Tommy described. They showered her with love and compassion. Her perplexed heart entwined with devotion for the important men who had raised her.

CHAPTER 109

2013

Three years after Tommy's death, Angie decided the time had come to sell the properties he left her. She put them out of her mind initially, but she had to deal with the memories of her emotional past and move on.

The properties in the United States were a good place to start. Las Vegas, New York City, and Waikiki held a multitude of recollections. Although Steve and their daughters offered to accompany her, she felt she had to travel this journey alone. Her life with Tommy ended many years ago, yet each place allowed her to reminisce privately.

Tommy updated the homes cosmetically to modernize with the times. A facelift had been afforded to each residence with new floors, fresh paint, and new appliances. Angie possessed an expert eye, and her skills as a Realtor allowed her to detect the quality of the renovations Tommy arranged.

Their house in Paradise had been a particularly special place. She and Tommy planned a future together in the kitchen where she stood. Angie remembered the green rotary phone that hung on the kitchen wall and the clock shaped like a coffeepot above the white range. The floorboard in the hallway that led to the bedrooms still made that squeaky sound when stepped on.

Once the US homes were prepared for sale, she flew to London to visit the flat. The red brick exterior of the building showed signs of damage. The street overflowed with tourists, appearing busier today than when Tommy purchased it in 1975. The inside would look charming after a good paint job and new carpet installation.

From London, Angie flew to Milan, rented a car, and drove up to Lake Como. The view from the balcony looked as breathtaking as she remembered. This penthouse should be vastly marketable. The charming, colorful scenery alone was worth a fortune, but she didn't care about the money.

Paris would be her final stop. She hadn't returned to this fast-paced city since her last trip with Tommy in 1980. The overwhelming, antiquated beauty of the fabulous city stirred excitement from within.

Her watch displayed five o'clock in Paris when a taxi stopped in front of the lovely vintage-looking building with black iron railings arched with a leaf design across the balconies outside of each dwelling. Angie glanced up at her Paris apartment from the busy street. The heavy rush hour traffic prompted crowded streets, incessant beeping of horns, and bikers shouting for their right of way.

She noticed a table and a pair of chairs sat outside on the balcony of her unit. She hoped the set hadn't been sitting out for years. She had no idea of the condition Tommy left the apartment in after his last visit.

Her stomach twisted, igniting a trembling sensation as she rode up in the clunky elevator. She realized she should have dealt with these properties sooner.

Angie's eyes took note of the number 1150 on the apartment door when she slipped the key inside the lock and entered.

She wasn't expecting the lights to work, but when she flipped the switch, strictly out of habit, the lights blinked on. She froze, noticing some clothing tossed over a chair and sliced fruit in a bowl alongside a water bottle on the kitchen counter. The TV was turned on to *Jaws* with that heart-pounding theme song, beating angrily.

She stepped back and glanced at the number on the door, confirming she had the right residence. Her feet inched further inside.

Tommy always closed up the place when he returned home, she thought. Why were the electricity and cable turned on?

Angie's heart raced as she heard footsteps approaching furiously from the other room. Her throat dried up, so she couldn't utter a word or scream for help when standing before her was a man wearing blue jeans and a gray T-shirt, holding a gun with the barrel pointed directly at her nose.

CHAPTER 110

The gun lowered to his side. He witnessed the surprised look on Angie's face and carefully placed the pistol on the table. "Angie? What are you doing here?" He stepped quickly past her body, peered outside into the hallway, and closed the apartment door. "Are you alone?"

It took her a moment to catch her breath, seeing his familiar muscular build. "Tommy?"

His lush brown hair was now streaked with silver strands. Dark-rimmed glasses sat upon the bridge of his nose. A few more wrinkles around his eyes, but it was Tommy in the flesh. He wasn't a ghost, and he wasn't dead.

"What the hell? You're alive!"

"Why don't you sit down?" He reached his hand out to nudge her to a chair, but she brushed it away.

"I don't understand. What is going on? Len told me you were... dead. I attended the will reading."

"I thought maybe you'd be a little happy to see me alive, Angie."

She dashed toward him, falling into his shoulder, her head against the crook of his neck. Soon, she released him from her grasp and took advantage of the chair he pulled out for her as she continued studying his face.

"You're still beautiful, sweetheart."

"You look good for a *dead man*." She stood back up, absorbed his presence, and sat down briefly, only to stand once again in sheer amazement. "Why did you point that gun at me? Why do you have a gun at all?"

His gray eyes displayed compassion. "I'm sorry I scared you. It's not like I was expecting you. I've been staying here. The building manager was new. I had a key to this place and told him I leased it from you, the owner."

"You've been staying here for the last three years?"

"It's best you don't know all the details, Angie. And if you plan to sell this place or use it, I'll move on. You haven't stopped by since I left it to you. I wondered if you were going to sell it. I figured, eventually, I'd get kicked out."

She shook her head. "I...I guess it was difficult to come here and to all of our special places to deal with the memories, your 'death,' and the media attention from your book."

He flaunted his sexy smirk, still intact after all these years. "Memories of you bring me peace. I think about the first time we were here and watched the Eiffel light up. Then your eyes lit up brighter than the tower."

Her mind wandered to the first time he brought her to this modest-size apartment with the wondrous view in their youth. "Stop distracting me! Why would you fake your death?"

"Didn't you read my book?" he laughed, then noticed the stern expression on her face. "Everything I wrote about you was true."

"Some details were a bit difficult to read. Not to mention *personal*, Tommy," she scolded.

He shrugged and nodded. "Your family." He let out a breath. "I didn't have my life story published to hurt you. I wanted you to understand all that was going on. You *should* know the truth. The truth about things I couldn't discuss with you years ago. I'm sorry if I hurt you, Angie. That wasn't my intent." His gray eyes displayed sympathy. Then he tossed her that infamous smirk. "Listen, I got jammed up. It's best that everyone believes I'm dead. The people after me would stop looking for me, and any threats against my son would die out too."

"Is Danny in danger?"

"Not anymore, but he could be if my cover is blown. These people may use my love for him against me. As much as I loved running the Montgomery, it came with a lot of trouble."

Angie turned away then stopped in her tracks, her finger lightly tapping her lower lip. "When I read your story and realized someone wanted you dead, I didn't know what to think. And that whole dramatic performance, having a will reading."

Tommy interrupted her. "The reading of my will was real. I didn't know what would happen to me. I needed to get my affairs in order. If whoever wanted me dead succeeded, I had to make sure my family was taken care of, the Montgomery would be in good hands, and my memoirs would be published. I didn't think you'd find me alive after all this time."

Her expression suddenly turned serious. "You talked about organized crime in your book." Her chin twitched, uncertain if she wanted to know about her family's involvement in criminal activity and possibly Tommy's rationale for hiding out.

He shook his head. "You left me before all this shit went down. You're married with children and grandkids. You're no longer associated with me, so you're not in jeopardy, and I don't want you involved. Believe me, it was changing my identity and faking my death or really dying. I chose this route."

"What can I do?" Her offer to help sounded sincere, yet sadness displayed through a few tears bubbling up in her gentle brown eyes.

"Why did you come here? The building manager never threw me out. I figured if you called to ask about this place, he'd mention someone was living here, followed by the French police at my door, throwing me into a jail cell for squatting or trespassing."

"Len told me I didn't have to lift a finger because he hired property managers to take care of all the places you left me. I merely had to pay taxes and fees to cover expenses. If there were any issues, I'd hear from someone." She paused, thinking. "I suppose Len's in on this, and he knows you're staying here. Uh! Of course, he arranged all of this! He probably wrote up a bogus lease for you to present if needed." With hands on her hips, she scanned the apartment and

began to pace. "Len's the attorney who handled your will and trans-
ferred ownership of the properties to me."

She shook her head at Tommy, who refused to acknowledge
her suspicion. "I didn't tell Len I was flying out here. He would've
warned you I was coming if I advised him about my travel plans. I
visited our other homes to put them on the market. Paris was my last
stop."

Tommy couldn't take his eyes off of her. Recollections of their
past flooded in. "Hey, I'm a resourceful guy. I'll be packed and ready
to go by morning."

"Wait." She waved her hand, then tapped her lips with her
pointer finger. "You can stay. If this place has been your safe haven, I
can't kick you out. I won't. Technically, it's your property."

"No, technically, it's *yours*. It's better if nothing is in my name."

"You said you have a new identity. How?"

His head swung from left to right. "You're impossible, you know
that? I'm leaving you out of this."

"When you spoke to me in your video will, you said you trusted
me with your *life*. Is that still true?"

He blew out a breath. "It's not about trust. It's about your protection. I left everyone I love behind to keep you all safe. Only a few
people, besides you, know I'm alive. The people who helped me fake
my death, my health records, death certificate, and the will reading.
I had a lot of money hidden in various places. I'm set for the rest of
my life financially."

"If you're my tenant, I should at least know the name you're
using."

Tommy thought for a moment, uncertain if he should reveal
his secrets, when the door flung open and an exotic-looking woman
entered with short red hair.

Angie studied her elegant aura. A younger, glamorous woman,
wearing a leather jacket, sharply pleated black slacks, and stilettos.

"Tim, aren't you going to introduce me? Who is our guest?" the
woman asked with a thick French accent.

"Charisse, honey, this is our landlord, Angie."

"Bonjour, Angie." She held out her hand to Angie for a shake.

Angie smiled back, hiding her surprise, and accepted the woman's hand with freshly painted midnight-blue polish. Naturally, Tommy would have a lovely younger woman in his life. "It's nice to meet you, Charisse. Since I was in town, I decided to stop by to see *Tim*. I'm glad we could meet in person. I hope you like the place."

"It's a charming apartment. Of course, you know how gorgeous the view is." Charisse pointed to the large screen door that led to the balcony with the magnificent Eiffel in sight.

"Any problems you need me to handle for you?" Angie asked, acting as a landlord would.

"We adore this place, don't we, darling?" Charisse said to Tim, placing her graceful arms around his neck. She kissed his cheek. Romance oozed.

Angie wondered if Charisse knew his real name and the real Tommy Cavallo or if she only knew him as Tim. The excessive amount of PDA before her became uncomfortable.

He released Charisse from his arms. "We have reservations for dinner tonight, baby."

"Yes, I need to shower and change, don't I?" She smiled at Angie. "Au revoir, Angie. I need to get ready." She tapped Tommy's chest. "So do you."

"Au revoir, Charisse." Angie waited for his girlfriend to leave the room, then she pointed to the gun he left on the table earlier.

Tommy picked up the pistol and stuffed it inside the back of his jeans.

"I guess I should get going." Her head lowered momentarily, deep in thought. "There's no expiration date on your lease. But if you decide to relocate, I'd appreciate you contacting me." She searched through her Louis Vuitton bag and pulled out a business card, circling her number.

He walked Angie to the door and whispered, "McGee. It was my grandfather's name, Timothy McGee. I do trust you, Angie, with my life."

Tommy stood close enough to Angie to feel her breath against his lips. His eyes set on hers as a swirl of memories rushed through his brain of the life they once shared.

She kissed her fingertips, then gently cupped her hand along the side of his cheek. "Be happy and safe, *Tim.*" Her eyes flooded with mild sadness mixed with a touch of relief.

He grasped her hand and left a delicate kiss on her palm, "Goodbye, Angie." Words he wanted to say directly to her for many years to establish closure. Slowly, Tommy freed her hand. Angie would always be dear to him, but he had already released her from his heart.

CHAPTER 111

Angie walked down the hallway, inching out of his view after a quick turn of her head for one final glance to confirm she wasn't dreaming.

Tommy stepped back inside, strolled to the bedroom where he placed the gun inside the nightstand drawer, and breathed a sigh of relief.

He removed his T-shirt and jeans, then pranced to the bathroom to join Charisse in the shower.

She opened the curtain and flaunted her dimples, allowing him room to step inside.

He embraced her before offering a gentle kiss.

"So that was Angie?" she teased as she lathered up his body with thick suds. "The woman you *hoped* I was the day we first met." She turned her back, tormenting him with mild jealousy.

He hummed, "Yes," as he kissed the nape of her neck.

"Why was she here? It's been three years."

"She owns the place. We talked about this. The day might come when we'd have to leave, but everything's okay."

"Hmm," she responded suspiciously. "She's quite stunning."

He knew better than to agree with her. "I think *you're* stunning, baby."

"Can you trust her, Tommy?" Her dimples diminished, seemingly worried.

Tommy gazed into her brown eyes filled with sorrow. He gently massaged his thumbs around her dimples and tenderly kissed the beauty mark beside her lips to soothe her worries. "She won't give me up. Even if she recognized you, Vicki, she won't hurt me or what we've built here together. Angie didn't watch sci-fi movies, and she left Nevada. It's not like she saw your face next to Atkins in political ads to easily recognize you."

"She could do research and look me up. I played quite a role in your book too."

"You look nothing like the photos the media displayed of you since you changed your appearance." He gently tugged at her drenched red hair before his hands wandered along her soaped-up body. "Nice touch with the French accent."

"Well, I didn't know who she was until you introduced us. Maybe we should start packing," she suggested, demonstrating disappointment. She loved this apartment and would hate to move.

"Do you believe in fate, babe?"

Vicki showcased a sultry grin, then nodded.

"Trust me, we are exactly where we're supposed to be, and we can stay here for as long as we want. Our life together in Paris is our destiny, Mrs. McGee."

CHAPTER 112

The legal documentation Len provided Vicki after Tommy's "death" included a passport, a birth certificate, and a driver's license under the name Charisse Yvette LaSalle.

She had a choice to remain part of the Hollywood scene and continue her acting career, keeping the money Tommy left her without the anchor of marriage to Jeffrey Atkins weighing her down. Or she could disappear with Tommy, changing her identity.

Her decision was simple. She followed her heart.

Jim, one of the few people who knew about Tommy's secret life, facilitated Vicki's meeting with Tommy.

Vicki cut off her long, dark layers and changed to a shade of rich red wine. The birthmark on her right cheek was hidden by makeup. Instead of contacts, she wore rose gold cat-eye lenses.

Even with the modifications to her look, Vicki might have been recognized flying out of Las Vegas. Jim drove her out of town to catch a flight to Paris, France, using her new identity.

Tommy anxiously awaited at Charles de Gaulle Airport for his love to arrive. She flew into his arms the moment she saw him holding a sign with her new name.

Len had the paperwork drawn for their name changes. Len's wife, Dr. Wanda Sherman, declared Tommy as deceased and signed his death certificate. A bit of deception to save the life of their good friend was worth it.

GINA MARIE MARTINI

Tommy and Vicki tied the knot under the names Timothy McGee and Charisse LaSalle. An eloquent exchange of vows took place with the Eiffel Tower as a gorgeous backdrop on April 22, 2012.

Vicki stayed out of the limelight, no longer a celebrity. Her B-level science-fiction films weren't popular in Europe to be easily recognized, especially since she fell off-the-grid three years prior.

A rumor started that she retired to a remote location in Montana. Buzz Olivia Crane had launched, based on some details anonymously sent to her.

The press attempted to track Vicki down for a statement about her affair with Tommy and divorce from Governor Atkins. It was Olivia who managed to obtain an exclusive statement from Tommy's grieving girlfriend. With her TV series ending, along with a bitter divorce and the painful loss of the man she loved, Vicki requested privacy. She announced taking a hiatus from her acting career.

Vicki's love and knowledge of art landed her a job at the Musée d'Orsay, greeting guests and explaining some wonderful masterpieces to tourists. She highlighted one piece of art to all her guests. The original Camille Pissarro oil painting, *The Boulevard Montmartre at Twilight, 1897*, hung prominently in the museum's impressionist section.

The long-lost painting was mysteriously shipped to the Musée d'Orsay, making headlines throughout Europe. This painting hadn't been seen publicly since 1941. Vicki included a stop at her favorite, priceless painting on all of her guided tours, explaining its history and miraculous return to the museum for the public to enjoy.

Before surprising Jeffrey with divorce papers, Vicki replaced the original painting locked in his storage unit with a fake. The same replica she was supposed to have hung on Trey Winters's wall in his apartment after stealing the original. With Larry and his hacker apprentice's help, they manipulated Jeffrey's alarm system and camera to swap the artwork without being spotted.

Should Jeffrey tell the police of Vicki's alleged theft, the art crimes unit would certainly label the painting she left in Jeffrey's possession a worthless imitation. Besides, the original had been shipped to the Musée d'Orsay. Her taped confession was destroyed, and the

358

Winters family never reported the painting stolen or that Trey had been drugged the night it vanished.

Tommy purchased a boat in Paris and launched his own business, taking small groups of tourists on cruises along the River Seine, pointing out the fantastic scenery and offering fun facts about Notre Dame Cathedral, the Eiffel Tower, the Musée du Louvre, and some hidden gems to share with the tourists. He could always tell a great story, and the visitors enjoyed his cruises and tall tales.

The couple created a simple, happy existence in Paris—finally free to enjoy life together. A life in Paris with beautiful antiquities to view each day was a poor attempt to conceal Tommy's sadness for parting from his family in such an intense manner.

Jim sent packages to Tommy regularly. Photographs and videos of Danny, Bianca, and his grandchildren, Emma, Kristina, and his twin grandsons, Thomas and Tyler.

How he'd love to see them all again—in person. Precious moments Tommy had to miss. Thanks to technology and his trusted friends, he was able to stay connected, in some small way, with those he left behind.

If Danny knew Tommy still lived and breathed, he could be in danger, or Tommy's cover could be blown. Danny and his family needed to believe Tommy died, at least until whoever attempted to kill him was identified and neutralized.

With the exception of leaving Tommy's family behind, hiding out wasn't as grueling a task as expected. He and Vicki enjoyed their destined life together. They often joked about Elvis being alive and living down the hall. If Tommy could fake his death and start a new life, surely Elvis could have too.

Next from the Entanglements series: *Lethal Revelations.* After reading Tommy's memoirs, Danny Cavallo is convinced his father was murdered. Danny challenges his father's enemies, pursuing justice for Tommy's demise. He attempts to reminisce through Tommy's past with the women closest to him: Sadie, Angie, and Vicki, searching for clues to catch a killer. Will Danny find the evidence he seeks, or will his life be shattered first?

The images captured of the artwork mentioned in this fictional story were found via internet searches.

Love Scene by Giulio Romano

The Boulevard Montmartre at Twilight, 1897 by Camille Pissarro

One of the many *Water Lilies* paintings by Claude Monet

Venus and Adonis by Peter Paul Rubens

Dogs Playing Poker from the series by Cassius Marcellus Coolidge

ABOUT THE AUTHOR

Gina Marie Martini is the author of the drama series, Entanglements, honored in 2020 with an American Fiction Award as a finalist in the Family Saga category for her debut novel, *The Mistress Chronicles*.

She was born and raised in Connecticut, where she lives with her family. She earned a bachelor's degree in psychology and a master's degree in health administration. Gina maintains a full-time career in the health insurance industry with a background in behavioral health and clinical programs.

Follow her at www.ginamariemartini.com, Facebook, Instagram, and Twitter.

CPSIA information can be obtained
at www.ICGtesting.com
Printed in the USA
BVHW081329131221
623924BV00001B/30